ARSENAL

WOLVES OF IRON VALOR MC BOOK 5

DEX HAVEN

UNDER A TEXAS SKY PRESS

DEDICATION

MEAN MAN

Life is fantastic; that's how good it is. That's mostly thanks to you.

EPIGRAPH

"Every saint has a past. Every sinner has a future."

-Oscar Wilde

CONTENTS

TRIGGER WARNINGS

All of my books contain graphic intimacy and violence (sometimes sexual)—but always with a triumph-centered resolution and a guaranteed HEA. I don't believe in giving away the journey before it begins, but I believe in honoring your peace. If you know certain topics are hard for you, I encourage you to trust your instincts and read with care.

That being said, I thought it was important to note that there are a couple of scenes in Arsenal that include non-consensual sex at the worst and dubious consent at best (mostly in terms of a twisted Alpha command dynamic or a witch-spelled consent). There is also nonhuman sexual contact. If this is painful or triggering for you in any context, I do not recommend you continue.

A complete list of warnings can be found on my website: www.dexhavenauthor.com

Chapter 1

Harper

I felt him before I saw him. The prickle on my skin, the sudden vacuum in my chest. Not the club's spotlight or even the acrid stink of beer and cologne—this was something cellular, a chemical alarm I hadn't heard in years. My wolf flared up, hackles raised inside me. *MATE.*

The word pulsed through my veins, a bass line louder than the club's thundering sound system. I didn't dare glance at the crowd, not even a peek from under my false lashes, but every muscle locked tight and jittery. I was halfway through my set, crawling on my knees along the catwalk in six-inch Lucite platforms, a string bikini top glued to my boobs and a scrap of glitter mesh covering what little else there was to see.

MATE. MATE. MATE.

My wolf vibrated with it, a dog with a scent she'd never forget, and I pressed my tongue to my teeth to keep from whimpering. My throat closed in on itself, and the velvet stage lights shimmered in that panicky way when you're about to pass out. Jess Regan was here. The mate I'd left almost five years ago. My *fated* mate, the only person in the world I'd spent more than a week imagining a life with.

The last person I ever wanted here.

My human side panicked. My wolf, not so much. She stretched out, tail flagged, ears up, thrilled at the chase. But I was smarter than she was. I was a prisoner here, and he and I both were in danger if I acknowledged his presence. My father made sure of that when he sold me off like fucking cattle.

I tried to focus on the music, to keep count of the measures and not of the beating in my chest. Jess was out there, and he was watching. Probably with those sniper eyes of his, the ones that made you feel like he'd calculated the wind speed and trajectory of every word you spoke.

My knees stung from the rough patch of stage carpet—nothing like the burn of my shame. I stretched my arms overhead, arched my back, forced a practiced smile. The men whooped and hollered and tossed crumpled bills, none of them meaning a damn thing. I could smell him now, a hint of gun oil and leather and that impossible, specific heat of pack. Not *my* pack, but I still knew his scent: chocolate, bergamot, and cayenne. It made my hands shake.

The ultimate shame came when I stripped off the bikini top I wore. The men in the audience went mad over my body. Since I no longer trained as a ballerina, my body had filled out. My breasts, which used to be much smaller, now were full and natural. My hands went to them; all a part of the routine. It's my job to work the crowd into a frenzy as much as possible. I'm the headliner. The only girl who is a professionally trained dancer, for all the good that did. Of course, I'll never be a ballerina again. Waylon Steiner, my Alpha, made sure of that. But I spin and crawl with the 85% motion my knees still have.

MATE.

I grabbed up the cash and tumbled off the catwalk with the last beat of the song, landed on my feet, and booked it for the dressing room. My ears rang with the music and the memory of my wolf's howl.

The tiny corridor behind the stage was a tomb, lined with gray lockers and the whiff of dying hopes. I hit my dressing room and collapsed into my chair, doubling over. I counted breaths: in, two, three, four, out, two, three, four. My hands clutched the edge of the vanity so tight my knuckles turned white. My pulse was a jackhammer in my throat. I hadn't been this close to accidental shifting in years. These days I stuck to full moon shifting, and that's it.

I squeezed my eyes shut, trying to shut out everything but the slow throb of a migraine coming on. My mind raced trying to understand how he had managed to choose this strip club to walk into. What were he and his cowboy friend doing outside of Houston?

Someone knocked on the dressing room door. I froze, and for a split second, the animal panic inside me shrieked that it was him, come to drag me out by my hair. But the door opened, and it was just Angel, the bouncer's girlfriend and sometime house mom, balancing a tray of tequila shots and cut lime. She winked at me.

"Harper, you okay, sugar?" Her voice was all cigarettes and warm honey.

I nodded, even though I was sweating through my rhinestone G-string. "Yeah. Just, uh. Low blood sugar."

Angel set the tray on the counter. "You get paid extra for looking like you're about to faint on stage? You oughta work that angle."

I made myself laugh. It sounded like a dying cat. "I'll keep that in mind."

She tilted her head, peering with a raised brow. "You want me to tell Waylon you're sick?"

At the sound of my owner's name—because that's what he was, even if the contract called me an "independent performer"—my stomach dropped. "No. I'm fine. Just need a minute."

She shrugged and left me alone with my reflection. I looked like a ghost. My face was still pretty enough, but my blue eyes were empty. No shine or life reflected back at me. My wolf huffed in disgust. We used to be something; she reminded me. We used to be star material. We should be dancing on a legitimate stage somewhere in toe shoes, not stripper heels.

There was a time, back in the Houston suburbs, when I was going to be a ballerina. I'd started dancing before I could read, and I was good enough that my mother told everyone at the country club that her daughter would be the next Misty Copeland. My father was less impressed. He'd been president of a financial services firm managing hedge funds before his little "problem" with wire fraud. The only dreams he allowed in his house were the ones he could pay for.

I had known Jess for most of my life. He was four years older than me and had gone into the military when I was in high school, and I hadn't thought much about him after that. Then, we reconnected when I was nineteen, at a coffee shop. He was home on leave, hair still regulation short and tan lines where his wedding ring would have been if he ever wore one. I didn't know what he was at first, just that he had the stillness of a predator and tattoos you wanted to trace with your tongue. I watched him stir his coffee, black, one sugar, and I realized that I'm sure I'd fail to matter in his world.

But then he looked at me. Really looked at me. And every cell in my body rearranged itself to fit the shape of that gaze.

We didn't talk about the mate thing, not then. But I knew. I knew by the way my skin ached to touch him, the way my heart sped up when he walked into a room. He knew too. He'd let his hand drift over mine on the little round table, like he was claiming me in public, and I'd felt the invisible chain loop around my soul. Finally, we both admitted it. It was undeniable.

It lasted three months. Three perfect, fragile, doomed months.

When I told my father, he lost his mind. Threw a glass across the kitchen, called Jess every ugly name he could think of—mutt, trash, criminal—and then told me if I ever saw him again, he'd see to it I lost everything. My tuition, my car, my spot at Julliard. My mother just watched, silent and brittle. I knew my father had plans to marry me off to some corporate partner he'd already picked out for me. He wouldn't let me spoil his plans. Then he threatened my little sister Brie. She was only 16 at the time. He swore he'd have her given to some old wolf as soon as he could if I didn't do what he said. It was hopeless. He took my computer and my phone and told me I'd better never contact Jess again. He told me to pack my stuff for New York that second. I did, and he had me on a plane that night.

I wrote a letter to Jess that I never had a chance to deliver.

The panic attack hit in slow waves now, less electrical and more like a fever creeping up my back. I gripped the countertop, tried to anchor myself in the here and now, in the low hum of the dressing room's neon and the steady drip of the leaky sink. It had been years since I'd let my wolf get that close to the surface. I'd trained her to submit, to roll over and play dead, same way I had.

But that voice—*MATE*—was a fucking sledgehammer.

What the hell was Jess Regan doing in my club? Maybe it was a coincidence. Maybe he hadn't recognized me. After all, the last time he saw me I was wearing a cardigan and ballet flats, not a thong and stripper heels. Still, I doubted there was a universe where he could forget my face.

I tried to think of what to do if he showed up backstage. The last time I saw him in person, he'd told me he loved me. That he'd wait for me, no matter what. He was stubborn, obsessive, relentless—the good kind of relentless, if you could stand being loved like that. I'd wanted it if I could've kept my sister safe and have it too.

"Breathe," I told myself, "just breathe." I counted out the seconds, but my mind slipped away again, back to that day at home. Back to the way my father's face looked when I told him I'd found my mate.

He'd gone red, then white, like all the blood in his body was trying to escape his own skin. He'd grabbed my wrist so hard I felt bone, and hissed, "Do you have any idea what you're throwing away for a boy who's not even worth a goddamn phone call?" Then he shoved me, hard, into the wall.

"You're going to Julliard, and you're never seeing him again," he spat. "Or I'll make sure you don't dance another day in your life."

I'd believed him.

He called the school, cut off my cards, arranged for me to be "escorted" to New York by one of his friends, a shifter with too many teeth and a wife who smiled like a barracuda. I never saw Jess after that. I don't know if he tried to find me. I liked to think he did, but I liked to think a lot of things that weren't true.

I remembered the call from my little sister Brie, the only person who still cared what happened to me. She'd whispered, "Dad's losing it. He said if you ever try to come back, he'll—" but she never finished the sentence. Brie was sixteen, soft as cream cheese and just as breakable. I'd promised her I wouldn't make waves. I'd promised her I'd survive.

MATE. My wolf wasn't letting it go.

Then I was at home on summer break after two years at Julliard. My father was on a rampage. He'd apparently been up to something illegal. A Ponzi scheme, from the sounds of things. I was so hopeful they would send his ass to prison and we'd be free of him. But apparently he'd found a money man in the form of the Morgantown Alpha, Waylon Steiner.

I had just come through the living room and come face to face with the Alpha. I knew from the look on his face that I was in trouble. An hour later, my father called me into his office. He told me he'd worked out a deal with Mr. Steiner. I was to leave Julliard immediately and go to work for the Alpha, dancing in his club. After three years, my father's debt would be paid. I lost it, screamed at the men that I would *not*. I was no whore. My father slapped me so hard my teeth rattled. Waylon grabbed my father and told him he'd never touch me again. What a joke. Like he was my savior. Then Waylon told me it would be me or my sister. And here I am three years later. I wish dancing were the only thing that were required of me.

I blinked, and time snapped back. My hands had stopped shaking, but the sick cold in my chest lingered. I put on fresh lipstick, adjusted the straps of my top, and braced myself for the inevitable. Either Jess would find me, or he wouldn't. Either way, I was going to finish my shift and keep my head down.

Angel poked her head in again. "You sure you're good? Waylon wants to see you after your next set."

I swallowed the bile in my throat. "Yeah. I'm good."

She closed the door, and I stared at my reflection, searching for any trace of the girl who used to have dreams. I found only the ghost of her. I tried to smile, but my eyes were still wrong.

On my way out, I forced myself to look at the crowd. Thank the Goddess, he was gone.

The dressing room was empty except for me and a pile of half-shed lingerie. I scrubbed my face in the little metal sink and fished out the old concealer stick from my purse, erasing what was left of my tears. No point in crying now. If Waylon saw I'd been upset, he'd have questions, and I never had answers he liked.

I didn't hear the door open. I only smelled the cigarettes and the sharp, medicinal tang of Waylon's aftershave, the one he ordered special from

London and wore like a threat. By the time I looked up, he was inside, and the door clicked shut behind him, no knock, no warning.

That was always his move—walk in, never ask, never announce. Just appear and let you feel the gravity of his presence. His eyes found me in the mirror, and I dropped my gaze, reflexive as a kicked dog.

"You making me proud tonight?" he said, voice slick and dead at the center.

"Yes, sir," I said, but it came out so thin I doubted he even heard it.

He stood behind me, so close I could see his reflection ghosting over my shoulder. He wore an Italian suit, the blue silk shirt unbuttoned just enough to show the anchor tattoo on his collarbone, his blonde hair twisted back like some fallen angel from a magazine ad. He ran his hand over my ass, slow, proprietary.

"You had a rough start, I hear," he said, smile not touching his eyes. "You need to get your head right."

I gripped the edge of the counter and nodded. "I'm sorry, sir."

He pressed his lips to my ear, just hard enough to remind me of the teeth beneath. "You're going to the VIP room. Right now."

My body reacted before my mind did. I stood and straightened my skirt, but my vision whited out at the edges. The familiar numbness crept down my arms and legs—my brain's way of padding me against the blow that always came after.

Waylon yanked open the door and watched as I slipped past, his hand low on my back, steering. I barely felt the club as I walked through it: neon streaking across the floor, music so loud it blurred into a single high scream, the mix of sweat and cleaning fluid and rotgut tequila.

Waylon led me through the heavy curtain into the back hallway, to the only private room with a real lock. He always kept it cold, and I shivered, goosebumps crawling over my bare arms and legs. The pole in the center gleamed under black light, the only bright thing in a cave of velvet and ruined dreams.

He shut the door behind us and twisted the lock. For a heartbeat I thought maybe he'd talk first, like last time, but he just sank into the leather couch and fixed me with that dead shark stare.

"You were off tonight, my little slave," he said. "You embarrass me in front of my guests?"

"No, sir," I said, careful not to let my chin rise.

He stretched out his legs, leather shoes crossed at the ankle, and folded his hands like a judge. "You're going to make it up to me now. I want you on that pole. Naked. Then you're going to crawl to me, take my cock out, and swallow it. All of it. You do it right and I'll forgive your little mood."

I swallowed, but my mouth was dry as sand.

"Yes, Alpha," I whispered.

My wolf thrashed inside, howling rage, but she was caged. I moved to the pole and peeled off my top, letting it fall to the carpet. My bottoms followed. I was cold, trembling, but Waylon's gaze never left my skin. I spun, slow, the way he liked, arching my back and letting my hair fall loose. He'd trained me for this—how to move, how to make it look like surrender when all you felt was terror.

After two turns, he snapped his fingers.

"Crawl."

I dropped to my hands and knees, the rug biting into my skin, and crawled the length of the room. I could see his cock straining against his pants, but he didn't touch himself, just waited for me to do it. When I reached his feet, I looked up. His face was flushed with a mean kind of pleasure.

He undid his zipper, slow, and let his large cock free. He was always rough at the start—one hand in my hair, pushing me down till my lips mashed against the base. I gagged, but held on, doing my best to breathe through my nose and ignore the panic that wanted to make me bolt.

He rocked my head on him, steady, saying nothing, not even breathing loud. The only sound was the wet click of my mouth and the soft beat of the music being piped into the room.

"Take it all the way down your throat little slave. Swallow my cock. I want my cum down your throat and then all over your tits." He growled.

My wolf yowled. I felt her claw at my insides, begging for escape, but I shoved her down. This was how you survived. You did what you were told and hoped it ended fast. He pushed his dick further down my throat. I wanted to grab at his thighs so he'd pull back but I didn't dare.

"Get ready, girl. Yeah, that's good. I like to see your throat bulge as you swallow me down. You have finally learned how to give a decent blowjob." His laugh was cruel, and I felt like I was suffocating.

He came with a grunt, jetting down my throat. He finally pulled out, his hand pumping his cock as jets of his cum still shot out across my face and chest. I coughed, but didn't dare wipe my mouth. I kept my eyes on the floor. He leaned back, sated, his pants still unzipped.

"I don't know what you were thinking about tonight, but you better clear your head, slave." He tangled a hand in my hair and jerked my head up. "You make me a lot of money, Harper," he said. "If you ever think about running, you know what I'll do to your sister."

I nodded. "Yes, sir."

"Now clean your cum covered self up my little slut. I won't send anyone else to you tonight. I'll have Rage drive you home, and I'll check on you when I get in. Remember slave, you are always being watched."

My head was still looking at my hands in my lap as cum dripped down to them. "I know, sir." And I did. My tiny apartment in Waylon's building was covered in surveillance cameras. I had no privacy.

He stood straightening his cuffs. "Next time you're on stage, I better see you smile, Harper. That's why they pay you."

"Yes, sir."

He left without another word. I sat there naked and cold, the taste of him thick in my mouth, and tried not to cry. I knew Jess and his friend had left. I looked for him when I made my way back to my dressing room. I was glad he'd gone. I hadn't wanted him to see what I'd really become. But deep down inside, I hoped he'd come back for me.

Chapter 2

Arsenal

The clubhouse was at its best before dawn. Most guys thought that was after hours, during the silent slot between bar close and the sunrise, when every surface still held a film of the previous day's sweat and gasoline but before anybody had the energy to spill blood or secrets. Me, I liked the hour when the only people inside were the ones you'd trust to hold your skull while you puked, or hide your body if you went missing. The Iron Valor MC clubhouse still looked newly built from its rising from the ashes of the explosion that killed Parker, Wrecker's mate. But the building crumbling on top of her couldn't keep her dead thanks to the Angel King. He brought her back to life. Now the Angel King is Big Papa's father-in-law. What a mind-fuck *that* turned out to be.

I showed up early, per habit. My boots didn't squeak on the painted concrete. I let the main doors swing closed behind me and stood there a second, letting the place tell me who was in it. Nobody in the lobby. Distant sounds—coffee percolator, sound of a shower, the quiet scrape of a barstool being set down—told me exactly who was already up. No danger. No surprises.

I passed through the main hall, where the faded American flag and the club's own heart and dagger insignia flanked the long table. Church, they called it, though the only worship happening here was of the tactical variety. I noted the fresh slug in the drywall from last night's argument—Wrecker's handiwork, unless I missed my guess. Menace's absence was palpable, now that he was running the Midwest. The whole building felt fractionally lighter, like a sandbag had been cut from the load.

I found Bronc alone at the table, salt and pepper head bent over a stack of handwritten notes and the inevitable legal pad, his reading glasses perched halfway down his nose. He looked up at my entrance, blue eyes registering and dismissing me in a single pass.

"Regan," he said. "Coffee's fresh."

I nodded once, no words wasted. Got myself a cup, black, one sugar and sat to the right of Bronc one seat removed. Bronc watched me, measuring, but I outlasted him easily. Silence didn't bother me.

Gunner arrived next, boots still muddy from chores, a plaid shirt clean but already untucked. He grinned at me, big dumb farm-boy energy, and clapped a hand on my shoulder. Most people hated being touched, but with Gunner you either accepted it or you ended up with a broken wrist. He slid in next to me, last chair in the row, then tried to flatten his wavy auburn hair with spit. It had never worked before; today was no different.

"Wrecker's running late?" Gunner asked, voice pitched low.

"Five says he's wrapped up with Parker," I replied. I didn't actually bet, but I liked the way Gunner's eyes lit up at the thought.

Bronc snorted. "Church will wait until VP's in the seat. He brings the intelligence; you bring the muscle, Gunner. Arsenal brings the fucking rules."

I shrugged. "Somebody has to." I sipped my coffee, savoring the burn.

Big Papa sauntered in, usual smile on his scarred face.

"Gentlemen. I think we're gonna be graced with a fantastic day." He placed two boxes of scones on the table, that everyone went for immediately.

Doc hauled his ass in on Papa's heels looking like Clark Kent, all dark hair, good looks, wearing black horn-rimmed glasses, stoic as ever. "Fellas."

At 5:47, exactly thirteen minutes before Bronc's scheduled start, Wrecker slid into the room. He wore a shit-eating grin, three days of stubble, and a fresh scar at the corner of his mouth. He shot me a sideways glance, then dropped into his seat like gravity was optional.

"All here, then," Bronc said, stacking his notes and folding his hands. Even after all these years, his knuckles looked like stone. "Arsenal, report."

I opened my folder and started in my voice flat, all data. "Recon on Morgantown Pack as requested. Alpha: Waylon Steiner. Born '86, took over at age twenty-five. Secondary: Cornelius Madsen, listed as Beta but no direct pack relation. Estimated pack size: eighty to ninety, but only fifteen in Morgantown proper."

Bronc raised an eyebrow. "Where's the rest?"

"Houston, mostly. The Woodlands. Steiner's operation is based out of a private compound north of town. Morgantown's just window dressing."

Wrecker leaned in, eyes narrowed. "Explain."

"Steiner controls a multi-front business: clubs, loan sharking, and adult entertainment. The strip club is the nerve center—called The Eyrie. Exterior security's excessive. Two perimeter fences, both electric. Interior: at least six armed guards per shift, rotating patterns. Private security contractors, not pack."

Gunner looked genuinely confused. "Who the hell needs that kind of security in a hoity-toity part of Texas?"

I didn't answer him. It was a rhetorical question, and it was the right one.

"His personal convoy consists of three armored SUVs. All custom—run-flat tires, bulletproof glass, police scanners. They rotate vehicles every two weeks and never park in the same place twice. Intel says he takes all his meals inside the club or at his own residence, or at his five-star restaurant called Savage Garden. It's located in a restored historic Houston mansion with a secret underground dining chamber accessible only by freight elevator, where the Alpha's closest associates feast on food prepared by chefs who've signed NDAs. My guess is he's paranoid, but with cause."

Bronc's mouth tightened. "Likely bad blood between him and any number of people."

"I'd guess if we pulled the blueprints of his club we'd find private rooms wired for AV and maybe video, and not just for security. He's probably up to his beady little eyeballs in blackmail, control, maybe even surveillance of his own men."

"Fuckers," Gunner muttered, shaking his head.

I continued. "Wrecker might want to get on this. Looked like money's moving fast. Too fast for a pack this size. Morgantown's population is tiny. But Steiner's bringing in Houston-level cash—property, cars, weapons. He's got high-end taste and the muscle to back it up."

Bronc let that land. "So what are we looking at? Cartel? Trafficking?"

"Could be both," I said, not liking the confirmation. "He's probably tied in with at least two other packs, but not as allies—more like subsidiaries. I think he's testing how much he can expand before someone pushes back. And let's not forget that those fuckers were involved with the witches who killed Papa." I looked next to me and saw Papa's knuckles go white as he gripped his coffee mug.

I squeezed his massive shoulder just to let him know how glad I am he's still with us.

Wrecker spoke up, voice just a rasp: "What's your angle on his pack? Anything unusual?"

"He surrounds himself with a lot of guys who aren't wolves. I don't get that. We're the best muscle you can get. Why have humans as security unless it's because they are expendable?"

That got everyone's attention.

I let the silence stretch, then finished. "He's not running a pack. He's running a business. The wolves are incidental."

He let it hang a second. "Arsenal, you and Gunner will handle another recon. Wrecker, dig into Steiner's contacts—see if there's a pattern."

I nodded, closing my folder. "Copy."

Bronc looked at each of us in turn. "We don't move on this until we know more. I want to get to the bottom of their involvement in Papa's abduction. I also want to know if they are flesh peddling. If it's trafficking, we end it."

"Roger that," Gunner said, a touch too loud.

Bronc's gaze landed on me. "Arsenal. If you see something—if there's a personal angle—bring it to me."

He didn't say it like a threat, but it didn't need to be.

I stood, saluted with my mug, and left the room first.

Church let out, and as bodies scattered, I intercepted Wrecker in the corridor. Parker joined us from the living room. Wrecker fell in behind me like we were back in formation, and Parker trailed with her usual soft-footed stealth. I cut through the admin hall to the back office, knowing we'd be undisturbed. Not even Bronc poked his head in; he knew when a room was about to get classified.

The office had been reinforced in the rebuild. What used to be a crappy room with rickety furniture, now had a nice wooden desk and several padded chairs. The only adornment was a Texas flag with a bullet hole dead center. I'd put it there the first day we got back inside; nobody dared to take it down.

I waited until both of them sat—Wrecker slouched, knees splayed, arms crossed; Parker on the edge, back ramrod straight, black nails clicking a nervous rhythm on the tabletop.

"Alright," I said, closing the door, "I've got something. You need to keep this off the record."

Wrecker's eyes went flat, all jokes off. Parker just raised one eyebrow, like she was waiting to be amused.

I braced my palms on the table and looked at the flag, not at them. "There was a dancer at the club. Her name is Harper Lawson. She's my mate."

The word hit like a stray round in the room. Wrecker's brow furrowed, then his lips parted. "You're shitting me."

Parker blinked once, then stared at me with an intensity I hadn't seen since Wrecker threatened to spank her in the middle of the club picnic a few weeks ago. "You have a fucking mate?"

"Had. She rejected me. Sort of. I haven't seen her since before I joined Iron Valor. Not since..." I trailed off, steeling myself. "Not since she walked out. Five years ago."

I sat down. My posture, normally textbook, slumped for maybe the first time in my life. "She was from my original pack, Rising Moon. Came from a wealthy family, went to Julliard. We knew of each other for years, but I'm seven years older. I never paid much attention. Until one day I was home on leave and I ran into her in a coffee shop. Didn't take long for the bond to show up."

"Then what happened?" Parker asked, her voice gone all soft as if she was a therapist and not a hacker with anger issues.

I stared at the tabletop. "Her father. Piece of shit hedge fund manager. He didn't like that his precious daughter was tied to someone with less money, less status, less everything. He made her choose. I figured we'd work it out, that he'd come around." My mouth twisted. "Instead, she ghosted me. No call, no message. Her father told me—after—he said she realized I was a 'low life loser' and she didn't want to give up her future for someone like me."

"Fuck," Wrecker breathed. "That's cold."

"It gets better." I flexed my hands, feeling the old anger like static under the skin. "She was nineteen. I was twenty-seven. Her father said he'd see me in jail if I tried to contact her again. Said I was preying on her. It was all legal; she was an adult, but I didn't want him calling command, raising a stink. It was a fucking nightmare."

Parker's eyes narrowed. "You think she believed him?"

I shrugged. "Doesn't matter. She left. I made my peace with it." Lie. But it sounded solid.

"So why bring us in?" Wrecker asked, always direct.

"Because that's not the life she wanted. She was going to be a fucking dancer. Not...this." I kept my voice steady, but the image of Harper crawling on that stage made me want to break something, preferably her father's jaw. "I need to know how she ended up in that club. And why."

"Trafficking?" Parker said, tone clinical.

"Or blackmail," Wrecker offered. "Pack feuds. There's a million ways it could go south."

I nodded. "Exactly. And I don't care what Bronc says about waiting—I'm not sitting on my hands if there's a chance she's in trouble."

Wrecker met my eyes, his expression unreadable. "You sure you can keep it together?"

"Wouldn't ask for your help if I couldn't," I said, and meant it.

Parker studied me, then leaned in, voice barely above a whisper. "You want us to dig?"

"Everything. Her, her family, the club, Steiner. Leave no stone."

She cracked her knuckles, grinned, and pulled out her tablet from a messenger bag. "I'll start digging right away."

"Do it."

The silence that followed was heavy but not awkward. Wrecker clapped a hand on my shoulder, then stood. "We'll figure it out, Jess. And if anyone's got her locked down, they won't live long."

He meant it. I trusted him more than anyone.

Parker was already typing, the blue light flickering in her eyes. "She's lucky," she said, almost to herself. "Not many guys would come after someone who left them."

I looked at her, then past her, to the flag on the wall.

"She never really left," I said, my voice a low growl. "Not from here."

Wrecker gave a rare smile. "That's the Arsenal I know. And brother, you can't keep this from the Alpha. He deserves to know."

I knew he was right. I couldn't have Wrecker and Parker go behind Bronc's back.

"I'll go to him. I won't have y'all involved in some kind of deceit."

They both nodded as they walked out. I knew they'd have the answers I needed soon. It was time to act. I'd spent my life being two things: a soldier, and a protector.

And I was done losing people.

⁂

I headed to Wrecker's house. Their tech room looked like something you'd see at the Pentagon. Wrecker broke down Harper's last knowns with the focus of a bomb tech; Parker set up two laptops and a burner phone, hands flying. I stood behind them, arms folded, willing myself not to pace. Years of discipline kept me in place, but my wolf was pacing circles under the skin.

"She was supposed to be at Julliard," I said, more to myself than anyone, "not dancing in a strip club for some sociopath's pleasure."

Wrecker grunted. "People change."

"She didn't," I shot back. "Not like that. Not unless someone made her." My voice was sharper than intended, but neither of them flinched.

Wrecker's fingers flicked through printouts from Parker's bag. "What's your take, then?"

I exhaled through my nose. "She was a prodigy. Ballet was everything. Her old man controlled everything else—her money, her future, her fucking phone. If she left, it wasn't because she wanted to." I felt my jaw click. "Someone boxed her in."

"Could be Steiner," Parker offered, not looking up from her screen. "He's got a way of taking what he wants."

I clenched my fist, knuckles bone-white. "Or maybe he just enjoys breaking people."

The silence was tight, but not uncomfortable. More like the loaded space before a breach.

Wrecker shuffled a file my way. "You ever try to contact her after she ghosted?"

"Once after I figured she'd graduated," I said. "Called her home line. Her father picked up. Told me she'd moved to Europe, had a new life, didn't want contact with anyone from Texas. Said if I tried again, he'd have my record splashed across the internet."

Wrecker rolled his eyes. "What record?"

"Exactly," I said. "He was bluffing. But I couldn't afford to push it. Not with her just starting out."

I hesitated, then nodded. "Never mailed it. Didn't want to look desperate."

Parker started printing out data. "If I were to guess, here's where things really went south. About the time she'd been at Julliard for two years, her old man was accused in a Ponzi scheme. He was arrested. Look at the dates."

She handed me a stack of arrest affidavits and other paperwork. Sure enough, he'd been indicted on several charges.

"Look at the attorney representing him. I swear I saw his name when I was pulling information on Steiner." I was trying to remember where I'd seen the name.

Wrecker was clicking away on his laptop. "Bingo! He also represents Steiner. That's not a coincidence."

"Fucking fuck! I bet he sold her out! That was the last time she attended Julliard. Can we find out when she started dancing at that goddamn club?"

"It's gonna take me a while, but I'm gonna get the timeline of when everything went down Arsenal. Just give me some time."

I nodded at Parker. I knew if anyone could get all the information on Harper, these two people could do it. I should have gone to see Bronc and Juliet. I shouldn't have kept this news to myself and tried to handle it like a lone wolf. That's not what we do here. Hell, nobody is more by the book than I am. I just couldn't risk his giving me the order to stand down.

CHAPTER 3

Harper

Three days after Jess walked into my hellhole life, I still wasn't sure if I'd hallucinated him. I'd sat at my vanity every shift since then, waiting for the world's axis to tilt again, waiting for him to stride in, blue-black eyes finding mine across the dark floor and every cell in my body shrieking *MATE*. But it was like he'd never existed. No sign, no hint, no tingle at the edge of my nerves. If it really was him, he'd taken one look at the disaster I'd become and left it to rot.

The dressing room was fluorescent bright, my reflection haloed in vanity bulbs. Even out of costume, I looked like the ghost of a dirty secret—stage makeup refusing to scrub off, hair stuck in last night's product, collarbones dusted with glitter that probably wasn't coming off until I molted. The silence was almost unfamiliar; even the club's morning cleaning crew was gone. It was just me, the clock on the wall, and the low-level hum in my chest that hadn't faded since the first time I saw Jess in a military uniform and thought: he could kill me and I'd thank him for it.

I sat up, rolled my shoulders, and realized they were actually loose for the first time in months. I exhaled deep, lungs expanding without that tight band of dread. Waylon hadn't been around for two whole days, and even if I was only breathing borrowed air, it was nice to have it to myself for a change. Not a single "special request," not a single bite of food brought in with that creepy little smirk, not a single hand on the back of my neck making sure I remembered my place.

The girls at the club called me "the princess," though not in a nice way. If you'd asked them, I was living the dream—Waylon's favorite, top billing, my own dressing room instead of a locker in the hallway. But I'd swap with any of them in a second. Most of the other dancers had normal lives outside this place. Husbands, kids, even just a boyfriend who'd pick them up after their shift. I had a one-bedroom apartment a floor below Waylon's penthouse, a TV that only allowed Netflix and Amazon, and only allowed food deemed appropriate to keep me at the optimum attractive weight. The only computer in my life was the one in the club's main office, and I wasn't allowed within ten feet of it.

I tried not to think about my family. I'd heard my dad had gotten probation for securities fraud thanks to Waylon giving him the money I was traded for. I think my mother had left him and taken Brie, my baby sister, and gone to Europe to escape the scandal. I wanted so much to talk to them but kept telling myself it was better this way. If I ever made it out of this place, maybe they'd be proud that I'd survived.

I could hear the other girls in the hallway, laughing at some inside joke, the kind that only made sense if you'd never spent a night with Waylon Steiner. I used to eat lunch with them in the lounge, but after a while it got old, listening to them complain about the shit I'd have given my left arm for: a phone that couldn't get a good signal everywhere, a boyfriend who could text you "I miss you," a bad date that ended with nothing more than a hangover. I hadn't even bothered to make up lies about my old life. It's not like anyone here cared.

If they resented me, it wasn't my fault. Waylon had made it clear on my first night that I'd never be "just one of the girls." He liked to parade me around like his prize filly, the one with the "real training," the one who could do a thirty-two-count fouetté while half-naked and never wobble.

He also liked to remind me that I was here because of my father, that every dollar I made was another drop in the bucket of his debt. The contract said three years, but I wasn't stupid. Nobody left Waylon unless they left in a body bag. He made sure I'd never go back to classical ballet. About three weeks after I'd arrived, I was attacked. They only went for my knee. I suffered permanent ligament damage in my left knee. I could still dance around a pole, but I'd never dance Swan Lake again.

I heard a clink from the hallway; a glass or bottle against tile, and I knew the witches were starting their morning shift. It always made my wolf's fur crawl when they came through—tall, pale, usually in black or gray, always with perfect lipstick that never bled no matter how many shots they poured. They didn't work the stage; they worked the bar and the office, counting money and keeping tabs on who owed what. I'd tried talking to one once, asking about a regular customer who hadn't shown up in weeks. She'd looked at me with amethyst eyes and said, "He's dead. Don't ask again." I never did.

If the dancers hated me, the witches hated me more. They watched me like I was a bomb about to go off. I was convinced they were the real reason Waylon kept me so close. He didn't care about the shows. He cared about leverage, about owning a piece of my old pack. Maybe the witches were there to make sure I didn't try anything stupid, like running, or talking to a customer who wasn't on his approved list.

My stomach twisted when I thought about Jess seeing me that night. If he'd recognized me, the stage name, the collar of black lace Waylon made me wear for the "VIP sets." He'd seen my wolf, beaten and hiding behind a plexiglass smile. I almost hoped he hadn't recognized me. I almost hoped he never came back.

But that was a lie, and we both knew it.

I reached for the makeup wipes, but my hand shook too hard to use them. I set them down, looked at myself in the mirror, and tried to see something worth saving. I thought about the ballet recitals when I was a kid, how I'd stand in the wings and press my fingers to my chest, feeling the wild stutter of my heart and the wolf inside me yipping at the scent of roses and greasepaint. I wondered if Jess still thought about me, or if he'd moved on, found a mate who could fight for herself. I wondered if I'd ever see him again.

The door opened, and one of the witches glided in—dark hair slicked into a bun, pencil skirt, and a clipboard in her hand. She gave me a look like she was measuring me for a coffin.

"Waylon wants you in the spa. Now," she said, voice flat as a funeral march. "We'll need you ready for tonight. He has a client coming in."

"Got it," I said, forcing my body to stand. I reached for my robe and wrapped it tight around my skin. I followed her down the hall, careful not to show my teeth or my fear. The spa was at the end of the corridor, past the locked door that led to Waylon's private office. I hated the spa. I hated the way they touched my hair, my skin, like they were scrubbing me down for auction. But I went, because I always went.

For a moment, as I passed the window and felt the sun on my face, I let myself imagine what it would be like to run. Just for a second, to shift and bolt across the parking lot, out into the trees and the dry grass and the endless Texas wind. I'd never make it, but at least I'd die running.

The witch with the clipboard smirked. "You're not special, Harper. Remember that."

I bit my tongue. "Yes, ma'am."

She ushered me through the spa doors, and the world went white and clinical. I braced myself for the day ahead, for whatever new ways they'd find to break me.

But somewhere deep in the shadowed part of my heart, I still hoped Jess would come back.

Maybe he already was.

The club called it a "spa," but the closest thing to relaxation I ever found there was the moment the steam got too thick to see anyone's face. The witches ran the place like an autopsy lab—clinical, cold, all white tile and the whiff of formaldehyde hiding under eucalyptus oil. I perched on a too-plush bench in the first treatment room while one of the salon girls, a junior witch named Aria, checked me in on her tablet. Her black hair was lacquered flat against her skull, and her talon-nails clacked like a woodpecker as she typed.

"Full moisture, scalp, and cuticle trim for Harper," she said to the girl behind her, not even bothering to look up. "No acrylics this time, per boss."

I could've told them my nails didn't need it; I never bit them anymore. There were better ways to cope. I tucked my hands under my thighs and waited for Aria's assistant—a redheaded shifter, not a witch—to lead me to the wash station. Every part of the process was designed for humiliation. You sat, they handled you; you kept your mouth shut. Most of the time the girls ignored me, but sometimes I'd catch them talking behind the rolling carts, eyes darting over to me like I was a specimen in a jar.

Today was worse than usual. The redhead started to massage shampoo into my scalp, and I flinched hard, pulling away before I realized what I was doing. Her hands paused mid-motion.

"You okay?" she said, softer than I expected.

"Fine," I said, forcing myself to sit still. "Sorry. Sensitive today."

She shrugged and finished the wash, but I saw the look she gave Aria—tiny, commiserating, as if to say, "See? Not so perfect after all." I wanted to melt into the seat, disappear into the drain with the dirty water and hair dye.

They did the moisture treatment next, wrapping my head in hot towels and leaving me to stew under the heater for what felt like hours. I stared at the floor, at my own bare feet and the pink-painted toes. Every little thing about this place was meant to make you feel like a princess. Every little thing made me want to peel off my skin and start over.

When they finally unwrapped me, Aria took over. She did the cuticle trim with the same skill she used to mix drinks—quick, efficient, and barely looking at what she was doing. "Any special plans tonight?" She said, voice like a plastic smile.

"Just the usual. Maybe a couple of VIP sets."

She made a face, just a flicker, then dug the trimmer a little deeper than necessary. I didn't flinch. I'd learned better.

"You know," she said, leaning in so close I could smell the sweet rot of her lipstick, "the other girls talk about you."

I didn't respond. I already knew what they said. Princess. Whore. The one who gets her own room because the boss can't keep his hands off her. I'd heard every version.

"They think you're better than them," she went on, voice low. "But I know what it's like having a man who owns you."

She smiled, showing the edges of her teeth. I wondered what they'd look like if she ever let her wolf out. I wondered if mine even remembered how.

Aria finished the manicure in silence, then ordered me into a steam cabinet for "pores and relaxation." She locked the wooden shell around my body, with only my head sticking out like a cartoon. The heat pressed in, baking my skin, and for a second I almost understood why people liked this. If you breathed deep enough, you could pretend it was just water and air, nothing else.

But my mind didn't let me rest. It wandered, like it always did, back to the night my father called me into his office and told me about the debt. He'd acted like he was doing me a favor, like giving me to Waylon was the only way to save what was left of our family. I hadn't even fought. Not really. I'd gone to the first meeting, let Waylon look me over like a cattle auctioneer, signed the "employment contract" without reading the fine print.

The worst part wasn't the dancing. I could handle that, even liked it, sometimes, when the crowd went quiet and I could pretend I wasn't naked. The worst part was the extra duties, the "special performances" in the VIP rooms, the expectation that my body was just another part of the show. I learned quick: when the Alpha said jump, you asked how high.

Waylon never forced me to mate him, not officially. He didn't want the mess that came with a bond. He wanted me compliant, pretty, and empty. He used alpha command sparingly, just enough to remind my wolf who owned her. Sometimes he'd look at me across the room, narrow his eyes, and I'd feel a sick warmth bloom in my belly, my limbs turning to water. I hated it. I hated how my body obeyed even when my mind screamed no.

I hated the way I'd started to crave it.

The steam timer dinged, and the cabinet opened. Aria's assistant handed me a robe and led me to the next station: blowout, makeup, and costume. We passed the break room where the other dancers clustered around a table, all heads turning as I walked by. Their eyes flickered with something mean and hungry, like hyenas watching a gazelle limp past. One of them, a tiny shifter with a scar down her cheek, muttered, "Here comes the Queen." Another snickered. I didn't dignify it with a look.

The makeup artist was a witch too, and she painted my face like she was prepping a mannequin: foundation, contour, lashes, lips. Not a word passed between us, and when she was done, she spun my chair to face the mirror. I didn't recognize the girl who looked back—a doll with perfect skin, lips the color of ripe strawberries, eyes rimmed in blue glitter.

"Knock 'em dead, honey," the witch said, and spun me right back to the hallway.

I wanted to cry, but I'd lost the ability years ago. I hunched my shoulders, fixed my gaze on the floor, and padded barefoot back to my dressing room.

Inside, I found the costume for the night's finale hanging on the door. Black mesh, studded with crystals, and a G-string so thin it might as well not exist. I changed in silence, fingers trembling as I adjusted the straps, then stood in front of the vanity and tried to remember how to smile.

For a second, I almost managed it.

I checked the clock. Thirty minutes until curtain. I sat at my vanity and stared at my reflection, searching for the girl I used to be. The one who dreamed of Paris and Broadway, who believed in mates and fate and happy endings.

She was gone.

All that was left was this: a body, perfected and prepared for auction, a voice that only mattered if it whispered "yes, Alpha."

I ran my tongue over my teeth and tasted blood.

The wolf in me whimpered, but she stayed silent.

She knew better.

When it came time for the final set, I was so tired I thought my knees might buckle before I made it to the stage. But you don't get to be Waylon's number one without learning how to fake it: how to move like your bones are made of champagne, how to arch your back just right so the crowd loses its mind, how to sell pleasure when all you want is oblivion.

I padded down the blue-lit hallway, mesh costume biting into my skin. Every heel-click echoed off the tile like a countdown to something. I reached the wings and stood waiting for my cue, listening to the DJ shout my stage name into the roar of a Friday night crowd. It was packed—wall to wall bodies, sweat, and noise, the stink of beer mixing with perfume and old lust. The air hit my bare arms like a slap.

"Showtime," I whispered to myself, and stepped into the light.

The glare of the spotlights burned away the world for a second. Then the crowd snapped into focus: dozens of faces, most of them leering or hungry, all of them trained on the body I was about to turn inside out for their entertainment. I took my place by the pole, smiled like my life depended on it, and let the music take over.

First twirl: slow and easy, hair flying, one leg hooked high to show off the mesh and the glitter. Money rained down almost immediately, dollar bills and twenties and even a couple of fifties, all of them just paper and sweat. The DJ had picked something sultry, bass-thumping, the kind of song you could get lost in if you didn't care who was watching.

I cared. Because tonight, someone was.

Halfway through my first rotation, I caught it: a flash of blue-black, a familiar silhouette in the far back corner, just outside the reach of the strobe. My heart lurched, and for a second I lost the beat. Jess. He was here, and every nerve ending in my body snapped to full alert.

Don't fuck this up, I told myself. You get one chance.

I locked my eyes to the mirror behind the bar, used it to scan the crowd while I danced. He hadn't moved, but I could feel him watching—so intense it made the air crackle. He wore a black t-shirt and jeans, nothing flashy, but he stood out like a wolf among sheep: still, patient, dangerous. The men around him hollered and shouted, but he didn't even twitch. He just watched, and it made my skin burn.

I went through the motions—spin, split, drop, arch—every move a reminder that my body wasn't really mine. I let the routine take over. At the bridge; I pulled off the top with practiced grace, tossing it to the edge of the stage where it landed on a pile of money. At the breakdown, I bent at the waist, hands flat on the floor, ass to the crowd. The room lost its mind. A shower of bills hit my calves and thighs, sticking to the sweat there. I reached back, grabbed my own flesh, gave it a squeeze. I looked over my shoulder and caught Jess's eyes, just for a heartbeat.

They glowed wolf-dark, full of something between anger and longing.

I wanted to run off the stage, wrap myself around him, beg him to take me away from all of this. Instead, I finished the set. On the last count, I did my signature move: a slow, teasing look over my bare shoulder, then a kiss blown to the darkness. The crowd howled, men pounding their drinks and girls throwing napkins and cash.

An usher ran to the stage, collecting all the cash.

I bolted for the wings, not daring to look back. My hands shook so hard I wrung them together to try to calm them. I took a detour through the service hallway, where Kenny the bouncer was waiting to walk me back to my room.

"You were on fire tonight, Harper," he said, grinning his gap-toothed smile. "Waylon's gonna be proud."

I forced a smile back. "Thanks, Kenny." He'd been nice to me, once, when I first started. I remembered how he used to bring me donuts during rehearsal, before Waylon got his hooks all the way in.

The usher moved around us and handed the cash to Kenny.

He walked me down the hall, money in hand, stopping only when we reached my dressing room.

"Darlene wants to see you," he said, voice dropping. "She's in the office. Probably about your take."

"Okay," I said, fighting the urge to collapse. "Just give me a minute."

Kenny nodded and left. I closed the door and braced both hands on the vanity. My chest heaved, lungs fighting for air. I stared at the girl in the mirror and tried to remember how to feel anything other than terror and shame.

Jess was here. This time he'd seen everything. He'd watched me sell myself to a crowd of strangers, strip down to my skin and act like it didn't matter. He got the entire show, saw what I was now—a whore in a pretty package, a wolf with her teeth filed down to nubs.

My hands wouldn't stop shaking. I pressed them to my face, breathed in the scent of sweat and stage makeup, and tried not to cry.

Someone knocked at the door. I straightened up, wiped my eyes, and put on my best "nothing to see here" face.

Darlene walked in, a stack of envelopes in her hand. She was one of the only humans who worked here, a fifty-something with hair dyed pink and a face like an old cartoon bird. She didn't like me, but she kept it professional.

"You think if you ignored me I'd go away?" The scowl on her face made her even uglier. I just stared at her. "You've got a VIP tonight," she said, not bothering to hide her disdain. "Big spender. Wants you in the champagne room at midnight. Don't fuck it up."

I nodded and gave her an emotionless answer. "Okay."

She set an envelope on the table. "Waylon's orders."

"Is he back?"

Darlene snorted. "Not 'til tomorrow. But he'll know if you don't deliver for the client." She lingered a second, like she was waiting for me to break down or complain, then rolled her eyes and left.

I slumped in the chair and stared at the clock. Thirty minutes until I had to go out there again, sell myself one more time.

I wondered if Jess was still here. If he'd try to save me, or if he'd just laugh while I burned.

Either way, I had to get through tonight. I smoothed my costume, wiped the runny mascara from under my eyes, and made myself stand up.

The wolf inside me bared her teeth.

I had no choice in the matter. This was my life, my shame through no fault of my own. I'd take the stage like I did almost every night, and I'd own it.

CHAPTER 4

Arsenal

The Eyrie stood two stories tall on the old business loop, every inch of its limestone facade bleached by years of the Texas sun. I parked in the alley like a good customer and walked around to the front. The entrance had all the signals: valet in a tailored vest, a security man in a tailored neck, a pair of bronze doors with etched glass and nothing to see inside. I stopped just shy of the entry, got my head straight. You only got one first impression in a place like this, and the wrong one would end you before you reached the coat check.

The vestibule was marble and velvet and expensive as fuck. They'd taken every cliché of a gentleman's club and upmarketed it until even the wallpaper looked smug. A hostess with a diamond chip in her incisor greeted me before I'd taken a full step inside. She wore a matte black sheath and heels that could've killed a small mammal. I noticed her scent: anxious, sharp, undercut by a designer floral that tried too hard.

"Good evening, sir." Her smile was professional, with a trace of the same smile a flight attendant gives to a man she's already decided is harmless. "Is this your first visit to The Eyrie?"

"It is," I said. I kept my voice pitched low, unthreatening. That always made them more nervous.

She showed me past the check-in podium. I scanned the room as we moved—chandeliers set to a dim gold, bars at each corner manned by white-jacketed staff, the stage dead center with a circle of dark wood tables radiating out like the rings of a target. I clocked two off-duty cops at the bar, sleeves rolled, eyes hard. The waitresses wore navy bustiers and garters but moved with the wary economy of people who knew exactly how fast a night could turn. The air hummed with low music and the metallic tang of old bills.

"The main floor's nearly full," the hostess said. "Do you have a reservation?"

"Friend of Mr. Corbin," I replied, dropping the name from our last recon. "Said I should check it out."

The smile stayed pasted on, but her pupils flared for a fraction. She nodded, led me past a pair of glowering bouncers, and seated me at a half-moon booth with a polished brass rail. "Service will be right with you. Anything else, just ask."

I watched her heels click away, then took a long scan of the perimeter. Two exits, one on each wing. Main stage up front, three dancer poles. There were at least eight servers on the floor, and I counted six cameras in sight. I ran a thumb over the ridge of scar on my left hand, comforted by the weight of the Glock at my back.

A server appeared at my elbow. He wore the same fitted jacket, hair slicked back, no jewelry. "Welcome to The Eyrie, sir. Will you be needing a drink menu?"

I told him just water, then looked up at the main stage as the lights faded and the music changed.

The crowd surged, not with hoots or howls but with the controlled anticipation of men who bought their excitement in measured, expensive ounces. The DJ didn't announce the dancer's name. She just walked out under the lights, and every eye in the place locked on.

Harper.

It was her, and the wolf in my chest nearly burst through my ribs. She looked taller than I remembered even from when Gunner and I were here a week ago. I was so shocked I barely noticed anything past her face. She looked like she had more muscle and curve in her hips, her long legs carving geometry out of the blue light. Her blonde hair, all one sheet, fell straight down her back like a curtain about to drop. She wore a mesh bodysuit that glittered at every angle and left nothing to the imagination but everything to want.

She didn't smile. Not in the way the other dancers did. Her face was blank as glass. She didn't flirt with the crowd; she looked above them, over them, through them. Every movement was deliberate. She took the pole with a single hand, spun a slow half-circle, and the mesh caught the light in patterns across her skin. The first drop brought her to a split, then she rolled up easy as breathing, never breaking rhythm. The bills started raining almost immediately—tens, twenties, a few hundreds. The other dancers worked the corners and the floor. Harper stayed in the light.

I couldn't stop watching. I told myself it was recon, that I was here to observe, but every flicker of her body called to the wolf in me and made it impossible to focus. I saw the way men watched her. I saw how their faces went slack, how their hands gripped their drinks tighter. One patron in a golf shirt leaned forward so far I thought he'd fall out of his seat. My hands clenched the brass rail. The urge to break his teeth buzzed in my forearms.

She didn't see me, not once. But I saw the way she watched the bouncers every so often, as if confirming which ones were on duty, which ones carried guns, which ones cared enough to do more than stare at her ass. She'd learned to scan the room the way I had—always knowing where the danger would come from.

She did a series of spins, fast and sharp, then landed in a crouch that sent a wave through the whole crowd. She made it look easy, but I knew how much control that took, even before whatever had made that left knee weak. She let her hair fall forward, hiding her face, and for one second she looked more animal than dancer—more wolf than girl.

When the song ended, the lights faded, and she gathered the bills with an efficiency that bordered on bitter. No blown kisses, no winks. She vanished offstage in a blur of pale skin and shimmer.

I took a breath. My water arrived. I sipped, then scanned the club again. The servers moved like chess pieces, always three tables ahead of the customer. The men drank slow, calculated. There wasn't the raucous energy of a regular strip club, no sense of release or abandon. Every man in here wore his mask tight to the bone; the only thing real was the hunger.

I slouched in the booth, arms spread. The upholstery was soft, but itched at my shoulders. I dialed up the burn in my glare, just enough to keep anyone from getting ideas about chatting me up.

I caught a fragment of conversation from the next table; a stocky guy with an oilfield tan and a thinner man in a checked shirt. "You see her?" the thin one whispered, low and reverent. "Fucking poetry, man."

"She don't fuck if you don't have enough cash," the stocky one replied, not taking his eyes off the stage. "That's what makes 'em want her."

"Bet you could break her if you had enough time," the other one said, and they both laughed, too sharp and too quick.

I memorized their faces. If they ever tried, I'd break them instead.

The show cycled through two more dancers before Harper reappeared on the floor, now in a cocktail dress and heels that looked less "stripper" and more "ambassador's mistress." She walked the floor with a tray, stopping at VIP tables and collecting compliments like arrows to the chest. She didn't touch, didn't smile, just nodded and kept moving.

I drained my water. The server came back. "Would you like to see a menu, sir?"

"I'm waiting on a friend," I said, and let my gaze linger just a hair too long. He nodded and left. I knew Wrecker was in place, covering the parking lot and the back door. All I had to do was wait for the signal.

Harper made her rounds. She never looked at me. I wondered if she recognized my scent, or if the years had burned that out of her nose. I watched her hands: steady, sure, never trembling. She was working. She was surviving. I respected that.

Another set ended. The crowd thinned a little as the clock edged past midnight. The club was quieter now, the soundtrack dialing down to a slow, orchestral pulse. I saw the manager, a tall, bleach-blond asshole in a sharkskin suit, make a circuit of the floor. He stopped at each dancer, whispered something in their ear. When he reached Harper, she stiffened, then nodded once. He kept his hand on her back for a second too long, then moved on.

My teeth ground together hard enough to rattle the fillings.

A couple in business casual moved to the bar near me. The woman wore heavy perfume, but underneath I caught her anxiety, the edge of some fight they'd been having all night. The man ignored her, watched the stage instead. The woman noticed me noticing, and for a second our eyes locked. She looked away fast, but not before I caught the look of "what the fuck are you doing here?" on her face.

It was a fair question. I didn't belong. But neither did Harper.

I counted out the seconds as she finished her floor rotation and disappeared into the corridor behind the bar. I considered whether to follow, but Bronc's voice in my head reminded me: patience. Mission first. Get the data, get the timeline, then get the girl.

But my wolf had other ideas. He wanted to kick down the door, take her by the hand, and run for the hills.

I checked my phone. A single ping from Wrecker: "Manager headed up to the VIP rooms. It's arranged."

Upstairs, it was all glass and hush. The main stage was a memory; up here, it was just corridors of carpet, soft gold sconces, and the quiet pulse of money moving unseen. I texted Wrecker: "Phase 2. Ten minutes."

When I made for the VIP corridor, the bouncer at the curtain looked me up and down. "You on the list?"

"You bet," I said. "Mike Rodgers."

I dressed the part. Black suit, crisp white shirt, gold cufflinks. Left my own boots but buffed them to a spit shine. The trick with these places: look like money, but not the kind that needed to brag about it.

I was at ease since I knew Wrecker would be shadowing the lot from a street over. My credentials tonight were the ones Parker had cooked up: forged driver's license, a pack of corporate credit cards tied to a legitimate Houston holding company, and a stack of hundreds to grease the right hands.

I was shown to the "Infinity Suite," which cost more than a month's rent in most places. The host swiped a card to let me in, then shut the door without a word. I stood there, letting my eyes adjust to the low light. The room was larger than an efficiency apartment. Real leather couches, a white marble bar with decanters pre-poured, and a crescent stage in the middle of the wall, empty but for a single pole lit by a cold blue spot.

I took the seat farthest from the lights, my back to the wall. I made note of the camera light in the upper right. With a twist, I yanked out the small jammer from my jacket and turned it on. The camera's red light blinked twice, then went dead. Thank you, Wrecker.

They made me wait ten minutes, just enough to remind me who controlled the clock. When she finally arrived, she did not look up. Harper's hair was down, silky and pale in the low light. She wore a black sheath dress, and her arms were bare but for a single silver cuff. She carried herself like someone heading to their own execution—measured, resigned, already halfway to the gallows.

She stopped five feet from me.

I let the silence draw out. It was a tool; silence. It let you see how long someone could last before their nerves snapped. Harper lasted longer than most. She didn't fidget, didn't speak. Her wolf was strong, even in this place.

After a full minute, I spoke. "Take off your dress."

She hesitated. Just a flicker, a ripple down her neck. But then her hands went to the zipper, and in one smooth motion, she pulled the dress off. She wore nothing underneath, not even the thin stage thong. Her body was paler than I remembered, but the muscle was still there, hard and clean. The mesh of old scars on her knee shone like a watermark.

She dropped the dress to the floor and waited.

"Your shoes," I said, my voice dry and flat.

She bent, slipped off her heels, and set them neatly beside the dress.

"Now dance."

The room's sound system was voice-activated; I whispered "play" and some slow, unfamiliar song started up, the kind meant for closing time and final calls. She stepped onto the stage, climbed the short riser, and put her hands around the pole.

For ten minutes, I watched her. Every turn, every climb, every split was measured, perfect. She didn't look at me or past me. She danced for herself, and the longer I watched, the more I saw that this wasn't about seduction at all. It was about proving a point: you can break a body, but not a will.

When the song ended, she came down from the stage, arms loose at her sides, and waited for my next order.

"Crawl."

She got on her knees, hands splayed on the thick carpet, and crawled to me. Her hair fell forward, veiling her face, but I saw the flush at her neck, the pulse at her throat. I wondered if it was anger or shame or something worse.

When she reached my feet, she knelt and waited.

I let the silence stretch again, feeling the electric push-pull of where our bond should be. My wolf clawed at my ribs, wanting to lick the wounds, wanting to pull her to us. But I made him wait, just like I made her wait.

I watched her breathing, slow and steady; the muscles of her back tensing and releasing. I wondered if she knew who I was. I wondered if it would matter.

I stood before her. "Lean up and take my cock out of my pants. Do not look at my face." I wanted to punish her. Wanted to make her feel the anguish and humiliation I felt the day I came for her to find she'd left me without so much as a goodbye.

She did exactly as I'd commanded. She unzipped my pants and took my rock-hard dick out with practiced hands.

"Now use your mouth and worship it like it's the alpha cock you always dreamed of," I said. The words tasted filthy, angry, but accurate.

She moaned deep in her throat, and took me in, inch by inch.

"I want my cock all the way down your throat. You need to suck it down as far as you can, girl. Use your tongue to lap up all of your spit around it. You know how to do it. I'm sure you've had a fair number of dicks in this mouth. Show me how deep you can take me. How much you want it."

She sucked my dick like it was the last one she'd ever have in her throat. Her groans only made it sweeter. I saw her clench her thighs together as her fucking pussy dripped for me. I wanted to shove my fingers inside her until she writhed.

I pulled her hair back so I could control her as I shoved my cock down her throat.

"That's it, baby. Take me all the way down. I can see your throat bulge with the tip of my cock. And when I come down your throat, you take it all. Don't spill a drop." Her moans told me she was ready for it.

"God, you feel so good. I can't hold it any longer." My release came in waves of cum down her throat, and even as she struggled, she swallowed, tears running down her face. From her moans and the way her hips shuddered, I knew she came right along with me. Incredible.

"Tell me something. You always make yourself come when strangers fuck your face?" I asked, voice ragged.

"No, I've only done that once. And it was this time. I think because it was for my fated mate," she whispered.

Her eyes slowly met mine.

"You owe me an explanation, Harper."

"I wish I could talk to you, but..." She cut her eyes to the camera in the corner.

"That camera isn't filming us right now." I helped her up and handed her dress to her and a bottle of water.

After putting the dress on, she sat next to me.

"There's too much to tell, Jess. Just know that I never wanted to leave you, and I never stopped loving you. I never rejected you. My father did all of that. All of this. I'm a prisoner here. Steiner would kill me or my sister if he knew I was talking to you or knew who you were."

My rage seeped out of me the more she spoke. I sat her on my lap so I could hold her for the few minutes I had left.

"I'm going to fix this and find a way to get you away from him. I'll keep you safe when I do. Do you trust me?"

"Always."

Then I kissed her. I tasted a trace of myself on her tongue, but I also tasted Harper. Peaches and vanilla and a flood of memories swept over my soul. At that moment, I didn't care who I had to kill; Harper Lawson was mine and I would claim her as soon as I could. Nothing and nobody would stop me this time.

Chapter 5

Harper

After Jess left, I didn't move for a full minute. I sat on the couch, dress loose around my body, hair hanging in my face like a shroud. My mouth tasted like him, and tears pooled at the bottom of my throat, but my eyes stayed dry. The wolf inside me howled against the inside of my chest, scraping for the door he'd just closed behind him.

The blue mood light of the VIP room faded from electric to ice as the minutes passed. My knees throbbed from where they'd been on the carpet, and my hands stayed clenched, nails digging little half-moons into my palms. I didn't let myself stand. It was easier to stay small, not give the cameras a better angle. I didn't doubt for a second that they'd be back on by now; I could almost sense the hum as the little red light rekindled in the corner of the ceiling, drinking in every second of my humiliation.

I'd barely managed to wipe my mouth with the back of my hand before Darlene came in. She didn't bother to knock, just shouldered the door and surveyed the scene with flat-eyed disappointment.

"Don't tell me you're falling apart now," she said. No "sweetie," no "hun." I guess I'd lost even that sliver of camaraderie.

I pulled myself together, dress up, hair behind my ears, and let her look at me. She didn't miss the red in my eyes or the roughness in my voice, but she didn't care, either.

"Get changed and wait by the staff entrance. Rage'll drive you home." She turned, but not before giving me one last once-over, like I was a steak she was sure had gone bad in the fridge. "And clean up before you go. Boss wants you looking presentable even for the bouncers."

I nodded. "Yes, ma'am."

My voice sounded like sandpaper, and she didn't respond.

The minute she was gone, I gave myself twenty seconds to break. Just twenty. I buried my face in my hands and pressed until my skull felt like it would split, until the roaring of my pulse covered every other noise in the world. I let myself remember Jess's hands, his voice, the way he'd said my name in the dark, the promise of "I'll get you out." It was the first real hope I'd felt since my father gave me away, and it was dangerous, like holding a match to a leaking gas line.

Twenty seconds. Then I walked to the tiny washroom and splashed cold water over my face until the sting replaced the ache. I toweled off, smoothed my hair, and stepped back into the hallway, leaving the memory of him locked up tight inside.

I moved through the backstage area like a ghost. The other girls were long gone, the rooms stripped of noise and perfume, leaving only the scent of cleaning chemicals and the static of old arguments. I checked my locker, but there was nothing inside except the club uniform. I knew the witches monitored everything, kept a file on even the most innocent interaction. If I so much as glanced at a forbidden name, they'd have me in Waylon's office before sunrise.

At the exit, Rage waited in the idling Mercedes. He was the only one of Waylon's crew who ever bothered with a real suit—black tie, white shirt, shoes that probably cost more than most people spent on a month's worth of groceries. He didn't look at me as I slid into the back seat, didn't comment on the swelling around my eyes or the way my hands trembled. He just adjusted the rearview mirror, watched me for a second in the glass, and then pulled away from the curb.

The ride to my apartment was fifteen minutes, but Rage made it in nine, never missing a red light or a speed trap. I pressed my forehead to the cold glass and watched the city scroll by. Houston at night was all taillights and shadows, a city made up of secrets you were never quite privy to. The sky was dotted with clouds, and the headlights carved tunnels out of the wet air. I tried not to think about what waited for me at home, or how I'd find a way to sleep tonight. My body was still electric with Jess's touch, but the rest of me was already crawling back into the hole it had spent the last three years digging.

Rage pulled up to the high-rise, didn't bother with small talk, just held the door as I stepped out.

"Walk straight in, ma'am. Cameras are live."

He said it quiet, almost apologetic. I gave him a nod; didn't bother with a smile. I doubted he'd know what to do with one if he saw it.

The lobby was marble and mirrored glass, the kind of place meant to look expensive but instead just made you feel like you were being watched from every angle. The doorman was a shifter, but not wolf; his ears twitched under his cap as I passed, and he gave me a nod so small it could have been a tic. The elevators were already called and waiting, the gold panel buttons reflecting the blue-white of the security lights. There was a camera in the elevator, too. I stood perfectly still, hands folded, face composed. A few years ago I would've made a face at the lens, stuck out my tongue, dared the witches to do something about it. Now I just pretended it wasn't there. I'd learned the lesson quick: every gesture was ammunition for someone else's gun.

My apartment was on the twenty-fourth floor, one below Waylon's penthouse. It wasn't a bad place—two bedrooms, open living space, little kitchen with granite counters and an oven I'd never used. But it felt more like a hotel suite than a home. Everything was uniform, pre-furnished, the art on the walls generic and soulless. There were no pictures, no souvenirs, not a single book that hadn't been checked by the pack's security team. The only personal item I had was a snow globe from Paris, a tourist trap from my first and only trip outside Texas, and I kept it hidden in a vent behind the washer.

I walked the perimeter, checking every window, every lock, just as I'd been trained. The surveillance panel above the TV flickered on as soon as I entered, scrolling through feeds of the building's hallways, the lobby, the garage. My own apartment was on constant view, every corner visible to whoever watched from the club's office. I pretended not to notice, but every step inside was a performance for someone else's eyes.

I set my bag down, shucked off the dress, and folded it neatly on the coffee table. I pulled on a ratty t-shirt and sweats, then stood by the window, looking down at the city below. It was almost 2:00 a.m. The traffic was thinning, but a few cars streaked along the freeway, taillights red and unhurried. Somewhere in the building, someone was playing classical music—Tchaikovsky, I thought, but I could've been wrong. The melody was warped by distance and the hum of the air conditioning. I let it fill the silence, just for a minute.

The apartment was supposed to be a reward for loyalty, a sign that Waylon "valued" me. But I knew the truth: it was a cell, padded and perfumed, but a cell all the same. The trackers in the walls, the locks on the bedroom door, the guard at the end of the hall. I was a trophy, nothing more.

I thought about Jess. How he'd looked at me in the VIP room, how he'd touched me like I was precious instead of ruined. It had been so long since anyone had seen me and not the mask I wore, the club's property. My wolf whimpered, remembering the feel of his hands on my skin, the sound of his promise: I'll get you out.

The hope of it scared me more than anything else.

I flicked off the surveillance panel and headed for the bathroom. I needed to wash Jess's scent off of me before Steiner had a chance to notice it. I stepped under the shower and the water hit me scalding and perfect, burning away the last traces of cold from the ride home. I braced my hands on the tile and let my head fall forward, eyes closed, and let the water hammer my skull until I couldn't tell where the pain stopped and the relief started.

I scrubbed hard, as if I could dig out every memory the club had left on my skin. I used the abrasive side of the washcloth, dragging it along my arms, my collarbones, the swell of my breasts. I left the inside of my thighs for last, working until the skin was pink and raw.

I didn't want to wash him away. But I had to.

The water turned cold, and I shut it off, letting the spray trail down until it was just a shiver. I wrapped myself in a towel and sat on the closed toilet, dripping, heart beating against the bones of my chest like it wanted out. I pressed my knees together, pulled my legs up, and let the towel fall open so I could look at what was left of me.

My left knee was a mess. The scar was barely visible—a white line along the side of the cap, faint but noticeable if you knew to look. The club doctor had wrapped my knee in a thin web of silver to slow the healing and to ensure it wouldn't heal exactly right. I ran my finger down the scar and tried not to remember the night they'd given it to me.

My first week at the Eyrie, I thought I could do it. I told myself it was just dancing, just performance, just three years and then I was free. I practiced my routines at night, learning the poles and the steps, the way the floor vibrated with bass and the way the spotlights could blind you if you didn't know how to move with them. I got it down fast. I quickly started earning more money than all the other dancers.

But a month in, I'd been cornered in my dressing room. Two men. Their only agenda was to damage my knee. They pulled me off my feet. I fought. My wolf fought harder. But one of them had silver knuckles, and he caught me on the knee with a punch so hard I heard the bone crack. I bit one of them, nearly took off his finger. But they just laughed, called me "freak," "bitch," "meat," and left me bleeding on the floor.

I managed to drag myself to the door. The club's witch medic patched me up with no words, just a tight smile and a needle full of morphine. By the time I woke up, Waylon was waiting. He told me my injury was "unfortunate." But he didn't seem too broken up about it.

He called in the pack doctor. I'd never seen a wolf so dead inside—pale, with eyes that looked right through you. He laid me on the exam table, strapped my wrists to the rails, and showed me the roll of silver wire. Said it was "for your own good, darling. You heal too fast. We need you a little more breakable." He wove the filaments around my knee while I screamed. Then he wrapped a kind of wrapping around the wires that a witch spelled, making it impossible to remove. He told me the wrap was just for a couple of weeks, then they'd remove it.

Once it was removed, the joint was healed, but not in the same way it would have been if my shifter healing had been allowed. I'd be 100% today. The joint never healed right. I could still dance, but not the way I used to.

Waylon made sure to watch the whole procedure. He liked to see his property getting customized. After, he kissed my cheek and told me I'd be "even more beautiful with a limp." He had just made sure I'd never be able to be a ballerina.

I sat in the bathroom, towel slipping off my shoulders, and looked at the knee until my eyes went blurry.

About two months after was the first time I had to work the VIP room. I tried to refuse. I told Steiner I couldn't, that I wasn't ready. He just handed me a dress, black mesh with a zipper that ran from neck to ass, and told me, "You'll do as your Alpha says." I went because I didn't have a choice. When I told him I was a virgin he stopped. "You just made me another $10k tonight my little slave. Thank you."

I threw up twice before they brought me to a suite with a mirrored ceiling and a semicircle of leather couches. But then, the witches had given me some kind of cocktail that had made me more compliant, and I no longer cared so much.

Waylon was waiting. Two other males were in the room with him. I smelled whiskey in the air. He told me to dance, so I danced. The dress had a slit that went from the floor to my hip, which allowed me to move freely. I wished that was all he'd ask of me. When the song finished, I knew my life was about to change forever.

Waylon snapped his fingers for me to come to him. He grabbed my arms and leaned me over the back of the sofa.

"Gentlemen, as promised, our beautiful angel is going to give me her cherry tonight. And you have paid to view the auspicious occasion."

He unzipped the dress and ripped my panties away. He bent me over further, exposing me to the disgusting men in the room.

"Have you seen a prettier virgin pussy?" He raked his fingers through my slit, and I jerked my body wanting to get away. That's when the first slap across my ass hit. He leaned over my back and bit my earlobe. Through gritted teeth, he warned me. "Do not embarrass me in front of paying clients, slave." He stood and looked back at his clients. She needs some priming. He licked his fingers and shoved them inside me, twisting them and moving them back and forth. "Make yourself ready for me, little slave." He used his Alpha command. And even though I was not his and he had no claim, I was his pack, and by virtue of what he was doing to my body, I felt my core clench around his fingers. "Ah, look at this, gentlemen.." He pulled his fingers out and to my shame, I knew they glistened with my wetness. I heard him suck his fingers. "I'd say she's ready for her Alpha's cock." And that was all the warning I got before he shoved his enormous cock inside me, ripping through my virginity in one thrust.

My body reacted violently, trying to straighten against the cruel invasion. The pain was almost unbearable. He didn't allow me any time to acclimate to his size before he was pounding into me again and again. His hips slapped against my ass and thighs. There was nothing pleasant or alluring about the way he took me. It's a small mercy that my body had created any slick for the bastard at all or I'd have been ripped to shreds. Tears streamed down my face. The entire experience was a nightmare come to life. He pulled out in time to shoot blood and cum all over my back.

"There you are, gentlemen. The evidence!" He shouted, proud of his gruesome accomplishment. Like he'd done something to be lauded.

When it was over, he leaned down and whispered in my ear. "You make a pretty picture when you cry."

Then he snapped his fingers again. The witches came in, took me to my dressing room, cleaned me up, styled my hair, powdered my nose, and sent me back on stage for the midnight set.

I never forgot that night. Every time I spun on the pole or visited the VIP room, the pain reminded me what I was.

Now, sitting in the dark bathroom, I let my hair fall forward and stared at the lines of my body. I traced the scars on my knee, the bruises on my heart.

I knew I'd have to face Waylon tomorrow, maybe even before. I hated him with every fiber of my being. I wanted him dead. But he held all the power.

I stood up, wiped the mirror, and looked at myself straight on. My face was gaunt, a little too hollow around the eyes, but my skin glowed under the red from the shower. I looked wild, dangerous, alive in a way I hadn't since I left Jess on that coffee shop patio all those years ago.

I dried off, slipped on a nightshirt, and crawled into bed.

I must have drifted, because the next thing I knew it was after three a.m. and my whole body was knotted with cold, despite the heavy covers. I rolled onto my side and tucked the comforter under my chin, hugging a pillow tight to my chest. I'd almost managed to lose myself in the rhythm of the city—cars on the freeway, an ambulance siren, the click and whine of the building's elevators moving up and down.

But the sound that finally broke through was the softest: the hiss of my bedroom door opening.

I froze. My heart thudded, once, twice, and then I forced myself to relax every muscle at once. If you tensed, he'd know. If you fought, he'd enjoy it more.

I kept my eyes shut. It was easier not to look.

The bed dipped behind me, the mattress bowing under Waylon's weight. He didn't say anything at first, just settled his body into the space behind mine, one arm thrown over my hip. I could smell the scent of him; cologne, liquor, the faintest metallic tang of blood. His hand was meaty and rough, fingers landing square on the bare skin of my stomach, then sliding down, slow, until he found the place between my legs.

He didn't even bother with foreplay.

His breath was hot against my ear as he moved his fingers inside me, not gentle, not slow, just insistent. I gritted my teeth and thought of anything else. My wolf curled up and whimpered, but the human part of me just wanted it over with.

"I heard another man looked at what belongs to me tonight," he whispered, voice so low it barely made it to my ears. "I watched you dance for him. Video quality was shit for some reason, but I know he paid handsomely for you to suck his dick." He bit down on my shoulder, hard enough to bruise. "How did he taste, little slave?"

I didn't answer. I just breathed, shallow and even, willing my body not to react.

He moved his hand, a sharp twist, and my body betrayed me with a tiny gasp. He grinned against my skin.

"I asked you a question, Harper."

I forced the words out, voice flat as I could manage. "Like any other ordinary rich guy."

"That's right," he growled. "Nobody compares to your master, right?"

He pulled my body flush against his, pinning me. He lifted my thigh and thrust inside, fast and brutal, like he was punishing me for something. Maybe he was. Maybe he always had been.

His free hand found my breast and squeezed, hard, thumb digging into the softest part. I held still, breathing through the pain, eyes fixed on the dark window. His rhythm was ugly, all dominance and no tenderness, and each movement jarred my bad knee until it sparked with fresh pain.

But the worst part was my body. He'd used his alpha power on me so many times, it didn't even feel like magic anymore. The commands were buried in my skin, my nerves, my blood. That and the spelled cocktails the witches had given me so many times had tricked my body into thinking it wanted this. My body flushed, responded, tried to draw him deeper even as my mind screamed for it to stop. He'd trained me well.

He licked the sweat from my neck and grunted, "Such a good little slut. Bet you came for him, didn't you?"

I didn't answer.

He pumped faster, hand on my hip, and I felt my muscles tighten against my will. When he hit the spot that always made me see stars, my body gave in, clenching around him as I shuddered. I bit down on the pillow, hard enough to taste blood.

"Fuck yes," he said, voice triumphant. "Nobody ever fucks you like your Alpha."

He pulled out, then stroked himself, coming across my lower back in hot, sticky stripes. He waited until the last shudder died in my body before he rubbed it into my skin with his palm, a final humiliation, the club's logo branded invisible on my flesh.

He got up, slipped on his pants, and yanked the covers off me. "Don't wash it off," he commanded. "You wear my scent until morning. Let every dog in this building know you're owned."

I lay there shivering, covered in sweat and semen, staring at the bright squares of city light on the ceiling.

Waylon paused in the doorway. "Always such a good fuck, my little slave." He didn't even look at me.

"Thank you, Alpha," I said. The words burned on my tongue after three years of repetition.

The door closed behind him, and I heard his heavy footsteps echo down the hall. I waited until the elevator whined him away before I let myself move.

I curled up, knees to chest, and pressed my face into the cold pillow. I didn't cry. I'd stopped crying a long time ago. But I let myself imagine Jess, just for a second, standing in the doorway, promising me that none of this was forever.

Hope was a razor. Its cut stung while you waited for the miracle you needed.

But I held onto it anyway.

I listened to the city until morning, counting down the hours until I could get out of bed, scrub myself raw again, and start over.

Survival. That's all I had left.

Until the day Jess kept his promise.

Chapter 6

Arsenal

The walk from the parking lot to Bronc's office was thirty-six yards, and I felt every inch. The clubhouse was quiet—too early for the regulars, too late for anyone coming down off a bender. Just the hum of the fridge in the kitchen, the soft tick of the hallway clock, and Wrecker's boots hitting the tile behind me in sync. I opened Bronc's door and let it swing wide, standing at the threshold until he looked up. I'd learned never to enter a man's office until invited, especially when his face looked like a heatmap about to go white hot.

He had both fists on the desk, knuckles flat and white as chalk. The veins in his arms looked ready to blow.

"Sit," he said.

We sat.

Wrecker took the left-hand seat, slouched low and casual. I stayed upright, elbows on knees, hands steepled. Parade rest, the way I'd been taught.

Bronc stood. He circled his chair like a caged dog, then planted his hands again and glared at both of us. His voice was low, but it had the resonance of a shotgun behind it.

"I got a question," he started, slow and deliberate. "At what point did y'all decide that the chain of command in this club was, what, a fuckin' suggestion?"

He fixed Wrecker first, then me. I didn't blink.

"You go off the grid in Houston," he went on. "You sniff around a rival's territory. You insert yourself into whatever backroom clusterfuck Steiner's got running. And the best part? You do it without so much as a phone call to your goddamn Alpha." He slammed his palm on the desk. "Are you both fucking brain-dead?"

Wrecker grinned, half-hearted. "Better to ask forgiveness than permission, boss."

Bronc ignored him and turned the full force of his stare on me. "Regan. You're supposed to be the stable one. The rules guy. Now I got Doc and Juliet blowing up my phone at four a.m. saying you're in the wind with my VP."

"Had to move fast," I said. "Didn't want to tip anyone."

Bronc exhaled, slow. "You didn't want to tip anyone. You didn't want to tip *me*. You understand how that sounds?"

I nodded. "Yes, sir."

He looked like he wanted to launch the nearest office chair through the window, but he kept his hands flat. "What the hell could possibly justify this?"

I glanced at Wrecker. He gave a subtle nod; the go-ahead. So I said it:

"Harper is my fated mate."

The silence was absolute. The hum from the fridge seemed to die. Even Wrecker, who knew, looked away.

Bronc just stared. No visible reaction for five full seconds. Then he sank into his chair and pressed his hands to his face. When he spoke again, the anger had gone flat and heavy.

"Of *course* she fucking is. Why wouldn't she be? Why the hell can't a female wolf in the state of Texas ever meet her mate like a normal goddamn person, huh?" He spread his hands, like we were all at a backyard barbecue and this was just a funny story about fate screwing him. "No, they gotta fuck it up. Get trafficked, or dealt some other kind of shit hand, get locked up by a psycho. Then they always land here. With Iron Valor. With me."

"I thought she had rejected me five years ago."

He pointed a finger at me. "You waited *five* years to tell me you had a fated mate? Guess that explains why you're such a fucking asshole to everyone who finds happiness with a woman."

I shook my head. "Well, fuck, Bronc. I didn't *know* she hadn't actually rejected me. Not until I talked to her."

His eyes went sharp. "You saw her in the club?"

I nodded. "She's at Eyrie. She's working the main floor and the VIPs. She's not a guest. She's on the menu."

Bronc's jaw bunched. "Was she trafficked in?"

"She says it was her father. Debt. Pack politics. She's been there three years. Longer than the news cycle on that whole Ponzi scheme."

Wrecker jumped in. "We think it's connected. Steiner owns Eyrie, but we picked up a bigger stink: witches everywhere, and maybe more. Arsenal thinks it's a front for something."

Bronc's eyes narrowed. "What kind of 'something'?"

Wrecker laced his hands behind his head, stretching. "There's way too much money moving for a strip club, even one with Houston clientele. Cash flow is more like a hedge fund. And the staff—several are witches, and the bouncers are human but with serious military backgrounds. Steiner's not running a pack. He's running a black site."

Bronc chewed on that, then looked to me for confirmation.

I gave it. "They're moving people. Maybe wolves if they are being subdued with spells. But Maltraz hates wolves; he'd do whatever it takes to humiliate them. And the sales are not domestic. That's the reason we've not really heard about it. Looks like they may transport them through the ship channel and then auction them once they get to their destination somewhere overseas. We also get the feeling Steiner's part ends at the docks."

He said nothing for a while. He just looked at me, then past me. Then he shook himself, like a dog snapping off rain.

"Why didn't you call me?"

I didn't have a good answer. "I just wanted to get to her fast. Guess I was afraid you'd make me wait until we had a solid plan in place, like any good ops leader would." I hung my head with the shame I felt at letting my Alpha down.

His gaze drilled a hole in my skull. "I'm not your enemy, Arsenal. I would've helped. You know that. But you could have put our entire pack at risk by going off half-cocked. And Wrecker, you should fuckin' know better. You're my VP. I expect better from you. Can I no longer trust the men who are supposed to be closest to me?"

I nodded. "Shit, sir. I just... I'd never felt driven like that. My wolf wanted to bust out of my skin to get to our mate. I know it was reckless." I stopped.

He let the silence hang. Then he looked at Wrecker. "What about you? Did I make a mistake picking you to replace Menace as my VP?"

Wrecker shrugged. "Somebody had to back him up. If he'd gone alone, he wouldn't have made it back alive. I'm certain of it. Plus, we got vital information while we were there. It was a fuckity fucked way of doing things, but we *did* accomplish a few things."

Bronc's mouth twisted. He tried simply to be mad, but I could see the worry underneath. He laced his fingers together on the desk, knuckles still white.

"Alright," he said, voice low. "Let's do it proper. Start at the top. Give me your full sitrep."

I did, breaking it down into five points, just the way I'd have done in the Corps.

"One: Harper is there under duress. Two: The club is run by Waylon Steiner, but there's clear evidence of witch coven involvement. They're not just employees; they're part of running the operations. Three: Physical security is ex-military, not pack. Four: Steiner is facilitating human trafficking. We suspect the supply goes through the Houston Ship Channel. Five: It's all being handled off-books. No good digital trails, but we think if we dig deep enough, we'll find ties to Maltraz."

That last word changed Bronc's face entirely. The anger melted off, replaced by a hard, cold focus.

"Maltraz," he said. "You sure?"

"As sure as we can be without further research. But we had our suspicions back when he was trying to infiltrate our bank accounts. That fucking demon king deals in the nastiest, most evil enterprises known to man. There are few things more evil or lucrative than human trafficking. We'd talked about his involvement in something like this before. This would be right in his wheelhouse. And I could swear I noticed a demon or two inside that club."

Wrecker chimed in. "We'll pull records of companies we had our eyes on back when he was trying to screw us over a few months ago, checking for shipping companies specifically. I guarantee we'll find trucking companies that drop cargo at the Houston docks."

Bronc leaned back in his chair and looked at the ceiling. Then he leaned forward again, elbows on the desk. "So Steiner, what, owns the docks?"

I shook my head. "Maybe. But it feels like he'd get more out of it than just doing what Maltraz says. Steiner's not the type to work for anyone. He's too proud for that. But no way he'd cross the demon king. The way he sets up his security, the way he acts around the witches. He knows that they have more power than he does."

Bronc stared at the desktop, then at us. "So what's your plan?"

Wrecker looked at me. I spoke.

"That depends on you. How far do you wanna go? The main thing I care about is extracting Harper. Getting her safe. Past that? It's up to you. I hate the idea that there are women, maybe wolves are being taken and sold or God knows what else. Don't know if you wanna just pass the info to Rafe and let the king take it and run. Maybe we need to bring him in anyway. If Maltraz is involved, it becomes bigger than Iron Valor for sure. I just want my mate back in my arms."

Bronc nodded, just once. Then he stood and came around the desk, standing over us.

"Alright. You're going to run this op. Both of you. But you're going to do it my way. That means no more cowboy shit, no more going off the reservation. You check in at least every other hour, even if it's just a ping. I want Parker working comms. You got that?"

"Yes, sir," I said.

He put a hand on my shoulder. Heavy, warm. "Jess. You get her out, and you bring her here. She's family now. But first, you gather every piece of information you can about their operation. And then you'll create an extraction plan and bring it to me."

I didn't say anything, but my wolf wanted to howl.

He squeezed once, then let go. "Now go. Brief Parker. I have to inform Rafe. The same way I expected to be informed as your Alpha, he expects it as my king. And if you even think about going rogue, I'll have Doc shoot you myself."

Wrecker grinned, stood, and clapped Bronc on the back. "Wouldn't have it any other way, boss."

I got up, and Bronc followed me with his eyes. "Don't fuck this up, Arsenal."

I nodded. "I'll do my best."

We left the office, and I could feel the shift in the air. The tension was still there, but it was pointed outward now. At an enemy, not each other.

We were a pack again. And nothing on earth or hell was going to keep me from getting Harper back.

Wrecker's tech room was the nerve center of the Iron Valor compound. He'd recently built an addition to his ranch-style house to accommodate more equipment. The large room was wired with enough power to light the Dairyville night. The inside was chaos: every inch of wall hung with monitors, whiteboards, cables, and at least three different flavors of tactical vest. The table in the middle overflowed with laptops, tablets, paper files, and coffee mugs of Parker's fancy pour-over coffee she was famous for.

Rocket, Parker's dog, was sprawled across the worn leather couch but hopped up the moment we entered. He made a beeline for me, tail a jet turbine, and jammed his head under my hand for a scratch.

"Somebody missed his boyfriend," Parker drawled from the swivel chair, legs tucked up, pink highlights shining through her dark brown hair, hoodie sleeves flapping as she typed. She didn't look away from her triple-monitor setup. "Wrecker's late with his breakfast again."

Wrecker grunted, dumped a box of scones from Aspen's bakery, and flicked Rocket's ear as he passed. The dog huffed, then went right back to licking my knuckles like they tasted like beef jerky.

Parker pointed a remote at the wall, lighting up the primary display. "Alright, gents. Here's the info." She hit a key, and the screen filled with a list of business holdings in Maltraz's portfolio.

Wrecker swept all the loose gear off the nearest chair, dropped into it, and started running his own laptop. "These all of 'em?"

"All as of the time he thought he was draining Iron Valor accounts," Parker said. "I've started working out from there. I'm focusing on warehouses and trucking companies now, looking for logos that carry his sigils."

The holographic display hummed to life, casting blue shadows across Parker's face as she leaned forward in the spinning chair. "Maltraz's empire's got more layers than a good lasagna," she said, fingers dancing across two keyboards at once. A spiderweb of corporate entities bloomed across the main screen - Cypress Holdings, Blackmast Logistics, a dozen others with innocuous names.

My finger traced a glowing connection between them. "Shell companies feeding shell companies. Classic laundering." My eyes adjusted to the light of the screens as they parsed data streams. "But there's a through-line here."

"Bingo." Parker punched a key, and six red pins stabbed into a map of the harbor district. "All these 'legitimate' shipping subsidiaries lease dock space from..." The screen zoomed in on a crumbling warehouse complex. "...Steiner Maritime Properties."

Wrecker's soda can crumpled in his fist behind them. "Our friendly neighborhood restaurateur and strip club owner owns the docks now?"

"Not directly." Parker spun up tax records that blurred at the edges - redacted sections glowing like infected wounds. "Steiner's got a silent partner. Something called Horizon's Reach LLC, registered in the Caymans." Her nose wrinkled. "Which just happens to share a P.O. box with Maltraz's 'retirement fund.'"

I tilted my head toward the shipping timetables suddenly scrolling beside the map. "These cargo manifests. The weight distributions are off."

"Like they're reporting half the containers they're actually moving," Parker nodded, pulling up customs documents that shimmered with digital tampering traces. "And guess which patrol routes get 'rerouted' whenever these ghost ships come in?" She threw military deployment charts onto a secondary screen, the gaps in coverage pulsing like open wounds.

The room buzzed with the quiet fury of puzzle pieces snapping into place. No smoking gun yet, but the shape of the gunpowder trail was forming; a shadow empire built on stolen lives, its roots sunk deep beneath legitimate businesses. I gripped the edge of the console, my voice a low growl.

"Find me a thread. However small."

Her grin was all teeth and reflected screen light. "Already tracing Horizon's bank feeds. If Maltraz sneezed near those docks, we'll find the tissue."

Outside, thunder rumbled - either a coming storm or the distant detonation of one of Wrecker's "stress relief experiments". The real explosion was happening here, in the electric space between data points and human desperation, where monsters hid behind spreadsheets.

I watched the screen, following the arrows and lines. "They're not moving drugs. Too careful."

"No," Wrecker said. "Bodies. Nothing that leaves a chemical signature."

I ran a finger over Rocket's spine, thinking. "If they're moving them by rail, the containers will be lined. Shielded."

Parker grinned, "Already on it. Most of the shipments are labeled as perishables—produce, seafood, that kind of shit. But when you cross-reference the weights, half of the containers are ten percent heavier than listed. That's a lot of celery."

"Or a lot of spelled people," Wrecker added.

He leaned in, scanning the scrolling data. "Notice the pattern? Every third Friday night, a double batch unloads from the railcar to the holding facility at the docks. Cargo then gets loaded onto a Maersk freighter."

I traced the route in my mind. "That explains why they have witches on the payroll. They have to have someone on hand to spell their merchandise and control the scene."

"That's my guess as well," Parker said. "And they ship these poor people overseas. Every final destination is either Korea, Thailand, or some private port in the Philippines."

Wrecker turned, eyes cold and bright. "That's a Maltraz signature if I ever saw one. It's evil. Only the sickos with enough money can buy a new pet every month."

Rocket whined and nudged my hand harder. I gave him a rub behind the ears, trying to steady the burn in my chest.

"Alright," I said, "so we know where they're going. Question is, how do they get them out? You can't just walk human cargo past customs, even spelled."

Parker grinned wider. "That's the sickest part. Most of the containers have a double wall—hidden space inside. Some even have oxygen tanks, rations. They're built for survival."

Wrecker's hands hovered over his keyboard. "You remember that story from last year? Four kids found alive in a storage unit, no memory of how they got there?" He didn't wait for a reply. "I'd bet that was a dry run. Now they've perfected it."

I felt my jaw grinding, a remnant of an old military tic. "How many have they moved?"

Parker scrolled, lips pursed. "Hard to tell. But by my count, at least three containers a month, minimum seven heads per."

I did the math. "Thirty a week. That's over 20 a month."

Wrecker nodded. "Now extrapolate that over a year. Between humans and wolves, they are devastating families and packs."

I sat back, Rocket's head in my lap, and tried to process it. I thought about Harper, about the girls at Eyrie, and wondered how many of them knew what waited at the end of that line. Probably none. Maybe all.

I forced my voice to calm. "What about the witches?"

Wrecker shrugged. "They handle logistics. Blackmail. Find a way to wipe the memories if needed. Remember, we have our own witch, and she is the most powerful of them all. She can make damn sure nobody talks."

I thought back to the way Aspen had disintegrated the Wyrdmother of the Verdant Hollow Coven when she tried to hurt Big Papa. That girl has witch and angel power. I wouldn't cross her.

Parker chimed in, "I'd bet most of the witches in that club aren't high-power. But the ones running security, they are likely carrying some kind of dark magic. I know my girl Aspen can wipe them all out, but you know her heart is as tender as can be. I hope it won't come to that. But she'd hate the idea of those women being taken. We'll just have to see how it goes."

Wrecker smiled, sharp as a blade. "We don't need the manifest. We need the list of drivers. Every one of them is either human or wolf, and nobody swaps runs without approval."

He gestured to the board. "We start at the port, work backward. Find the last-mile guys, squeeze them until they break. Once we have a name, we track the holding facility. That's where they keep the girls before shipping."

I picked up a pen and circled the warehouse address. "We hit this site first. Parker, you keep tracing the digital. Wrecker and I will do recon, see if there's a weak link in the fence."

Parker raised an eyebrow. "And Harper?"

I swallowed. "We extract her first. If she's still at the club, I'll go in. Alone."

Wrecker's eyes flicked up. "Not happening. You get her out, but you're not soloing the hit."

I met his gaze. "You want her safe? This is how it has to be. They know my face. She knows my scent. If I don't do it, nobody will."

The tension stretched until Rocket barked, snapping us all out of it. Wrecker laughed, dry and low. "Fine. But if you go dark for more than five minutes, I'm calling in the National Guard."

Parker turned back to her monitors. "And I'll have drones on standby, just in case."

I grinned. "Good."

I stood, gave Rocket one last pat, and walked to the board. The addresses and names blurred together, but one word kept burning: Harper.

She'd spent three years in that place, waiting for a miracle. She was going to get one.

I traced my finger along the shipping route, from the docks to San Pedro, then up the coast to some no-name town in northern California. I remembered Maltraz's signature: hit fast, hit hard, then move before anyone can follow. This was his hand. Maybe even his endgame.

Wrecker came up beside me and clapped me on the shoulder. "You got this, Jess."

Parker wheeled her chair over and bumped my hip with her knee. "Go get your girl, Arsenal. We'll cover the rest."

I nodded, took a breath, and looked around the room. The screens flickered, the lines pulsed, the data crawled across the glass in cold logic. But under it all was the heat of the hunt. The promise of violence, of righting a wrong the world had let fester.

I checked my phone. One unread text: a photo of the vacant lot next to Wrecker's house. A piece of land I'd always meant to buy, but never had the time or the nerve. Now, I looked at it and saw something different: a blank slate. A start.

I closed my eyes and pictured Harper there, sun on her hair, bluebonnets at her feet. I sketched a house in my mind: strong walls, wide windows, a porch that ran the length of the front. Room for our own dog, and maybe a pup or two.

But first, I had to get her out. Whole.

"Alright," I said. "Let's do this."

The team moved, each to their station. Wrecker prepping surveillance, Parker hacking deep, Rocket wagging his tail like the world was already fixed.

I watched the board, the route, the future I could almost see.

And for the first time in five years, I believed in it.

CHAPTER 7

Harper

Two weeks with no sign of Jess, no chance at a phone, no hint of rescue. I'd spent every night under black lights and the gaze of men who'd never learn my name, and the only thing keeping me upright was the stupid animal hope that maybe he'd come for me. I tried to burn that hope down to cinders, but it never really died. It just smoldered in the pit of my chest, waiting for something to ignite it again.

Tonight the club was packed. Wall-to-wall bankers, oilmen, frat boys in knockoff designer suits, and the businessmen who decided if they were going to be more than predictors of prey. The lighting was bluer than usual, maybe to match the night's "Arctic Goddess" theme; maybe a cold theme was indicative of what this place was. Cold, indifferent, unfeeling.

I had a third set. I stood in the wings in my sapphire mesh and tried to breathe through the pre-show nausea, not that it did any good. Every girl in the lineup glared at me like I was the prom queen about to ruin their night. They hated me for a lot of reasons, most of which weren't my fault. I was always the "Princess." They still called me that when they thought I wasn't listening. Sometimes they didn't bother to lower their voices.

The real reason was Steiner. He made a show of favoring me—extra spa time, a nicer room, the best costumes. He wanted me bright and shiny for his high rollers. The rest of the girls didn't get shit except broken nails and maybe a night off if they blew the manager hard enough. I'd have traded every favor for a day with a regular job and no eyes on me.

I heard a commotion at the back exit and looked out to see what was happening.

Rage, one of Steiner's bouncers, stormed through with a girl in a headlock. She was small, brunette, maybe twenty. Not a shifter—her scent was all fear, no wolf. She kicked and screamed, shoes flying off her feet and nails scoring angry red lines across Rage's arm. He didn't even flinch. He just dragged her through the door.

The girl howled, "Let me GO!" Rage ignored her. He shoved her forward, hard enough that she hit the tile and skidded.

I knew what came next. They'd parade her through the back for "processing." If she were lucky, she'd end up waiting tables or dancing on the side stages. If she wasn't, Steiner would make an example of her.

Vespa, one of Darlene's witches, followed behind in her little leather skirt and heels, clipboard held like a judge's gavel. She barely even looked at the new girl. Just wrote something down and stalked off toward the manager's office. When Rage hauled the girl to her feet, she tried to bite him. He laughed and slapped her so hard her head snapped sideways. I felt the blow on my own jaw.

Vespa reappeared and motioned for Rage to bring the girl to her. She pulled out a tiny black vial and uncapped it, waving the open end under the girl's nose. The girl tried to turn away, but Rage held her by the hair. Vespa said something in a language that made my scalp crawl, and the girl's body went limp.

The girl's head lolled, her eyes half-closed, and Vespa grinned. She pushed a strip of tape over the girl's mouth, then motioned for Rage to take her to the green room.

"See you on stage, honey," Vespa cooed. Then, softer, "if you last that long."

They disappeared into the gloom. I didn't envy the girl. Not because of what was going to happen to her, but because I'd been here long enough to know that the real horror wasn't the pain. It was the way it numbed you, day by day, until you stopped feeling anything at all.

The rest of my shift went by like every other: a blur of hands and money and the constant, low-grade terror that one wrong step would end me. I watched from the hallway as the new girl took her first turn on stage. She wore a red mesh bodysuit and nothing else. Her movements were jerky at first, then smoother, as if she'd suddenly remembered how bodies were supposed to work.

But there was nothing behind her eyes. They were blank as marbles, not even tears left in them.

The crowd cheered, threw cash, screamed for her to go lower, bend deeper, show more. She did, because there was no other choice.

That was the part that made me sick: not the humiliation, or the pain, but the certainty that this place would eat you alive and spit out only the prettiest bones.

After her set, the girl was gone. I didn't see her in the locker room, or in the bathroom, or even huddled outside for a smoke. Sometimes, they vanished after a night or two, "transferred" to another club or "let go." I'd stopped asking questions. The last girl who asked ended up with her head shaved and her tips docked until she left on her own.

I didn't even get a chance to take off my shoes before Darlene stormed into the dressing room. She didn't knock—she just threw open the door, eyes already locked on me like I was the only thing standing between her and a five-minute cigarette break.

"Lucky night, Harper," she drawled, lips twisted into something that wasn't quite a smile. "Steiner wants you for a VIP. Right now."

I looked down at my smeared makeup, my hair stuck to the sweat on my neck, and tried to make sense of it. "I'm supposed to have a finale set. Two more rotations—"

She cut me off, snapping her fingers so hard the fake diamond ring nearly broke the sound barrier. "Not tonight, sweetheart. Tonight, you're the main event."

Darlene set a Styrofoam cup on the vanity, the heat of it already wilting the cheap plastic lid. The liquid inside was the color of pond sludge, and it steamed up a sour herbal reek that made my stomach clench.

"Drink this," she said.

"No, thanks," I replied, and reached for the makeup wipes instead. My hands were trembling, and I hated her for noticing.

Her eyes narrowed. She didn't raise her voice, didn't get physical. She didn't need to. She just said, "Drink," again, and this time it hit my body like a shove.

I curled my fingers around the cup, trying to resist, but it was like my muscles belonged to someone else. My wolf howled in protest, but even she couldn't override the compulsion. My lips touched the rim, and I tasted the bitterness before the smell even registered.

It was foul—burnt citrus, spoiled honey, and something metallic underneath. I gagged, tried to pull back, but the words Darlene hissed next—soft and in some language that sounded like broken glass—made my hands tip the cup further, until I had to swallow or choke.

The tea seared down my throat, blooming cold and hot at the same time, and I could feel it spreading through me: a shiver, then a numbness, then a faintly pleasant fuzziness at the edge of my brain.

Darlene watched, arms folded, smug as hell. "You can try to resist my orders, you little shit. But you'll always do what I say. And you think that drink was bad?" She leaned in, her perfume a sickly wall of gardenia and nicotine. "Just wait until you see what's waiting in that VIP room."

She laughed, not like a person, but like someone auditioning for a horror movie. Then she yanked open the costume rack and pulled out a dress I'd never seen before. It was black leather, so tight it looked spray-painted, with a neckline that plunged to my navel and a hem that barely covered my ass.

"Put it on," Darlene said.

I started to protest, but the words caught in my throat, sticky and foreign. My hands moved on their own, stripping off my stage gear and sliding into the dress. It fit like a second skin—if your skin was made of latex and hopelessness.

Darlene tossed a pair of stilettos at my feet. "He wants you in these. Walk careful, wouldn't want you to break anything important."

I slipped them on, each step a little more unsteady than the last. The tea's warmth had settled in my chest, dulling the fear and replacing it with a strange, syrupy calm. I knew I should be panicking, or at least running, but my body just kept moving forward, obedient and empty.

Darlene checked me over with a critical eye, then grabbed my wrist and pulled me down the hallway, past the mirrored walls and the still-humming green room. The other girls barely looked up as we passed; they'd seen this before, and nobody wanted to catch the curse by accident.

At the end of the corridor was the elevator—real, not the decorative fake one in the lobby. Darlene punched a code into the keypad and the doors slid open with a hiss. I stepped inside, the world tilting slightly as the floor rose beneath me.

We went until we stopped on the second floor. The doors opened onto a short hallway lined with black marble and gold-framed mirrors. The air was cooler up here, thinner, and every surface gleamed like it had just been cleaned for a funeral.

Darlene pushed me out of the elevator, towards the door her grip iron on my arm. She put the code in another door and left me in the room. "Good luck, princess," she whispered, then turned on her heel and left me standing in Steiner's private VIP room.

I tried to steel myself, but the tea made it hard to care.

The door closed behind me with the click of an electronic lock, but I wasn't alone.

The suite looked like a murder fantasy designed by a luxury architect—black marble floors, oil paintings that oozed sexual violence, a chandelier dripping with smoky quartz. The curtains were drawn, but even with them shut, the parking lot light's glow found its way in, crawling over the surface of the bar and the low velvet couches.

Waylon Steiner stood in front of the minibar, swirling something brown in a glass. His suit was navy, his shirt open just far enough to show off the fresh tattoo on his collarbone—Greek letters, I guessed, but I couldn't read them. He didn't bother to turn as I entered. His attention was on the other guest.

The man—no, the creature—standing beside him was nearly seven feet tall. He wore a Tom Ford suit that looked tailored for a pro wrestler, and his skin was the shade of old slate, smooth and matte. His face was sharp angles and shadow: high cheekbones, black hair razored close on the sides with a braid running to mid-back, and a nose like a blade, ridges from bridge to nostrils pierced with three gold rings. His eyes glowed red, but not like a wolf's; the irises were vertical, a cat's eye that shimmered and narrowed when it caught the light. His mouth was wide and full of fangs, the canines more saber-toothed than human. His hands were massive, with fingers tipped with black, lacquered claws.

I'd seen monsters before. This one was bored.

"About fucking time," Steiner said, setting his drink on the bar. "Slave, get over here."

The tea was still in my system, dulling the panic, but not enough to override the fresh spike of fear. I forced my body to move, stepping forward on the too-high heels. The demon (because what else could it be) watched with the air of a food critic sent to review a McDonald's.

Steiner walked around me, eyeing the leather dress and my bare legs. "You look like a dime-store fuckdoll," he said. "Perfect."

The demon's gaze raked over me, assessing, then flicked to Steiner. "Is this the one?"

"That's the girl I told you about. Strong as hell, but she'll fold if you put the right screws to her." Steiner grinned. "She's the best piece of ass in this place."

The demon inclined his head, polite. "I'll be the judge of that."

Steiner pressed a hand to my lower back, right above the tailbone, and forced me to stand still. "Strip."

He didn't say it with any emotion, just as a statement of fact. The magic in my blood thrummed. My hands moved to the zipper without waiting for my permission. I peeled the leather dress off, folding it over a chair, then stood there naked except for the shoes. My skin broke out in gooseflesh from the sudden chill.

Steiner made a show of looking me over, then turned to the demon. "You want a drink, Maltraz?"

So that was his name. I'd heard it whispered in the club before. Maltraz, the business partner. The one even the witches were afraid of.

Maltraz waved a hand. "Later. Have her dance."

Steiner grinned, teeth showing. "You heard the man, slave. Put on a show."

I wanted to run, or at least punch someone. My wolf screamed at me to move, to fight. But the spell worked better than any collar. I walked to the pole on the slightly raised stage and wrapped a leg around it and spun. My routine was certain; my steps sure. When my feet met the stage, they slid apart, hips rolling. I danced, slow and sinewy, arms above my head and hair swinging in front of my eyes. I pretended I was someone else, someone who wanted this and not who I was—a woman buried in humiliation.

Steiner leaned against the bar. Maltraz just watched, expressionless, as I moved, bending, twisting, grinding my body into the nothingness between us.

"She's graceful," Maltraz said finally. "I see the slight scars. I like them."

Steiner snorted. "Cost me. Had to cripple her old career to kill her dreams."

Maltraz made a low sound, somewhere between a laugh and a growl. "You mortals. Always so wasteful."

He gestured to me. "Come here, girl."

I stopped dancing. My heart thumped loudly in my chest, but I obeyed. I crossed the floor to him, my knees threatening to buckle at the way his eyes drilled through me. When I got close, he reached out and tilted my chin up with a single claw.

"You know who I am?" he asked, voice like gravel dragged over silk.

"Yes, sir," I managed.

He cocked his head. "Say my name."

"Maltraz."

He smiled. "Say my title."

I hesitated.

Steiner barked, "For fuck's sake. He's the Demon King! Don't say you know who someone is if you don't *really* know who they are, my dumb little fuck slave. Think of him as *your* king tonight, slut. Get on your knees and show him respect."

My knees hit the floor before I could even think. Maltraz stood in front of me, looking down with absolute, predatory patience.

He moved over to one of the velvet couches and unbuttoned his jacket and the bottom button of his vest.

"Crawl to me, and when you get here, you can unzip me," he said.

I hated this man, but I did it. I crawled the short distance to the sofa and got back on my knees. My fingers shook as I worked the zipper down of his expensive pants, revealing a cock that was, of course, as inhuman as the rest of him: gray-black, ribbed, with a subtle spiral to it, and a double row of piercings running along the shaft. I could feel the magic in the air, crackling like ozone, making every hair on my arms stand up.

"Worship it," Steiner hissed, somewhere behind me.

"Yes, get my cock good and wet with your mouth, girl." Maltraz looked down at me as I took him in my mouth, the way I'd done for countless others, but the taste was different: salt and burnt metal, and something else, something ancient and wrong.

"Now spit on it and use that pretty little tongue to work that spit all around." When I started, his cock jerked. I'd never seen anything like this in my life. I admit I'd have found it a bit fascinating if I weren't being forced and humiliated. And if I hadn't been programmed to respond to this type of sexual humiliation. I hated myself for feeling my pussy clench. "Steiner, I smell your slave's arousal." He was laughing at me. I wanted to die.

"For a girl that I know hates me and hates being forced, she's quite a cum slut." Steiner laughed, and I realized he had his own cock in his hands, pleasuring himself.

I ran my mouth and tongue over the demon a few more times before his massive clawed hands picked me up by my upper arms and slammed me down on his lap and onto his massive cock. The pain was excruciating, and I cried out, praying he didn't rip me open. He just groaned with satisfaction, throwing his head back. He then started to piston into me from below; my pleasure was not a consideration in the least. I was glad of it. I did not want to reach an orgasm while this vile creature found his release. The only good thing to happed was he came quickly, spilling inside me his cum running out of me and down his pants. I wanted to laugh at the nasty mess he had made. I kept my face stoic. He lifted me and unceremoniously tossed me onto the sofa as he went into the adjoining bathroom.

Steiner still had his cock in his hand, pumping it faster. "Come here and finish me slave. On your knees." I crawled to him. Hating my life more than I ever had. I hoped and prayed that Jess had found a way to rescue me from this literal hellish nightmare that was my life.

Steiner thrust himself into my mouth a few times before he pulled out and shot streams of cum onto my face and chest. He grabbed a handful of my hair and twisted hard, making me look up at him. "Now you see what real power looks like, don't you?"

I didn't reply fast enough.

He slapped me open-handed, and my cheek went hot. "Answer."

"Yes, Master," I said.

I still knelt on the floor, eyes to the ground as Steiner grabbed a towel and wiped himself off and zipped up his pants.

Maltraz had re-entered the room, straightening his jacket. He looked down at me, face unreadable. "You did well," he said. "Perhaps next time, you'll remember my title."

He walked to the door, nodded to Steiner, and vanished into the hallway.

Steiner looked down at me, still kneeling, still dripping. "You're nothing," he said. "Not even a wolf anymore. Just a hole for men better than you."

He turned and left, slamming the door so hard the chandelier rattled.

I stayed on the floor for a long time, trying to pull my thoughts together, trying to remember what it felt like to have control over anything.

Eventually, I went into the bathroom and wiped myself off with a towel and put on the dress I'd worn up here. Then I'd left the room for the elevator.

As I rode down to my dressing room, I looked at my reflection in the black glass walls. My face was smeared, my body marked, my eyes red and raw. But somewhere deep behind them, I could still see a flicker of something that refused to die.

Maybe Jess would come for me. Maybe he wouldn't.

But if he did, I'd make sure he burned this place to the ground.

CHAPTER 8

Arsenal

The alley behind Eyrie was a channel of silence, hot and breathless. City steam curled around the dumpster in the corner, rolling slow in the streetlight. The three of us were hidden in the shadow of the fire escape. I had Big Papa to my left, his titanic presence a calming force as always. Wrecker was on my right, boots planted, jaw locked. We looked like we belonged there. We didn't, not really. Well, we looked that way to ourselves, anyway.

I checked my comms for the third time, thumbing the mic twice—a short pulse for "status good." On the other end, a faint click in the static. Parker's line, at the far end of the alley, tucked in the battered Sprinter van painted utility gray. If you stared long enough, it flickered, like a mirage. Aspen's work. Her cloaking spell was holding; to normal eyes, the van didn't even exist. Just like we didn't exist.

The smell of burnt coffee and ozone rolled from the van's exhaust. I catalogued every scent—Eyrie's kitchen grease, the spilled gin in the trash, the faint mineral of last week's rain. But it was the undercurrent of blood and terror, the trace of magic in the brick, that set my nerves to vibrating. Wolves were supposed to be predators. Tonight, we were prey, waiting for a gap in the trap.

Big Papa kept one hand inside his jacket, the other on a pocket rosary. He said he didn't need it, but he worked the beads when he was thinking. I saw his lips move every so often. Praying, or cussing out his dead enemies, maybe both. I'd known him ten years; he was the only guy who made me feel short.

Wrecker never stopped moving, even when he was still. One knee bounced, fingers drummed, shoulders flexed every time the wind shifted. His face was stone, but his eyes never stopped working. He kept glancing at the exit route, to the left, then right, then up the fire escape, then down to the van. We all knew the plan, but we rehearsed it in our bodies, over and over. That's how you made it home.

Two weeks of planning, one week of dry runs, three sleepless nights waiting for the right window. Eyrie's shifts ran late—girls got off at two, cleaning crew at three, but the guards worked in pairs and cycled out every ninety. The only thing we had on them was the element of surprise, and the fact that the best shifter-ops team in the state had my back. And, well, Aspen's cloaking. That was the real ace; if we could get to Harper and hit her with the smoke, the club's cameras would see her vanish into thin air.

I unsnapped the safety on my SIG, felt the weight settle into my palm. I always carried with a round chambered, but I still checked, every time. Ritual, not paranoia. Wrecker favored a trench knife, brass-knuckled and bladed; he spun it in his palm, back and forth, never drawing attention. Big Papa didn't carry at all, but if you ever saw him fight, you'd know he didn't need to.

At 11:38, a van pulled up. The back door rattled open, and a bouncer stepped out, hauling a girl by her upper arm. She was slight, maybe one-twenty, with long black hair. She had on a pair of cut-off jeans and a tank top. I saw the cut on her lip. The bouncer was ex-military; you could see it in the way he moved, knees soft, scanning every window. He shoved the girl against the wall and waited.

A second later, a witch in a pencil skirt and heels stepped out, clipboard in hand then nodded to the door. The girl tried to resist, but the bouncer hauled her inside.

"Dammit," Wrecker whispered. "She's not a wolf. Likely someone they grabbed or took in exchange for a debt."

I nodded. "Fuckers."

Papa grunted, "That shit's coming to an end as soon as possible."

Midnight. What the fuck? A limo rolled up. Black-on-black, windows smoked, tires shining wet even though it hadn't rained in a week. The engine didn't idle; it just cut to silence. I felt the air pressure change, like the world sucked in its breath.

The door opened, and Maltraz stepped out. He didn't bother with his human skin. He must be going straight to a room out of sight. You couldn't miss this fucker. Almost seven feet tall, with skin the color of molten iron, eyes black as gun oil except for the red glow. He wore a suit that cost more than my first car, and his hair was braided back in a way that made you think of snakes. He walked slow, unhurried, and the bouncer at the door snapped to attention, then bowed.

My wolf surged, primal and ugly. Every muscle in my body tensed. I had to lock my knees to keep from lunging. Wrecker's hand shot out, clamped on my wrist. It didn't hurt, but it was enough.

Big Papa leaned in, voice almost inaudible. "Hold, brother. Not yet."

Maltraz took his time up the steps, pausing at the door. He turned, looked straight into the alley. I knew he couldn't see us, not in the darkness and distance, but for a split second, I swore he was looking at me. He smiled, a slow, cruel thing, then went inside.

I let out a breath I'd been holding. Wrecker did the same. For a minute, nobody spoke. We just listened to the city, and our own heartbeats.

"Parker, sitrep," I whispered into the comm.

Her voice came back, low but clear: "Van holding steady. Oscar's on the roof. Cloak is at ninety-eight percent. Aspen's prepping the charm."

I looked down the alley. The Sprinter glimmered in the weird light, a shimmer that bent the edges of reality. Aspen was in the passenger seat, eyes closed, lips moving. Her familiar, Oscar, sat on the roof, head swiveling. You wouldn't see him if you weren't looking, but I'd learned to pick out the faint blur of his fur. He was the best spotter we had, rodent or not.

I checked my watch. The sweep team would be back in eighteen minutes, the girls would start lining up for exit around two. That's when Harper would come out, if she was on tonight. If she were alive.

My brain wanted to spiral, but I forced it down. Focus. Nothing else mattered.

"Status," I said, more to myself than anyone.

Big Papa shifted, body loose, the way only giants can be. "We're good, Arsenal. We got you."

Wrecker flicked his knife back into his belt, flexed his hands. "I got left. Papa's got right. You move on her, we move with you."

I nodded once. "Copy."

We waited.

Minutes crawled. The only sound was the hum of transformers and the far-off pulse of club music. I found myself counting my own breaths, keeping my heart from jumping. Every sense dialed up: I could hear the whisper of Parker's typing, the rustle of Oscar's claws on sheet metal, even the faint pulse of blood in the witch's throat as she checked the alley again, ten minutes later.

I thought about Harper. I thought about what she'd endured, and what it had cost her. I thought about the time I saw her dance, when her body moved like she was making war against the world. I thought about what I would do to the men who tried to break her.

Mostly, I thought about the moment I'd see her again. What I'd say. What I'd do if she said she didn't want saving.

I ran my thumb over the scar on my palm, grounding myself.

The door opened again at 2:00. The same bouncer, walking a troupe of girls. This time, they were chatting and laughing walking towards the parking lot. I heard a couple of snide remarks about "Steiner's little princess." They seemed to be under the impression that Harper lived some kind of life of luxury and not the hell she'd implied to me. That made my stomach twist. That can't be true. I saw the stress on her face. She was a prisoner, I was certain.

"Two minutes," I said. "Last sweep."

Wrecker checked his watch, then the door, then the street. Big Papa rolled his neck, a slow crackle of vertebrae. I felt them at my back, solid, ready.

Parker's voice again: "Get ready, boss. Aspen said the veil is strongest at 2:17."

"Copy."

The waiting was the worst part. Waiting for the op to start. Waiting to see if your best was enough. Waiting to find out if you were going to be the hero, or just another name on the wall.

I kept my eyes on the door, breath steady, gun tucked tight in the holster.

Tonight, I was both wolf and soldier. And nothing on earth or in hell was going to keep me from my mate.

The minutes ticked down, and the world held its breath.

This was it.

At 2:14, the club's back door stuttered open and Harper stumbled into the alleyway. My pulse spiked, but my hands stayed steady. She was shadowed by the regular bouncer, a slab of meat with a shaved skull and navy suit, the kind that flexed on ex-cons to make sure nobody forgot who ran the world. He held her by the wrist, none too gently.

Even from a distance, I saw she'd been through something awful tonight. Her hair hung loose past her shoulders; the blonde seemed colorless in the poor light. She wore a t-shirt dress that sagged off her frame.

Her body was fit as always, but everything else about her screamed she was unwell. Her face was a wreck—mascara streaks, a split at the corner of her mouth, eyes lifeless. It was as though she'd somehow lost her will to go on. That changed tonight.

The bouncer marched her to the waiting Escalade, same as every night. He did a sweep of the alley and didn't see us. Why would he? He was human. He unlocked the driver door, leaving Harper standing at the passenger side. She wrapped her arms around herself, shoulders hunched against the chill. I counted the steps, readying myself.

Wrecker murmured, "Go."

I moved.

Six strides, and I was behind her. My hand covered her mouth before she could scream. Her body locked up, and the shock rolled off her in a shudder. I angled my face down, speaking low into her ear. "It's me. I've got you."

She stilled, pulse going wild against my palm. I felt her inhale, a long, desperate drag of air, and then her whole body went slack. It was almost as though she'd expected me.

"Do you trust me?" I whispered.

She nodded, just barely.

I released her mouth and caught her before she fell. She nearly collapsed, knees gone, so I hoisted her upright with a grip under her arms. I didn't carry her. Didn't want to hold her so intimately.

We hurried down the alley, tailing Big Papa and Wrecker to the van. Her scent, even masked by the reek of perfume and city filth, was enough to drive me mad.

Big Papa looked at her with something between rage and pity. "Let's move, brother."

Wrecker took point, scanning for movement. We broke left, through the chain link, past the dead security light, and made for the Sprinter. Parker already had the rear doors open; Aspen stood inside, hands up, eyes blazing emerald. The moment we crossed the threshold, Aspen hissed a word that crackled with raw power, and the world shimmered. For a second, I thought we'd stepped out of time. The city noise went hollow, and the light shifted blue. A ripple went through me, head to toe, but Harper didn't flinch. She just went boneless, arms dangling.

Oscar, Aspen's familiar, sat on her shoulder, prairie dog nose twitching. He studied Harper with a little tilt of his head, then chittered to himself. "She's very brave," he said, accent crisp and British. "Very brave indeed."

I set Harper gently on the bench seat, hands on her shoulders to steady her. She didn't look at me, not at first. Her eyes were wide, glassy, fixed on the far wall of the van.

Parker slammed the doors shut, hit the locks, and called out, "We need to roll."

Wrecker did a circuit, checking every window, then turned his attention to Harper. "Need to do a sweep," he said, voice low and even. He pulled a scanner from his bag, ran it behind her neck, down her arms, over her dress. The machine went red.

"Fuckers chipped her," Wrecker spat.

He fished a small knife from his belt, glanced at me. "You want to do it?"

I nodded. "Where?"

"Behind the ear."

I crouched in front of her, brushed her hair aside. She didn't flinch, just stared through me. I found the bump—hard, round, right at the hairline. It took five seconds to cut it out. Harper didn't even make a sound. Wrecker held out a sterile pad; I pressed it to the wound, wiped the blood, then tucked her hair back.

"There's another one," Wrecker said. "Purse."

He opened the clutch bag slung across her chest, rifled through the lining. He found the tracker—about the size of a pea—sewn into the seam. He yanked it out, crushed it under his boot.

Harper blinked finally and looked at me. Her eyes weren't bluebonnet-bright anymore, but dark, rimmed with red. She tried to say my name, but nothing came out.

"You're safe," I told her. "You're with me now."

Big Papa found a wool blanket and placed it over her lap. He didn't say anything, just held her hands for a long minute. She leaned into him, eyes shut, and for a second I thought she might break down. But she didn't.

Parker started the engine, and the van pulled away from the curb, silent as a dream. Aspen came forward and knelt in front of Harper, and grabbed her hands. "You're safe," she said, soft as velvet. "You're goin' to a place where nobody's gonna hurt you." Her sweet Georgia accent shone through as it always did in tense situations.

Harper nodded, but her jaw shook. She turned to look out the window, arms locked tight around her stomach.

I watched her, feeling the old helplessness creep up my spine. I wanted to hold her, fix her, kill every bastard who'd touched her. But I knew better. You can't fix the kind of broken that comes from a place like Eyrie. You can only get them out alive.

Wrecker sat next to me, elbows on knees. "You good, Arsenal?"

I shrugged. "I don't know."

"Never seen you freeze like that before," he said.

"I didn't freeze."

He grinned, humorless. "Whatever you say."

Harper didn't look back at us for the rest of the drive. The team worked around her, efficient as always—comms checked, escape routes mapped, next steps briefed in shorthand. We were a machine. She was the mission, but she wasn't part of it.

She sat shivering in the middle of the van, surrounded by warriors, a witch, a prairie dog in a suit jacket and plaid vest, and looked like she'd never be warm again.

I wanted to tell her it was over. But I knew better than to lie.

Instead, I watched her, and waited.

She was alive. That would have to be enough for now.

It took us an hour to make it to the old municipal airstrip. The fence was a joke; the camera feed looped on a thirty-second delay, thanks to Parker. I watched our plane through the windshield: a Gulfstream, white as bone, engines idling, lights on but cabin dark. It looked out of place on a strip built for crop dusters and medevac.

We pulled up fast, killed the engine. Wrecker and Big Papa took point, first out, guns ready and eyes scanning the perimeter. Nothing moved out here but tumbleweed and oil-sheen puddles. Parker slid the van door open and helped Harper to her feet. She was shaking, but tried to cover it with a fistful of her skirt. I hovered, a hand at her back, but didn't touch unless she needed it. She hated being touched when she was scared.

We walked the tarmac single file, Oscar scurrying rode on Aspen's shoulder who followed with a clutch of blankets and a medical kit. The wind was cool even though it was early spring; it went through her dress and left Harper's skin stippled with goosebumps. She moved like her body didn't belong to her. I kept pace at her side, fighting the urge to pick her up and carry her the rest of the way. Soldier overruled wolf, for now.

Inside the jet, the lighting was soft and gold. I guided Harper down the aisle, careful to keep my movements slow, predictable. She flinched when my hand grazed her elbow, then shot me a look—guilty, ashamed, all nerves. I let go.

She slid into the plush seat I pointed to. I strapped her in, the belt loose enough not to pinch. She let me. Her hands trembled as she clutched them in her lap. The dark under her nails made me want to smash things.

I handed her a bottle of water. She clutched it with both hands, staring at the condensation. Wrecker took the seat behind us, feet up and eyes shut, already detached. Parker and Aspen sat opposite, both angled toward Harper, giving her space but not ignoring her.

"We'll be in the air soon," I said, voice low. "It's a three-hour flight. Nothing to do but rest."

She nodded, still not looking up.

Parker started talking, voice soft, like a lullaby. "Hey, Harper. You got this. We're all gonna help you get through it."

Harper gave a small nod.

Aspen reached over and covered her with a blanket and then patted her arm, feather-light. "We're Iron Valor. You're safe. Nobody's gonna hurt you, okay?"

Harper tried to answer, but her throat closed. She nodded again, too fast, and blinked hard at the carpet. Her hands picked at the seatbelt.

I watched her. My wolf wanted to drag her into my lap and keep her there until she was warm and whole again, but the human part of me remembered everything—the way she'd left, the years of silence, the misery of missing her. I held back, knuckles white on the armrest.

The engines spooled up, and the cabin vibrated. The pilot's voice came on: "Wheels up in five." Big Papa came down the aisle, handed me a granola bar, then sat facing the aisle, feet planted, arms folded. Guardian angel mode.

As we taxied, Harper grew smaller, eyes sinking. The motion of the jet made her eyelids droop. She fought it, tried to sit up straight, but the water bottle drooped in her hands and nearly spilled. Parker rescued.

Aspen whispered, "Try to rest, honey. It'll help."

Harper nodded, blinking slowly now. Her head lolled back against the seat, lips parting. She was asleep before we left the ground.

I watched her, memorizing every change in her face. The dark circles were worse in this light. The bones in her cheeks stood out sharp. Her lips were pale, almost cracked. Every few seconds, her hands jerked with some dream or memory. I wanted to reach for her, but didn't.

We hit cruising, and the cabin settled into a hush. Parker and Aspen whispered at the far end, voices low and private. Wrecker snored, feet up, arms crossed.

I watched Harper and waited for the anger to burn off.

It didn't.

I raised the armrest between us. Her head slumped sideways. I caught it, guided it gently to my lap, and then let her sleep there. I brushed a hand over her hair, slow and careful, until the shaking stopped.

I sat that way for two hours, the hum of the engines a lullaby.

At sunrise, the plane banked left. I looked out the window.

Below us, the land was flat and gold. Dairyville, ten miles to the east, dusted in morning light. At the edge of the tarmac, I spotted a truck: Bronc's fancy Ford idling. Waiting for us to arrive.

I woke Harper with a hand on her shoulder, soft as I could manage. She jerked awake, then went still when she saw it was me.

"We're home," I said.

She looked out the window, then at me. There was nothing in her eyes—not fear, not hope. Just exhaustion. But she nodded once, and let me unbuckle her.

I led her down the aisle and out into the new day.

Bronc and Juliet stood on the gravel tarmac, faces in the sun, Alpha and Luna there to receive a new member of their pack.

I'd brought her home. Now the real work started. For both of us.

CHAPTER 9

Waylon Steiner

Thirty minutes after closing, I sat alone in the Eyrie's top-floor office with a $400 bottle of bourbon sweating on the credenza and a sea of midnight black glass reflecting my kingdom. Every inch of this place had been custom: the Italian leather on the desk chair, the mahogany that looked like it was whittled out of a Rothschild's casket, the embedded safe I'd had welded to the foundation and hidden behind a wall-sized lithograph of a dying bull. Even the lamplight was calculated—two yellow halos burning the corners into shadow, leaving just enough dark for secrets to hide.

The club's earnings for the week loaded on my laptop, columns of green digits stacked like casino chips. I could have watched them pulse all night, each line a tiny confirmation that I'd won, again, while the world's suckers slouched toward their cubicles with nothing to show but pay stubs and a half-hard-on for retirement. Even with the bonus Maltraz had scraped off the top for "consulting," the take was obscene. My share alone would cover five years' tuition at the kind of prep school that built Supreme Court justices.

I lit a cigar, not because I needed it, but because the smoke curled in the air and clung to the skin like a velvet glove. The night had been slow, but there was a residual hum in my veins—maybe the aftershock of watching Maltraz, or maybe just the satisfaction of seeing a job done right. I'd always been a sucker for good craftsmanship, even when it was evil.

Maltraz had come early. Rage delivered him through the back corridor, where the sensors were dead and the girls didn't go. The demon was dressed in Tom Ford, black on black, hair slicked to his scalp and tied off with a braid that looked like it would cut your palm if you grabbed it. He filled the room with the heavy iron stink of his kind, even as he smiled and shook my hand like we were closing a real estate deal instead of planning a felonious future.

He didn't bother with pleasantries. He wanted his girl.

Harper was brought in, docile and glass-eyed, still under the aftertaste of whatever shit Darlene had slipped her. She walked like a wind-up doll with a dead battery. I made her dance and then kneel at his feet. Maltraz didn't hesitate. He wanted her to swallow that monster-sized pierced and twisted cock down her throat. And my slave slurped it until his demon moans filled the room. When he couldn't stand another minute, he jerked her up onto his lap, impaling her on the iron rod. I'll admit I winced to myself with a tiny bit of worry that she'd incur an injury, but her cries only made me harder. The demon king used her the way a wolf uses a kill—brutal, fast, purposeful. She made no sound after the first whimper, and the only proof it mattered at all was the way her hands curled into the velvet cushion. Maltraz grunted, finished, and licked the blood from his own hand where his claws had dug into her hips, like it was caviar. Then he wandered into the bathroom to clean up.

We wound up back here in my office to discuss business. He wanted the next shipment accelerated. Asia this time, not Europe. He'd sweeten the pot by covering customs and providing a witch for logistics. In return, he wanted "dividends" up front: first pick of the talent, plus a fifty percent cut of the net until the channel stabilized. It was extortion, but I nodded. The truth was, without his shadow, none of this worked. I was the face and the spreadsheet, but he was the engine. My hands were clean—he kept them that way, so long as I paid.

As he left, Maltraz paused at the door. He said, "The girl is wasted here. You know that, right?" And then he was gone.

I poured myself a double, let the cigar burn down to a cold inch, and replayed the scene over and over in my head. Harper's body—pale, perfect, marked with old scars and new bruises—made me think of nothing except the opportunity cost. I could've sold her to any high roller in the South for ten times what she made onstage, but I kept her because she was rare. Because she made the other girls work harder, and the clients spend more. Because, somewhere deep down, I hated my father for breeding a pack that valued only brawn and violence, and I wanted to show him that you could dominate the world with nothing but leverage and a knife's edge.

I thought of the other girls, the ones I had broken and remade, and how none of them ever lasted as long as Harper. I wondered if she even remembered her old life anymore, or if the club had become her entire existence. I wondered if she hated me, or if she had learned to love the leash.

I told myself it didn't matter. Not anymore. The money, the power, the connections—those were the only things that counted.

I was about to shut down the computer when the door banged open so hard the hinges groaned. Rage stumbled in, red-faced and panting, like he'd run the length of the building with a wolf on his heels.

He didn't even bother with a preamble. "She's gone," he blurted, voice trembling.

I let the words hang in the air, like the smoke. "Explain."

He swallowed, looked down at the floor. "Harper. She didn't make it inside the truck."

My hand tightened on the bourbon glass until I thought it would shatter. "You're supposed to walk her out you dumb fuck."

Rage flinched. "I did, boss. I walked her to the Escalade myself. She was behind me the whole time. I checked the rear lot before I got in. I unlocked the doors and got in. She never got in the backseat."

He looked up, desperate for forgiveness, but all I saw was a liability.

"Part of the protocol is that you personally open her door and strap her the fuck in!"

He looked at the floor. "I understand, boss."

I stood and set the glass down with surgical precision. "Show me," I said.

He didn't hesitate. He hustled out, and I followed, my body moving with a cold efficiency I hadn't felt in years. We moved through the private corridor, past the guest suites, past the dead-eyed bouncers who watched us with the same numb indifference as always. Rage led the way to the loading dock, where the Escalade sat in the alley by the back door.

The spot was empty. The gravel showed no marks except the usual tire tracks and boot prints.

I scanned the ground, then the fence line, then the roof. "Pull the tapes," I said. "Now."

The security room was a frigid little box, all cinderblock and the humming blue heat of a hundred screens. The staffer on duty—a bland, balding drone with a face like a collapsed soufflé—looked up and nearly fell off his chair when Rage and I stormed in. The air stank of burnt circuits and energy drinks, a kind of electrical desperation that never left the place, no matter how many times I made them swap out the carpets.

I let Rage take the lead. His hands hovered over the keyboard like he were trying to defuse a bomb, sweat dripping down his wrists onto the cheap plastic. The room filled with the click-clack of keys and the static of skipped time as he scrubbed backward through the night's footage.

"There," he said, jabbing a finger at the screen. "Twenty-three fifteen. That's when she leaves."

He played it in real time. Harper moved through the corridor, head down, body language deadened. She didn't look left or right, just kept to the wall. Rage appeared a minute later, carrying the go-bag and a set of keys. He never looked at her.

They hit the alley. Harper hung back, just out of the reach of the lights. Rage circled to the driver's side, did a perfunctory scan, and unlocked the Escalade. Harper reached for the passenger door.

Next frame, she was gone. No blur, no struggle, not even a shadow. Just empty space.

I watched the loop five times, each repetition grinding another layer of patience from my nerves. By the sixth, I wanted to put my fist through the monitor and into Rage's face.

"You didn't even watch her get in the car," I said, voice flat as a morgue slab.

Rage tried to stand straighter, but even his size couldn't cover how small he felt. "I—I always do, boss. She's never run before. Three years, not one problem. I thought—"

"You thought wrong," I snapped, eyes never leaving the freeze-frame. "She's not a girl, she's a product. You don't leave a product on the dock and hope it loads itself."

He said nothing. The security tech pretended to be absorbed in the next screen over, but I could smell the terror sweat from across the room.

I pulled out my phone and dialed the club's main number. "Get Darlene to the security office. Now." I hung up before they could answer.

The wait was measured in heartbeats. Darlene arrived in two minutes, heels stabbing the tile, the slit of her dress running thigh-high and her face a mask of perfume and contempt. She gave Rage a look that could have killed a weaker man, then focused on me.

"What's the emergency?" she said. Her voice was sugar, laced with arsenic.

I pointed at the screen. "Watch."

She did, and her mouth curled at the edge, not in surprise, but in recognition.

"You said the cameras are top of the line, right?" She asked the tech.

He nodded, nervous. "Redundant system, multiple angles. Nothing gets missed."

Darlene smiled, with a smear of lipstick on her teeth. "Except this."

She leaned closer, peering at the frozen frame, and whispered something I couldn't hear. The air shimmered, just a little, like a drop of oil on water. She put her palm on the monitor, held it there for five seconds, then let go.

"It's a spell," she said. "Very expensive, very clean. Probably a charm of disappearance or misdirection, layered with a time-warp. Whoever did this was either a professional or an older witch with access to ancient magic."

My jaw tightened. "You told me the covens wouldn't work in Houston anymore."

"They won't," Darlene said. "Not for you. But there's always someone willing to do business if the money's right."

I didn't bother asking how much. If it was enough to get a girl out from under my nose, it was enough to make a dent in a mid-sized nation's GDP.

Rage hovered by the console, desperate for absolution. "You want me to hit up our sources? See if any witches came into town the last week?"

I nodded. "Do it. Check the hotels, the airports. Pull the guest lists for every room in the building since Friday."

He was already on his phone, dialing with a trembling finger.

Darlene turned to me, one eyebrow raised. "You want me to track her?"

"Yes."

She grinned. "I'll need a sample. Blood, hair, saliva. The usual."

I didn't have to ask where to get it. The demon king had left plenty of Harper's DNA on the velvet couch upstairs. I sent the tech to fetch it.

Darlene watched him go, then lowered her voice. "You know this was a pro job, right? Harper didn't do this on her own. Someone wanted her out."

"I know," I said. "But who?"

Darlene tilted her head. "We had that client a couple weeks ago. The one who paid so much money for her. Remember? The cameras were wonky the entire time. She blew him; they talked but we couldn't get the conversation because of bad audio. I know you remember."

She was right. I remembered that fucker. I asked Harper about him, but she acted nonplussed about him, so I blew it off. Should have trusted my instincts.

Darlene continued. "The VIP suite log showed it was a Mr. Rodgers who'd left a huge tip and bugged out without so much as a fingerprint on a glass. At the time, I'd written it off as a rich pervert's night out."

I turned to Rage. "Pull his receipt. Get his card info. Pull the camera footage for the club for the entire night. Then I want club footage gone over for the days before that night. Find out if he was watching her, or if he had a witch helping him."

Rage nodded, chin-to-chest. "On it."

The security tech returned with a ziplock of stained velvet. Darlene took it, inhaled, and closed her eyes. She murmured something in that strange witch language, and the hairs on the back of my neck prickled.

"She's alive," Darlene said. "And she's moving fast. Someone's got a vehicle, maybe even a plane."

"Can you trace?"

She grinned. "Always."

I watched her work, thinking about Harper out there, running. Wondered if she was scared, or if she believed in whatever fairy tale had been promised her.

Mostly, I thought about the guy who'd had the nerve to cross me. I imagined his face, the shape of his skull, how easy it would be to break every tooth in his mouth.

Darlene finished the spell, tucked the velvet into her purse, and turned to leave. "You'll have your answer by morning," she said. "If she leaves the country, I'll know."

Black smoke started pouring from her purse as she walked away. She let out a startled yelp as she tossed it off her shoulder.

"Dammit!" She opened her bag. Everything in it was covered with a green glowing goo.

She raised her eyes to me. "Sorry boss. It seems I won't have an answer on Harper's location in the morning or any other time. Whoever this witch is, she has put a powerful protection spell on her that prevents scrying or tracking. If you want to find Harper, you'll have to do it the old-fashioned way."

"FUCK!" I wanted to break bones.

I turned back to Rage, who was sweating bullets onto the keyboard. He looked up, face pale as death.

"If I don't get her back," he whispered, "what happens?"

I leaned in, let him smell the bourbon and the old blood on my breath.

"If you don't," I said, "I'll feed you to Maltraz in pieces. Starting with your tongue."

He nodded, throat bobbing, and turned back to the screens.

I stood there, watching the monitors, waiting for Harper to appear again, even as a part of me knew she never would.

But that was fine.

Because the next time I saw her, it would be on my terms.

And there would be no one left to save her.

CHAPTER 10

Harper

The jet's stairs dropped with a hiss and a shudder. I blinked at the gravel-paved tarmac, watched the shadow of the wing cut a blade of darkness across my bare legs, then braced myself for whatever came next.

I'd left Eyrie in a blur of shadows and sorcery, but arrived in Dairyville under a sky so clean it almost hurt. The air here was a dry slap—bright, unfiltered, heavy with nothing but sun and the faraway promise of rain. I should've felt exposed. Instead, I felt lighter. Like I'd been exhumed.

There were people waiting. Three of them. The first was the Alpha, no question. I knew before my eyes adjusted. He was a slab of a man, the kind you could build a courthouse out of. The sunlight caught the silver in his beard and the blue in his eyes, making him look both ancient and brand new. Next to him was a woman so tiny I thought at first she was a kid until she turned and revealed a belly you only get when you're six months along with twins or an eight-pound linebacker. She wore a yellow sweater dress and a pair of tall brown boots.

I was the last off the plane. Jess tried to hang back like he wanted to help me walk, but I felt the gravity of him even with his hands in his pockets, jaw locked, staring at new grass springing up through the rocks. The bond between us had gone from silent to symphonic since the rescue, the notes all muddled together: rage, panic, a lust that made me want to laugh and cry in the same breath. Underneath it all, a bleed of hope so sharp it bordered on delusion.

The wind whipped my dress against my knees as I descended. My legs nearly gave out, but I steadied myself, chin up. The Alpha met me at the bottom, his shadow eclipsing mine. For a second, I thought he might go for a handshake. Instead, he just nodded, blue eyes taking in every inch of me; the mess of my hair, the bruises, the scab on my lips where I chewed them to pieces.

"Welcome to Iron Valor," he said, voice deep enough to rattle my bones. "I'm Bronc. I'm the Alpha of this pack, but this is the real boss." He jerked a thumb at the blonde.

The woman closed the gap in three quick steps, grabbed my hands, and pulled me into a hug that left no room for protest.

"You must be Harper," she said into my shoulder. "We're so glad you're safe." She pulled back and gave me a once-over, the look that said she's already picking out pajamas for you and warming soup on the stove. "I'm Juliet, the Luna of this bunch. But if you call me Mrs. Baucaum, I'll bite you."

I tried to muster a reply, but my voice didn't want to cooperate. I heard myself croak out a "Thank you," and a tear slipped down my face.

Juliet didn't flinch. She gripped my hands tighter and shot a glare at the two men, daring them to say a word about it. "Ignore them," she whispered, big smile on her face. "They're tough, but they turn to jelly when a woman starts sniffling."

Behind her, Bronc gave an eye roll so practiced it probably counted as a legal signature. "I'm serious, Harper. You're safe here. And I'm not just saying that for show." He let the silence hang for a second, then added, "We know you must have been through hell. Some of us have lived through our own versions of it. Iron Valor isn't like those other packs."

My throat ached. "I—I know," I managed, forcing the words out through gravel. "Thank you for letting me come here."

He crouched a little to meet my eye. "You're one of us, if you want to be. But after the last few months, we have to ask for a small courtesy."

I tensed, bracing for a contract, a test, or a tracker in my neck.

"It's nothing bad," Juliet rushed to add, waving a hand. "Just a pack vow. Old-fashioned, I know, but we got burned a while back. Some wolves turned traitor, and nearly all of us were killed. So now Bronc asks everyone new to swear it. Just a loyalty thing."

Bronc nodded. "It's just words. Of course, there's pack magic attached to it. But you should know the drill. You swear to honor the pack, not betray it, and protect your brothers and sisters if you can. That's it."

The tension in my shoulders bled away. I looked between them—Bronc with his hands behind his back, waiting with the patience of a father, and Juliet, vibrating with nervous energy and some kind of fierce, maternal fire. I wanted to belong here. Maybe more than I'd wanted anything since I was twelve and still thought ballet was magic.

"I'd be honored," I said, and meant it.

Juliet grinned like she'd won a carnival prize. She squeezed my hand, then glanced at Bronc. "Go on, big guy."

Bronc placed a hand on my head, gentle as a benediction. His palm was warm, but I felt the static charge of Alpha power even through my hair. "Repeat after me," he said.

The vow was simple, and I didn't trip over any of the words. I didn't realize until halfway through that my wolf was echoing each phrase, a low harmony under my breath. When it was done, Bronc removed his hand and smiled, the lines around his eyes deepening.

"Welcome home, Harper," he said, and for the first time in years, I felt like I actually *was* home.

Juliet looped her arm through mine, steering me away from the jet and the others who had flown with us. She walked me across the tarmac, moving at exactly my speed, never too fast or too slow, as if she could feel the tremor still working its way through my nerves. We got to the edge where the grass line started; where the world shrank to the hush of insects in the air.

She was all business now. "You must be running on fumes. We have a room ready for you upstairs in the new pack house. It's not much yet—Maddie, Bronc's sister, tried to decorate it, but she's got no taste, bless her. You'll get some time to rest, and then I'll come up and see if you want something from the kitchen. If you'd rather be alone, just—"

"I'll be with her," Jess barked from behind us, too loud in the sudden quiet.

Juliet stopped so abruptly that my inertia nearly toppled us both. She turned, boot toe to boot toe with Jess. There was a full foot and a half of height difference between them, but she stared him down like she owned the planet and all the air above it.

"Last I checked, Arsenal, you haven't yet claimed this woman. That means she gets to decide where she wants to be. Are we clear?" Her Midwest accent came out thicker now, along with the beginnings of a Texas drawl and something more lethal underneath.

Jess's jaw bunched. He looked at me, then at Juliet, then back at me. "She's not safe unless she's with me." His tone was respectful and quiet.

Juliet arched an eyebrow so high it nearly left her forehead. "Bullshit. That might be the case, but I think you might just want to keep her in a box so you can watch her. Maybe you want to be sure she stays put. Be sure you really just want to keep her safe, buddy and aren't worried about control. I won't allow choices to be removed. Not in my pack."

The power in the air was thick enough to chew. I felt my wolf stir, trying to make sense of the signals. Jess's bond screamed at me: panic, shame, and a hunger that made my thighs ache. Juliet's, on the other hand, was a blanket of calm fury—clean, maternal, but with a knife edge under the surface.

Bronc strolled up, hands in his pockets, face unreadable. He leaned down and whispered something into Juliet's hair, then kissed the side of her neck. Instantly, her hackles flattened. She grinned, relaxed, and shook her head like she'd just remembered it was a party and not a murder trial.

She looked at me, eyes softening. "Sorry, Harper. Old habits." She gave my hand a gentle squeeze. "There was a time that I spent trapped by someone in a cage. I swore I'd never let another woman feel that way. You can stay wherever you want. We've got the best security in the country. Nobody can get to you without going through two dozen armed shifters and a witch with the power of God."

I heard myself laugh, weak and threadbare, but real. "Thank you, Juliet. I appreciate it. But... it's okay." I turned to Jess, whose shoulders had just now begun to un-knot. "I want to stay with him. If that's alright." The words burned on the way out, but I made myself say them.

Juliet was quiet for a second, searching my face like she were looking for some sign of coercion. When she found none, she let out a breath and nodded. "Alright, then. But you ever want a change of scenery, you come see me, and I'll move you myself. No questions asked."

Bronc put a hand on Jess's shoulder and squeezed, hard enough that Jess winced. "Walk with me, Arsenal," he said. They moved off toward a row of black SUVs, talking in low voices. I watched Jess's head sink, his hands shoved deep in his pockets, and wondered if I'd just made a mistake.

Juliet gave me a side-hug, belly hard as a basketball against my ribs. "We're here for you," she said, dropping her voice to a whisper. "Even if you can't be here for yourself."

She released me, then stalked away, boots crunching across the gravel. For a moment, I just stood there, the sun glaring off the hood of the nearest car; the wind snagging my hair and tangling it in my mouth. I looked down at my hands, still shaking, and tried to remember the last time I'd chosen anything for myself.

When I looked up again, Jess was returning, head down. He stopped a few paces away, not close enough to touch.

"Sorry," he said. "I didn't mean to…" He trailed off, clamped his mouth shut, and ground his teeth together until I thought they'd shatter. He looked like a man whose every instinct told him to run, but his body refused to budge.

I shrugged, a small motion, not sure if I forgave him or not. "It's fine. I just want to rest."

He nodded once. "We should go."

I followed him to the truck. As we walked, I could see Bronc out of the corner of my eye, arms crossed, watching us like a sentry. Juliet stood beside him, hand on her belly, eyes bright and unblinking. For the first time, I realized how fiercely these people protected their own. It was a different kind of leash than Steiner's, but it was one I thought I could live with.

I slid into the passenger seat and let the door slam me back into reality. Jess started the engine, and we rolled out of the lot, the dust from the tires painting a gold veil over the last sliver of morning sun.

The Iron Valor compound awaited—a fortress, a home, a holding cell. For now, I didn't care which.

All that mattered was that I wasn't alone.

The drive from the airstrip to the Iron Valor compound took less than ten minutes. The scenery was all fence-line and dust; the world flattening out into a panorama of brittle yellow grass and sagging power lines. Jess kept both hands on the wheel and said nothing, eyes locked on the horizon. His knuckles were white. I wanted to break the silence, maybe ask a question about the pack or the rules, but my words just pinballed around my mouth and vanished.

At the door, two women waited.

The first had her hair cropped short and spiked up with streaks of pink. She wore a hoodie so enormous it looked like it could have eaten her, and a pair of black leggings that did nothing to hide the bulk of muscle underneath. The other woman was her opposite in every possible way—tall, dark hair parted dead center, and a kind of quiet, unassuming beauty that made you do a double take when you caught it in the right light. She wore a yellow sundress with white polka dots and a big white collar. She had on white tights and brown boots.

I recognized them both, but only distantly. They'd been in the van and on the plane, hovering at the edge of my vision, making the trip feel less a true rescue. I remembered the smell of Parker's coffee, the way Aspen sang to herself under her breath.

Jess parked the truck and jumped out, rounding to my side and opening the door before I could even reach for the handle. I tried to climb out on my own, but my knees locked and I nearly ate it on the step rail. He caught me, one hand under my arm, and then let go as soon as my feet touched ground.

"Hey, Harper!" the short one called, voice big as a freight train. "Remember me? I'm Parker. Wrecker's mate." She bounded over, and for a second I thought she might tackle-hug me, but she just stopped short and grinned. "Glad you made it."

The other hung back, with a half-smile on her lips. "You probably don't remember me, honey. I'm Aspen. I'm the local witch. I'm mated to Big Papa. He's the one who helped make you feel so calm in the van. He's the best." She's clearly head over heels in love with her mate. "I own the local bakery. You'll be getting some goodies soon. I make the best blueberry lemon scones you ever ate. Just prepare your tastebuds to be dazzled." Her southern accent washed over me like warm water, and I hoped we could become friends. "If you need anything, you come see me."

A third figure darted from behind Aspen's dress; an eighteen-inch-tall prairie dog, wearing a tiny vest and a pair of wire-framed glasses. He bowed with such grandeur I almost snorted.

"Miss Harper," he said, voice crisp and British. "Oscar B. Wild, at your service. If you require assistance, do not hesitate to call upon me. I am highly discreet." He flashed his incisors and then ducked back into Aspen's skirts.

I blinked. "Is he... is he always like that?"

Aspen giggled. "Oscar's my familiar. He's very proud. He'll keep you safe, no matter what."

Parker leaned in, lowered her voice. "If you need clothes or, like, anything at all, Bronc's sister Maddie brought you a duffel bag. It's waiting outside Arsenal's door."

I nodded, trying to smile. "Thank you."

Aspen tilted her head. "Are you okay, darlin'?"

I wasn't. My skin crawled with a thousand memories, every nerve ending screaming to be scalded clean. The demon's touch clung to my body, sticky and sour. I wanted to scrub every inch until I bled, and even then I wasn't sure it would be gone. My eyes started to sting, and I forced myself to breathe. "I just need a shower," I said, voice flat. "Maybe two."

Jess's posture changed in an instant. He stepped between me and the others, arms loose at his sides, shoulders squared. "We'll head up," he said. "Thanks for the help."

He didn't wait for a reply. He walked me past the main building—big, low-slung, with a wrap-around porch and windows painted a blinding white. The sun was at its peak now, no shadows left to hide in. Every inch of the property screamed order and security, but there were splashes of comfort here and there: a wind chime, a porch swing, an old Radio Flyer wagon tipped over on the lawn.

The living areas were on the second floor of the large pack house. The hallway smelled like fresh paint and carpet. Jess's door was easy to spot—it had a battered Marine Corps sticker next to the peephole, and a pair of muddy boots lined up perfectly against the jamb.

A duffel bag leaned against the threshold, stuffed to bursting. Jess picked it up in one hand, unlocked the door with the other, and stepped aside for me to enter.

I hesitated, then went in.

The place was spotless—minimal, almost severe, but not unfriendly. The living room had a gray sectional, a wall-sized TV, and a small kitchen tucked behind a peninsula bar. The appliances gleamed. The only decoration was a single framed photo on the counter: Jess and Bronc, both in uniform, both with arms around each other and shit-eating grins.

Jess set the duffel on the sectional and pointed down the hall. "Bedroom's through there. Bathroom's attached. You can... do what you need. I'll get you some towels."

He left without another word. I listened to his footsteps fade, then collapse into the quiet.

I took a minute just to stand there, hands dangling, head empty. My heart still hadn't slowed, and my skin still felt wrong. But at least here, I could close the door and pretend.

I found the bedroom. King bed, fluffy comforter, a mountain of pillows that all matched. There was a row of hooks on the wall for jackets, and a heavy safe built into the closet. The only personal item was a battered copy of "Lonesome Dove" on the nightstand.

The bathroom was gleaming white tile, the shower big enough for three. There were three bottles of soap lined up—no flowery scents, just plain blue gel and a bottle of Head & Shoulders. I almost laughed.

I closed the bathroom door, locked it, and let the silence take me apart piece by piece. The tile was freezing under my feet, but I barely felt it. I stripped off my t-shirt dress, peeled away the old underwear, and looked at myself in the mirror. The bruises were yellowing out. My hair was a tangled mess.

A knock at the door made me jump.

"Harper?" Jess's voice, awkward and careful. "I brought some stuff that Maddie dropped by. You probably don't want to use my cheap soap."

I yanked the towel around me and cracked the door. Jess stood there, eyes on the floor, holding a canvas tote stuffed with bottles and a hairbrush and what looked like half the personal care aisle from Target. He set it on the counter without looking at me.

"Thank you," I whispered, voice barely audible.

He nodded, jaw flexing. "Take your time. I'll be in the living room." Then he vanished.

I closed the door again, pressed my back to it, and slid to the floor. My towel bunched around my waist, and I let my knees draw up to my chest. That's when it hit me—no warning, no gentle ramp up. Just a flood, like someone had torn open a dam.

I sobbed. Not dainty, pretty tears, but a full-body, retching howl that left my throat raw and my stomach knotted. I pressed my fists into my eyes, trying to block it out, but the crying only got worse. I wept for every moment in Eyrie, for every night I'd spent wishing for rescue, for every piece of myself I'd bartered just to stay alive. I cried for Jess, for what I'd done to him, for what he'd just done for me.

When the tears finally ran dry, I sat there in the half-light, chest heaving, head spinning. I let myself lean into the sadness, the fear, the shame. I let it hurt.

Then, slowly, I stood up.

I set the new toiletries on the edge of the sink and picked up the brush, running my fingers over the bristles. I uncapped the bottle of real shampoo and sniffed it—jasmine and lemon, nothing like what I used at the club. It was perfumed like Eyrie. *This* was the smell of regular life, the smell of people who weren't constantly running from the past.

My hands still shook as I turned the shower on, as hot as I could stand. The room filled with steam in seconds. I stepped in, closed my eyes, and let the water carry everything away.

When I was done, I wrapped myself in the fresh towel and stood there, staring at my reflection.

I was still a mess. But I was alive. And I'd made it this far.

That would have to be enough for today.

Chapter 11

Arsenal

I stood outside my bathroom, a grown man with a silver star and several combat tours, and listened to Harper fall apart on the other side of a three-panel wood door. The tile on the walls amplified every sound—the retch, the wet hiccup, the way her knuckles must be white on the towel as she tried to stitch herself back together. I could see the veins on my own wrists, blue and raised and angry, my hands shaking with the urge to rip the door off its hinges, gather her up, and force the universe to apologize for what it had done to her.

My wolf howled at me, every instinct in my body boiling down to a single command: go to her, hold her, don't let go until the air in her lungs was steady and the whites of her eyes were no longer visible. My human side said nothing. It just pulled its own tattooed arms tighter around my chest and reminded me that five years ago, she'd chosen to walk away. It reminded me that I'd spent half a decade learning to close doors and build new ones out of steel and willpower.

So I stood there, hands jammed into the pockets of my sweats, jaw working until I tasted blood at the hinge. If I opened the door, I knew what would happen: I'd fall to my knees, beg her to tell me it wasn't real, and then end up drowning in the same helplessness that had nearly gotten me killed a dozen times over in some shit-smeared part of the world.

I couldn't afford to lose myself. Not when the pack needed me. Not when she needed me.

The crying tapered off after a while. The shower switched on, and the hiss of water masked whatever came next. I braced my hands on either side of the door frame, staring at the grain of the wood, and counted the seconds like I used to count the beats between sniper shots: one, two, three, steady, release.

Five years. Five years since she'd ghosted me, left me with nothing but a memory of bluebonnet eyes and the echo of her wolf. I'd told myself that I didn't care. That I could move on, build something new, learn to be a person instead of an animal trained for war. But the truth was, I'd gone to hell and back for the chance to feel her in my arms again, even if it was just to say goodbye.

She could have called. She could have written a letter, sent a text, done literally anything but disappear into the wind and end up as some other man's toy. Her first stop wasn't that club. She'd been at Julliard. For two fucking years. Never once did she try to make contact. Instead, she let me rot, let me sign up for every black-bag mission with a life expectancy measured in hours. I'd gotten good at dying. Bronc said it was my only flaw—no self-preservation, no care for my own body. He was right. I didn't want to live if it wasn't with her.

It was Bronc who'd saved me, in the end. Dragged me out of a bullet-stained mudhole in Kandahar and put a beer in my hand, told me there was a place for me in the world. That was the day I learned to call Iron Valor my family, and I'd never looked back.

Until today.

The bathroom door clicked open. A billow of steam rolled out, heavy with the clean lemon-and-cedar scent of the soap Maddie stocked for her. Harper stepped out, wrapped in a towel the color of wet ash, her hair plastered to her skull and dripping down her back. She looked smaller than I remembered, and in that moment I hated myself for noticing how the curve of her collarbone still made me want to sink my teeth into her.

She stared at me, eyes red and swollen, cheeks patchy from tears. For a second, neither of us moved.

"My bed is ready for you," I said, my voice coming out flat as a firing range.

She blinked, startled, like she'd forgotten there were other people on the planet. "I can take the couch," she whispered. "That'll be fine." Her Texas accent was muted now, softer at the edges. I almost didn't recognize it.

"I said my bed is ready for you." My voice gruffer than I'd intended.

Her eyes snapped up to mine. "I just... that's fine."

I stepped aside, letting her limp past on a bad knee. She moved with the practiced grace of someone who'd had to hide pain for a living. She walked past me and gently sat on the edge of the bed, towel clutched to her chest like armor. "Is there any coffee?" she asked, voice trembling. "Or maybe tea?"

"There is. Meet me in the kitchen."

I filled the electric kettle and set it to boil. My hands wanted to shake, but I made them move slow and steady, the way you're supposed to handle plastic explosives or infants. I found the good tea—the one with the lavender on the label, the one Juliet said was best for nerves.

Harper had changed into a pair of gray joggers and a t-shirt that said "Cute Girls Read Smut" in bubble letters; no doubt Parker's contribution. Her hair was twisted in a towel. She looked up at me, eyes wary.

"Have a seat." I pointed to the low bar stool at the peninsula and handed her the cup of tea. "You need to eat," I said, setting a plate of scrambled eggs and sausage in front of her.

"I'm not hungry."

"You haven't eaten in at least a day," I countered. "Your body needs protein if it's going to heal. Eat, or I'll call Juliet and have her force-feed you." I meant it as a joke, but it landed flat.

She picked up the fork with her left hand. I'd almost forgotten she was left-handed. She poked at the eggs and took a bite. "They're cold," she said, but not like she was complaining.

"Sorry."

She took a bite, chewed slow. I watched her jaw move, remembered the way she used to smirk around a mouthful of barbecue on Saturday afternoons. Now, every movement was measured, small. Like she was afraid the food might fight back.

We sat in silence for a minute. I sipped my own tea, watching the way the light traced the lines of her face. I noticed what looked like a fresh scar under her chin that hadn't been there before. I wanted to ask how she'd gotten it, but I bit my tongue instead.

"I know you're angry," she said, not looking at me. "You don't have to hide it."

I set the mug down. "I'm tired, Harper."

She snorted, a sound that was almost a laugh. "That's a lie. You're furious. You've been grinding your teeth since I got here."

"Would you prefer I yelled?"

She shrugged, a slow, careful movement. "I don't know. Maybe."

I looked at her then, really looked. The bones in her wrists stood out sharper under the skin. She was thinner than I remembered, but every muscle was still mapped out under the bruises and the fading marks from God knows what. I wondered if I could love a woman who'd been broken so many times, or if I was just chasing the ghost of who she used to be.

"What happens now?" she asked, pushing the plate away.

"Now you rest," I said. "Tomorrow we talk to Bronc. Then we figure out what you want to do."

She wiped at her mouth, even though there was nothing there. "What if I don't know what I want?"

"You're not on a timeline. I don't know everything you've been through. Trauma and healing take time. Nobody is going to rush you."

The words hung in the air, heavy with everything unsaid. I finished my tea, set the mug on the counter, and grabbed her plate. Harper headed back toward my bedroom and had crawled under the comforter. I draped the blanket over her and tucked it in around her shoulders. I wanted to touch her hair, brush the damp strands away from her face, but my hands stayed at my sides. The old ache flared up in my chest, but I let it burn.

"You're safe," I told her, voice rough. "No one can hurt you here. Not Steiner. Not anyone."

She looked up at me, and for a second, the blue in her eyes flared alive. "Thank you," she whispered. "For getting me out."

I didn't trust myself to speak, so I just nodded and stepped away, pulling the door shut behind me. I listened for a minute, heard the whisper of her breathing settle into something slow and even.

For the first time in years, I felt a piece of myself click back into place.

But the rest of me was still broken.

I spent an hour pacing the perimeter of the pack house before Bronc's text came through: *Ten minutes. Debrief. My office.*

That gave me just enough time to scribble a note for Harper. I left it on the nightstand, along with a glass of water and a burner phone programmed with only my number. If she woke up alone, I didn't want her thinking she'd been abandoned.

Her breathing was soft and deep. I stood in the doorway a moment longer than I should have, then snapped the lock and let the old habits take over.

I walked downstairs to the basement, shoulders squared, making myself ignore the eyes I could feel from people I'd passed in the hall. The rumors would be flying by tonight: that I'd brought home a broken girl, that the infamous Arsenal had finally found his own weakness. Let them talk. I'd survived worse.

When I walked into the meeting room, the entire command staff was there: Bronc at the head; massive scarred hands clasped on the table. Wrecker, as always, wore a look like he knew something you didn't know and he'd be happy to fight you over it. Gunner leaned his chair back against the bookcase, arms folded, looking for all the world like he'd just wrestled a steer and made the animal regret its choices. Doc, glasses on his nose, eyes on his laptop, still in his lab coat; the dashing doctor curing what ails everyone. And finally, Big Papa, hands steepled, his presence grounding the whole room.

Six pairs of eyes tracked me as I slid into the seat between Bronc and Big Papa. Wrecker grinned, teeth sharp. "Late, Arsenal. Slipping in your old age?"

"Had to make sure the guest of honor made it to sleep without incident," I said.

Wrecker gave a slow nod, like he approved. "Uh huh. Sleep."

Bronc got serious. "How's she doing?"

I shrugged. "Alive. Exhausted. She showered and crashed."

Bronc wasted no time. "Good. We'll keep it short. Report."

I kept it clinical, just the facts: the infiltration, the extraction. I didn't mention the way Harper looked at me when I pulled her from the van, or the way her body had collapsed into mine when she realized it was real. I didn't mention the part of me that wanted to run back and check on her every five minutes, or the wolf inside me that kept howling for more.

Wrecker interrupted. "Maltraz showed up two hours before extraction."

I nodded. "Yup. Full regalia. Steiner was playing the lapdog, but make no mistake—Maltraz owns that operation."

Bronc frowned. "Trafficking?"

"Confirmed. Humans, wolves. All spelled and bound. They move them through the city and out by the ship channel. That's where Steiner comes in. He owns the dock. The club looks like a pit stop. The real work happens though the train yards."

Wrecker's chest puffed out. "This info comes from Parker's endless research."

I wanted to shiver. "Seems last night was more than just a business meeting, however. He was there for a VIP room visit."

I hesitated, and as sick as it made me, then told the truth. "Harper was given to Maltraz for the VIP session. When we pulled her out, she was... not herself. Wrecker can confirm—she didn't even react when he cut the tracker out."

A ripple of anger went around the table. Gunner's jaw ticked. Big Papa let out a quiet breath and closed his eyes for a second.

"Goddamn," Bronc said. "Any risk she's been spelled?"

I shook my head. "Aspen and Oscar swept her. No residue."

"She's not a danger to the pack," I said, my voice harder than I intended. "If she were, I'd have taken her far from here.."

Big Papa's hand landed heavy on my shoulder, steadying. "Nobody doubts you, Jess."

Wrecker leaned in. "Question is, what's our next move? You know Steiner will come looking. And Maltraz will want a pound of flesh."

I spoke with confidence. "He's gotta figure out it was us first. We blocked the cameras. When I was with her two weeks ago, I scrambled audio and video. I don't doubt they'll figure it out eventually, but it'll take them a while."

Bronc didn't hesitate. "We need to tighten up security. Wrecker, you and Parker get surveillance juiced up. We'll continue with recon. Papa, if Aspen and Oscar could maybe work on wards around the compound and be sure Harper is protected with some magic as well as muscle?"

Papa gave one of his famous small grins. "I can tell you they put an anti-tracking ward on her when we were about ten miles out of The Woodlands. She'd asked me about it, noting that Steiner has a few witches on staff. Any decent with can scry a location if they had the right tools, and she wanted to prevent them from tracking Harper."

Bronc shook his head. "You know, for your little witch to have been a dud her entire life, she sure has embraced her new powers. We are blessed to have her in our pack."

Papa beamed. "She will be thrilled to know you said that, Alpha. I assume it's fine for me to relay?"

"I'll tell her myself if you don't," Bronc told him before telling me to stay with Harper until we knew more.

I nodded. It wasn't an order so much as a benediction.

Pearl's head popped through the doorway, hair piled high and a tray of coffee mugs balanced on one hand. "Y'all look like death warmed over," she said, setting the tray down. "I brought scones—Aspen's latest. Blueberry lemon. Eat, or I'll tell the world you boys are a bunch of ninnies."

She made her rounds, kissing each of us on the cheek, but lingered a second longer on me. She whispered, "It's all gonna be okay sweet boy. It'll be better than you could ever have dreamed." Then she sailed out, singing Patsy Cline off-key.

Gunner snorted into his coffee.

Bronc shook his head. "Best damn mama in the state," he muttered.

He turned back to business. "Gunner, get the security teams spun up. I'll coordinate with Rafe's people. I want the king to know what's coming. The last thing we need is another dead alpha laid at the feet of Iron Valor. I don't want another Council inquiry with our name on it."

Wrecker saluted, mock-serious. "Nothing more I'd love to do than kill that motherfucker myself. But yeah, let's let the king's men take the heat."

The meeting broke up fast. I made it to the end of the hall before Big Papa caught up.

He stopped me with a look. "You alright, son?"

"I'm fine," I lied.

He didn't buy it. "You're not fine. You're angry, and you're scared."

"Shouldn't I be?"

He shrugged. "Maybe. But you don't have to carry it alone."

I stared at the floor. "She already left me once? What if she doesn't want to stay?"

Papa's smile was slow and sad. "Then you let her go. But you give her the chance first."

He patted my back, almost knocking the wind out of me. "Remember: 'Freedom is a gift, not a test.'"

I managed a smile. "Thanks, Papa."

He squeezed my shoulder once more, then headed upstairs.

Outside, the sun was high and sharp, bleaching the grass to bone. I felt the itch under my skin—the urge to run, to shift, to let the wolf take over.

Gunner appeared at my side, hands in his pockets. "You wanna run?" he asked.

I grinned. "Hell yes."

Wrecker materialized out of nowhere, already stripping off his shirt. "Last one to the ridge buys first round at Pearl's tonight."

We took off, laughing like idiots, and didn't stop until the trees swallowed us whole.

We bolted across the compound like we were being chased by devils. Maybe we were. Gunner led, legs eating up the ground with an easy cowboy lope. Wrecker pushed hard, staying just behind him, his hair flying in the wind like a banner of war. I brought up the rear, steady as a metronome, refusing to give them the satisfaction of seeing me sweat.

We hit the tree line at full speed, and nobody hesitated. Gunner peeled off his shirt, boots flying in opposite directions. Wrecker yanked his jeans down in a single rip, leaving them inside out and abandoned in the leaves. I waited until the last possible second, then stripped to the skin, letting the cold air hit me all at once. For a second, the world was nothing but heartbeats and the tang of pine in my nose.

Then I shifted.

Bones went soft, then hard. Muscles stretched, snapped, reformed. My hands curled into claws, my vision exploded from gray-scale to Technicolor, and every sound in the world dialed up to eleven. My wolf came roaring to the surface, a surge of pure animal that wiped away every thought of Harper, every memory of loss, every worry about tomorrow. All that mattered was the run.

I loped after them, paws hitting the earth in a rhythm older than language. Gunner was already ahead, his wolf a big, russet blur tearing through the brush. Wrecker's gray coat flickered in and out of the shadows, always doubling back to snap at Gunner's heels or circle around and try to trip him up. We were three points of a triangle, each pulling the others forward, faster and faster until the world blurred into streaks of color and scent.

We hit the first ridge, and Gunner jumped it in one bound, tail flagged in challenge. Wrecker slid sideways, grabbed a mouthful of Gunner's ruff, and yanked him off balance. They rolled together, a tangle of fur and bared teeth, until Gunner broke loose and sprinted for the next rise.

I let them fight it out for the lead. I liked the view from the rear, liked the way the sun dappled through the branches and made every hair on my pelt stand on end. I could smell everything—the old cigarette butts from last year's poker game, the loam where Parker buried her coffee grounds, the musk of deer hiding somewhere to the left. I catalogued it all, sorting friend from foe, threat from safety. My wolf thrummed with the knowledge that nothing in these woods could hurt us.

We ran for miles. Sometimes we split up, carving new paths through the scrub and fallen logs; sometimes we regrouped and chased each other like pups. Wrecker was the fastest, but Gunner had stamina, and I had the patience to wait for my moment. When it came, I cut hard right, launched myself over a fallen log, and knocked both of them into a heap at the base of a pine tree.

We wrestled in the dirt, three grown men reduced to snarling, yipping idiots. It felt good. It felt clean.

When we tired, we lay side by side, tongues lolling, the steam rising off our bodies in the cool late morning air. For a long time, none of us moved. The only sound was the wind in the needles and the soft whuff of our own breath.

This was freedom. This was the only place in the world I didn't have to think, didn't have to carry the weight of my own history.

Wrecker stood first, shook the dirt from his coat, and nudged me with his nose. Gunner groaned, rolled over, and then we all three started running again, faster this time, pushing until our lungs burned and our paws bled.

We chased the sun all the way to the top of the high ridge, where the whole of Iron Valor's land spread out below us in gold and green. We stood together, side by side, and howled. The sound echoed down into the valley, wild and fearless, a reminder to every creature for miles that this was our territory.

For a moment, I forgot about everything else. There was no Harper, no Bronc, no Steiner, no past or future or second guessing. There was only the run, the wind, the brotherhood of the pack.

I laughed—a wolf's laugh, sharp and bright—and the others joined in, voices mingling and rising until it felt like we could shatter the sky.

We were alive. We were together.

And for the first time in as long as I could remember, that was enough.

Chapter 12

Harper

I woke up to the sound of nothing at all—a stillness so complete that for a second I thought maybe I'd died in my sleep. Then I remembered: I was in Jess's apartment, in a comfortable bed, wearing a t-shirt that didn't have Steiner's scent clinging to it. For a dizzy heartbeat, I didn't know what to do with the absence of threat. My brain pinged the usual danger zones—the door, the window, the closet—but there was nothing lurking. No monster waiting on the other side. Just a breeze, just the day.

My body felt like it belonged to me for the first time in months. There was an ache deep in my hip, a couple twinges in my back, but they were plain old aches, nothing like the panic-clenched nausea that had lived in my gut for three years. I lay there a moment, listening to the hum of the fridge and the way the blinds rattled when the HV/AC kicked on. In the time since I'd last had a safe place to sleep, I'd forgotten the luxury of small sounds.

I sat up and looked around. Jess's place was the same as when I'd gone to sleep: clinical, almost, but not unfriendly. Everything was squared off and in its place. The comforter was tucked with a hospital corner I'd never bother trying to replicate. On the nightstand, next to a phone and a bottle of water, was a slip of paper. A note written in his rigid, all-caps hand:

HARPER- MEETING THEN GOING FOR A RUN WITH THE GUYS. BACK LATER. HELP YOURSELF TO ANYTHING. J.

There was a pen line beneath my name, as if he'd almost written more but then stopped himself. The thought made my chest feel fizzy.

I shuffled to the edge of the bed, wincing a little at how tight my thighs had gotten. The floor was cold. My feet left little sweat halos on the hardwood as I walked to the bathroom. In the mirror, I hardly recognized myself. My hair had dried wild and full, frizzing out in every direction. My eyes were puffy, but not nearly as wrecked as I expected. The bruises on my arms had gone yellow and green overnight, making it look like I'd lost a paintball war. The cut on my lip was almost healed. The only real difference was my face: it looked... softer. Like my skin wasn't being pulled tight by terror anymore.

I splashed water on my face and remembered, with a start, the duffel bag that had been left for me. It was on the dresser, right where Jess had dumped it. I tugged it open and peered inside.

It was like Christmas. New underwear, still in the Hanes bag; jeans with the tags attached; a sky-blue tank top and a pale pink sweater. New clothes that normal people wore. There were even a pair of white tennis shoes and a bag of hair ties. I nearly laughed out loud.

I changed into the jeans—they fit, mostly, if I rolled the cuffs—and pulled the tank over my head. It felt like wearing hope. The sweater was light and soft, not the cheap acrylic I was used to. I did a little twirl in front of the mirror, just to see if it was real, then made a face at myself. What a dork.

I rummaged through the bag and found a small cosmetic case. Inside was tinted moisturizer, eyeliner, some mascara, and a nice quality tinted balm. The sight made my eyes sting. I hadn't put on anything but stage makeup in so long that I'd forgotten the ritual of it, the way it could make you feel like a person instead of a product. I dabbed on the moisturizer, traced a thin line of black along my lashes, and brushed the mascara over the tips. My hands didn't even shake.

I added the lip balm last, careful to keep from reopening the cut. The cherry scent was pleasant enough. I stuck my tongue out at my reflection, then grinned. I almost looked alive.

I grabbed my toothbrush and gave my teeth a good brushing. I was rinsing my glass when there was a knock at the door. I froze, every muscle going wire-tense. The old habits didn't die easy. I slid to the wall, heart hammering, and peered through the peephole. My brain took a second to process what I saw.

It was Parker, bouncing on the balls of her feet, wearing a tie-dyed hoodie and bright blue yoga pants. She was flanked by a tall, dark-haired beauty in a sundress and denim jacket. The brown-haired girl had her arms crossed and was watching the hallway like she expected to be mugged by a Girl Scout.

I exhaled and opened the door. Parker grinned. "Well, well. Look who's up before noon."

The blonde gave me a big wave. "Hey. I'm Maddie. I brought you some stuff." She held up a paper sack, the logo from Buttercream & Blessings bakery visible on the side. She strolled in like she owned the place. I heard she's the Alpha's sister, so I guess she kind of did.

Parker followed her. The room instantly felt brighter.

"We figured you'd be in need of some company," Parker said, shoving her hands in the pockets of her hoodie. "Also, we're all meeting at Aspen's for lunch. Thought you could use a break from...well, everything."

I nodded, still a little shell-shocked by how normal this all felt.

Maddie set the bag on the kitchen island and smiled. She had the same eyes as Bronc—ice blue, but warmer. "I brought cinnamon rolls. Aspen says, everybody needs sweets to brighten up their lives."

I took the sack, mouth watering at the smell of sugar and yeast. "Thank you," I said. "I'm not... I mean, I haven't eaten with people in a while."

Parker gave me a look, not pitying, just sharp. "Yeah, well, welcome to the circus. Aspen is already at the bakery making enough food to feed the entire county. If you want to bail, just say the word and we'll cover for you."

I shook my head. "No, I want to go. I just need to, uh—"

Maddie interrupted, "You look great. You'll beautiful girl, and you'll fit right in." She smiled. "Anyways, we don't stand on formalities. We're a strictly come as you are pack."

I laughed, and it was so startling that I had to pause and catch my breath. "That's a good thing, cuz I'm definitely out of practice when it comes to normal social situations."

Parker snorted. "Good thing none of us are normal, then." She jerked her thumb toward the hallway. "You want to grab your stuff? We'll wait."

I nodded, ducked back into the bedroom, and paused and thought I should leave a note. I found a post-it and scribbled, *"Out with Parker & Maddie. Will be back later. Thank you for everything—H."* I set it next to Jess's original note, overlapping the corners.

Back in the kitchen, the girls were waiting. Parker had already opened the cinnamon rolls and was licking frosting off her thumb.

"Ready?" Maddie asked.

"Yeah," I said. "Let's go."

We stepped out into the morning together, and for the first time in years, I didn't worry about what would happen on the other side of the door.

I'd expected Dairyville to be more like a ghost town, the kind of place where the main street was a straight shot between a gas station and a funeral home. Instead, it looked like something off a Hallmark movie set. There was a town square, honest to God, with a big limestone clock tower and benches painted every shade of pastel. The storefronts were trimmed in all colors; the awnings matched the doors. There was even a tiny bandstand in the center of town, decorated with crepe paper streamers.

Parker drove like a woman who'd never seen a speed limit enforced. We rocketed ten miles between the pack compound and Buttercream & Blessings in under 15 minutes, her fancy sports car humming every mile. Maddie rode shotgun and played DJ, flipping through local country stations until she found one with an actual yodeler. The song sounded like a coyote being drowned, but nobody seemed to mind.

When we pulled up outside the bakery, the first thing I noticed was the light. Aspen's shop was painted the color of lemonade, with a yellow and white awning and flower boxes bursting with actual marigolds. The sign was hand-lettered, no stencil, with the name in curly script and a tiny prairie dog painted beneath it, wearing a monocle and bow tie.

Maddie hopped out first and grabbed my hand. "I know you've met Aspen, but you'll love her more and more the longer you know her," she said. "She's like, the opposite of me. Where I'm all a bull in a china shop, she's made of sugar and optimism."

Parker snorted. "You're both dorks."

We ducked through the front door, and I was hit with a wall of smells: vanilla, melted butter, and just a hint of lemon. The shop was empty except for Aspen. She wore a pale blue swing dress with white daisies and white tights, her black hair pulled into a high ponytail. She looked like a retro pinup, if pinups came with flour up to their elbows and a dishtowel slung over her shoulder.

She glanced up, and her smile was so bright it made my teeth hurt. "Y'all! I thought you'd never make it!"

Aspen's accent was pure Georgia, the vowels stretching out like a hammock. She swept around the counter and hugged me first, wrapping both arms around my ribs like she'd known me forever. For a second, I almost cried again.

"Good to see you again, Harper. Welcome!" She pulled back, eyes sparkling. "I got the table all ready. Maddie, Parker, go get the pot of tea. I'll show Harper the spread."

The table near the window was set for tea, but not in a fancy, stuffy way. There was a three-tiered stand with finger sandwiches—cucumber, egg salad, pimento cheese. There were scones and quiches and little tarts filled with what looked like lemon curd and berries. On one side, a wooden board was covered in cubes of cheddar, slices of apple, and pecans candied in something sticky. The plates were mismatched china, every cup painted with a different flower.

It was a world away from the crystal chandeliers and granite counters of Eyrie. The kindness of it nearly bowled me over.

A scuffling noise came from the kitchen, and a moment later, Oscar the prairie dog appeared, standing on his hind legs. He wore a plaid vest and had a small napkin draped over one paw. He gave me a deep, theatrical bow.

"Miss Harper. It is a delight to see you among the living."

I blinked. "Uh...thank you, Oscar. That takes some getting used to doesn't it? A talking animal, I mean."

Aspen nodded. "He does. And if he gets a bit too much up in your business, just tell him so. He loves a bit of sass."

Oscar wriggled his whiskers. "I only wish to serve," he intoned, "and to sample the occasional sweet treat." Then he scampered to a table, where he began to meticulously organize the sugar packets.

I sat at the table, feeling weirdly exposed by the sun streaming through the window. The girls arranged themselves around me—Aspen to my left, Maddie to my right, Parker across, one leg tucked up in her chair.

For a while, we just ate. Nobody asked me questions; nobody pressed. Aspen insisted I try everything, and I did, even though my stomach wasn't sure it wanted company. The food was incredible—real butter, sharp cheese, soft bread, and quiche that melted on my tongue. I forgot I was supposed to be on edge.

When we'd demolished most of the food, Parker cleared her throat and leveled a look at me. "So, Harper," she said, "you feel comfortable talkin' about it?"

My fork froze mid-bite. "I'm sorry?"

Aspen shot her a glare. "Don't mind Parker. She's got the subtlety of a sledgehammer."

Maddie squeezed my hand under the table. "It's just… you don't have to tell us. But it might help. Or not. Whatever you want."

I looked at all three of them, expecting the usual hunger I saw in club girls when gossip was about to be served. Instead, I saw nothing but patience. I took a deep breath.

"My dad forced me to leave Jess," I said, voice quiet. "I grew up in a wealthy household in the Rising Moon Pack. Like, really wealthy. Jess was from the other end of pack territory. Where the blue-collar families lived. I didn't really know him growing up because he was so much older than me, but I saw him one day after I'd turned 19 and we both recognized immediately we were mates. He had already been in the military for several years, and I was committed to going to Juilliard. I used to be a ballerina." Considering where they'd found me, I could only imagine what they thought of me. But I continued.

"Jess was home on leave for a couple of weeks, and we saw each other every day. I knew my father would not approve. He'd had several high-powered wolves he wanted me to meet when the time was right. Before Jess was set to deploy, I thought I'd tell my mother about him. I had hoped she'd talk to my father and help me convince him that my happiness was what was important. She told my father, and he lost his mind. He told me if I wanted to go to Julliard I'd have to cut ties with Jess. My plan was to make my father think I agreed and let Jess know we'd be together after I graduated. But my father had me on a plane that night. I didn't expect him not to allow me to talk to Jess before I left. He confiscated my phone, my computer, iPad, everything. Jess deployed the next day." I took a sip of my tea and then continued.

"I had no idea he'd told Jess I had rejected him. I was for sure that we'd be together again. But, he deployed, and I never saw him again."

Maddie's eyes got big and wet. Aspen covered her mouth with one hand, tears already welling up.

"I hated my dad for it," I went on. "But I was too scared to fight him. I just kept telling myself it was temporary. Then everything went to hell when I was twenty-one. My father got caught up in a big Ponzi scheme. He'd invested heavily in it and basically lost everything. He still had to defend himself in court, and I guess he was desperate for money. No bank would lend him any, so he turned to the Alpha of the Morgantown Pack, Waylon Steiner, who, besides owning several successful businesses, is some kind of loan guy. My dad was a hedge fund guy; you'd think he would have known better. He loaned my dad I don't know how much money, but there was no way he could pay it back. I was still at school, and in the meantime my mom had divorced my dad and taken my younger sister to live somewhere in Europe. I was home for summer break when I discovered my family had fallen apart." I continued with how Steiner had seen me and offered the deal of taking me in trade for his debt. I explained how he threatened to take my sister instead since she'd turned 18, and I couldn't let that happen.

"He told me it would just be dancing, nothing else, just until the debt was paid."

Parker snorted. "Bullshit."

I nodded. "Yeah. That's when I figured out what kind of man my dad really was. But he said to think of Brie, and that was all it took. That's why I went willingly."

Aspen reached over and grabbed my arm, squeezing tight. "You poor girl."

I shrugged. "It was hell, but my baby sister would never have survived it. I figured I could survive anything for three years."

"But you think he wouldn't have let you go?" Maddie guessed.

"Yeah. The 'contract' was just a lie. Steiner told me himself. Said I belonged to him now, and that if I ever tried to leave, he'd send someone to kill my family."

There was a pause, broken only by the clink of Oscar setting a tea-spoon precisely parallel to the table edge.

Parker said, "So you survived. You're here now. You can do whatever you want."

I laughed, but it came out like a hiccup. "Not really. Jess thinks I rejected him. I never did. I just... disappeared. He's so angry. He won't even touch me. He doesn't want me now. And why would he? You have no idea what my life was like. What I was forced to do."

Aspen's face went stormy. "Don't say that. That boy is in love with you. He's part of your soul. He's just been angry for so long. When you carry that kind of hurt for so many years, it just takes a bit to move past it. You're going to have to let him work it out. He knows anything that happened in that club was against your will, sweetie. He knows."

Maddie nodded. "He's filled his life with sad imitations of what love should look like. When you know your mate is out there, there is a void that simply cannot be filled with anyone else. And believe me, there are plenty of women who have wanted to be the one to fill it. But he'd never entertain that. He's been no saint, but he's never been with any woman long term. He's been waiting for you."

I blinked. "Are you serious?"

Parker laughed. "He's an ornery idiot a lot of the time, but he's loyal. If you want him, you won't be able to keep him away."

I thought about the look on Jess's face when he saw me at the airstrip—the way his mouth twisted up like he was fighting back a scream. I thought about the way he'd clenched his fists, like he could squeeze out the poison just by holding me tight. I thought about the note he left me this morning, and how he almost wrote something else.

I wanted to believe them, but a tiny, poisonous part of me whispered that I'd ruined my only chance.

"He seems so enraged," I said. "I just wish he'd reject me officially, so I could move on. If that's what he's going to do."

Aspen shook her head. "Don't say that, honey. Your wolf would never forgive you."

She was right. Even now, the thought made my skin crawl. The idea of being alone—of never feeling the mate bond, was like staring into a black hole.

Parker grinned. "So what are you gonna do?"

I set my jaw. "I'm gonna go home, and I'm gonna tell him the truth. If he still wants to reject me, I'll take it. But if he doesn't, I'll never let him go again."

Maddie and Aspen whooped, and Oscar let out a high-pitched "Bravo, Miss Harper!" from the corner.

I stood up suddenly lightheaded. The sun was brighter than ever, and for the first time since I was a teenager, I felt like maybe I could survive another day.

"Thank you," I said, voice catching. "For everything."

Aspen hugged me again, and this time I let myself lean in, just for a second.

Parker jingled her keys at me. "Ready to go home?"

I nodded. "Ready as I'll ever be."

We said our thank yous and goodbyes to Aspen and Oscar after offering to help clean up. Maddie, Parker and I stepped into the daylight like we belonged there.

Parker drove her sports car like a bat out of hell, so the trip back to the pack house took no time at all. Parker dropped me at the curb and shot me a wink before peeling off, tires chirping on the hot blacktop. The air had shifted while we were at lunch, growing thicker and a few degrees warmer. Storm coming, maybe, or just the pre-dinner lull that always made Texas afternoons feel heavy as a wet blanket.

I climbed the stairs, clutching the paper sack with the leftover scones, and paused at the landing. I could hear my own breath, fast and shallow. There was a confidence in my stride that hadn't been there this morning. I thought about what Aspen said about how you can survive anything if you have a reason. I punched in the entry code and listened for the beep before turning the knob.

The apartment was silent.

But the air was wrong. Dense. Every hair on my arms stood up.

I stepped inside, took two steps, and stopped dead.

The place seemed off.

The coffee table was overturned, books scattered here and there.

My legs went cold, then numb. I scanned for blood, for signs of a fight, but there was nothing—just the raw aftermath of something volcanic. The air was thick with the smell of sweat, and, underneath, the copper tang of rage.

"Jess?" I called, voice cracking.

Nothing.

He wasn't here. Then I remembered that Parker and Maddie had mentioned the bonfire and barbecue that were happening tonight. I figured he must have gone without me. All the good feelings I had felt from the afternoon with the girls vanished.

Chapter 13

Arsenal

I returned from the woods with my lungs scraped clean, sweat drying cold on my skin and the metallic aftertaste of brotherhood still stinging my tongue. Wrecker and Gunner had peeled off to shower and then pregame at Pearl's, leaving me to stalk the perimeter in silence, the edge of the run still itching at my bones. The animal in me was sated for maybe a minute and a half before the human side took over, reminding me that tonight was supposed to be a turning point, that I had a job to do, a mate to protect, a future to reclaim.

I trudged up the back steps of the apartment, mud spackling my shins, muscles vibrating like live wires. The sun hadn't set yet, but the shadows inside my place were already deep and mean. I kicked my shoes off by the door, leaving them where they fell. A fine dust hung in the entryway, swirling up from the entry rug like ghosts off a battlefield.

Empty. The apartment was empty. She was gone. Every muscle in my body knotted at once.

The next few seconds blurred. I flipped the coffee table; books flew across the room. The TV remote vanished into the couch cushions. I crossed the room in three strides. I almost sprinted to the bedroom to look for clues. I flipped the comforter off the bed, the familiar rage driving my actions. A paperback was flattened against the nightstand, open to a page I'd read three times but never dog-eared. A glass of water tumbled to the floor in the aftermath. That's when I noticed the note on the nightstand, all-caps in blocky, black ink: "OUT WITH PARKER & MADDIE. BACK LATER. THANK YOU FOR EVERYTHING—H."

A laugh bubbled up in my chest, so sharp it made my throat sting.

Just another sign I was fucking out of control. She was gone alright, but just for the afternoon, nothing dramatic. My wolf wanted to chase her, to track her, to hunt her down and haul her back by the scruff of the neck. It wanted to remind her who I was, what we were, why she didn't get to just leave without warning.

I tried to shake it off. I paced the apartment, hands clenched, jaw ticking so loud I thought it might shatter. For a moment, I let myself imagine she'd been taken, that someone had breached the pack perimeter and spirited her away while I was running through the trees, laughing like a dumb fucking animal. It was easier to think she'd been abducted than that she'd simply chosen to be somewhere else.

Then my mind did what it always did: it spat out images, one after the other, raw and unfiltered. Harper on her knees in some VIP suite, Harper dancing for strangers, Harper bent over a velvet couch while a man with too many rings gripped her hair. My stomach turned to lead. I saw her hands—her real hands, delicate and long-fingered—wrapped around the base of a cock that didn't belong to me. I saw her body, the body I'd memorized down to the smallest scar, used as currency in a room full of monsters.

My canines threatened to drop. A growl rattled in my chest, so deep and ugly I didn't recognize it as my own.

I wanted to smash my fist into the kitchen wall. But I didn't. I still had some semblance of control. As small as it was.

The note was still in my hand, balled so tight the edges cut into my palm. I uncurled it, read it again, searching for hidden meaning. "OUT

WITH PARKER & MADDIE." No subtext. No secret code. Just a woman trying to be normal for once in her goddamn life.

I slumped onto the sectional, elbows on knees, and stared at the wall for a long time. In the silence, I heard every memory Harper had ever left behind: her laugh, her moan, the little gasp she made when I kissed her collarbone. I heard the way she said my name. Then I remembered that I wasn't even the one she had given her virginity to. I missed out on that first. It had only been a few months from the time we learned we were fated mates until she'd fucked me over and left me. I thought I'd have time to claim her officially with a ceremony; to make it special. I'd had years to stew on that.

After a while, I remembered that tonight was the monthly pack barbecue. I was supposed to help set up, haul coolers, keep the new pups from eating the potato salad. I was supposed to be a good soldier, a good wolf, a good brother. Instead, I was sitting here, choking on the scent of a woman who I might not ever stomach accepting again even though I knew I did want her.

I pushed off the couch grabbed a quick shower and then pulled on some clean jeans. I grabbed a clean Henley from the closet and looked at myself as I brushed and pulled my hair up with a tie. The man in the mirror looked feral—eyes too bright, jaw tight, no sign of a guy anyone would want to be around. I wondered what Harper would think if she saw me like this.

I slipped on my cut and left the apartment, locking the door behind me, and walked toward the clearing where the pack would be gathering. The sky was turning purple at the edges, streaks of cloud lit up like brush fire. I felt the old adrenaline start to build, a sense of purpose returning with every step. There were things to do, jobs to finish, people to protect.

Harper would be there eventually. She seemed like she wanted to be here.

Until then, I'd burn off the anger the only way I knew how; with fire and smoke and the company of men who understood what it meant to hurt.

The pack clearing was already alive by the time I got there. The sun was just a memory, but the sky was still bright at the edges, burning off the last of the day like a piece of flash paper. The bonfire crackled in the center of the yard, thick logs stacked in a pyramid, flames reaching for the sky. Pearl's boys; the ones she trusted to man the smokers, had bare arms glistening with sweat and barbecue sauce. The whole place reeked of smoke and meat and the tang of a party about to head on into chaos.

I liked the setup. It was efficient. Six long tables lined the north side of the clearing, covered in cheap plastic tablecloths and bowls of potato salad, slaw, chips, pickles, and deviled eggs on ice. Half a dozen coolers were packed with beer and soda and, somewhere at the bottom, the homemade plum wine Juliet brewed in her spare time. There was a makeshift bar by the porch, stocked with every liquor you could imagine and a few you wished you couldn't. The lights strung up around the perimeter were already blinking on and off, moths orbiting every bulb.

People were everywhere. The cubs—kids, really, but wolves grew fast—were running circles around the tree line, playing some kind of feral tag that was equal parts tackle and shriek. The older teens clustered by the fire, sneaking beers and pretending not to look at the girls. The women of the pack had claimed the picnic benches and were setting up paper plates, arguing over which batch of brownies would disappear fastest. A few of the men were already lined up at the brisket station, gnawing burnt ends and talking shit about the Cowboys' season.

I grabbed a stack of folding chairs from the back of the lodge and hauled them around the bonfire, ignoring the way people watched me when they thought I wasn't looking. I set up the chairs in a perfect arc, measured down to the inch, and then stepped back to check my work. Satisfied, I drifted to the edge of the firelight and posted up, hands in my pockets, watching the flames eat through the logs.

I didn't want to go looking for Harper. I told myself it was because she was not here, or having a good time, that she deserved a night with friends, but the truth was, I didn't want to face her. Not yet. Not with all this poison swirling in my head.

Big Papa found me before anyone else did. He moved through the crowd like a tank through wet cement, every inch of him battle-scarred and calm. The firelight made the old burns on his face look fresh, a topographic map of every fight he'd survived. He stopped next to me and said nothing for a minute. He finally spoke. "Aspen said the girls had a great time this afternoon. Said Harper opened up a bit. Mentioned something about how she had wound up where we found her. Said it was a rough story."

I was running low on compassion at that moment. "We all got our sad stories I guess, huh, Papa?"

I saw the disappointment in his eyes. That just about gutted me. The one person around here you don't want to disappoint is JT "Big Papa Rice." The man had been wounded by a roadside bomb and carried scars all over his body, and he was about the best goddamn man you could ever meet. He could kill a man with his bare hands, but he also would pray with you if you asked. I'd never been happier than when he'd found his true made, that little witch Aspen, who remarkably is a hybrid. Her daddy is the King of Angels on the earth. How perfect it that? Papa deserved that woman. Maybe I deserved the hell I was wallowing in. He shook his head and walked away from me.

Gunner was next in the little parade of officers coming my way. He's the youngest and newest of our crew. He was selected as an officer when

Menace became the fucking King of the Midwest Territory. Yeah, I rub elbows with a king. Gunner is way smarter than he's given credit for. Has a cattle ranch and is a cowboy through and through. He wants to find his mate more than anything and thinks I'm a fucking moron for not grabbing Harper with both hands and letting bygones be bygones. He'd never felt the sting of rejection, though. Never lived through years of gut-spilling emptiness knowing the person created for you didn't want you, or so you thought. It fucks with your heart, your head, and your soul.

He handed me a beer without comment.

"So," he said after a long pull. "You gonna stand around broodin' all night or are you gonna actually enjoy yourself?"

I ignored him.

He grinned, teeth perfect and a little too white for a real cowboy. "You ever think about how stupid it is, makin' yourself miserable over a girl who's right here, wantin' you?"

"She doesn't want me," I muttered. "She wants a life that never happened."

Gunner rolled his eyes. "She's here, isn't she? She's your mate. She's sleepin' in your bed. What the hell else does a woman have to do, paint it on your truck?"

I didn't answer.

He finished his beer, set the empty on the ground. "You know, when I was a pup, my mom used to tell me that wolves who waste a second of happiness are dumber than a bag of hammers. Cuz not everybody gets a second chance." He leaned in, voice dropping. "Don't waste yours, Jess."

I wanted to punch him. Instead, I drained my beer and stared into the fire, watching the way the coals shifted, the way the flames licked the logs and left nothing but ash.

Around us, the pack kept up the party. Laughter rolled across the clearing, high and wild. Kids shrieked. Music blared from somebody's Bluetooth speaker, a mix of country and classic rock and one or two pop songs I'd never admit to liking. I watched the couples move through the crowd, arms linked, heads tilted close. I saw Wrecker and Parker sneak off to the shadows, her hand buried in his back pocket. I saw Big Papa wrap Aspen up in a bear hug, spinning her around until she screamed with laughter.

I watched it all, and for the first time, I didn't feel like I belonged.

I sat there, bottle sweating in my hand, and tried to remember what it felt like to be whole.

I couldn't.

I let the heat from the fire numb my face, the smoke sting my eyes, and waited for the night to end.

I didn't know what tomorrow would bring, but I knew it would hurt.

I could only hope it would be worth it.

The fire burned higher as the night got drunker. By the time I'd grabbed my third beer, the pack clearing was thick with noise: laughter, shouts, the clatter of plates and the whine of a country tune. Every table was packed, and the air was heavy with the smell of sweat and mesquite and charred sugar from the s'mores kits the kids had started raiding early. I parked myself at a picnic table on the far side of the fire, facing the flames and the silhouettes that flickered beyond them, my back to the crowd. The heat felt good on my face. It was the only thing I trusted to burn hotter than the mess inside me.

A shadow detached itself from the mass at the brisket line and drifted my way. I knew the scent before I could even make out the face. Marisol. She walked with a sway that made the wolf in me perk up and wag, the kind of confidence that said she'd never once been afraid of rejection. She had on cutoffs and a white crop sweater that showed off the ink across her ribs, her long black hair in a braid that whipped at her hips as she closed the distance.

She didn't say a word, just slid onto the bench beside me, so close that her thigh pressed against mine. I kept my gaze straight toward the fire. She grinned like she knew exactly what I was doing.

"You look like a lost little pup," she said, pulling a cold beer from the six-pack and popping the cap on the edge of the table.

"Thanks, Mari."

She shrugged, took a long drink, and let the silence stretch out. She was never one for small talk. After a minute, she leaned in, her lips so close to my ear I could feel the heat of them.

"Rumors are goin' 'round," she said, soft enough that it wouldn't carry. "I'm sad if they're true?"

I stiffened, but nodded. "They're true."

Marisol considered that, then draped her arm around my shoulders, fingers digging in just enough to remind me of the fun we always have. "Good for you," she said. "But you know you don't have to be miserable about it, right? You ever need to forget, you know where I live."

She nuzzled the side of my neck, a flash of teeth and tongue, and I felt my wolf go slack with comfort. It wasn't sexual—well, not only sexual. It was the kind of touch that said you weren't alone, that the world hadn't yet managed to break you all the way through. Marisol had been my anchor more times than I could count. I'd let her hold me together more than once when the darkness got too heavy.

She pulled back, eyes glinting in the firelight. "I'm gonna miss you, Arsenal." Then she leaned in and bit my ear.

Then she caught my jaw in her palm and turned my face to hers.

She surprised me with what she said next. "She's not the enemy, Jess. You're your own enemy." She let the words hang there, her hand still on my cheek.

I wanted to argue. I wanted to tell her she didn't understand, that the weight of Harper's absence had hollowed out every part of me, that I didn't know how to be a man anymore, let alone a mate. But Marisol didn't do pity. She did action, and right now, action meant finishing her beer, setting it down, and pulling me into a sweet sideways hug.

I let her. I even hugged her back, burying my face in her hair for half a second and inhaling the sweat and smoke and wildness that was Marisol. It felt good. It felt easy.

She let me go, pulled back, looking into my face. She was about to kiss me when she froze. Her nose twitched. Her eyes narrowed, scanning the darkness beyond the fire.

I turned, following her gaze.

Maddie came around the edge of the bonfire first, her hands full of paper plates and a pie tin. She was laughing, her head thrown back, and it took me a second to see who was behind her.

Harper.

She looked different in the firelight. She wore jeans that actually fit, a soft blue tank top and pink sweater, and her hair wavy and loose around her shoulders. Her cheeks were flushed from the heat, and her eyes—the bluebonnet eyes I'd spent five years trying to forget—were fixed right on me.

For a second, nobody moved. Maddie stopped, pie hovering in the air, and followed Harper's gaze. Harper stood perfectly still, a smile frozen halfway on her lips, as she took in the sight of me and Marisol, locked together on a bench with her arm still slung around my neck.

The world went silent. The music, the laughter, the crash of voices—all of it faded out, replaced by the pounding of my own heart. I could feel every set of eyes on us, the entire pack going still as they waited to see what would happen next.

Marisol's fingers tightened on my shoulder, then relaxed. She followed my gaze, saw Harper, and in that instant, I watched her whole body change. The easy grin vanished, replaced by something colder, harder. She let her arm drop and straightened up, chin tilted high.

Harper's eyes widened, a flicker of hurt crossing her face before she shuttered it away.

I tried to speak, but the words stuck in my throat. I wanted to run to her, to drag her away from the fire and the eyes and the old wounds. I wanted to tell her that Marisol was nothing, that she was just a friend, that I'd never wanted anyone but her.

But I didn't move. I just sat there, trapped between the past and the present, unable to choose.

Marisol broke the silence first. "Looks like you got company," she said, loud enough for everyone to hear. "Don't let her down, Arsenal."

She pushed off the bench, shot Harper a glance that could have shattered granite, and stalked away toward the woods. Maddie muttered something under her breath and hustled after her, leaving Harper standing alone in the glow of the fire.

I stood, slow, feeling every muscle in my body rebel against the movement.

Harper looked at me, and for the first time since that night at Eyrie, I saw real fear in her eyes. Not terror, not panic—just the simple, awful fear that comes from realizing your worst fear is about to come true.

I crossed the clearing, not caring that everyone was watching. The fire threw our shadows out ahead of us, twisted and huge.

I stopped a few feet away from her. She didn't back up, but she didn't come closer, either.

"And the hits just keep on coming," she said, her voice barely a whisper.

I tried to smile, but it felt like my face might crack. "I'm here."

She nodded, then looked past me to where Marisol had disappeared. "Clearly. You, her, my humiliation. Gang's all here."

"She's a friend."

Her mouth twisted. "She looked like more than a friend."

I shook my head. "She was... comfort. That's all."

Harper's eyes filled with tears, but she blinked them away. "I don't blame you. It's no more than what I deserve. If I had been stronger, none of this would have happened. I understand. I want you to be happy, Jess. It's truly all I want. If I need to leave to make that happen. I'll go."

I wanted to scream. I wanted to tell her I'd waited, that I'd never stopped waiting, that even with every woman in the world on their knees, none of them were her.

But all I said was, "You can't leave me again."

She smiled, small and sad. "I'll give it some time. But I can't see *that*. I won't watch *that*." She nodded in the direction Marisol was walking away. "So if you need *that* to be happy. Please, I'm begging you, let me go."

We stood there, the fire crackling, the night closing in around us, the several members of the pack pretending not to listen.

She spoke one more time.

"I also can't do this in front of the pack. I've been humiliated every day for the past three years." She finally looked at me. "I'm done with that."

Fuck. In all of this, I kept forgetting she was innocent. I was the worst kind of man; victim shaming, even if it was in my mind. I had to do better—*be* better. I'd been so caught up in my own hurt I hadn't truly considered hers. The fire popped, and I'd turned toward the sound. When I turned back toward her, she was gone.

Chapter 14

Harper

The moment before Jess had walked over to me had seemed like an eternity. I watched him with that woman draped over him, her dark hair swaying like a tail every time she laughed. She nuzzled her cheek against his jaw with a practiced rub, marking him with her scent even in human skin. Then she leaned in and bit the bottom of his ear, hard, until he jerked away with a smile and a barked "Watch it." Everyone nearby saw it. Until she noticed me and walked away, Maddie following her.

My wolf made a noise I didn't recognize. Half snarl, half plea, all humiliation. I dug my nails into my palm until the pain became sharp enough to dull everything else.

I was still in the clothes from this afternoon. They'd been perfect then, a costume for the world I'd imagined could exist: soft blue tank, slouchy pink sweater, jeans without a single run or stain. My hair was in waves twisted into pretty spirals by Maddie's careful fingers. I'd spent fifteen minutes making sure my eyeliner was perfect. Now I wondered if I should have left the makeup off, left the bruises visible, made it easier for the crowd to point and say: there, that's the whore who let the world eat her alive.

The bonfire heat painted my skin and filled my nose with the crackle of sap and fat. I wanted to run, but my legs refused to work. My insides churned. For a moment I was back at Eyrie, the spotlight hitting my face, stage smoke curling up my thighs. Rage in the front row, his mouth open in a leer, and the demon king's voice in my head: Good girl, now make it look like you want it.

I did. I always did, because the witches made sure of it.

Steiner's club employed three different witches, all with their own specialty cocktails of compulsion. I still remembered the first time I tasted the "blue smoke." It came in a shot glass rimmed with black salt, and the moment it hit my stomach, it was like someone had pulled my soul out and replaced it with honey. My body would flush, lips swell, thighs go slack and hungry. Every nerve lit up. It made me want to writhe, to please, to be touched, to be watched. It made me want to perform so bad I would claw my own skin off if I weren't allowed on stage.

But none of that desire was mine. I'd be screaming inside the whole time, watching myself move and touch and moan, knowing that no matter how much I begged to stop, nothing would obey except the mask. I became a marionette, a living wet dream with no driver behind the wheel.

That was what the men paid for. Not just the body, but the obedience. The blankness.

I knew that was all Jess saw now. I was a haunted house, and he wanted no part of the ghosts rattling in the attic. After I told him I didn't want to do this here, he'd turned back to the fire—didn't even notice I'd walked away.

The air shifted behind me. I tried to step back, but nearly collided with a circle of three women, all holding red plastic cups and all wearing the same shade of judgmental smirk. I didn't know them. Their names were irrelevant; they were always some variant of Lauren or Kaitlyn or Jessa.

One of them—the tall one, pretty in a fake-tan, gym-hard way—leaned in and stage-whispered, "Well, at least she's not on a pole tonight."

The others tittered, glancing at me sideways.

The laughter cut through me sharper than any knife. I couldn't speak, couldn't breathe, could only turn and walk as fast as I dared, keeping my chin up. If I were going to be the pack's latest charity case, I'd at least do it with my spine straight.

Their voices followed, softer but not soft enough:

"Poor Arsenal. Can you imagine? Your fated mate is a—"

"Don't say it."

"I *will* say it. She's a stripper. And probably more than that."

"You know Arsenal. He likes 'em easy."

My wolf whimpered again. I wanted to run, to shift and tear something to pieces, but all I could do was drift toward the shadows at the far end of the clearing.

Past the bonfire, the land dropped off into a gentle slope, studded with picnic tables and old farm implements that someone had painted turquoise for a "rustic" vibe. Most of the crowd was clustered by the fire, but a few couples had paired off here, away from the chaos. I saw Bronc at one of the tables, Juliet in his lap. They were an odd pair—the Alpha so big he looked like he could break her in half, and the Luna curled up against him like she'd never known anything except safety.

I wanted to hate them for how easy it looked. Instead, I hovered nearby, letting their voices roll over me like static.

"You know what I think?" Juliet was saying, her hand tracing circles on Bronc's forearm. "I think they are just about the two most broken people I've ever seen. It breaks my heart."

Bronc grunted, but he didn't sound annoyed. "You said it your-self—everybody's broken. Some of us just hide it better."

Juliet kissed his neck, soft, then said, "I just hope they figure it out. Otherwise, she's gonna end up running. And we both know what happens when a wolf starts running."

Bronc's voice dropped so low it was almost a growl. "If she tries, Arsenal will hunt her to the ends of the earth. It's how he's built."

There was a silence. Juliet leaned back and looked her mate full in the face. "He looks at her the same way you looked at me when you pulled me out of that jungle. You thought I was too broken. You didn't think I'd make it all the way back to you."

"You scared the shit out of me," Bronc said, his mouth quirking.

She gave him a gentle smile. "I was afraid I was too broken to love. But you loved all the pieces back together."

Bronc squeezed her to him. "Maybe they can love each other enough to put their pieces back together."

I clung to those words, let them echo in my head as I turned and kept walking. The pack's laughter faded behind me, and the darkness ahead looked softer, more forgiving.

I didn't know if my pieces *could* be loved back together.

But for the first time since I left Eyrie, I wanted to try.

The walk back to the pack house felt like wading through tar. I was out of breath by the time I reached the porch. I wanted to climb the stairs straight to Jess's apartment and hide in the dark. I had to go through the common room to get to the stairs.

The entryway was all glass and warm wood, a living room lined with nice couches and overstuffed chairs. The place was empty except for the faint glow of the kitchen light and a few wall sconces until I stepped inside and realized I was wrong.

The women were waiting.

There were four of them this time, not counting the toddler in a unicorn onesie who sat quietly on the carpet, stacking blocks. The grown-ups perched along the far couch, heads bent in close, but the second I walked in, they turned as one and smiled.

It was the smile of predators who had just found a wounded rabbit in their den.

"Hey, Harper!" chirped the one with a platinum pixie cut. She wore a pink track jacket and a pair of Lululemon leggings that made her legs look like they belonged on the cover of some fitness magazine.

The others followed her lead, all chorus and echo. "Oh, hi! We were just talking about you!" "Come sit down! We want to get to know you." "Are you feeling better after your long day?"

I froze. My first instinct was to flee, but then I heard Maddie's voice from this afternoon: "You look great. You'll fit right in." I could do this. I could pretend.

I stood stock-still. "I was just heading upstairs."

They came to me, blocking my way.

We all stood in a small circle. The air around me prickled with perfume and competition.

"So," said the pixie, "how are you settling in?"

I hesitated. "Okay. Just getting my bearings, you know?"

The second woman, tan and tight-faced, her lips the color of an angry plum, leaned forward. "You were a dancer, right? At that club?" She said the word like it was a diagnosis.

I nodded. "I was a dancer, a prima ballerina. I trained at Juilliard for two years." Maybe if I reminded them I was once respectable, it would blunt the edge.

The third, a redhead with a margarita in her hand and bitterness in her eyes, pounced. "Juilliard? That's like really impressive. But what kind of dance do you do now? I heard it was... uh..." She glanced at the pixie for backup.

"Pole dancing," supplied the fourth, a round-cheeked blonde who looked like she'd been pretty before she'd had three kids and decided the world owed her an apology. "Isn't that what you did?" Her smile was wide, but her pupils never left my face.

I felt my cheeks flush. "Yeah. I mean, I don't..." I started, but was immediately cut off.

"But you did more than just dance, didn't you?" asked the blonde, voice sticky-sweet. "I mean, I have a cousin who bartended at clubs, and she said sometimes the girls do… other things for money. Not that I'm judging. We all do what we have to."

"She's not judging," repeated the redhead, nodding solemnly. "We all know how hard it is for single girls. Sometimes you just need to survive."

I tried to back away so I could make it to the stairs, but they had my exit blocked. My skin itched under my clothes.

The toddler, oblivious to the tension, upended her block tower and let out a little whoop.

The women ignored her. They'd found better prey.

The pixie pressed, "You and Arsenal are fated supposedly, but he never claimed you. That's so odd! Like I'd guess he'd think twice now."

They all made a noise at this, a blend of ahh, right, the sound people make when the plot twist lands exactly where they expected it.

"Well, he's always been such a stand-up guy," the blonde said. "Everyone says he's the most loyal wolf on the planet. Which is why it's so… surprising. I mean, not that it's any of our business, but we were just shocked to see him bring you here. Like, of all people."

"Of all people," echoed the redhead, teeth bared in a smile.

"Guess it was difficult, going from Juilliard to, like, the pole?" asked the pixie, too casually. "It must have been so different. All that discipline, then… that."

I stared at my hands. "Yeah," I muttered.

The tan woman—who hadn't spoken yet, just stared at me with hooded eyes—finally said, "I just think the standard for our MC and pack officers' mates is usually higher. That's what's most surprising about Arsenal bringing you here. Do you expect him to claim you?" She asked like she couldn't imagine he would dirty the pack with me.

The conversation devolved from there. Every question was more pointed, more invasive. Did you ever date customers? Did you like it? How much money did you make? Did you ever get recognized on the street? Was it weird to be watched all the time? Was it hard to keep yourself clean? Did you have to do drugs to get through it?

I answered each one as flatly as possible, hoping they'd get bored, but every answer only seemed to make them hungrier.

By minute ten, my head felt like it was filling with helium. I tried to leave, but the redhead's hand landed on my forearm, holding me in place.

"We just want to be sure you're a good fit for the pack," she said, her nails digging in a fraction too hard. "It's nothing personal. We're just very protective of our own."

That was when I realized I'd never be one of them. No matter how many muffins I ate at Aspen's, no matter how many picnics or potlucks I showed up for, I'd always be the girl who was too damaged to love.

My wolf rolled over, baring its belly.

"I should go," I whispered. "It's late."

The pixie pouted. "So soon? We hardly got to know you."

She reached for my hand, and for a second I thought she was going to kiss it, like some weird Southern debutante, but instead she just patted it twice and said, "Maybe next time you can tell us about your favorite routine."

The laughter that followed was the worst yet—sharp, cold, the kind that leaves bruises.

I took a backward step toward the stairs, and then—

The air changed. A sound like a thunderclap, but lower, deeper, vibrating in my teeth.

A growl.

Every head snapped toward the entryway. Jess was there, hair pulled tight in a knot, eyes black and bottomless, the lines of his face gone sharp as a guillotine.

He took in the room—me, hunched and humiliated; the women, clustered together like a murder of crows—and said, in a voice that could cut through steel:

"What the fuck do you think you're doing?"

Nobody answered. The toddler started to cry.

Jess didn't move, didn't even blink. "Everyone of you better know that I will be confronting your mates. If you don't have a mate, I'll be chatting with your fathers. They will know how shameful everyone of you has behaved toward my mate. If this behavior *ever* happens again, you will take it up with the Luna. And then I'll handle it myself."

A tremor ran through the group. The pixie opened her mouth, but Jess's stare pinned her shut.

"I've been nice. I've let the pack handle its own. But this ends now." His voice never rose above a whisper, but it carried to every corner of the room. "Harper's with me. You don't know her story; her sacrifice; you've not walked in her shoes. Spread the word. If anyone disrespects her again, there *will* be hell to pay. If you have a problem with that, you come to me. Not her. Not ever. Don't talk to her. Don't *look* at her unless it's with the respect she rightly deserves."

The silence was absolute, except for the snuffling toddler and the sound of my own pulse in my ears.

"Go," he said, not to the women, but to me.

I moved. I floated past the couch, the kitchen, the judgment, until Jess's hand closed around mine, warm and steady. He didn't tug, didn't squeeze, just let me know he was there.

We climbed the stairs together, not speaking, not looking back. The door to his apartment shut behind us, and the world outside collapsed into a single, blessed point of quiet.

He let go of my hand then, but not before squeezing it once, hard enough to remind me that not every part of me was breakable.

Some pieces, it seemed, could be mended.

We didn't speak for a long time. Jess dropped my hand at the door and motioned for me to sit, then locked the deadbolt with an unnecessary click. He moved through the room like a caged animal, pulling a throw blanket off the back of the sectional, rearranging pillows until there was a small fortress built for me in the corner of the couch. I let him, not wanting to break the fragile peace his presence offered.

He gestured to the nest. "Sit."

I did, crossing my legs at the ankles. He dropped down beside me, not touching but close enough to radiate heat. He took a deep breath, staring at his hands, and then—almost tender—reached for my boots. I jerked back on instinct. He stilled, waiting. When I didn't protest further, he tugged them off, one by one, setting them upright against the sofa. Then he lifted my bare feet and set them on his lap.

He ran a thumb along my instep, finding a knot there and working it loose. My eyes closed on their own.

"They're so fucking ignorant," he said so quietly I almost missed it. "That group of them, anyway. The way they look at you. The things they said. They thought I couldn't hear them, but I did. There's a reason they were inside instead of out with the other women. They've burned all their bridges with them. None of the other women can stand that little clique. But, I'm not sayin' other women won't talk, Prima. They will."

I didn't know what to say, so I said nothing.

His grip tightened a fraction. "If you want to leave, I'll take you wherever you want to go. But if you stay, I won't let anyone harm you. Not again."

His jaw worked side to side, the vein in his neck visible. "I know I'm the worst of them."

A thousand responses crowded my tongue, but none seemed right. I wanted to ask why after all this time; he cared. I wanted to ask what happened to the man who used to laugh with me on the lakeshore, who said I had eyes like Texas wildflowers.

Instead, I asked, "Why did you let me go, Jess?"

He looked like I'd slapped him.

He didn't answer right away, just kept kneading my foot with the careful brutality of a man who'd learned to heal with his hands only after he'd broken everything worth fixing.

Finally: "I didn't let you go. I didn't have a choice."

He dragged his palm down his face and exhaled hard. "After that night at your house, your dad told me you'd changed your mind. That you were gone and weren't coming back, ever. That you didn't want a wolf with nothing to offer, not when you could have a future. I tried to call, but you blocked my number. Your mom wouldn't even let me on the property after that. I thought you had been given a choice, and you chose another life. That you'd right and truly rejected me."

"But it's not true," I said, hating the desperate note in my voice.

He nodded, slow. "I know that *now*. But back then? You were gone, and I was filled with rage. I left for deployment early. Didn't look back. I figured if I wasn't good enough for you, I'd make myself good enough for someone, or die trying."

He traced a circle on my heel, eyes locked on the motion. "Spent the next five years doing exactly that. Recon, then Delta."

He looked up then, and his eyes were dark, almost black. "That's where Bronc found me. I served with him. When he became Alpha of Iron Valor, he asked if I wanted to join him here. Told me I could have a pack, a purpose, something bigger than my own pain. I've been here ever since, and it's here I've found my true family. I don't get back to Rising Moon to see my parents and siblings very often anymore. I've tried to bring them up here, but for some reason they'd rather wallow in their poverty down there."

"But you never stopped waiting," I said. It wasn't a question.

He shook his head. "Not really. I had no idea how you'd ever make it back to me. I tried to move on, but once you know your mate is out there somewhere, there is nobody else. So no. I never stopped waiting."

We sat in silence, his hands moving up to my ankle, thumb pressing small, perfect circles into my skin.

"When I saw you that night in the club, I was on recon for an op. I couldn't believe it," he said, voice low. "I thought we'd made eye contact. Did you see me?"

I nodded my head.

He smiled, crooked and sad. "Before that, when you were dancing, it wasn't like you noticed anyone. You were just... in the moment. Lost in the music. For a second, I thought maybe you were happy."

My throat closed. "I wasn't. I never—"

He cut me off. "I know. When you finished, I saw you rush off stage like you couldn't get away fast enough. I knew you didn't want to be doing that. I knew you were made for more."

His hand moved up to my calf, massaging the muscles there, working out tension. "That's when I knew you were still mine. That you'd never stopped being mine."

I let the words settle over me, heavy and warm.

His hands stilled, holding my leg in place. "I know you're scared. I know you think you're broken, and I haven't done a single fucking thing to help put your pieces back together. But if you'll give me another chance; give *us* another chance, I'd like to try."

He pulled me onto his lap my legs draped to the side, careful as if I might shatter. He settled me against his chest, arms circling my waist. I could hear his heartbeat through his shirt—strong and steady. I could feel the heat of his skin, the tremor in his muscles.

For the first time, I let myself lean into him, just a little.

"I want to stay," I whispered, so soft I wasn't sure he'd hear.

His arms squeezed tighter, just for a second.

"You don't have to decide tonight, Prima," he said, using the name he used to call me again, breath tickling my ear.

But I already had.

I was done running. I was done with being a haunted house. I wanted to be the place where he could come home.

I pressed my face into the curve of his neck and breathed in deep. I could smell the smoke of the bonfire, the sharp scent of his sweat, and—underneath it all—the wild, warm promise of what we could still be.

My wolf stirred, lifting her head without whimpering for the first time in years.

I let it howl.

Chapter 15

Arsenal

I'd barely gotten the door shut before I smelled blood. Not the metallic tang of violence, but the thinner, more caustic scent of fresh humiliation. It rode the air from the common room, thick as smoke after a house fire. Underneath was the cheap cloy of vanilla-sugar body spray—an assault of synthetic sweetness that made my teeth ache—and beneath that, Harper's clean, lemon-and-linen scent, wound tight as a wire.

I let the door click behind me, every sense sharpening. The pack house was built for maximum openness: a sweeping entrance with a cathedral ceiling, glossy wood floors, thick throw rugs and a pair of fire-places at opposite ends of the great room. Juliet had gone full Southern Gothic when she decorated, so the place was crowded with battered armchairs, velvet settees, and floral prints on every available wall. The air tonight vibrated with a different kind of drama.

I followed the hum of voices—female, high and hungry—until the sight line opened up. Harper stood alone, arms wrapped around herself, facing a semicircle of pack women arrayed by the leather sectional like a goddamn tribunal. They had her boxed in against the credenza, between the chipped paint of a plant stand and the cold marble of the coffee table.

The ringleader was a bottle-blonde in athleisure, her nails weaponized into pale pink daggers. The others flanked her: a brittle-faced redhead in Ugg boots, a puffy-faced brunette yoga wannabe queen, and a mousy little thing whose eyes darted between them, feral and eager.

They hadn't seen me yet. Harper's eyes had, though. I caught them for a split second—blue and glassy, pupils wide with animal panic. Her lips barely moved, but I read them like a prayer:

Help.

"I just think," the blonde was saying, voice pitched to carry, "that you might not be up to the standard of pack material."

The redhead snorted. "Arsenal is a pack official after all."

"Yeah," said the brunette. "You may be off the pole *now*, but…" The laughter that followed was brittle, sharp enough to cut.

I saw Harper flinch, just a tremor through her shoulders, but she didn't respond. Didn't even look at them.

The blonde leaned in, lips peeled off her teeth in a smile. "Is it true what they say? The more money they give the more you give out?"

The wolf in me went incandescent. My vision rimmed out. I saw everything: the heat rising up Harper's neck, the twist of her hands in the hem of her shirt, the way her nails pressed hard enough to leave half-moons in her skin. I saw the smugness in the pack women, the absolute certainty that they were untouchable.

I stepped into the space; ice-cold and clinical. A growl preceded my words.

"Is there a problem here?" I asked, letting the words knife through the air.

The blonde barely flinched. "Not at all, Arsenal." She drew out the name like it was a joke. "We were just welcoming your guest to the pack."

I ignored her, looking only at Harper. She stared at the floor, jaw locked. The tremble in her left hand had migrated to her knee, and I recognized the signs of collapse.

I closed the distance. "You want to come upstairs?"

She started to answer, but the blonde cut in. "She's fine, Arsenal. We're just having girl talk. You know, about pack traditions."

"Let me make something clear," I said, voice low enough that every syllable was freighted with promise. "You do not speak to my mate. Ever. Not unless it's with the respect owed to a member of this pack—especially a pack officer's mate. If I hear so much as a whisper about her past, I will drag each of you in front of Juliet and let her decide what to do with you." I let the threat dangle, then added, "And if that doesn't get through your skulls, I'll have a chat with your fathers. And then your mates. You will not like how that ends."

The redhead's face went white. The brunette shrank into herself. Only the blonde held her ground.

"Are you threatening us, Jess?" she asked, voice brittle.

I stepped in, chest to chest. "You forget yourself. Jeanette." I growled through clenched teeth, my wolf coming forth. These bitches seemed to forget that every pack officer in Iron Valor was an alpha in our own right. We chose to bow to Bronc. "You should expect a visit from the Luna, you little insignificant piece of shit. And it's best you remember, I don't threaten," I snarled. "I promise." She shrank almost to her knees.

I held her gaze until she looked away, then turned to Harper and took her hand. Her skin was clammy, the pulse in her wrist fluttering like a trapped bird.

"Go," I said, not a question.

Harper didn't speak. She just nodded, eyes fixed on the floor. I led her toward the staircase, feeling the weight of the room shift, every head tracking our progress.

As we climbed, I glanced back. The redhead was already in tears. The blonde was staring at her hands, nails digging into her own palm.

I didn't enjoy it. I wanted to, but all I felt was rage: at them, at myself, at the entire fucked-up hierarchy of the world that made a girl like Harper the target of so much hate.

On the landing, I paused. Harper was shaking harder now, not with fear, but with the effort of keeping it all contained.

"I'm sorry," I said, voice breaking a little. "I should have been here."

She shook her head. "It's not your fault."

"It is. I'm Sergeant at Arms. I protect the pack. That means you, too. Especially you."

She smiled, just a ghost of one, but it was enough to make my chest ache.

We reached my door. I unlocked it, pushed inside, and closed the world out behind us. For a minute, neither of us moved.

Then Harper let out a breath, long and shaky. "Thank you," she whispered.

I could still feel the adrenaline in my blood, the edge of violence fizzing just below the surface. But when I looked at her, at the way her hands had gone slack, all I wanted was to fix her. To hold her together until the world stopped tearing at her seams.

I reached for her, slow this time. She let me pull her in, let me guide her to the couch, let me tuck her in beside me like she belonged there.

The wolf inside me howled for blood. But the man just held her, as gently as I could, until the shaking stopped.

And for once, I didn't want to let go.

After I'd pulled her into my lap, she'd relaxed against my body.

"You can ask," she said, voice so low I almost missed it.

I kept her head tucked under my chin. "Ask what?"

She shrugged. "Whatever it is you want to know. I'd rather you heard it from me."

I shook my head. "I don't want the story unless you want to give it."

She let out a short defeated laugh as she pulled back so she could look at me. "It's going to be the elephant in the room forever if I don't tell you."

I nodded. "Alright, Prima. Tell only what you're comfortable telling."

"Okay," she said, moving from my lap to the spot next to me. She pulled her knees up to her chest, sitting sideways facing me. "Here's the short version."

I placed some pillows in the corner of the sectional so she could get more comfortable, then I pulled her feet into my lap. Pulling her boots off, I gently started to massage her feet as she began.

She took a breath and started, slow and steady.

"You know how I wound up in that awful place. I had no choice. The first week I was at Eyrie, Steiner took me to a witch in River Oaks. Her name was Lilah. She ran a kind of spa for 'special clients.' I was told it was to 'prepare' me for what was coming. I didn't want to go, but my dad's debt was hanging over my head like a noose, and the more I fought, the more Steiner reminded me he could take Brie instead. My baby sister, Jess. She was only seventeen. Still in high school."

My hands stilled. I forced myself to breathe. I angled my body to face hers.

Harper kept talking.

"Lilah made me drink a blue liquid. I don't know what was in it, but it hit me like a sedative. For three hours, I was awake but not. She made me recite mantras, over and over: 'I am valuable. I am wanted. I bring pleasure. I obey.' She said they were—affirmations, but with a kick." She paused, wiped her nose with the back of her hand. "After three sessions, I couldn't say no to anything. I realized later they were powerful spells. Not that it mattered. Steiner always got what he wanted no matter what."

I tried to keep my face neutral, but my teeth ached from clenching.

"The day of my first show, Lilah came to the club and dosed me with something else. This one made my skin feel electric. Every touch, every breath, was like—" She broke off, searching for the word. "Like being tickled from the inside out. When I went on stage, I couldn't stop myself. I danced my heart out." She looked up at me, almost apologetic. "After the first month, I was attacked in the hallway. Someone went for my knee. They bashed it. Steiner had the club doctor look at it. He said I tore a meniscus. While it was healing, he had the doctor wrap the outside of my knee in thin strips of silver. Steiner wanted to be sure that it didn't heal as well as it could. I'd never dance ballet again. It was effective. My knee healed eventually, but I still have pain when I make some moves. And I can't do some steps at all."

A sob worked its way up her throat, but she swallowed it down.

I wanted to kill. I wanted to rip out every vein in Steiner's body and spell out the word MONSTER with the pieces. I reached for her hands.

"I worked six nights a week at the club. After the first six months, the witches' potions weren't needed anymore. My body just... did what it was told." She flexed her toes as if remembering the phantom instructions. "VIP rooms started after month two. Mostly it was blow jobs, hand jobs. Some men just wanted me to dance or watch. Some liked it rough. There were nights I thought I'd die in there."

Her voice dropped lower.

"Steiner took my virginity. He did it in front of several clients. They paid handsomely for the privilege. Then he made a big show of it, paraded me through the main hall letting everyone know." She shuddered. "After that, I belonged to him."

My vision tunneled, black at the edges. The wolf in me screamed, but the soldier kept it on a tight leash.

"He kept me in an apartment a floor beneath his own. It had bars on the windows and an armed guard at the door. I was let out for shows, for VIP sessions, and sometimes for dinner with the other girls. Steiner came down four nights a week, sometimes more unless he was out of town. He said I was his 'favorite.' He said I should be grateful, because he was a man of his word and hadn't hurt Brie. But he always hinted he could change his mind."

She was shaking now, the fine tremor spreading from her knees to her jaw.

"Last week, I'd asked about the contract. I thought it had to be getting close to the end of the three-year obligation. But Steiner told me he'd never let me go. He said there were clients coming in from out of town, that my price had gone up. That's when I started looking for a way out. It was a miracle when I saw you the night you were at the club. I knew the goddess was going to fix things."

I told her I didn't believe in coincidences either.

She nodded. "I thought I was hallucinating. You looked like a ghost. But then you walked out and never looked back."

I remembered that night—the way my heart leaped when I caught her scent, the way my bones nearly vibrated out of my skin. I'd left because I couldn't risk blowing the mission, but in that moment, I'd almost thrown it all away for a chance to touch her.

"I wanted to call out to you. But I was so ashamed," she said her voice small.

I brushed her hair back from her face.

"The last night at the club," she said, voice thin as wire, "they told me a VIP was coming. Maltraz. They made me wear the black dress, the one that barely covered my ass. Darlene, the club witch, gave me some kind of tea. It made me feel strange. I remember how tall Maltraz was. And his eyes. The smell of sulfur and cologne. He was monstrous; his skin was gray like iron and every part of him was inhuman. He put his hands around my neck and made me do things. Made me beg." She trailed off, eyes unfocused. "It hurt. Then when Maltraz left the room to clean up, Steiner made me finish him." She shuddered. "After I changed clothes, Rage walked me to the alley where the truck was waiting to take me home like every other night. But you guys were there. Then you, Wrecker, Papa, and the girls all saved me."

I wanted to hurt something. I wanted to put my fist through every wall between here and Houston. But I kept my voice level.

I pulled her back onto my lap. "You're safe now," I said. "He can't touch you again. I swear it on my life."

She shook her head, a miserable, fragile arc. "It's not over. He'll come for me. He doesn't like to lose."

I reached up and took her hand. "Not while I'm breathing."

She tried to smile, but failed. The tears ran down her face in perfect silence.

I wiped them away with my thumb, marveling at the resilience of the girl who once pirouetted across summer lawns, who could now sit here and bleed without ever raising her voice.

When the silence settled again, I said, "You're the bravest person I know."

She huffed a laugh. "I'm a coward. If I were braver, I'd have run years ago."

I shook my head. "If you'd run, they could have killed your sister."

She closed her eyes. "It doesn't matter now. My mom got Brie out before Steiner could find her. I think they may be hiding in France. I've caught snippets of conversations Steiner has had with his men, angry that he can't find them."

I had to ask the hardest question. "Why didn't you contact me before you'd gotten into the situation with Steiner? While you were still in school?"

She shook her head as if she were trying to figure the answer out. "That's the stupidest thing of all. I didn't know how to find you. You had deployed, and I was young and dumb. My father had taken away every way I'd had of contacting you; my phone, computer, everything. I seriously thought I'd be able to find you after I graduated and we'd be able to be together no matter what my father said."

"Hmm. I guess I can understand that." That was the best response I could come up with. Time and age had taught me that people do dumb things, myself included. Tonight showed that.

We sat there; the fire casting long shadows on the wall until her breathing slowed. When I was sure she was asleep, I lifted her up and carried her to my bed. I tucked her in, set a glass of water by the nightstand, and made sure her phone was within reach.

Then I sat on the edge of the mattress, watching her chest rise and fall, fighting the urge to run through the night and tear the world apart.

For now, my job was to protect her. Later, I'd see about revenge. Beg for her to forgive me for being so covered in my own selfish grief that I failed to consider hers.

But for tonight, this was enough.

When I woke, the sunlight was already slanting in through the open window, a wedge of gold splitting the bedroom in two. Harper was still asleep, one hand flung out across the comforter, hair sprawled like a field of fallen wheat. She hadn't moved since I'd laid her down hours before. For once, her face looked peaceful—soft, almost young. I made myself memorize it. There weren't many times in my life when I'd seen that kind of peace on anyone's face.

I moved slow, not wanting to jar her awake. My every instinct said to stay, to keep the world out, to let her rest until she was ready to meet it again. But my wolf was on high alert—pack business never stopped, not even for love or heartbreak—so I left a note on the nightstand, the same blocky all-caps as before, and let myself out.

There were meetings that morning. Bronc wanted a sitrep on Eyrie; Wrecker had heard rumors of a new shipment at the rail yard. I went

through the motions, nodding when expected, barking orders when necessary. But all the while, my thoughts drifted back to the girl sleeping in my
bed.

When I got home, Harper was up and about. She was in the kitchen,
standing on tiptoe to reach a mug from the upper shelf, wearing nothing
but a pair of my old army sweats and a pink tank top I didn't recognize.
She'd made coffee—strong enough to burn a hole through the cup—and
had started to pour a mugful.

She didn't notice me at first. Her focus was absolute, mouth twisted
in concentration. It was how she used to look at crossword puzzles, or the
maps we'd trace with our fingers, charting the distance from Texas to New
York and back. For a second, I just watched her, letting the sight stitch
something together in my chest.

She glanced up and caught me staring.

"Morning," she said, eyes wary but not unfriendly.

"Morning," I echoed, and crossed to the fridge. I grabbed a bottle of
water and drained half of it, then leaned against the counter, arms crossed,
waiting for her to set the tone.

"I read your note," she said, voice careful. "Thank you."

I shrugged. "Didn't want you to wake up alone."

She traced the rim of her mug, not meeting my eye. "I don't know
what happens now. I don't even know who I am anymore. Everything that
made me me is gone."

I closed the distance and set my hands on her shoulders, firm but
gentle. "That's bullshit. You're still you. You just get to decide things now."

She gave a bitter little smile. "You're just saying that because you want
it to be true."

"I want you to believe it," I said, squeezing her shoulders. "You survived three years in hell, and you came out the other side with your soul
intact. That's more than most people can say." I paused, letting the words
land. "I know I can't fix everything. But I can be here for whatever you

need. I know I've started on shaky footing. I didn't know what happened, and I've felt sorry for myself for years. I've been so fucking angry every day for as long as I can remember. But I never stopped loving you. I want to be here for you. Even if I've fucked things up until now. I'll be here for you for as long as you want me."

She looked up then, really looked, and her eyes were fierce. "Even after everything? After what I let happen?"

My hands tightened. "None of that was your choice, Prima. Not a single second. You were forced. You were manipulated, tortured, and made into something you never wanted to be." I bent down, putting my forehead to hers. "To me, you're still the girl who used to drag me out to the lake at midnight to count shooting stars. You're still the only woman I've ever wanted. The goddess gave me you. If you want to say no, I'll let you walk out the door and never stop you. But I'll never stop loving you."

She closed her eyes, a tear leaking out. I caught it on my thumb before it could fall.

"I was never strong enough to escape," she whispered. "Not because I was afraid for myself, but because I knew he'd go after Brie. After my mom. Steiner told me, if I ever ran, he'd kill them both and send me the proof."

I nodded, understanding settling in my gut like a stone. "That's what I would have done."

She looked up, surprised. "You think I did the right thing?"

"I think you did the only thing you could. You protected your family. You did what a wolf is supposed to do. You kept the people you loved alive, even if it meant dying yourself a little every day." My voice broke, but I kept going. "I'm proud of you. I'll always be proud of you."

She reached up then, fingers trembling, and touched my jaw. "You're not mad at me?"

I huffed a laugh. "Mad at Steiner. Mad at the world. Not at you. Never at you."

The tension left her all at once. She slumped against me, letting me catch her weight. I scooped her up, one arm around her shoulders, the other under her knees, and carried her to the couch. She clung to me, face pressed into my shirt, as if she could burrow inside and hide there forever.

I let her. I let her breathe, let her cry, let her shake until she was empty. Then, when the silence got too heavy, I asked:

"Do you remember the last night we were together?"

She smiled, eyes puffy but alive. "You mean the night before my father lied to you and told you I rejected you?"

"Yeah. You wore that white dress with the little blue flowers. I couldn't stop staring at you."

She flushed. "You kept calling me bluebonnet."

"You hated it."

"I loved it," she admitted. "I just didn't want you to know."

I brushed a strand of hair off her cheek, tucking it behind her ear. "You look even more beautiful now."

She shook her head, embarrassed. "I look like shit."

"You look like my mate," I said, and kissed her forehead.

She went quiet, then: "Do you still want it?"

I arched an eyebrow. "Want what?"

She swallowed, then met my gaze, pupils blown wide. "To claim me. I want you to do it. If you still want me."

My heart nearly stopped.

I nodded, slow. "You know what that means?"

"It means you'll never let me go," she said. "It means I'll always belong to you. And you to me."

I stood, lifting her into my arms. She weighed nothing. I carried her to the bedroom, set her down on the edge of the bed, and knelt before her.

"Are you sure?" I asked, voice hoarse.

She nodded. "I've never been more sure of anything in my life."

I pulled her onto my lap, her body flush against mine, her curves molding to me like she was made for it. Her lips parted, and I dove in, claiming her mouth with a hunger that had been simmering for years. Our tongues tangled, hot and slick, and she moaned into me, her hands fisting in my shirt like she was afraid I'd disappear. But I wasn't going anywhere. Not now. Not ever.

Her breasts pressed against my chest, her nipples hard even through the thin fabric of her tank top. I slid a hand underneath, cupping her, feeling the weight of her in my palm. She arched into my touch, her breath hitching as I thumbed her nipple, rolling it between my fingers. Fuck, she was soft. Soft and warm and perfect, and I couldn't get enough.

"Jess," she whispered, her voice trembling. "Please."

I laid her back against the pillow and continued reacquainting myself with her beautiful body. My hand ran down her side, tracing the curve of her hip, the dip of her waist, until I reached the waistband of my sweats. She lifted her hips, letting me slide them down, and fuck, she wasn't wearing anything underneath. My cock throbbed at the sight of her, her pussy glistening, already wet for me.

"You're so fucking magnificent," I growled, my hands loving the feel of her. She stared up at me, her eyes dark with need, her lips swollen from my kisses. I kneeled between her legs, spreading her thighs wide, and leaned down to taste her.

Her pussy was sweet and tangy, and I groaned as I licked her, my tongue flattening against her clit. She cried out, her hands knotting in my hair as I ate her like a starving man. I circled her clit with the tip of my tongue, teasing her, making her squirm. Her hips bucked against my face, and I grabbed her thighs, holding her still as I devoured her.

"Oh God, Jess," she moaned, her voice breaking. "Please, please don't stop."

I wasn't planning on it. I slid two fingers inside her, curling them just right, and she moaned, her body trembling as I worked her. Her pussy clenched around my fingers, dripping wet, and I added a third, stretching her, fucking her with my hand until she was begging. I moved my tongue in small circles around her clit as I pumped my fingers in and out of her. My eyes lifted to see the bliss reflected on her face. I'd never seen anything more beautiful.

"I'm gonna come," she gasped, her thighs shaking. "Jess, I'm gonna—"

I didn't let her finish. I sucked her clit into my mouth, flicking it with my tongue, and she came with a cry, her pussy pulsing around my fingers. I didn't stop working her through it until she was whimpering, her body wrung out.

"Jess," she breathed, her chest heaving. "I need you."

I was already stripping out of my clothes, my cock aching, throbbing with need. I climbed over her, my body pressing hers into the mattress, and kissed her again, deep and hungry. She wrapped her legs around my waist, her pussy slick and hot against my cock, and I groaned, the sensation almost too much.

"You're mine, my mate. And I'm never letting you go again," I growled, lining myself up with her entrance.

"Yes! I'm yours," she whispered, her eyes locked on mine. "Always. Yours."

I thrust into her, hard and deep, and she cried out, her nails digging into my back. Fuck, she was tight, her pussy clenching around me like a vice. I held still for a moment, letting her adjust, then pulled out and slammed back in, hitting her core with every stroke.

"Yes," she moaned, her hips meeting mine thrust for thrust. "God, Jess, yes."

I fucked her like that, hard and fast, my cock driving into her again and again. Her pussy was so fucking wet, her juices coating my cock, dripping down our thighs. I reached between us, rubbing her clit, as she writhed, her pussy pulling me in deeper.

"Fuck Prima. You feel like home." Her pussy gripped my dick so tight, and I had never felt anything so perfect.

"Come for me," I growled, my knot swelling at the base of my cock. "Come on my dick, on my knot as I claim you and love you."

She moaned, deep, her body shuddering, and I almost lost it; my cock pulsed. My knot swelled, and her pussy stretched to accommodate me. I looked down between us, so fucking turned on at the sight of the way she took me.

"Look at you, my mate. My knot has you stretched so perfectly. I can feel you pulling me inside your sweet pussy. I've never felt anything so amazing."

I felt my canines elongate, ready for me to claim her.

"Are you ready for me to claim you, bluebonnet?" I asked her with a feral grin.

She bared her neck to me as her body writhed as much as was possible. "Please, Jess! Mark me as your mate so I'll be yours forever. I love you!"

"I love you, my mate, my heart, my soul," I said as my teeth found their mark at the base of her neck and shoulder. We both shattered with my bite. I'd never felt an orgasm like that. I felt our bond snap into place. Her blood filled my mouth, and I drank it down. I licked her wound, and it healed immediately. Then, I bared my neck to her. "Please mark me as your mate."

Her elongated canines sank into my neck and shoulder, and my orgasm flared to life again. I felt her soul connect with mine. When she released, I saw tears streaming down her face.

"Mine," I whispered, my voice rough.

"Yours," she breathed, her hands stroking my back. "Always."

But it wasn't over. Not yet. My knot was still locked inside her, and she was still trembling, her body humming with need. I kissed her again, slow and deep, and started moving, fucking her with shallow thrusts that made her whimper.

"Jess," she moaned, her hips rocking against mine. "More."

I gave her more, my cock sliding in and out of her as much as the knot would allow her pussy gripping me like a glove. I felt Harper's very essence flow through my soul. Her joy, her sadness, everything that was her became a part of me. The years of longing for each other became a part of our souls.

We were a mess, sticky and sweaty and spent, but I didn't care. She was mine, and I was hers, and nothing else mattered. I held her close, my knot still buried inside her, and kissed her forehead.

"Sleep," I whispered, my voice rough. "I've got you."

She nodded, her eyes drifting shut, and I lay there, watching her, my heart pounding in my chest. She was safe. She was mine. And I'd die before I let anyone take her from me again.

Chapter 16

Harper

The first thing I noticed was the hush. Not just the absence of fear, or the hush that came from living in a world where nothing wanted to eat you alive, but a deeper, almost holy quiet. I was wrapped in Jess's arms, head pillowed on his chest, his heartbeat thudding beneath my ear in time with the distant ticks of the kitchen clock. For a moment, I didn't know where I ended and he began. I didn't want to know.

Sunlight crept across the bed in a razor-thin slash, filtered through the split in the window curtains. Dust motes danced like tiny fairies, shifting in the stream of morning light. I reached out, running my hand through the bright, warm band, and the motes scattered and then, just as quickly, realigned. The skin on my wrist looked translucent, veins glowing blue in the gold. When I flexed my fingers, I caught the hint of a tremor—not from fear, but from the sudden, silly giddiness of knowing that this was all real.

I closed my fist and felt the press of Jess's arm around my waist. His hand cupped my hip, splayed warmth with his thumb resting in the soft hollow at the top of my thigh. There was nothing sexual in the touch—not yet. Just a claim, as old as the world and twice as sure.

"You awake?" he said, voice thick with sleep and something heavier.

I smiled into his chest. "Barely. You?"

"Uh huh. Just wanted to be sure I wasn't dreaming."

I propped my chin on his pec and stared at him. "If this is a dream, I wouldn't wanna wake up."

He grinned, slow and lopsided, the lines around his eyes softening. "It's nice to be living a dream and not a nightmare anymore, bluebonnet."

The name. It fizzed across my skin, sweeter than any pet name had a right to be. "Guess you're droppin' Prima and going straight for bluebonnet, huh?" I asked, with a tease in my voice. I acted irritated with the nickname, but I think he knows I kind of love it.

"It suits you," he murmured, brushing the backs of his knuckles down my cheek. "Your bluebonnet eyes never left my memory."

I didn't say anything because words would have just gotten in the way. Instead, I lifted my leg over his hip and straddled him; the sheet slithered down to pool at our knees. Jess's hands came up automatically, palms to my ribs tracing their contour as he caressed my sides. I leaned down, pressed my lips to his, and let the kiss build from soft to urgent.

"You're the most beautiful thing I've ever seen," he said, voice low and fierce. "I'd take a thousand bullets before I'd let anything hurt you again. Fuck, Harper," he said. "You don't know what you do to me."

His hands—those massive, calloused hands—cupped my face like I was something sacred, something he fucking worshipped. I was straddling him, my thighs pressing into his hips, and his naked chest was a furnace against mine. The heat of him was intoxicating. His palms slid down my sides, rough yet tender, and I couldn't help but arch into his touch. My fingers tangled in his hair, holding myself up on my elbows as I hovered over him. His fingertips grazed my ass, just a feather-light caress, and I fucking whimpered.

I could feel him—his cock—hardening beneath me, pressing insistently against my soaked pussy. I didn't even try to stop myself; I rolled my hips, grinding against him, craving the friction. My wetness was already slicking his cock, and damn, the sensation was electric. His voice, low and gravelly, spilled filth into my ear, and it drove me wild.

"The way your pussy is dripping down my cock makes me want to do the nastiest things to you, bluebonnet."

Then his arms wrapped around me, muscular and unyielding, and he flipped me onto my back like I weighed nothing. I gasped and gave a giggle, my breath hitching as his mouth descended on me. His lips were relentless—trailing kisses down my neck, nipping at my collarbone, before he locked onto my nipple. Holy shit. He sucked hard, his teeth grazing the sensitive peak, and I cried out as I arched into his mouth, my hands clawing at his scalp. He released it with a wet pop, his tongue flicking over the swollen bud before moving to the other breast to give it the same brutal attention.

I was trembling, my legs spreading wider as he worked his way down my body. His tongue circled my navel, teasing, taunting, before he reached the apex of my thighs. His hands gripped my legs, spreading me open, and I was exposed, dripping and aching for him.

"Hold these legs open for me, baby," he growled, his voice thick with lust. "Let me see every inch of this perfect fucking pussy. Christ, you're so wet for me. Look at you just begging for my touch."

And then he dove in.

His tongue was a secret weapon, plunging into me, lapping at my slick walls like he was starving for it. I shoved my elbows beneath me, propping myself up so I could watch him feast on me. His eyes met mine, dark and wicked, and stars, the way he smirked as he devoured me. It was too much. His tongue flattened against my clit, and I jerked, a whimper tearing from my throat. But he didn't stop. No, he kept going, fucking me with his tongue, his lips, his teeth, until I was a shaking, moaning mess.

Then he crawled up my body, his mouth claiming mine in a kiss so possessive it left no room for doubt that I was his. His cock, thick and throbbing, pressed against my entrance, and he didn't hesitate. He thrust into me in one brutal stroke, and I shouted his name, my head slamming back into the pillow. He filled me completely, stretching me, taking me so deep I felt him in my very soul.

My hips rose to meet his, every thrust driving me closer to the edge. Our bodies moved together like we were made for each other, and the power of it—Jesus Christ—it was overwhelming. His knot swelled inside me, locking us together, and I came undone, my orgasm crashing over me like a roaring tidal wave. He grunted, his own release spilling into me, and I clung to him, my nails digging into his back as he claimed every inch of me.

We stayed like that, locked together, our breaths ragged, sweat slicking our skin. His forehead rested against mine, and for a moment, there was nothing else—just him, just me, just this amazing perfect connection that felt like it would never end.

And it didn't end.

He pulled back slightly, his cock still buried deep inside me, and his lips crashed into mine again. His hands slid under my ass, lifting me slightly, and he began to move again, slow and deliberate, dragging his cock against that sweet spot inside me. I moaned into his mouth, my legs wrapping around his waist, pulling him closer.

"You're mine," he growled against my lips, his thrusts growing harder, deeper. "Every fucking inch of you belongs to me."

And I wholeheartedly agreed. I belonged to him; body, soul, and everything in between. His hands gripped my hips, guiding me as he pounded into me, each thrust sending shockwaves of pleasure through my entire body. I could feel another orgasm building, hot and urgent, and I clutched at him, desperate for release.

"Come for me, Harper," he commanded, his voice rough, and holy crap, I obeyed. My orgasm hit me like a freight train, tearing through me with such intensity that I screamed, my body shaking uncontrollably. He followed me over the edge, his cock pulsing inside me as he emptied himself into me once more.

We collapsed together, a tangled mess of limbs and sweat and cum, and I buried my face in his chest, breathing in the scent of him. His arms wrapped around me, holding me close, and I knew, oh yes, I knew, there was nothing that would ever compare to this.

He was mine, and I was his, and that was perfect.

For a while, we just lay there, tangled up and panting, his forehead pressed to mine.

"I love you," he whispered, so quiet I almost missed it.

I smiled, running my fingers through the sweaty tangle of his hair. "I love you more."

"That's mathematically impossible," he said, kissing the tip of my nose.

"You're not the only one who can do math," I shot back, grinning like a kid.

He laughed, then buried his face in my neck and just breathed, as if he could live on nothing but the scent of my skin.

Eventually, the sunlight shifted and blazed a stripe across the bed. I sank into its warmth, feeling the slow melt of contentment settle into my bones.

For the first time since I could remember, I was happy.

Not the borrowed happiness I'd faked for strangers, not the brittle kind I'd rationed out in stolen moments.

This was the real thing.

And I never wanted to let it go.

When we finally rolled out of bed, it was past eight, and I felt like I'd slept for a year. The pain in my knee was just a dull echo, the old bruises faded to faint shadows, and I could walk without flinching. Jess made coffee, strong enough to strip the enamel from your teeth, and I drank it black, just to prove I was as tough as he was. I wore nothing but his battered college t-shirt and a pair of black leggings. I'd pulled my hair into a high ponytail, which hung down my back in a riot of blonde curls. He looked at me like I was a miracle.

It was a cool early spring Texas morning, the wind still damp from last night's rain. We hopped on Jess's bike and cut through town, weaving through the side streets to avoid the rush at the middle school. Dairyville was smaller than any place I'd ever lived, the kind of town where there was a gas station when you entered the city limits and one when you left. Most of the houses were squat, white brick, with blue tin roofs and chain-link fences out front, the yards a mix of winter-brown and wildflowers already trying to take over the cracks in the sidewalk. Others were ranches with land and cattle or crops. The downtown area was something out of a Hallmark movie. Cute businesses lined the town square with colorful awnings and park benches. The center of town even had a white gazebo that just needed a little band playing to complete the scene.

We parked outside Aspen's bakery—Buttercream & Blessings—and for a second I just stared at the place. It sat center of the hardware store and a hair salon and was painted the color of an Easter egg with a striped yellow-and-white awning and window boxes full of marigolds. Even with the glass front door closed you could get a wave of sugar and cinnamon that hit me like a memory of every good thing I'd ever tasted. Through the front window, you could see the racks of scones and the chalkboard menu, written in perfect swooping script.

Aspen herself was at the counter, perched on a stool and hunched over a stack of receipts, her long black hair pulled into a messy ponytail. She wore a swing dress the color of robins' eggs, dotted with daisies, and white tights with black ankle boots. When she saw us, her whole face lit up.

"Well, look what the cat dragged in!" she said, voice syrupy-sweet with a hint of mischief. "And by 'cat' I mean the world's scariest wolf."

Jess gave her a little salute. "Morning, Aspen. Is it too early for the good stuff?"

She hopped off the stool and circled the counter, beaming. "For you two? Never. I made blueberry scones and the brown butter coffee cake. Harper, you'll die when you taste it. I used the special cinnamon from Mexico that Wrecker smuggled back last month."

Before I could even thank her, Aspen enveloped me in a hug, squeezing until my ribs creaked. "You look so much better, honey. I could just cry."

I squeezed her back. "You might be the only person in this whole state who gives a damn if I live or die."

She snorted. "Nonsense. Everyone in the pack gives a damn. Some are just better at hiding it." She gave Jess a wink, then shooed us to the corner table.

As we settled in, the bell over the door gave a little trill, and I turned to see her little prairie dog familiar standing at attention on the floor. He wore a navy blue bowtie with his vest and jacket, and his whiskers twitched with focus.

"Miss Harper," he intoned, "may I wish you and Master Arsenal a beautiful good morning on behalf of my lady Aspen and myself. If you require anything, do not hesitate to summon me."

I choked back a laugh. "Thank you, Oscar. You're looking very dapper today."

He nodded sincerely. "The occasion merits it. The Sergeant at Arms is not often seen with such radiant company."

Aspen returned with a tray, setting out thick mugs of coffee and a plate heaped with scones, still warm and studded with berries that bled violet into the crumb. She set a tiny cup of creamer in front of Jess and another in front of me, even though I hadn't asked. "Just in case," she said, conspiratorial. "I always liked mine with cream, but nobody here does, so I started drinking it black to fit in. Don't ever let them change you, Harper."

It struck me as the most honest advice I'd heard in months.

We ate in silence for a few minutes. The coffee cake was impossibly tender, soaked in butter and sugar, and I nearly moaned out loud when I tasted it. Jess noticed and smirked, but said nothing, just nudged the plate closer and refilled my mug whenever it dipped below half.

Aspen left us alone, after dropping a little curtsy to Oscar, who then padded off to the kitchen, muttering something about "a backlog of invoices and utter chaos in the pantry." It was just Jess and me, the bright morning, and the smallest bakery table in the world.

I took a breath. "I'm worried about my sister," I said, not even bothering to ease into it. "When Steiner realizes I'm gone, he'll be furious. He always said, if I ever disappeared, he'd send someone after Brie."

Jess reached across the table and covered my hand with his. "She's in France, right? Or was that just a cover?"

"She was," I said. "At least, that's what I overheard Steiner saying. I'd caught snippets of conversations where he had been complaining about how he couldn't find her and that last he'd heard she was there. She went to college in Texas. Then past that, I have no idea. I heard Mom left my dad after the Ponzi scandal. But it's been years since I've seen any of them. The last time I saw them, Brie was probably nineteen." I wiped a tear away with my napkin.

He squeezed my hand. "You think they'll come back if you ask?"

I shook my head. "I don't know. I don't even know if they want to see me. I barely know them anymore." The words stung. "Steiner might find them first. Or maybe he already has, and he's just waiting for the best moment to use them against me."

"We'll do our best to keep that from happening." His voice was so certain I almost believed he could pull it off. "I'll talk to Bronc and see what we can do. Wrecker and Parker are the best at finding people, even if they're halfway across the world. We'll get them to safety."

I gave him a small smile. "I just hope if we find her she won't hate it here."

Jess cocked an eyebrow. "Why do you think she might?"

I looked down at my coffee. "Because it's a dusty little town in the middle of nowhere, and Brie is... well, if I'm being totally honest, she's a little bit spoiled. I love her with my whole heart, but my dad always gave in to her. She likes nice designer clothes, shoes, cars, and things like that. She likes getting her way. And she loves big cities. She wanted to marry a wealthy man and live in the lap of luxury. Now she'll probably end up in a cabin, eating barbecue and dodging gossip from all the women in the pack who think she's a snob."

He grinned. "If she's your sister, she'll adapt. She might even like the quiet. Lord knows you needed it."

I thought about that for a while, picking at the edge of the scone, letting the jam bleed onto my fingers. "Do you think we'll ever be normal?" I asked, half to myself. "Like, actually normal, not just pretending for a weekend?"

He leaned in, serious for once. "No one's normal, Harper. That's a lie people tell so they can sell more magazines. What we are is what we are. But we're good. And I'm not letting anything hurt you, not ever again. That's my only job now. Besides, nobody was wealthier than Juliet, our Luna. She came from a top Wall Street family. Talk about the lap of luxury. And for fuck's sake, Menace's mate was a goddamn princess! Hell, he's the fucking king of the Midwest, and Savannah is now the Queen! So if your sister is into all that shit, she cannot get any more hoity-toity than our friends."

I nodded, letting the truth of it settle.

The bell over the door chimed, and I glanced up, expecting a random customer. Instead, Big Papa filled the entry, ducking his head to clear the frame. He wore a black long-sleeve Henley with his Iron Valor cut and faded jeans, his hair slicked back and his beard combed neat. He spotted us, raised a hand, and made his way over.

Jess's whole body changed. He got a weird, pinched look in his eyes and stood straight-backed and formal.

"Morning, Papa," he said.

"Morning, Arsenal. Miss Harper." Papa gave me a smile that could have healed the world, then turned back to Jess. "You got a minute?"

"Of course." Jess looked at me, eyes softer now. "Be right back."

They walked to the far end of the bakery, heads bent together in low conversation. Even though I couldn't hear them, I saw the way Jess's shoulders squared, the way his jaw set hard. He looked like a soldier reporting for duty. I wondered if he'd ever be able to stop.

Aspen slid into the chair across from me, her hands cupped around a mug of tea.

"Apparently Jess had something unkind to say to Papa at the bonfire," she said. "Big Papa loves these guys and won't let anything come between them. He's the best man I know. He treats some of the guys more like sons sometimes even though he's nowhere near old enough to be their dad."

I nodded. "I get it. Jess was never really close to his dad. And I know he'd never want anything to come between him and his brothers."

Aspen smiled, soft. "It's hard for wolves like him. He's always protecting other wolves; sometimes he forgets."

I blinked, surprised by how much I needed to hear that. "He's so stubborn."

"Well, you sure must be strong to have endured everything you have and still kept your mind strong. I admire you. You're good for him. I know he's not perfect. I had to prove myself to him. But he had my back when it counted."

We sat in silence for a while, watching Oscar march between the tables, stopping every few steps to fuss at a crumb or reorganize a stack of napkins.

"He really loves you," Aspen said. "I knew it from the second I saw the way he looked when we pulled you from that awful place."

I blushed, unable to help it. "I love him, too. I just hope I don't bring any shame to him."

"You won't," she said. "Because you haven't done anything to be ashamed of Harper. Don't forget that. Don't let anyone talk you into believing things about yourself that just are not true."

At the end of the counter, Papa and Jess clasped hands, then embraced. Papa pulled back, slapped Jess on the shoulder, and said something that made him laugh for the first time all morning.

When they walked back to the table, I saw the difference in Jess. He looked lighter, easier. He dropped into the chair beside me and pulled me close, his arm around my waist.

Papa stood over us, hands on his hips. "You two look good together. And your mate mark is a nice look."

"Thank you," I said, trying not to squirm.

He nodded and then turned to Jess. "You take care of her."

"Always," Jess said, voice steady as stone.

Papa grinned, then bent down and kissed Aspen on the head. "You coming to the pack run tonight?"

Aspen glanced at me, then smiled. "Wouldn't miss it."

Oscar piped up from under the table. "May I attend as well? I will be most discreet."

Aspen laughed. "You're part of the pack, Oscar. You have to come."

He puffed up, proud. "Excellent. I shall prepare accordingly."

Papa left, the bell chiming as he went. Aspen started clearing our plates, but not before sneaking a second scone onto my napkin.

Jess leaned in, lips at my ear. "You okay?"

I nodded. "I'm happy," I whispered, surprised by how true it felt.

"Good," he said. "I'm happy too."

We sat there for a while, just watching the sun work its way across the table, turning the coffee brown and the scones gold. Jess traced little circles on my wrist with his thumb, and I let myself hope that maybe, just maybe, this could be the start of something right.

I closed my eyes and offered a silent thanks to the creator.

Thank you for saving me.

Thank you for keeping him safe.

Thank you for today, and every day after.

When I opened my eyes again, the world was still there, waiting.

And I was finally ready to meet it.

CHAPTER 17

Waylon Steiner

The office was glass and steel and mirrors, a penthouse on the top floor above the club. I paced in a twelve-foot line, wearing a trench into the imported Turkish rug that cost more than some people's houses. Every two minutes, I'd pass the bank of security monitors, their cold blue glow strobing across my skin. Half the feeds showed the floor of the club, a slow-motion parade of silicone, sequins, and slavish devotion. The other half were trained on the shipping docks and train yard, where the real business happened.

Leo sat in one of the expensive leather guest chairs, legs crossed, tablet on his lap. He could have been a banker or a lawyer—his suit was pressed, cufflinks the size of chickpeas, even the shaved lines in his hair were symmetrical. He watched me pace like a man timing laps at a track meet, which was one of the reasons I kept him around. Leo never flinched, never looked away, never let my moods make him blink. I needed that right now.

"You keep that up, boss, and you'll wear a groove in the floor. Not sure we have a guy on the payroll who can repair that kind of damage." His eyes didn't leave the tablet, but the joke hung in the air, polite as a smoke ring.

"Shut up, Leo." My voice was a fucking cheese grater tonight. I ran both hands through my hair, then let them clench at the base of my skull, just shy of tearing out a chunk.

I could feel the anger in my blood, running just below the skin, itching to break through. I'd lost things before—money, girls, product, my own goddamn dignity—but nothing burned like this. Harper had vanished. Poof. Gone from my hand like a magician's card trick, and I was the mark, staring at my empty palm with a big, dumb smile.

"I should have fucking claimed her," I said, not for the first time. "Should have bitten her. Made the bond. Then I could have tracked her to the ends of the earth, no matter how many goddamn shadows she ran through."

Leo didn't say anything. Just kept scrolling. I hated how calm he was, but that was the job. He was my number two, my consigliere, the man who handled things, so I didn't have to. Most nights, that was a blessing. Tonight, it was sandpaper on my brain.

"I told you," I said, my voice rising. "I fucking told you, Leo. The minute you get soft—one fucking inch—they take a mile. These bitches, they can smell weakness. That's how she got out. That's how she played me."

He shrugged, a tiny motion. "She was on a short leash. We had eyes on her every second. The only time she left the building was for work, and even then she had Rage on her like white on rice."

"Rage is a fuck-up." I slammed my fist into the edge of the desk, just enough to rattle the monitor. "I should have had Viktor do it. Viktor never lets his dick think for him. Never gets distracted."

Leo looked up finally. "If it's any consolation, we still have the list. Seven tonight. Three wolves, four humans. All in the manifest, all tagged and processed."

That calmed me a little. At least the rest of the operation was on track. Tonight's shipment was the kind of thing that kept the lights on and the right people in my pocket. Seven girls—no, women, I reminded myself, always use the legalese—shipped out in a custom rail car, destination: Maltraz's cargo ship waiting at the edge of international waters. Three of them were high-bred wolf bitches, the kind that could pass for Instagram influencers, except they'd been drugged into submission and weren't likely to make any more duck-face selfies. The other four were top-shelf humans, all virgins if the paperwork wasn't forged. And Leo's paperwork was never forged.

The clock on the wall read 10:36. The first wave would be on the loading dock in less than fifteen minutes.

"Show me the manifests," I said, and Leo flicked the file onto the main screen.

He had them color-coded and bullet-pointed, like a grocery list for cannibals. I scanned the names, the stats, the photos. Half of them looked like they could have been the face of a makeup ad. The others were pure muscle, bred for labor and obedience. I liked a balanced shipment. Gave the buyers more to fight over at auction.

I felt the old pride flare up, the satisfaction of a job run with military precision. But it curdled instantly, soured by the empty spot in my chest where Harper used to be. It wasn't love, don't make me laugh, but there was something about her, some kind of crackle in the air when she was around. I'd always thought I could train her, break her, build her back up into something I could use. Instead, she'd found the gap in the fence and slithered through.

"We'll get her back," I muttered, more to myself than to Leo.

He took the hint. "First priority is the shipment. After that, I'll deploy the dogs. But I need to know if I'm using velvet gloves or steel. What are we doing if we actually catch her?"

I smiled. That was the best thing about Leo: he didn't flinch at the ugly questions.

"We bring her in alive. No marks above the neckline. If she's got a mate or a pack, we cut them off at the knees first, then bring her back." I let the words hang there, then added, "But I want her to see me first. I want her to know I won."

Leo tapped a note into his file. "And if the client asks for an update?"

I had to laugh. "Which client? The one with horns, or the one with the blue blood?"

"Both."

"The demon gets whatever he wants. The hedge fund asshole can suck it." I glanced back at the monitor, watched as the first of tonight's product was dragged across the dock, her hands zip-tied behind her back and her hair trailing like a white flag. "Let's make sure this one goes smooth. No fuck-ups. No drama."

Leo nodded, stood, and straightened his lapels. "I'll be on the floor if you need me."

He left, closing the door with a soft click. I waited until the echo died, then slumped into my chair and let myself breathe. The office was too quiet now. The hum of the building, the low whine of servers, the distant thump of bass from the club below—it all faded into nothing.

I swiveled to face the window. The city spread out beneath me, lights twinkling like a million tiny lies. Somewhere out there, Harper was hiding. Somewhere, she thought she was safe.

She wasn't. She belonged to me, and I always, always collected what was mine.

But maybe it was time to diversify. I thumbed the edge of my desk, let the thought turn over in my mind.

Brie Lawson. Harper's little sister. Same blood, same eyes, same pedigree. I pulled up her file on the secondary monitor, let the images flicker by. She was in Paris, or so the PI claimed. Living under an assumed name, wasting her talents on art and dance instead of anything profitable. I could almost taste the bitterness in her smile, the way she'd crumple the second I put my hand on her shoulder.

I grinned. If I couldn't have the wolf, I'd settle for the lamb. Maybe even both, if I played it right.

The knock was more of an explosion—three hammer-blows that rattled the door on its hinges and set the glass in the windows humming. A split second later came the smell: sulfur, hot metal, the sharp sting of ozone and scorched plastic. It rolled through the air like a living thing, coating the back of my tongue.

I swore under my breath, straightened my shirt, and opened the door.

Maltraz filled the frame—literally. Seven feet if he was an inch, broad as a lineman, but with the proportions of a nightmare. His skin was iron-gray, hairless, with a polish like slate that caught the light. His eyes were the worst: a pair of red-glowing coals, slit like a cat's, set deep in sockets lined with black. The irises weren't circles, but a vertical slice, and if you looked too long, it was like staring into a well that had no bottom.

Tonight he wore a suit from the most expensive tailor in Paris, and he made it look like a Halloween costume. The jacket was obsidian, no vent, the cut so sharp it could take off a finger. The shirt underneath was blood-red, open at the throat to show a lattice of gold chains and two heavy nose rings, both gleaming in the overhead. The horns had been filed down for the occasion—maybe to look less conspicuous, maybe just to fuck with my head.

He smiled, and the teeth behind those lips were rows and rows, shark-style, all white and needle-fine.

"Evening, Mr. Steiner," he said, and the voice was all silk, every syllable buffed to a mirror shine.

I felt my heart try to crawl up my throat, but I forced it down. "Maltraz. I didn't expect you so early."

He stepped into the room. Didn't ask. Just moved past me, his cologne colliding with the sulfur until the whole office was a chemical soup. The guy could have run a chemistry set out of his pores.

"I had business in town," he said, glancing at the monitors. "Thought I'd check in on my favorite supplier."

He settled into my chair, behind my own desk, and stretched his legs out. He didn't even try to hide the claws—black, shiny, curling out of his fingers like sculpted obsidian. I'd seen what they could do to a human skull, or a reinforced car door. The fact that he could use a cell phone without carving it in half was almost comical.

I took the seat across from him. The table between us felt as useful as a wet tissue.

"Everything is in motion," I said. "Tonight's shipment leaves at midnight. Seven packages, all handpicked. The train car's been spelled by your friend in River Oaks. Should be zero chance of escape or interference."

Maltraz nodded. He reached into the breast pocket and produced a slip of paper, unfolded it, and ran his claw along the line items. "Three wolves," he said, more to himself than to me. "Good. The Asian one—she's the singer?"

"She is. Fresh off the plane last week. Never even seen a Western city."

He smiled. "That's how I like them. Pristine. Uncontaminated by American pop culture."

He flicked the paper onto the desk. "And the rest?"

"All virgins. All debt-encumbered, none with parents in-country. We'll have them drugged, bound, and on the boat by dawn."

Maltraz steepled his fingers, watching me over the points of his claws. "Efficient, as always. I admire your devotion to the craft."

I tried to keep my hands from trembling. The air was getting thicker by the second. Every breath felt like I was huffing a glue stick.

"We aim to please," I managed.

Maltraz laughed—a dry, barking sound that set the windows quivering again. "You always have, Waylon. But tonight is special. Tonight, I want a demonstration of your loyalty."

My spine went cold. "Anything."

He leaned forward; the chair creaking under his mass. "I want the Lawson wolf. The dancer. I want her in the VIP suite, ready for me before midnight. No substitutions. No excuses."

Shit.

"Of course," I said. "She's been prepped. I'll have Rage bring her up as soon as you're ready."

He smiled again, and this time the teeth looked even sharper. "You are a man of your word."

He leaned back, plucked a gold cigarette case from his jacket, and tapped one out. The tip was already smoldering. He didn't light it. It just burned, exuding the same sulfur-and-honey stench that was pouring out of his skin.

I could feel the sweat rolling down my back, pooling at the waistband of my slacks.

Maltraz flicked his eyes to me. "You're sweating, Mr. Steiner."

I tried to laugh. "Comes with the territory. Some of these clients are more dangerous than the product."

He considered that, then shrugged. "True enough."

He tapped ash onto the Persian rug, watching the embers fizzle out. "I have a particular fondness for the Lawson girl. Her bloodline is rare, almost extinct. Did you know that?"

I nodded, keeping my face blank. Of course I knew. I'd had her file run through three different labs, just to make sure she was as clean as she looked. But I hadn't known what it meant until Maltraz showed up last month, offering twice the market rate for a confirmed Lawson.

"She's a special case," I said. "Very valuable."

"Indeed." Maltraz uncrossed his legs, stood, and circled behind my chair. "It would be a shame if anything happened to her before the transfer. Accidents are so... inconvenient."

He was close enough now that I could feel the heat radiating off him. The hair on my arms stood up.

"She's secure," I said. "No one even knows she's in the building. Not even the staff."

Maltraz's hand settled on my shoulder. The pressure was light, almost friendly. But the claws dug in, just a hair.

"Excellent. Because I would be very, very unhappy if she vanished."

I swallowed. "Understood."

He let go, stepped around to face me, and smiled once more. "I'll be in the lounge. When you're ready, have her brought to me."

He left without another word; the smell lingered like a bad memory.

The door closed with a soft, final click.

I sat there, staring at the empty chair, trying to keep my heart rate below triple digits.

There was only one problem: Harper wasn't here. Harper wasn't anywhere.

She was gone, and now the most dangerous thing on earth was hungry for her blood.

I had ten minutes to invent a miracle, or I was dead.

No—worse than dead.

I was a liability.

I grabbed the phone, punched in Rage's number, and tried not to scream.

"Find her," I said when he picked up. "And if you can't—fake it. Use one of the lookalikes. Just don't let the demon know we've lost the real one. Not until we have a plan."

Rage grunted, then hung up.

I wiped my hands on my pants, leaving two wet streaks.

I had nine minutes left.

The devil was waiting.

I'd barely gotten my pulse under control when Maltraz called me to the lounge. The VIP suite was a converted library, all mahogany and velvet, the air humid with spilled liquor and centuries-old books. The demon sat at a poker table, shuffling a deck one-handed, claws flashing in the lamplight. The smoke from his cigarette twisted in the air, coiling into animal shapes that vanished just as quick.

A girl in a blue silk robe knelt by his side, hands folded in her lap. She was pretty enough, but her eyes were empty—dosed to the gills, probably, or just resigned to whatever was coming. Rage stood in the corner, arms crossed, looking everywhere but at the demon or the girl. He caught my eye and gave the smallest shake of his head.

We were in deep shit.

Maltraz beckoned me closer. "Have a seat, Mr. Steiner."

I obeyed, trying to look casual. The girl trembled when Maltraz ran his hand through her hair, but she didn't flinch or cry.

"Where is my toy?" the demon asked, voice a purr.

I went for the lie, praying it would stick. "She's on her way up. The handlers are prepping her."

Maltraz's smile was gentle. "Is that so?"

He snapped his fingers. The girl at his feet jerked upright, then toppled forward, face down on the carpet. Out cold. He leaned forward, folding his hands over the cards. "Let's not do the dance tonight, Waylon. You know I hate it when people waste my time. You dared to lie to me? You know that my boss is the father of lies."

I dropped the pretense. "She's gone."

He stilled, every muscle locking in place.

"Explain," he said, and the word shook the table.

"She was taken," I said. "Last week. Out of the alley. No trace. We've combed the city, the cameras, everything."

Maltraz stood, slow, letting the chair grind against the floor. He was on me in a heartbeat, faster than I could react. One clawed hand wrapped my throat; the other slammed into the table, splintering the polished wood. He lifted me until my feet left the floor.

"Who took her?" His breath was pure brimstone.

"We don't know," I choked out. "Someone good. They wiped our security, spoofed our trackers. It was clean."

He squeezed just a fraction. "You have ten seconds to give me something useful."

I flailed, desperate. "I have the footage. The week before she was taken. There was a man who paid large for her. But the video footage was blurred. We got one shot from the main floor. But it's just a face."

He dropped me. I collapsed onto the carpet, gasping.

Maltraz knelt beside me, his face a mask of rage. "Show me."

I staggered to my feet and led him down the hall to the surveillance room. The wall was a mosaic of monitors, all blank except for one, playing a loop of the alley behind the club. I cued up the footage, hands shaking.

"This is the last sighting," I said, voice hoarse.

The video showed Harper walking to the truck behind Rage. He rounded the truck. When she grabbed the door handle, she vanished. Then another monitor showed two weeks before when a man paid for her in a VIP room. Before the video blurred, there was a second his face was clear.

Maltraz leaned in, nose inches from the screen. His eyes glowed brighter, casting a red light over the keyboard.

"That's the only good frame," I said. "Everything else is static. But the way he moved—military, for sure. Special ops, maybe."

Maltraz was silent for a full minute. Then he smiled wide and terrible, showing every tooth in his head.

"Arsenal," he said, savoring the word. "Iron Valor Pack."

The name hit me like a punch to the gut. Iron Valor. The pack we'd crossed a few months ago, when we'd paid back a debt to Verdant Hollow by allowing them to use Morgantown in some messed up shit against Iron Valor.

Maltraz turned to me, his expression flat. "Sorry Waylon. Our little slave is off the table."

I shook my head, not trusting my mouth to work.

"The Council is watching me when it comes to Iron Valor. It means I cannot touch her or them, at least for now." He flicked a claw at the screen. "She is off the table. Unless something changes."

I swallowed, my mind racing. "You want me to let it go?"

His eyes narrowed. "No. I want you to find something better. Something more valuable. The sister, perhaps."

I tried to hide my relief. "We have a line on her. Paris. We don't have an exact location, but we're close."

Maltraz's mood changed instantly. The monster faded, replaced by a slick, predatory calm. "That's different," he said, voice almost playful. "As long as she's not in Iron Valor hands, she's fair game."

He clapped me on the back, hard enough to rattle my bones. "You usually deliver, Waylon. Don't disappoint me again. And if you ever lie to me again, it will be the last time."

I nodded, already plotting the next move.

Maltraz left the surveillance room with a swirl of sulfur and smoke. The air cleared, and I was alone, staring at the frozen image of the man who'd cost me my prize.

Arsenal. That son of a bitch. I called Leo in. "Pull a file on Arsenal from the Iron Valor Pack."

He had it in my hands in less than an hour. I scrolled through every detail: ex-military, owns a gun shop, Iron Valor's Sergeant at Arms. The kind of guy who'd cut your throat and eat a sandwich while you bled out.

I stared at his photo, memorizing every line.

The game had changed, but I was still in it.

Tonight, I'd lost a pawn. Next time, I'd take the queen.

"Prep the Paris team," I said. "We're moving on Lawson's sister."

Leo didn't ask questions. "ETA?"

"I want to move on this within the week. I want her on a plane as soon as possible."

"Understood." His fingers flew across his keyboard.

I sat back, letting the tension melt out of my shoulders. The club below throbbed with bass, a thousand strangers getting off to the women grinding before them oblivious to the war brewing above their heads.

I watched the monitors for a while, letting the city's light blur together.

Let them think they'd won. Let Iron Valor celebrate.

The next round was already mine.

Chapter 18

Arsenal

I woke before sunrise, a habit I'd never managed to break, and rolled out of bed with Harper still curled against the pillow, her hair spilled in a golden snarl. She barely stirred. I stood for a full minute just watching her chest rise and fall. She looked better in sleep, the sharp lines of her face relaxed, her lips parted, her cheekbones less hollow. Some of the tension had left her body, but not all. Even in rest, she clung to the edge of the mattress, as if the world might tip her off any second.

I showered and dressed in the dark, pulling on jeans and a clean Iron Valor tee, careful not to make a sound. I caught my reflection in the bathroom mirror: my eyes were brighter than they'd been in years; my skin had life. I pulled my hair up into a loose bun and brushed my teeth. My mind kept flashing back to the way Harper had screamed my name when she came all over my cock last night over and over again. I swear my mind was clearer this morning than it's been in years. She's fucked life back into every facet of my being. Our bond had connected more than her soul to mine. It's like it's enhanced every part of me. Shit. I looked in the mirror again. This is what happiness looked like.

The kitchen was quiet, the digital clock on the stove glowing 5:42. I brewed a pot of coffee. Not the freeze-dried shit I'd lived off of in

Afghanistan but robust gourmet stuff you buy in a bag. I drank it standing up, bare feet cold on the tile. Each sip scalded my throat, but I didn't care. I needed to be awake, clear-headed. Today, I would have to eat the biggest crow of my entire fucking life.

I mentally replayed my apology a dozen times before I finished the mug. It was simple enough: I'd acted like an asshole to my brothers for years, resenting every one of them who found a mate or a little patch of peace. I'd shit on their happiness, insulted their women, made a goddamn art of being impossible to love. If I were being honest, I'd never expected to get called on it. Iron Valor didn't do therapy sessions, and we sure as hell didn't do group hugs. We did violence, and we did loyalty, sometimes both in the same breath. But Bronc had called church, and that meant this was the perfect time for facing the music.

I set the empty mug in the sink, shrugged into my cut, crammed my feet into my boots, and scribbled a note for Harper in block letters:

WENT TO THE CLUBHOUSE. BACK LATER.

<u>WAKE UP SLOW</u>. EAT SOMETHING.

LOVE YOU.

—J

I hesitated, then underlined "WAKE UP SLOW." She needed the rest. She needed to know I'd be coming back.

I made my way downstairs as slowly as possible, keeping my head down, replaying every instance of my being a prick to the people who were my family. The list was too long. I didn't know if I'd ever make it right. Maybe that wasn't the point. Maybe you just started with today and hoped it stacked up.

The first floor of the pack house was dark except for a couple of wall sconces. I could smell the slow burn of last night's embers, the faint trace of beer and barbecue. I walked through the great room heading toward the basement stairs, reveling in the stillness. I was early, of course—old military habits and a lifetime of being the first one into the breach. I headed for the den, only to find Bronc already there.

He sat on the leather couch, boots up on the coffee table, staring into the fire. Even in the dim light, he looked like a statue: ramrod spine, arms folded, eyes set in that blue steel. The only thing that gave him away as human was the mug of coffee cradled in both hands. I realized, not for the first time, that Bronc had a way of commanding the room even when it was empty.

"Morning, boss," I said, keeping my voice low.

He looked up, face unreadable. "Arsenal. Couldn't sleep?"

I shrugged. "You know how I do when I got things."

Bronc grunted, which was as close to a laugh as he usually got. He gestured to the opposite chair. "Sit. Might as well get this over with."

I sat, hands knotted together, elbows on my knees. For a while, neither of us spoke. The only sound was the low pop of a coal in the fireplace.

Finally, Bronc broke the silence. "I know you've got a lot on your mind." He sipped his coffee. "But I need you dialed in today."

I nodded. "You'll get my best. You always do."

"Not always," Bronc said, his tone so flat it almost stung. "You give your best to the job. Not to the people."

I flinched, because he was right.

He looked at me for a long time, those blue eyes boring right through all the bullshit. "You got something to say, Jess?"

I swallowed, forcing myself not to look away. "I've been a dick to the brothers. And to you. For a long time."

Bronc raised an eyebrow. "And why's that?"

I chewed the inside of my cheek. "Because every time I saw one of you find your mate, or make a life, it felt like getting a bullet in the gut." I let the words hang there. "I didn't trust it. I thought it was a weakness. I thought it would get us all killed."

Bronc set his mug down, leaned forward. "That what you still think?"

"No," I said. It came out harsh, almost a bark. "Not anymore."

He let out a long, slow breath, as if he'd been holding it for years. "You know what I think, Arsenal?"

I shook my head.

"I think you're scared. I think you always have been. Not of dying, but of being left behind." Bronc's voice didn't soften, but it lost some of the edge. "You lost your brother when you were just a kid. Then you lost your mate before you ever got to claim her. That shit leaves scars."

I felt my jaw flex. "He was the good son," I said, almost under my breath. "He was the one who made Dad proud."

Bronc snorted. "Your old man is a mean old son of a bitch, from what I hear."

"Yeah," I said. "After Ben died, he barely looked at me. I was just a hired hand who worked for free. Didn't talk unless it was an order. Never asked if I was hurting."

"That's why you signed up?"

"Yeah. I knew a lot of wolves did. Seemed easier to take orders from someone who didn't have to pretend to give a shit."

Bronc nodded, like he'd heard it a hundred times before. Maybe he had.

He picked up his mug and took another slow sip. "So what are you gonna do about it?"

I didn't have an answer. I looked at the wall, at the framed pictures of every Iron Valor patch since the club was founded, every face caught in that moment of pride. There were men on that wall who'd died for the pack, some I'd served with, others who'd bled out before I was born. I thought about what it meant to have a family, to be worth something to anyone.

"Maybe start with an apology," I said, the words tasting like vinegar.

Bronc grinned, just a flicker at the corner of his mouth. "It's a start."

He leaned back, legs sprawled wide, taking up as much space as possible. "You know, when I took this job, I had no idea what I was doing. None of us did. We were kids with guns and motorcycles, thinking we could fix the world by force of will. Truth is, we fuck up just like everyone else. I saw my dad do it for years. Thought when he died I'd slide right in and become him."

He looked at me, a real warmth in his face now. "Didn't quite go that way. I've fucked up. But then I try again. That's the difference."

I nodded, not trusting myself to speak.

Bronc stood, stretched, and clapped me on the shoulder with a hand that could have snapped my collarbone if he wanted. "I depend on you, Jess. Don't forget that."

"I won't."

He held my gaze for a second, then looked at the clock on the wall. "We got twenty before the rest of the idiots roll in. Want to run through the briefing?"

"Yeah," I said, my voice steadying. "Let's do it."

We walked to the war room together, side by side, the silence not awkward anymore but comfortable. I realized, maybe for the first time in my life; that I belonged.

When the time came, I'd stand up and face my brothers. I'd take my lumps. I'd own the past.

And with Bronc's hand on my shoulder, I knew I could do it.

The war room had filled with the six men who'd made Iron Valor more than just a club: Bronc at the head of the table, Wrecker to his left, then Doc, wearing a lab coat and stethoscope instead of his cut. Big Papa was to his right, then my chair, then Gunner, and Menace's face filled one of the new big screens on the wall, his white-blond hair catching the light like a ghost. He sat in his fancy office already dressed in a navy suit complete with black tie. Looked like he belonged on the cover of fucking GQ magazine. I'd asked for him to join us for this part of our meeting.

I sat at the table, hands locked together so tight my knuckles went white. I'd spent the last ten minutes rehearsing my speech in my head, but it still came out raw.

Bronc started, thanking Menace for joining us. Told him to bear with us as he went through the basics—status updates, shipments, Wrecker's quarterly numbers, which he delivered in three words: "We're still solvent." They saved my part for last. When the silence came, all eyes locked on me. Even Menace seemed to lean in.

I stood, because sitting would have made it worse.

I cleared my throat, then just said it: "I owe every man at this table an apology."

Wrecker arched an eyebrow, the only sign he was listening. Papa just stared, his huge hands folded in front of him, scarred from a roadside bomb.

"I've been an asshole to everyone of you who found a mate." My voice didn't crack, but I heard the tremor in it. "I told myself it was because mates made us weak, made us a target, but that wasn't it." I looked up, meeting their eyes one at a time. "The truth is, Fate had given me a mate. One I loved with everything I had in me. Fulfilled me. Made me whole. And before I had a chance to claim that mate, I was told she had rejected me. I felt like half of my soul had been ripped from my body. And it's a shitty excuse. But I carried that soul-crippling hurt for years."

I swallowed hard. "And when you found your mates, I hated it. I resented it. Not just because it felt like you'd all left me behind. I just knew you couldn't trust them. That they would for sure hurt you the way mine had hurt me. And I couldn't stand the thought of you being crushed like that. And then, when they turned out to be amazing, I guess I was jealous. Why couldn't I have that kind of happiness? I knew I would be alone forever because I had a mate, and she didn't want me."

Menace's face stayed stone still. Wrecker just blinked. Papa gave a slow nod, as if cataloging the words for later.

"I'm not proud of how I treated any of you," I said. "And I'm not proud of how I treated your mates. Especially you, Big Papa. Aspen deserved better than what I said about her."

Papa shrugged, but the set of his jaw told me it mattered. I pressed on, knowing I had to get it all out before I lost my nerve.

"I've claimed Harper. She's mine, officially, and she's here to stay." I let the silence stretch, then added, "And the shit people have been saying about her? None of it was her fault. She was helpless. She did what she had to so her family wouldn't get hurt." I swallowed, trying to keep my hands from shaking. "She's the bravest person I've ever met."

Wrecker glanced at Bronc, then back at me. "So, you're apologizing for being a prick, and you want us to slow down on the whore talk?"

A bolt of anger shot up my spine, but I forced it down. "Don't ever call her that again."

Wrecker shrugged, but there was the hint of a smile behind his teeth. "Just checking. I mean, you suggested taking Parker out. You hinted at killing her. Potato, po-tah-toe."

"That's fair, Wrecker. I also had Parker's back when the chips were down."

Wrecker nodded. "Also fair. And I'd take a bullet for Harper."

The tension eased between us.

Menace's voice, piped in over the Surface speakers, was cool and precise. "We all read the file. We know how bad it got." He paused. "What's your plan for the fallout?"

I squared my shoulders. "I'm handling it. Any problems, they come to me. Not her. Not ever."

Bronc spoke next, his voice slow and deliberate. "You mean the shit that went down last night in the common room?"

I nodded. "Yeah."

He turned to Big Papa. "What'd Aspen say about it?"

Papa rubbed his beard, eyes distant. "She had trailed in behind Arsenal. She caught only the last part of it right before you walked in. She said Harper handled herself, but it was ugly. She's tough. She'll be okay." He looked at me. "But next time, don't be a part of it. Don't give them fuel for their fire."

Juliet's voice cut in through the office door and the war room. "WHAT?"

Bronc rolled his eyes. "Here we go." He said with a sigh.

The door opened, and our pregnant Luna waddled into the room. Even though she was only about four months along, her tiny Omega size and the fact she was carrying twins made her look like she was much more pregnant than she was.

"Did you say something ugly went down in the common room last night with Harper?" Her tiny hands were on her hips.

I sat back down and addressed her. "Yes ma'am. Several women had her cornered and were reading her the riot act. Grilling her about being on the pole. And telling her they didn't think she was Iron Valor officer mate material. I set them straight and told them if they ever said anything like that again, I'd have words with the Luna and you would visit them personally."

Color ran up her neck to her face. "I want the names by the end of this meeting."

Bronc was rubbing her back. "Now, little wolf, take it easy. You're carrying my pups, and I don't want you dealing with things that can cause you stress."

She looked him eye to eye since he was still seated. "You listen to me, Alpha. I won't have any members of my pack bullied and disrespected. Especially not an officer's mate. It won't take long I can assure you. I'll get the names, and you can call them, their mates or fathers if they don't have a mate, in for a quick meeting. And I will address it. Boom. Easy peasy."

I hid my smile as Bronc smiled at his mate and agreed as Juliet looked my way.

"Harper doesn't need to worry about ever having that happen again, Arsenal. I can promise you that. I can't stop people from judging her, but I can damn sure stop them from doing it out loud in public." She patted my shoulder as she walked out of the room.

"Yes, ma'am," I said.

Gunner leaned forward, arms folded, eyes sharp as razors. "I gotta say, you look different."

I met his eyes. "I feel different. Settled."

He grinned big and goofy, but you just never know with Gunner. Those light-hearted waters run deep.

Bronc continued with more Harper business. "Do you think Steiner is going to come for Harper?"

I looked to Wrecker since he's had the tech end covered.

Wrecker jerked his chin at the screen. "No sign of heat in the region."

"Steiner's gonna change targets," I said. "He won't like losing her. She said he's a win at all cost kind of guy. He lost his prize possession, but he's not stupid enough to go up against Iron Valor in a fight. He'll want to hurt her, but not directly."

Bronc dragged his hand down his face. "The sister."

"Yeah," I said. "But Harper's got no clue where she is exactly. She just knows her dad was arrested for the Ponzi scheme thing years ago and her mother and sister fled sometime after. She thinks they went to France after she overheard Steiner say something about their being in Paris. I've been poking around, and I found out something she doesn't know. Looks like her father's questionable business partners had had enough of him. He was murdered last month. The man never learned. No witnesses, no prints. Probably a mob hit. I haven't told her yet."

The air in the room went glacial. Bronc's eyes narrowed, but he kept his voice even. "Why the fuck not?"

"The man destroyed her life," I said, and my words surprised even me by how they landed. "He told me she had rejected me and then he sold her to Steiner. He's the cause of all her pain. This is going to reopen those wounds. Maybe she'll be glad to hear it. But she's not the type to celebrate death. And this news isn't gonna help us get to her sister."

Wrecker grunted. "Shit. Well, you just have to frame it around the fact that it was information uncovered in trying to find Brie. It's a tragic end to a tragic life. You need to remind her that getting to her sister before Steiner does is the most important thing right now."

I nodded my head. "My guess is Steiner's already got contacts in Paris. The second Brie pops her head up, he'll have her bagged and in a shipping crate. Maybe less than a week, if he pushes hard."

Bronc leaned back, massaging the bridge of his nose. "So we're racing a multimillionaire with a fucking trafficking empire and a demon king on speed dial. Wrecker—run down every travel manifest in the Schengen Zone to see if Brie has an alias. Get Parker to see if she can backtrace Harper's old numbers—her mom's burner might have left a trace. Make it fast," Bronc said, not as an order, just a fact of nature. "If this goes to shit, I want a team on the ground before we can fall any further behind. And I'm bringing Rafe in on this. Having the southern king work with us will go a long way should the Council get wind of it. Menace, you may need to vouch for us too, but I won't have you or your men involved. This is strictly a Southern pack issue, and Rafe needs to step up with muscle. If there is going to be an injured or dead Alpha as a result, I don't want Iron Valor's fingerprints to be on it. We've already taken out two kings and two Alphas on my watch. Another big kill and the Council will be out for our blood."

Menace straightened in his chair. "I don't like it, but I understand and respect your wishes. I'd like to be on the call when you contact Rafe."

Bronc nodded. "That would be helpful. Thank you, brother. Now Wrecker, how fast can you get a twenty on the girl?"

Wrecker cracked his knuckles, then typed in a few commands. "If she's in the city, I'll have her location by sundown. If she's not, it'll take a little longer to find the places she stops for Wi-Fi or a pastry. But nobody ghosts the net completely."

Bronc looked at me again, like he was giving me the floor. I ran a hand over my jaw, felt the rough bristle there. I appreciated my brothers more than I could say.

"I need to go to Harper," I told them. "I need to prep her. There's no guarantee Brie will run to us even if we get to her first. If she doesn't understand the danger, she'll keep running until she ends up in a crate."

Wrecker smirked. "When are you gonna tell Harper about the old man?"

I nodded once. "Today."

Parker blew into the room wearing her usual workout gear. Short dark hair with pink highlights shining. "Thought the conversations would be easier if I were here instead of my monster there texting everything." She blew a kiss toward Wrecker.

The conversation turned to logistics, air travel, the best way to get boots on the ground in France without triggering every customs agent on the continent. Bronc talked about safe houses, about which allies might be bribed to provide muscle or extraction. Wrecker suggested two, maybe three pack members from Rafe's friends in Paris. Parker said she'd ping her old boss at Cisco to see if anyone could offer coverage on phone possibilities in France.

The longer we talked, the more I felt the old machine switch on in my head: objectives, contingencies, risk assessments, everything falling into grid lines and checkboxes. It was almost soothing. Like violence was just another word for control.

Then Bronc ended the meeting with his usual precision. "Wrecker, Parker, keep working to get me a fix on Brie. Arsenal, keep Harper on lockdown and ready to move at a moment's notice. If Steiner moves first, we go full wolf pack. No prisoners. That's it."

Wrecker flicked a salute, gathered his gear, and was gone. Parker lingered, eyes flickering between Bronc and me, then stood and left without a word. Bronc was last, but before he went, he clapped a hand on my shoulder, the kind of grip that could bend rebar.

"Y'all will be fine," he said. "Fate made her for you. You know she's gonna have to go to France with you. Her sister won't come with you without her. You gonna be able to keep your head?"

I nodded. "I want to end this. She's fucking smart and brave. Her mind and body are clear of the poison that son of a bitch had pumped into her system. She can do this."

Bronc held my gaze. "That's all I wanted to hear."

When the room was empty, I sat for a long time, finishing my coffee. I thought about what it would mean to Harper, losing her father like that. He's the one who fucked her life up. She'd probably be relieved.

Then I remembered the last thing Harper had said to me before we left the bakery that morning. "Do you think Brie will ever want to see me again?"

I'd hoped I wasn't lying when I said. "She'll run to you the second she's in trouble."

But the truth was, I didn't know. There were some wounds you couldn't cauterize, no matter how many times you bled for them. And there were some sisters who'd rather burn alive than admit they ever needed saving.

I stood, my legs cramping from sitting too long, and headed for the door. There were errands to run, messages to send, weapons to clean. But before I did any of that, I let myself imagine what I'd do to Steiner if he ever touched Brie.

It was a long, ugly list.

The world was a meat grinder, and my job was to keep Harper and her family out of it. I'd failed once. I wasn't about to let it happen again.

So I made a promise right then, in that empty sunlit room. I'd find Brie and Harper's mom. I'd bring them home, even if I had to drag them across an ocean and through hell itself. And I'd never let another monster touch what was mine to protect.

Not while I was breathing.

CHAPTER 19

Harper

The kitchen glowed with that particular morning gold that follows a frosty night, sunlight sharp enough to make the crumb-strewn countertop glitter. I'd been awake for hours, all showered, dressed in soft leggings and an oversized sweater, my damp hair curling at the ends. The memory of Jess's hands on my skin kept me warm. Three empty coffee mugs bore witness to my waiting, the fourth nearly slipping through my fingers as I chased the ghost of last night's pleasure—his mouth between my thighs, the growl in his voice when I came the third time, how he'd cradled me afterward like something precious.

Crumbs from yesterday's pastry dusted my notebook, my sweater, and the patch of bare knee peeking through the torn fabric of my leggings. I didn't brush them away. The stillness felt fragile, like the world was holding its breath.

The front door sighed open at noon. Jess stood framed in the doorway, morning light catching the damp ends of his hair. His knuckles shone raw and pink. He'd been at the gym again, punishing the heavy bag or maybe just his own regrets. My chest tightened when his gaze found me, that familiar ache blooming under my ribs.

"Hey," he rasped, voice rough as gravel. I wondered if he'd spoken at all during the pack meeting.

"Hey yourself." My mug clinked against butcher block. "How'd the meeting go?"

A muscle jumped in his jaw as he crossed to me. "Gave my apologies for being a colossal dick for the past however many years. Told them I'd been a jealous bastard. That their mates deserved better than my..." His fingers brushed crumbs from my knee. "My shit."

The touch sparked memories. Those same fingers inside me last night, coaxing sounds I didn't know I could make. Heat flooded my cheeks.

"You didn't have to..."

"I did." His hands engulfed mine, warm and sure. "For years, I let anger rot me. Punished you for surviving. Punished them for..." His thumb traced my pulse. "For finding what I thought I'd lost."

The confession hung between us, fragile as the sugar crystals on my sleeve. I wanted to kiss it away, to drag him back to bed where words didn't matter. But his eyes held a new softness; the black irises rimmed with gold like a solar eclipse in reverse. I stayed still.

"You don't owe me..."

"Let me." His forehead pressed to mine. "Let me be better."

The refrigerator hummed. The clock ticked. His thumb kept circling my wrist as shadows moved behind his eyes. The unspoken things waiting in his throat.

"I need you to sit down," he said, pulling me to the couch. I followed and sat on the edge of the cushion spine straight. His voice had gone formal, like he was reading a bad report and didn't know how to soften the blow.

He poured himself a mug of the now-cold coffee and walked back over to me. He sat across from me on the new coffee table, set the mug down and put his hands on his knees. He wouldn't look at me for a full fifteen seconds. Finally, he cleared his throat.

"We were working on finding your sister. Wrecker and Parker ran all the numbers, all the addresses. I was searching too, and I found something. A file from Houston PD. Seems your father hadn't stopped dabbling in illegal shit when he'd been convicted in that Ponzi scheme. He must have gotten mixed up with some really bad men who did really bad things." He squeezed my hands. "I hate to be the one to have to tell you, but he was killed last month."

The world stopped. For a full minute, I didn't understand what the words meant. Then they clicked together, cold and smooth and permanent.

"How?" I asked. My voice sounded flat, like it was being piped in from another room.

"Hit in a parking garage. Execution style. The news called it a robbery, but the report says there was nothing missing. There were just two bullets to the back of the head. *We* think it was a mob hit. Or maybe something to do with the Ponzi scheme. He'd made a lot of enemies."

I felt the edges of my vision go white, the way it sometimes did when I'd danced too long without water, when my blood sugar would crater and the world would shrink to a single, ringing note.

I didn't cry. I didn't scream. I didn't do anything but breathe, slow and careful, until the feeling passed.

"I should feel something," I said after a long while. "I should at least want to cry over the death of my parent. But I don't."

Jess moved off the table, then knelt in front of me. "That's okay."

"I mean, I'm sure he didn't cry for me when he sold me to a monster." My lips twitched, a ghost of a smile. "Guess karma got the last word, after all."

He looked up at me, eyes full of something that wasn't pity, wasn't sorrow. It was just real. "I'm sorry."

"Don't be," I said. "I'm not."

We sat there like that, frozen. The sun broke through a cloud and lit the room, warming my bare feet. I pressed them against the tile just to remind myself I was still here, still alive, and not just some ghost sitting here.

Jess ran his thumb along my knuckles, slow and steady, not forcing anything.

When I finally looked at him, I could see the struggle on his face. He wanted to fix this, but there was nothing to fix. All he could do was wait until the ice inside me melted, until my blood started moving again.

"Thank you for telling me yourself," I said. "I would have hated to find out from the news."

He nodded, like he didn't trust himself to speak.

I closed my eyes, let the sunlight pour over my eyelids, and imagined a world where the dead stayed dead, where the only monsters were the kind you could outrun, or outlast, or out-love.

I opened my eyes, and he was still there. Solid. Unyielding. Still my wolf.

"I don't know what I'm supposed to do now," I said.

He gave me a sad smile. "Whatever you want."

I nodded, and for the first time in my life, I believed it might actually be true.

"We need to talk about next steps," he said, settling on the edge of the sofa. His hands flexed, restless, then stilled as he met my gaze. "First priority is getting to your sister. Bronc says the odds are good Steiner's already got teams looking for her."

The name landed like a fist to the ribs. "So she's in danger," I said.

"She's not safe," Jess agreed. "But we're better. Wrecker and Parker are on it. They're trying to get a trace on your mom in Paris. Menace has contacts there, being a royal and all." He paused. "It's possible they know someone is after them and they're running."

My pulse stuttered, then evened out. I tried to recall the last time I'd talked to my mom. It was a voice memo, not a call—her voice disguised, heavy with code words. I'd deleted it a minute later, like I always did. She'd said, "Your sister is painting now. She's got a good studio and friends she trusts. Don't worry about us. We love you forever." Then, it was gone.

"Could she be hiding?" I asked. "I mean, Mom was always good at that sort of thing. She made it through the IRS scandal, the pack betrayal, all of it. She could vanish if she wanted."

Jess nodded. "If she's trying, she's doing a decent job. But we have a couple of advantages Steiner doesn't."

He didn't elaborate. He didn't have to.

I chewed on my thumbnail, then stopped. "What do you need from me?"

"Any way to contact her, any numbers you remember, any old passwords or codes. Even if it's just a maybe."

I shook my head, frustrated. "At Eyrie, they changed my phone every week. Sometimes twice. Steiner's people monitored every call, every text, every breath I took online. The only number I ever really memorized was the one I got for my sixteenth birthday. It doesn't even work anymore."

Jess leaned in, eyes sharp. "You sure?"

I thought for a minute, then closed my eyes and let my brain flicker back through the years. "It was a 713 number. Then they changed the area code, I think. It was the only one Mom ever called directly."

He handed me a battered spiral notepad. "Write it down."

I did, my hand shaking just a little. "That's all I've got."

"It's enough," he said. He was already dialing Wrecker before I finished the sentence.

I watched him cross to the sliding balcony door, back straight, shoulders squared. He spoke low and fast, tossing off codes and acronyms like a man born for this. I could see the animal in him now—alert, dangerous, a wall you could crash a truck into and still not dent.

When he hung up, he turned to me. "Wrecker says he'll have a hit within the hour. If it's live, we move. If not, we go anyway. We can't let Steiner get to them first."

"Do you think Brie will even talk to me?" I hated how small my voice sounded.

"She won't come willingly to anyone but you," Jess said. "She's still your sister, even after all this."

I wanted to believe him. But I knew Brie. She'd spent her entire life having everything given to her. She always got her way. I love her, but she's spoiled rotten.

Jess must have seen the worry on my face, because he sat next to me and pulled me onto his lap. My body molded to his instinctively, like it had been waiting all day for this. He held me there, arms wrapped around my waist, and for a long time neither of us spoke.

Finally I managed, "If she doesn't come with me, she'll wind up with Steiner. Or in a train car. Or heaven forbid, in the arms of that demon king."

He buried his face in my neck, breathing deep. "You'll need to drive that home to her if she resists. Scare the shit out of her. Even if she still resists, that's not going to happen. I won't let it."

I nodded, even though I didn't believe it completely.

"Go pack," he said gently. "Travel light. If it goes down tonight, we leave in a matter of hours."

My legs were numb when I stood, so I leaned against the counter for a second before heading to the bedroom. I grabbed a selection of the new sweaters, jeans, and leggings that I'd gotten since I arrived here. Jess had gotten me a pair of soft leather boots that had become my favorite footwear, so they went in the bag.

It felt surreal, packing for a mission I might never come back from. I should have been afraid, but all I felt was the buzzing numbness of adrenaline. I tucked a small bottle of perfume in the side pocket, then added a dog-eared paperback, just for the comfort of it. At the last second, I crammed in a notebook and a new pen. For Brie, I told myself. She'd want something to draw with.

When I zipped the bag, I realized my hands were shaking. Not a little, but a lot.

I carried it back to the living room and set it by the door.

Jess was standing there, just watching me, his expression soft. "You ready?" he asked.

"Not really," I admitted.

He smiled. "Me neither."

But we both knew we'd go, anyway.

The next few hours passed in a blur of waiting. I drank more coffee, picked at the split ends in my hair, and paced in circles around the kitchen until I thought I might wear a rut in the laminate. Jess busied himself with weapons—cleaning, packing, checking each one with the careful love of a man who trusted metal more than luck. He didn't say much, but every few minutes, he'd look up and check on me, like he needed the reassurance that I hadn't disappeared again.

At three, my phone buzzed. It was Wrecker, the message short and to the point:

PILOT GOOD TO GO 4AM FLIGHT. PACK LIGHT. MEET AT PEARL'S TONIGHT, 7. BRING ALL ESSENTIALS. -W

I read it twice, then showed it to Jess. He nodded once, snapped the magazine into place with a click that echoed in the tiny apartment.

"We leave at four," he said, voice even. "Tonight we eat, then go dark. No social, no phones except the one Wrecker gives you."

"Where are we going until then?" I asked.

He smiled, that half-crooked thing that had won me over in the first place. "I want to show you something."

I didn't press for details. I just shouldered my duffel and followed him down the stairs, out into the chilly spring afternoon. The sky was the color of dishwater, but sunlight kept punching through in random spots, setting the wet grass ablaze. Jess's truck was waiting at the curb, a big Ford with plush leather seats. He popped the lock and held the passenger side open for me, just like before everything went to hell. Always the gentleman.

We drove west, deeper into pack territory, past several houses. After about ten minutes, the land spread out flat and endless, a checkerboard of pasture and wildflowers, bluebonnets and Indian paintbrush crawling up the bar ditches. I rolled the window down and let the wind tangle my hair, the air sharp with the smell of green things growing.

"Where are we going?" I asked.

"Not far," Jess said. "Just trust me."

We took a left at a mailbox painted with cartoon cows, then rumbled down a dirt road lined with cedar. At the end of it was a wide metal gate and a hand-painted sign: WRECKER & PARKER, in bold red. Jess keyed in a code, and the gate swung open with a whine.

He parked at the edge of a wooded lot, then killed the engine. "C'mon."

I stepped out, the soles of my sneakers sinking into the soft earth. The whole place smelled of cedar, moss, and the faint sweetness of honeysuckle on the wind. We skirted the side of Wrecker and Parker's place; a pretty ranch house with a wraparound porch, every inch of it hung with wind chimes and dream catchers. Parker's touch, no question.

Jess took my hand, pulled me through knee-high grass and down a gentle slope. I could hear water, and a few seconds later we came to a little creek, maybe six feet wide, the banks crowded with willows and wild plum. Jess stopped at a break in the trees, then turned to face me.

"This is it," he said, voice gone soft. "This is where our house is gonna be."

I stared, trying to picture it: a flat acre of grass, the creek curving along the back; the trees throwing shadows like a cathedral. The afternoon light caught in the leaves and made them shimmer, pale green and silver. For a second, I couldn't breathe.

He put his arm around me and pointed to a spot halfway up the rise. "I want a white board and batten. Big porch facing east so you get all the morning light. Gray sage shutters. Inside, just one level, ranch style, but with a huge kitchen. Big eating area, because you like when people come over. Stone fireplace. Three, maybe four bedrooms. Enough for a couple of pups, if you want them."

His words made my heart trip and catch. I squeezed his hand so hard he winced.

"You mean, you want a family?" I said.

He looked at me, really looked, then nodded. "If *you* do."

I thought about it for half a second. I pictured little kids running through the grass, arms out like airplane wings. I pictured the two of us sitting on that porch, watching the sunset and maybe not being haunted anymore.

"I do," I said.

Jess let out a breath; a look of relief on his face. "Good."

We stood like that, staring at the empty lot, until my toes started to go numb from standing still.

I leaned my head on his shoulder. "Can I tell you a secret dream?"

"Anything."

"If we ever make it back from France, and if we have the money, I'd like to open a dance studio in town. Nothing fancy, just a little place for the kids. Maybe the moms wouldn't think of me as the town whore and would let their little girls learn ballet from me."

There was a long silence. Then Jess said, "They'd be lucky to have you."

I snorted. "You're biased."

He wrapped his arms around my waist, pulled me close. "Maybe a little."

We watched the creek for a while. I listened to the water, the wind in the trees, and the far-off bark of a dog. It was all so normal, so possible, that for a minute I almost forgot about Paris, about the pack, about everything waiting for us on the other side of the ocean.

"This is just the first days of our dreams coming true," Jess said, his voice muffled against my hair.

I closed my eyes, letting myself believe it.

When we finally walked back to the truck, the sun was low in the sky, painting the world in bronze and blue. The shadows were long, but the air had warmed, and I could almost taste the fullness of spring.

We drove in silence. When we reached town, Jess pulled into the lot behind Pearl's, parked in the shadows, and turned to me.

"You ready for this?" he asked.

I stared at my hands, the way they shook just a little.

"No," I said. "But I'm going, anyway."

He reached over, laced his fingers with mine, and squeezed.

And for the first time, I felt like we might be all right.

Chapter 20

Arsenal

Pearl's Bar & Grill looked like a place that had been born old and gotten better every year since. Yellowed glass, battered wooden door, a crooked neon sign in the window that read "Open 'Til the Cows Come Home." It sat right off the Dairyville courthouse square, the same place it had been since before the first Iron Valor patch got stitched. The parking lot overflowed with pickups and battered imports and one ugly, sky-blue Harley with a cartoon octopus on the tank—Gunner's latest Frankenstein project.

The second I opened the door, the world hit me in the face: the tang of hickory smoke, fried onions, and a low, throbbing mix of country radio and football highlights. Friday night at Pearl's meant every square inch was packed, but in the far corner, a long row of tables had been bolted together. That was us. The pack.

Bronc and Juliet sat at the head, Juliet's hair a waterfall of gold, her belly round and radiant in a black cotton dress. Bronc had his hand on her back, thumb idly tracing the curve of her spine. I caught his eye, and he raised two fingers in greeting before pointing me to the empty seats halfway down. Wrecker and Parker were already parked across from them, Parker's "Spicy Book Club" hoodie nearly glowing in the dim light, leggings stretched over the kind of ass that made a grown man lose a step mid-stride. Parker had her feet up on the seat beside her, a glass of whiskey balanced on her thigh. Wrecker, the contradiction; a monster of a man who'd rather read than fight, but he could kill you with his bare hands.

Big Papa and Aspen took up the next slot, Papa in his usual black thermal, Aspen in a sleeveless turquoise dress and a white cardigan she kept pulling over her hands. Oscar, the prairie dog familiar stood guard at her feet, only his inquisitive nose and two black eyes visible above the lip of her purse. Doc was next, crisp as a new scalpel in a checked shirt and jeans, his glasses catching every stray bit of light. Gunner sat between Doc and Bronc, a wolf among wolves, his boots caked in the mud of whatever field he'd run through on the way here.

Harper hesitated just inside the doorway, shoulders pulled up like she expected someone to lob a grenade at her. I felt it in my teeth—the old ache, the one that wanted to snap at anyone who looked at her wrong. I touched her elbow, soft. "They're all glad you're here," I said.

She nodded, but her hand had a tremor in it as she tucked her hair behind her ear.

I guided her through the crowd. There was a beat where all the conversations at the table paused, every face tracking us in that hypervigilant way only a pack could. Then Parker called out, "Well, look who finally decided to show up!" and the table erupted, the tension snapping like an old rubber band.

We wedged in at the only open slot: Harper to my right, Doc to my left. She perched on the chair, ankles crossed, making herself smaller. I kept my arm over her chair-back, not touching, just staking the ground.

Menus got passed like hand grenades, drinks ordered by the pitcher. Pearl herself strolled over, hair in its usual silver helmet, and banged down two Mason jars of sweet tea. "I put the order in already," she barked, "so don't go messin' up my system. And I want to see every plate clean, or you'll have to answer to me." She winked at Harper. "You too, sweetheart."

"Thank you, Mrs. Baucaum," Harper said, voice so pretty and careful it made Pearl beam.

"You got a good one here, Arsenal," Pearl said, not bothering to hide it from the table. "Pretty and polite. About time you brought home something worth showing off."

Wrecker snorted. "Yeah, we were starting to think he liked his rifles more than women."

Parker poked him in the ribs. "He still might. You've seen the way he oils his barrels?"

There was a round of groans and laughter, and the table broke into the easy chaos of family—everyone talking over each other, stories and jokes ricocheting around like spent casings. Bronc kept a hand on Juliet, always. Aspen leaned into Papa, her hair blending with the plaid of his shirt. Gunner made a show of draining half a pitcher of Shiner, then offered some to Harper. She took a sip, face twisting, and set it down.

"How's the bakery?" Parker asked Aspen, voice pitched to reach over the noise.

Aspen's face lit up. "It's been so busy I haven't had time to catch my breath. Every Friday, the high school football team comes in and buys out the cinnamon rolls before ten. I have to hide an extra pan in the back for Oscar." She looked at the prairie dog, who gave a solemn little bow.

Parker beamed. "That's what you get for being the best in three counties."

Harper smiled, the real thing this time, and I felt the win deep in my chest. Every time she let herself belong, I wanted to howl it from the roof.

Bronc raised his beer, voice carrying down the table. "Quick announcement before Pearl brings out the feast." The table went still. "My son finished his service last week. Tyler's coming home."

There was a thunder of applause and a chorus of "Semper Fi!" from the old Marines at the other table. I saw the flicker of pride on Bronc's face; the way Juliet leaned into him, eyes shining.

"That's wonderful," Harper said, soft. "You must be so proud."

Bronc grinned at her, warm. "We are, ma'am. It'll be good to have the whole family together again."

Pearl returned, three pack members in tow, arms loaded with platters: brisket, sausage, fried catfish, mashed potatoes drowning in brown gravy, platters of biscuits. They stacked the table high, then vanished as quickly as they'd come.

The next fifteen minutes were all eating, hands and forks and stories of old times. Harper tried everything. She picked at the sausage, then went back for seconds, then thirds. She laughed at something Doc said, and for a moment, she leaned into my side, just a brush of skin, but I could have died happy.

Gunner gestured at Parker's shirt. "Is that new?" he asked, mouth full.

She glanced down. "Yeah, 'Spicy Book Club.' Got it at the gas station in Amarillo. You like?"

"I do," Gunner said, voice solemn. "It's very... you."

Parker rolled her eyes, but she blushed. "You're not in the club. You couldn't handle the dark stuff."

"Try me."

She shot him a look that made my skin prickle. "I'll bring you a reading list."

Wrecker raised a glass. "Speaking of clubs, how's the gun shop, Arsenal? You running out of inventory yet?"

I shrugged. "Damn near. Every month it's three days of restock and then we're dry again. I got a line on a new shipment, but it's stuck at the border." I looked at Bronc. "Supposed to be clean. I trust the source."

Bronc nodded. "Good. We'll need it."

For a second, the air changed. I saw the old wariness pass between Bronc and Wrecker and Papa, the way their eyes flicked to Harper and then back to me. They were all thinking about what came after tonight, what waited on the other side of the Atlantic.

But for now, it was family. For now, it was food and laughter and the kind of comfort you only got after you'd bled for each other.

Big Papa wiped his mouth and leaned over to Harper. "You settling in alright?"

She nodded, a curl of hair falling over her cheek. "I am. Everyone's been really kind for the most part."

He smiled big and soft. "That's because you're good people." He jerked his chin at me. "Arsenal ain't always easy, but you keep him in line. We all see it."

She ducked her head. "We're good for each other."

I watched her, watched the way she started to relax by increments, her hand coming to rest on my thigh beneath the table, fingers tracing slow circles. My wolf inside settled, content.

Oscar the prairie dog crawled out from under the table, circled the group, then stood up in Aspen's lap. "Miss Harper," he intoned in his tiny, perfect British accent. "Should you require additional cutlery, I am at your disposal."

She clapped a hand over her mouth to keep from laughing. "Thank you, Oscar. That's very sweet."

He bowed and vanished beneath Aspen's chair, mission complete.

As the meal wound down, the noise level ramped up. Parker and Harper huddled close, talking about some trashy romance novel. Gunner taught Aspen how to blow straw wrappers across the table. Papa and Doc argued about the best whiskey in Texas. Bronc and Juliet conferred in low voices, her hand never leaving his.

I leaned into the noise, the closeness, the feeling of being part of something that was bigger than myself. I watched Harper's face light up, watched her walls come down, watched as she let herself belong.

At some point, Parker dragged her to the bathroom. As they left, I caught Parker's eye. She winked, and for the first time in a long while, I trusted her to have Harper's back. There was no threat at this table, not tonight.

When they returned, Harper's cheeks were pink, and she was laughing. Parker had her arm looped through Harper's, and they slid into their seats with the easy grace of old friends.

Wrecker glanced at the clock. "Time?"

"Just past 2100 hours," I said.

He nodded, finishing the last of his beer. "We should go soon."

Bronc stood, clearing his throat. The table went quiet.

"Thank you, Pearl, for feeding the wolves," he called, loud enough to reach the kitchen.

Pearl popped her head out. "Don't mention it, sugar. Next one's on the house, so y'all better come back alive."

That hit harder than anything else all night.

We rose as a pack, chairs scraping, bodies moving as one. The old men at the next table gave us a wave and a half-drunk "Oorah." Oscar scurried up Aspen's sleeve and disappeared into her purse.

On the way out, I paused at the door. Harper hovered behind me, her eyes wide but steady. I bent down, putting my lips to her ear.

"You did great," I said.

She squeezed my hand. "I felt... safe."

That was the whole point.

We stepped out into the cold, the smell of barbecue clinging to our hair and clothes, the echo of laughter still ringing in our ears. The stars were bright in the night sky; sharp and blue against the black.

I took her hand and led her to the truck, the engine already running warm.

Inside, with the doors closed, I let myself smile.

Maybe I was still scared. Maybe tomorrow would rip it all away. But tonight, we'd had something close to perfect.

And it was enough.

Three giant monitors glowed on the wall above the whiteboard, and every square inch of table was covered in laptops, maps, open manila folders, and enough caffeine delivery systems to keep a battalion awake. The war room had been readied for us to learn all we could for our trip.

Most nights, the pack house had the low-key, lived-in comfort of any family home: dog hair on the rugs, mismatched mugs in the sink, a faint smell of Pine-Sol and bacon that never fully left the air. But on mission nights, the place vibrated at a different frequency. There was a ritual to it. Shoes left at the entry, phones in the Faraday box, everyone moving with a shared sense of urgency.

Harper entered ahead of me, her hand tight in mine. The mood in the war room was already serious: Bronc at the head, chair tilted back, arms crossed like a general waiting for battle; Juliet beside him, now in jeans and a faded "Cowgirl Up" tee that somehow made the bump of her pregnancy look dangerous. Wrecker and Parker flanked the screens, each with a laptop open and a stack of files between them. Doc and Big Papa had staked the side wall. Aspen sat with Oscar at her feet, a grimoire and a spiral-bound notepad in front of her. Gunner sat, boots up, chewing on a toothpick, eyes on the door.

We dropped into the two open chairs at the foot of the table, me on the end, Harper to my right. I scanned the room: all eyes forward, all business. The table was littered with enough weaponry—disassembled, legal, and less-than-legal—to make an ATF agent twitch.

Wrecker kicked things off. "Alright, ladies and wolves. We fly out at 0400. King Rafe made it happen: Instead of taking the Iron Valor jet; we're going in his private Gulfstream out of Amarillo. We'll land at Le Bourget–Seine-Saint-Denis and have customs help from Rafe's witch Gwen."

He clicked the remote, and a map snapped onto the central monitor, a red line tracing the flight plan. "From there, Rafe's men pick us up, get us into the city."

Parker slid folders down the table, one for each person. "These are the files on our contacts in France, plus any known hostiles. All up to date as of four hours ago. I've burned the important stuff onto flash drives, too." She handed Harper a folder and a small drive. Harper took them, knuckles white.

"Our targets," Wrecker said, "are Harper's sister, Brie, and her mom, Nanette. We believe they're living under assumed names. At one point they had been in Montmartre where Brie was showing paintings under a fake name, but that had changed. Best guess, they're moving as often as they think they need to."

He pulled up a dossier. "Steiner's got a Paris team. Muscle, not brains. They'll likely try to snatch-and-grab, not subtle."

"Any indication Harper's mom has taken another mate?" Bronc asked, his eyes narrowed to slits.

Wrecker shook his head. "No, but she's not above hiding in plain sight. If she did, it'd be a power move: tying her wagon to a Paris pack, maybe one of the old bloodlines." He glanced at Harper. "Sorry, but we have to consider it."

She nodded, lips pressed tight.

"Brie?" I said. "Any boyfriend, girlfriend, mate?"

Wrecker raised an eyebrow. "No mate on record, but she's been seen with a couple of Parisian wolves. We don't know if it's social or if she's in bed with them, but they're definitely not human."

"Shit," I muttered.

Harper's voice was thin. "Is that... is it dangerous?"

Parker shrugged. "Depends. Could be they're protecting her. Or could be they're the honey trap, holding her until Steiner pays up."

Big Papa's baritone rolled out. "Either way, we go in assuming they're compromised. Trust nobody who ain't on our payroll or in the pack."

"Copy that," I said.

Parker switched screens. "The other thing to know: Paris PD is on the take, and most French wolf packs play both sides. If we go loud, it'll get ugly fast. If we go quiet, we might have a shot at pulling them out before anyone knows we're there."

Wrecker smirked. "But if it does go loud, I brought toys." He slid a sheet across to me, a detailed checklist of hardware stashed with Rafe's men at the airstrip. I read it, lips twitching.

"Nice," I said. "But I'll still bring my own."

Doc piped up, quiet but firm. "Extraction plan?"

Wrecker looked at Parker, who answered. "There's a secondary airstrip on the south edge of the city. If we can't get back to the original, we'll drive them to the fallback. Rafe's guy will meet us there. Ten-minute runway window, then it's a hard exfil."

"And if we're separated?" I said.

Parker didn't miss a beat. "Each team has a burner. If one team gets split, rendezvous at one of the safe-houses listed in your file. They're in code, but the GPS is already programmed. You get there, you lock down, you wait for the go signal."

Bronc leaned forward, voice like gravel. "Everyone got their role?"

One by one, we nodded.

He pointed at Wrecker and Parker. "You two are brains and comms. Doc, you're transport and medical. Papa, you run point on physical extraction. Aspen, you and Gunner will work your comms from here. Arsenal, you keep Harper glued to your hip at all times. Her safety is the mission. If Steiner or anyone else gets near her, you go full combat on their ass. Keep Rafe's men up to speed and near. I want their team running second on this. If Steiner is taken down, I want plausible deniability. Our most important asset will be Gwen. She is an incredibly powerful witch who has been with

Rafe for years. She'll be able to create a veil that will shield y'all from human and supernatural eyes. As long as she's okay, you should be able to get in and get out without too much trouble. But prepare for all contingencies."

I straightened. "Yes, sir."

Juliet smiled at Harper, a little flick of warmth. "You'll be okay," she said. "We have the best in the world with you."

The briefing rolled on. We hashed every contingency, every backup plan. If the house were burned, we'd regroup at a safe-house. If the police got involved, Parker had bribes ready for at least two captains in the 18th arrondissement. If the worst happened, Wrecker would blow the fallback airstrip with C4, and everyone would run for the train.

It all made sense, and it all felt like it could go to shit in one bad minute.

The conversation turned to the targets: Brie, Harper's sister, last seen at an art show. The mother, last confirmed at a French bakery near the Marais. There were photos, blurry but good enough. Harper stared at the pages like she could will them into reality. The wolf friends were the only unknowns.

I flipped through my own file, scanning every page. Patterns, schedules, possible chokepoints. My mind raced with tactical overlays, possible ambushes, fallback positions. The more I saw, the more I liked the plan. The only part I didn't like was the unknowns.

"Steiner's men," I said. "How many?"

Wrecker grunted. "Four confirmed, maybe two more. They're ex-military, mostly US or Polish mercs, with a couple of shifters for muscle."

"Names?"

He passed a sheet. "Best we could do. These are ugly dudes, Arsenal. Not the kind that scare easy."

I memorized every name and face, then slid the page to Harper. She studied it, brow furrowed.

Parker asked, "You recognize any?"

She shook her head, then stopped. "Wait. The one on the left. I think I saw him in Houston. He was... he came to the club with Steiner once. He was quiet, but he watched everything."

Wrecker grinned. "That tracks. He's ex-Polish GROM. Likes knives."

I felt Harper stiffen beside me. I put my hand on her knee under the table and gave her a squeeze.

Wrecker summed it up: "These aren't dumb goons. They'll improvise."

Bronc looked at me. "You ready?"

I nodded. "Let's do it."

Papa clapped his hands together, the sound sharp as a pistol shot. "Then it's settled."

Juliet collected the folders, giving Harper's an extra squeeze. "You'll do great," she whispered.

Everyone broke up, heading out in ones and twos. Wrecker and Parker lingered, heads bent together over a laptop. Bronc walked us to the door.

On the porch, under the bare bulbs, he paused. "She'll be safe," he said, looking me dead in the eye.

"I know," I said, and for the first time, I believed it.

We walked up to my apartment in silence. I could see the fear in her, but I could also see her bravery.

At the door, she stopped. "Do you think we'll get them out?" she asked.

I looked at her, really looked, and saw the future mapped in the lines of her face.

"We'll get them," I said.

And I meant it.

Tomorrow, we'd fly to Paris.

Tonight, I'd keep watch over her dreams.

Inside, she dropped her bag on the bedroom floor and went straight to the bathroom. The water ran; I heard the clink of glass against porcelain, the faint rattle of pill bottles. She was prepping—safety, ritual, anything to keep from thinking. I put my own bag down and loaded two mags into the bedside Glock, stashed it in the drawer by the lamp. I checked the window locks; then did it again. Some habits never leave.

She came out in a faded tee and nothing else, hair up, face bare. She padded to the kitchen and poured herself a glass of water, drank half, then just stood there. I could see the current running under her skin: adrenaline, fear, anticipation, all twined tight.

She looked up, and the rawness in her gaze leveled me.

"I'm scared," she said.

"You're not alone," I told her. "You don't ever have to be alone again."

I carried her to the bed and set her down and carefully peeled the tee off over her head. Her body was all muscle and soft, healed scars and lines of strength. I undressed, stripped down to skin and nothing else, and crawled onto the bed beside her. She watched me, her eyes glistening with lust-filled anticipation.

I started at her neck, kneading the tight muscles under my thumbs, working them until she groaned and her head lolled back. I moved to her shoulders, slow circles, then down her arms, forearms, hands. She relaxed by increments, eyes half-closed, mouth slack.

When I got to her thighs, she parted them without asking. Her pussy was already wet, slick and hot, and I took my time with her, tracing every inch, every edge, with my mouth and hands. I didn't rush, not even when she whimpered. I wanted her to feel everything, to remember what it was to be touched with love, not power.

I sucked her clit, slow, gentle, just enough to make her squirm. She came quickly, her heels digging into my back. I kept going, licking her through the aftershocks, then slid up beside her, holding her face in my hands.

She pulled me in for a kiss, tasting herself on my tongue, and for a moment she looked so vulnerable I almost couldn't stand it.

"Again," she whispered. "I want more."

I rolled her over, face-down, her arms stretched above her head. I started at her shoulders, massaged down her spine, stopping to kiss each vertebra, each scar. When I got to her ass, I squeezed, then spread her, buried my tongue inside until she was begging.

When I couldn't wait anymore, I grabbed her hips and raised her ass up in the air. I lined up and pushed inside her, slow and deep, letting her feel every inch of my rock-hard erection. She arched back against me, taking all of me, gasping out my name in a voice I'd never tire of hearing.

I fucked her like that, slow and steady, her body stretched beneath mine, her cunt squeezing my cock tighter every time I pulled back. The mate mark on her neck glowed red, and I felt the answering throb in my own, our bond a live wire between us.

"Mine," I growled, biting her shoulder.

"Yours," she sobbed, "always."

I felt my knot start to swell, and I gripped her hips, slamming into her harder, her ass bouncing under my hands. She came again, body shuddering, and I went with her, my knot locking us together as my cum filled her up. Her orgasm continued as my body shuddered and rocked inside her. Nothing ever felt as fucking good as being inside my mate, her body clenched around my cock.

I collapsed on top of her my forearms taking my weight so I didn't crush her beneath me. We lay there, bodies fused, sweat cooling on our skin. I kissed her back, her neck, anywhere I could reach. When my knot finally softened, I pulled out and went into the bathroom to soak a washcloth in steaming hot water. I came back and cleaned her gently and then cradled her to my body.

"I love you, bluebonnet." I whispered in her ear.

She looked up at me with those same blue eyes and grinned. "I love you, Jess."

The alarm went off at 2:45 a.m. I rolled out of bed, showered, dressed in black jeans and a long-sleeve tee. Harper showered after, slicked her hair back in a ponytail, and dressed in simple travel clothes: jeans, a tee, running shoes. She wore no makeup, but she didn't need it.

We ate a quick breakfast of toast and black coffee. She said little, but I could see the steel had returned to her spine.

At 3:30, we were out the door. The pack house van was waiting, Gunner at the wheel, Doc riding shotgun. We tossed our bags in the back, then climbed in. The van was silent except for the hum of tires on the highway.

Gunner pulled into the private hangar with five minutes to spare. The Gulfstream sat on the tarmac, lights on, engines ready. Wrecker and Parker were already there, arms crossed, bags at their feet. Bronc and Juliet were there too for the send-off.

We got out, shouldered our gear, and met the others at the steps. Parker hugged Harper tight, then whispered something in her ear that made her laugh.

Bronc pulled me aside. "Bring them home," he said.

I nodded. "Count on it."

He clapped my shoulder, hard. "You always were the best at bringing people home."

We climbed the steps, took our seats, and buckled in. As the engines spooled up, I reached over and took Harper's hand, squeezing it until she looked at me.

"We'll be okay," I said.

She squeezed back. "I believe you."

The plane rolled down the runway, gathering speed. As it lifted off, I looked out at the dark Texas sky, the lights of Dairyville shrinking behind us.

CHAPTER 21

Harper

I'd never flown private before, but I guess if you're running a paramilitary rescue mission in Europe, you might as well do it in style.

King Rafe's Gulfstream G7000 was less an airplane and more a horizontal skyscraper: all panoramic windows, leather upholstery so soft it felt like memory foam, and hand-stitched wool rugs underfoot. The first step inside, I almost tripped over my own shadow, stunned by the glare from the overheads bouncing off the polished walnut. I'd grown up with luxury; flown first class, the works. But this; this was something completely different. Here, two flight attendants stalked the aisle like a pair of magazine models: both six-three, both wearing white shirts so tight across the shoulders it looked painted on. Male shifters. They had the bored confidence of men who took zero shit from anybody. I appreciated that Rafe wanted to take care of the people on this flight both protection and otherwise.

Jess and I took the seats at the back of the main cabin, a window booth set a little apart from the rest. He looked completely at home, legs stretched in the aisle, his arm draped over the seat-back. The only sign of tension was the way his thumb kept tracing the inside of my wrist, a tiny, circular motion over the skin. He kept his eyes on the door until the last of our crew was on board, then nodded to the taller flight attendant, who responded with a crisp "Roger that, sir," and vanished behind the galley curtain.

Across from us, Wrecker and Parker sat next to each other, Parker's laptop balanced on her knees, Wrecker's own device open on the tray. Their heads bent together, pale and dark, a study in opposites. Parker was talking so fast her words tripped over each other, but her fingers flew even faster, tapping out code or maybe just nervous energy. Wrecker grunted occasionally, low and deep, but didn't look up from his screen.

Toward the front, Doc and Big Papa had commandeered the only table in the cabin. Doc had a binder open, cross-referencing a stack of dossiers, his glasses slipping down his nose as he read. Papa just sat, arms folded, a serene mountain of muscle and patience, eyes closed like he was already forty thousand feet up and dreaming of the landing.

The last to board was Gwen, and even in this zoo of power, she was hard to miss. Barely five feet tall, maybe a hundred pounds in heels, with white-blonde hair twisted into a perfect chignon. She wore an unstruc-tured navy suit; the pants cropped at the ankle to show off blue suede pumps. She carried a clutch and a slim leather satchel, not a weapon in sight. The minute she cleared the cabin threshold, the temperature dropped ten degrees. I felt the goosebumps on my neck before she'd even made it to her seat.

She smiled at us, a little too wide, and slid into a single seat two rows up, nearest the galley door. "Wolfsbane, right?" She called, glancing at Jess. "You always sit where you can see the exits. How delightfully retro!"

He gave her nothing but a nod. She winked and settled in, crossing her legs and tucking her bag under the seat. I tried not to stare, but failed. Even at rest, Gwen hummed with a strange, glassy energy, like her whole body was two seconds away from snapping into a thousand splinters.

The engines spooled up, a vibration that worked its way through my sneakers and up into my jaw. I looked out the window, watched the tarmac flicker past, the glow of Amarillo's runway lights retreating in a blur. Jess leaned in, his lips close to my ear. "Relax," he said, a whisper only for me. "No one here wants to see you fall."

"Easy for you to say," I muttered. "You've done this a hundred times."

He squeezed my hand, the calluses rough against my palm. "You've survived worse than this."

I had.

The jet rocketed down the runway, the takeoff so smooth I barely felt the nose lift. The world outside went black, then blue, then nothing at all. Inside, the lights dimmed to a moody, cinema-level glow. The flight attendants made their first pass, carrying a tray of white porcelain cups and a glass carafe of coffee so strong I could smell it from ten feet away. The taller one—Nils, according to his nameplate—smiled at me and poured, not a drop spilled.

"Cream? Sugar?" he offered, voice clipped and efficient.

"Both, please," I said, and he obliged, folding the paper-wrapped sugar into the mug with the skill of a magician. I took a sip. It tasted of burnt molasses and adrenaline.

Beside me, Jess waved off the service, focused on his phone. He scrolled through encrypted messages, thumb flying. I peeked at the screen and caught a list of logistics: safe houses, contact codes, gun runners in Lyon. It was less a rescue mission and more a small war.

I nursed my coffee and tried to get comfortable. The seat was impossibly soft, but my body wouldn't settle. Every few minutes, I checked on the others.

Wrecker and Parker argued about some digital dead-end, Parker's voice rising. "That's the difference between a real hacker and a script kiddie, Eli. If you'd just let me set the sniffer—"

"No." Wrecker's reply was a flat wall. "Last time you 'set the sniffer' you bricked the whole firewall for three hours. And then you crashed the pack's Netflix."

"Because you wouldn't give me admin—" She stopped herself, then started again, softer. "It won't happen again."

He grunted, but a corner of his mouth quirked. "I'll believe it when I see it."

I looked to the front, where Doc and Papa had gotten into a low-voiced conversation. Papa spoke first, a rumble like rolling thunder. "What's your read on the witch?"

Doc answered, calm as ever. "Powerful. Young, but not inexperienced. If she wanted us dead, she could do it a hundred ways without lifting a finger."

Papa nodded. "So we trust her?"

"No," Doc said. "But we need her more than she needs us."

I watched Gwen, wondering if she could hear them. She just sat, legs crossed, reading from a slim paperback whose cover was in Cyrillic. Her lips moved as she read, a silent incantation, or maybe just a nervous habit.

The cabin lights dimmed another notch, and outside, the sky stretched endless and dark. I sipped my coffee, then curled my legs under me, trying to force myself to relax. I reclined in my seat as Jess's hand found my knee and rested there, a silent anchor.

I closed my eyes. Sleep hovered at the edges, then fled. Every time I drifted, the darkness filled with images: the club in Houston, the feel of Steiner's eyes on me, the way Maltraz's claws had dug into my waist. And then, always, my sister's face, half-hidden behind a curtain of hair. I'd barely recognized her in the files: the old softness scrubbed away, replaced by something sharp and metallic.

What if she didn't want to be saved? What if we made it all the way to Paris and she just spat in my face? The fear settled under my ribs, cold and bright.

I opened my eyes and glanced around. No one was looking at me. Good. Maybe they'd think I was tougher than I really was.

Three hours into the flight, the attendants dimmed the lights entirely and moved through the cabin with water bottles and single-serve pastries. Parker had collapsed against Wrecker's side, feet in his lap, asleep and drooling. Wrecker didn't move, just scrolled on his phone, eyes bright in the faint glow.

Jess read something on his tablet, his free hand still wrapped around my thigh. His grip never slackened.

Gwen stood and padded silently to the rear bathroom. When she passed, she paused, her eyes on me. "You sleep yet?"

"Trying."

She crouched beside me, her perfume sweet and chemical. "Nerves?"

I nodded.

She smiled, and for a second she looked much younger, almost my age. "Don't worry. When we land, I'll walk you through the next bit. It'll be like a school field trip, but with guns."

"Is that supposed to make me feel better?"

Her smile widened, flashing even white teeth. "No. But it's honest. We need you sharp. No one else can get your sister to trust us."

I swallowed, not trusting myself to speak.

She straightened and turned to Jess. "Wake time is in ninety minutes. Customs will be tight, but I'll shield you until the cars are ready."

He nodded. "Appreciate it."

She vanished into the bathroom, and I let out a deep sigh.

Jess set his tablet down and looked at me. "You okay?"

I shrugged. "Nah, but I'll fake it."

He smiled, the rare, crooked one. "Faking it is how the best get through."

"Is that how you do it?"

His hand slid higher, fingers pressing into the muscle of my thigh. "I used to. Now I just want to get you out alive."

I turned and watched the sky outside. It was pitch black, but the window reflected us: two scared animals, bracing for whatever came next.

I thought about Paris. I thought about the way they said my mother and Brie had made a life, even if it was only a shadow of one. I thought about the men who were coming to kill us, and the demon who wanted to buy my sister as a substitute for me. The world felt so much smaller up here, and the stakes so much larger.

I leaned into Jess and let myself hope, just for a second, that maybe the people who'd risked everything to bring me this far actually knew what they were doing.

But hope was dangerous. It was the thing that got you killed.

So instead, I clung to the familiar: the smell of jet fuel, the weight of Jess's hand on my body, the faint hum of voices in the dark.

Somewhere over the Atlantic, I finally drifted off. I dreamed of wolves in the snow, howling at a moon they could never reach.

And in the dream, I ran with them beside a beautiful light brown wolf with dark knowing eyes.

The wheels hit French tarmac with a jolt that shook me from the dream. Outside, the lights of Le Bourget–Seine-Saint-Denis glared through a curtain of rain, streaking the glass with long, twitching veins of water. We'd crossed an ocean, and still the world looked the same: wet, cold, and dark.

The flight attendants snapped back into motion, serving bottled water and packages of those dry European biscuits that shatter into sugar dust the second you bite them. I ignored both, pressing my forehead to the window, watching the plane taxi past the FBO and out to a cluster of black SUVs parked at the far end of the lot. All around, puddles caught the blue strobe of police lights. It made the whole runway shimmer, a migraine made physical.

Jess put a hand on my knee, squeezing once. I looked down and realized I'd been bouncing my leg hard enough to make the tray table rattle. Across the aisle, Wrecker yawned, stretching his arms over his head, then leaned in and muttered something to Parker. She rolled her eyes, but the tension in her jaw said everything. Up front, Doc was already on his feet, sliding files back into his briefcase, while Papa ran a palm over his beard and cracked his neck.

I counted the seconds until the seatbelt sign blinked off. Gwen was the first up, zipping her jacket over a crisp white blouse. She checked her watch, then reached into her bag and pulled out a small glass vial—something pale green and thick, like melted Jell-O. She uncorked it, dabbed a drop onto each wrist, then massaged it into her skin with quick, practiced circles. Her lips moved as she did it, but I couldn't catch the words. Not a prayer, exactly. More like a password.

We filed down the aisle, bags slung over our shoulders. Jess walked ahead, flanked by Papa and Wrecker, all three moving with a confidence that might have fooled anyone who didn't know what they were up against. Parker trailed behind, hands jammed in her hoodie pocket, head down but eyes flickering everywhere. I stuck close to Gwen, who barely came up to my chin, but had the presence of a full-grown wolf.

We hit the bottom of the stairs, and the cold smacked me in the teeth. Paris in spring: I'd imagined some faded movie postcard, but in reality it felt like the kind of wind that cuts straight through clothes and into bone. I pulled my jacket tighter, grateful I'd thought to pack it on top when I'd changed clothes when we'd gathered our bags. Black leggings, black turtleneck, the boots Jess bought for me at the Dairyville feed store—nothing fancy, but enough to make me look like I belonged in the city. Or at least, like I hadn't just crawled out of a bunker.

FBO handlers in matching gray jackets rolled up with luggage carts. I watched as they loaded the gear, handling each case with a reverence that bordered on the religious. Gwen hovered over them, her hands folded, lips moving faster now. When one of the handlers reached for the heavy weapons case—the one that held enough firepower to flatten a city block—she caught his wrist, fingers barely grazing the latch.

"Allow me," she said, her accent as smooth as honey but with a hard edge behind it.

The man stepped back, eyes glassy. She pressed her palm to the case, and for a split second, I felt the world stutter. The air thickened; the rain slowed. Everything in the periphery blurred, like a camera lens knocked out of focus. I blinked, and when my vision cleared, the handlers were loading what looked like ordinary hard-shell suitcases. The weapons case had vanished, replaced by a battered Samsonite plastered with airline stickers.

I looked at Jess. "Did you—"

He nodded. "That's the veil. Only works on humans and shifters allowed to see it. To us, it looks normal. To them, it's just luggage."

I stared at the handlers, who went about their work, oblivious to the fact that they were pushing enough armament to start a coup. My skin prickled.

"Does it work on cameras?" I asked.

Parker answered a few steps behind. "If the witch is good, yeah. Even the digital stuff shows what she wants it to show. But it's not perfect. Stronger magic can break it, and so can the right tech."

"So we're not actually invisible."

Wrecker snorted. "We never are. Best you can hope for is to be overlooked."

A line of customs officers appeared, waving us toward the VIP entrance. The lead officer wore a sleek gray suit, his badge gleaming under the fluorescent overhang. He scanned our group with the disinterest of someone used to high-rollers and celebrities. Still, my pulse jumped when he locked eyes with Jess, then with Gwen.

"Bienvenue à Paris," he said. "Your paperwork, please."

Gwen stepped forward, produced a sheaf of documents, and handed them over. The officer leafed through, pausing to inspect a pair of blue passports, then the stack of letters on Iron Valor letterhead. He lingered on the weapons permits for a beat too long, then looked up.

"Business or pleasure?" he asked in English this time.

"Business," Jess answered. "We're here on a private security contract. Clients are already at the hotel."

The officer grunted, then glanced at Gwen. She flashed a dazzling smile. "My employer is very serious about safety," she said. "Especially for his American guests."

He handed back the papers. "You'll find Paris to be very... interesting these days. I recommend you avoid the Champs-Élysées after dark."

Jess smiled, a wolf baring its teeth. "We'll keep that in mind."

The officer waved us through. We moved as a single unit, the way packs do when the world feels hostile. The luggage carts were waiting, each loaded with duffel bags and cases, the witch's charm holding strong. Jess grabbed the largest and motioned for me to follow.

The SUVs sat idling on the far side of the lot. Three of them, all black, all identical. The drivers wore gloves, faces obscured by the gloom. Jess opened the rear door, then turned to me. "Stay close," he said. "This is the hard part."

Inside, the seats were cold leather, and the air smelled of air freshener. Gwen slid in up front, beside the driver. Jess and I took the middle row, with Wrecker, Parker, and Papa crammed in the back. Doc took the shotgun seat in the second vehicle, barking instructions into his phone.

For a minute, no one spoke. The city flashed by outside: streetlights, skeletal trees, a tangle of overpasses painted with graffiti. I saw a kid on a bike, weaving through traffic, and wondered if he had any idea what was rolling past him in the night.

Gwen turned in her seat, looking at me. "You okay?"

I nodded, but she frowned. "You need to breathe. Hyperventilating makes you useless."

I sucked in a lungful of air, held it, then let it out slow. It helped a little.

The convoy pulled to a stop at the edge of the customs lot. Another set of agents waited, one of them carrying a clipboard. He made a show of counting the cases, then frowned.

"There is an error," he said, flipping the page. "This crate is not on the manifest."

He pointed to the big black Samsonite—our magic weapons case. My heart skipped.

"It's just audio-visual equipment," Gwen said, voice bored. "For a meeting. The client asked us to bring it last minute."

The agent considered, then reached for the latch. For a second, my whole body went cold. If he opened it and saw what was inside...

Gwen's hand moved so fast I barely saw it. She tapped her wrist, just once. The agent blinked, stepped back, and looked at his clipboard again.

"Ah," he said. "There is a correction. You may proceed."

Jess exhaled, the tension draining from his shoulders. I glanced at him, and for the first time, I saw real fear in his eyes. Not for himself, but for all of us.

We rolled past the checkpoint, then out into the wet Paris night. The cars merged with the traffic, headlights painting the world in strobes.

Only when we were a mile from the airport did anyone speak.

"That was too close," Wrecker muttered.

Parker shivered. "Witches. Fucking terrifying."

Gwen smiled, catching my eye in the rearview. "Magic is just a trick. You get used to it."

I watched the city flicker past, each building a blur, every street a maze. Even with all the power in this car, I'd never felt smaller.

The rain kept falling, soft and relentless. I wondered how many eyes were already on us, how many traps had been set.

In that moment, I realized: the only thing scarier than being seen was being truly invisible. Because then, nobody would ever come looking for you.

And in this city, that was the easiest way to disappear.

We followed the lead car through the periphery of Paris, headlights cutting ribbons through the rain, every intersection marked by the flicker of yellow streetlamps and the sudden, glimmering eyes of city cats perched on stoops. The soundproof glass made the world feel far away—a silent movie, all glow and shadow and the streaks of water that mapped every curve in the street.

Gwen's outline glowed blue whenever we crossed beneath a streetlight. She'd anchored something magical to the dashboard, a tiny rune-scarred stone wedged behind the coin holder. Every time we slowed at a checkpoint or roundabout, her fingers brushed it, lips moving in a silent chant, keeping the veil around our convoy tight. Nobody looked twice, even when we double-parked on the Rue de Rivoli and a city cop walked right past our bumper. Maybe it was the magic, or maybe it was Paris being Paris—indifferent, eternal, and tired of its own drama.

The city was more beautiful than I'd expected. Not the cold, touristic grandeur of the postcards, but an intimacy: the way the rain pooled gold beneath the lamps, the way bakery lights burned behind fogged windows, the way each building wore its centuries like a comfortable old coat. Even the people looked better here—every umbrella a fashion statement, every sidewalk argument a scene from a movie I could never quite translate. I watched the world slide by and wondered if, in another life, I might have lived here. Danced here.

I thought of Aspen suddenly. "Papa, you need to bring Aspen here when this madness is over. If anyone would love this place, it would be her."

I looked over my shoulder and saw the face of a man rapturously in love with his mate. "There is no question but that my Sunshine would find herself in heaven in the bakeries here. It's keeping Oscar hidden away that would be the challenge." He gave a small laugh that we all shared. That brief moment of levity was so needed at that moment. But that's what Aspen did. She brought happiness. I hoped I could be a little like her someday. Jess squeezed my hand.

Thirty minutes later, the convoy snaked around a block-long park and stopped at the entrance to our hotel. Not just any hotel, but the Hôtel de la Reine: a five-star palace in the 2nd arrondissement, all carved limestone and black wrought-iron balconies, glowing like a beacon in the gloom. The awning was striped navy and cream, the kind of touch that made my heart skip with nostalgia for things I'd never actually had. Jess leaned in, voice low.

"You ever been someplace like this?" he asked.

I shook my head, unable to hide my awe. "I've stayed in five-star hotels with my family before, but *this* is beyond."

"Don't worry," he said. "We'll come back sometime when we can actually enjoy it."

The doors opened in sequence; the drivers popping out to help with the bags. Gwen met us at the curb, her blue pumps soaked but her smile bright as ever.

"First priority is inside. I'll check the perimeter. Parker, you're on comms with Wrecker. The rest of you—upstairs, low profile."

Even in English, the words came out like orders barked on a drill field. It was strangely comforting.

We followed the valets in, our boots squeaking on the marble. The lobby was a dream: two stories of crystal and gold leaf, a fireplace as big as a Volkswagen, and the air thick with the scent of peonies and whatever expensive cleaning fluid the French used to polish centuries of secrets. For a second, I almost forgot why we were here.

The night manager appeared, a wisp of a man in a silk suit, his face an unreadable mask of efficiency. He spoke rapid French with Gwen, glancing at the rest of us only when absolutely necessary. He pointed us toward the private elevator at the end of the hall.

In the glass, I caught our reflection: six shadows, moving as one. Even Wrecker, who could never pass for anything but dangerous, managed to look like just another American tourist with too much gym time and not enough sense. I pressed close to Jess, who kept one arm braced protectively at my back.

The elevator ride was slow, old gears grinding up through the levels. We spilled out onto the penthouse floor, where the suite door opened at Gwen's touch. Inside, the suite was absurd: three bedrooms, each with its own velvet-draped balcony; a kitchen stocked with enough wine and cheese to feed a small army; a living room with a view of the Eiffel Tower, lit up like a promise. The moment the door latched, the spell broke. Everyone went to work.

Parker and Wrecker set up laptops at the dining table, unzipping cases and laying out an arsenal of gadgets. Papa disappeared into the kitchen and returned with six tumblers and a bottle of whisky, pouring two fingers for everyone, no questions asked. Doc checked all the windows, running a hand along the frames, then set up a med kit by the fireplace.

Jess pulled me aside into the hush of the master bedroom. "You okay?" he asked, searching my face.

"My legs are shaking," I admitted.

He smiled, softening. "If they weren't, I'd be worried. We did good tonight. Tomorrow is what matters."

I nodded. I felt confident next to him; like I was more powerful than I was alone.

He held me for a minute, his chin resting on my head, then kissed my hair and guided me back to the main room. Papa handed me a glass. I took it, letting the whisky burn a line down my throat.

Through the balcony doors, the city glimmered. I could see the lights of Montmartre, and I imagined my sister somewhere out there, maybe even seeing the same sky. Maybe feeling the same fear.

We gathered around the table, each of us silent, waiting for Gwen to report back. I drank my whisky and let the warmth spread through me, chasing away the last of the cold.

After ten minutes, the suite phone buzzed. Jess answered, listened, then hung up. "Clear for now," he said. "No tails. We hold here until dawn, then Gwen takes us to the rendezvous."

I nodded. I was so tired I could barely keep my eyes open, but the determination in my chest burned hotter than ever. I would find my family. I would get them out. Nothing else mattered.

The others drifted off to their rooms in ones and twos. Jess stayed beside me on the couch, arms wrapped tight around my waist. We watched the city together, neither of us speaking.

Somewhere out there, my sister and mother were waiting. And this time, I would not let them go.

We made it back to our beautiful bedroom suite where I showered off the day's travel and dressed in my comfortable flannel pants and sweatshirt. Jess pulled me to his chest when we made it to the bed. Sleep came easy and dreamless. The only thing I carried into the dark was hope.

Chapter 22

Arsenal

I woke to the silence of the Paris penthouse, the sky still black outside the cathedral-height windows, and for a moment, I'd almost forgotten where I was. The suite's air hung heavy with last night's cologne of jet lag, city rain, and suppressed fear. I padded barefoot through the hushed corridors, shirtless, scars and all, straight to the kitchen and the squat Italian espresso machine, a brushed-chrome cannon that hissed and gurgled with every shot.

By my second cup, I felt human; well, as human as I *was*. By the third, I was a goddamn machine.

The penthouse had three bedrooms—Harper was dead asleep in ours, her hair a lion's mane spilled across white linen—but I needed a table, a big one, with good sight lines and bad chairs. I found it in the glass-walled "library" off the main hall: a twelve-seat slab of reclaimed oak, flanked by shelves of unread hardbacks and a disused wet bar. I dragged in a stack of tourist maps, the latest intel from Rafe's Birmingham office, and a roll of Paris street grid printouts that Wrecker and Parker had marked up on the flight. Every marker was a wound: blue for safe houses, and green for likely routes. Our last intel had put Brie and Nanette with the Renault Pack. Figuring that remained the same, we'd marked that area in red. By the time the sun edged over the Seine, I had the city's skeleton sketched in front of me like a murder board.

At 6:04, Wrecker stomped in, already in jeans and a gray tee, hair still wet from the shower. He poured himself a mug, ignored the little cup the Italians wanted you to use, and leaned over my shoulder. "You sleep?" he asked.

"Some." I flicked the topmost printout. "You see this?"

He did. "Renaults moved their base of operations from the outskirts to right here." He pointed at the block just west of La Défense. "That's a change. They usually keep a low profile in suburbia."

"Means they're either scared, or showing off."

Wrecker grunted, then thumbed through his phone. "Got word from Marcel. They're on their way. Bringing the new guy."

"He solid?"

"Rafe says he's ex-Legion. Wolf and a half."

I liked the sound of that.

Behind us, I heard the faint snap of slippers on hardwood. Parker drifted in, this time in an "In My Smut Era" hoodie, and yoga pants. Her face was all sharp planes and half-lidded electric blue eyes, but she moved like she'd never slept at all. She surveyed the table, snagged a mug for herself, and perched on the edge of a side chair.

"This is it?" she said, gesturing at the maps.

"Start here. Build out as we get eyes," I told her. "We're looking for patterns."

She nodded, clicking on her phone, scanning for any overnight pings. "Witch is still asleep?" She asked, meaning Gwen.

"Not for long," Wrecker said. "She's got a hard-on for morning rituals."

"Gross," Parker deadpanned.

At 6:13, the secure phone buzzed. I answered, voice low. "Arsenal."

A half-second delay, then a baritone with a hint of Marseille: "This is Marcel. We are downstairs."

"Come up. Room's open." I killed the call, then looked at Wrecker. "He said 'we.'"

"They always move in pairs. Etienne's the backup."

"Fine by me."

I heard the lock cycle and went to the door. The first thing you noticed about Marcel and Etienne was that they didn't look like wolves, not at first glance. Marcel wore a black windbreaker over a suit that screamed unlicensed security, and his hair was shaved on the sides with the top swept back and slicked down. Etienne was shorter, stockier, with an old rugby player's nose and a faded tattoo that ran from the base of his left ear to the edge of his jaw. Both moved with the loose, dangerous grace of men who'd broken a lot of bones in their lives, most of them not their own.

Marcel carried a battered messenger bag. He offered a hand, and when I shook it, I saw the old Legion scar across his palm. "Arsenal," he said, voice level. "You look like your reputation."

"Thanks. Coffee's in the kitchen. We're in the library."

He nodded to Etienne, who peeled off, probably to sweep the suite. Bronc would have approved.

We sat around the slab of a table, Wrecker and Parker on one side, me and Marcel opposite. Marcel unrolled a tube of blueprints, layering them over my tourist maps, and we got to work.

"King Rafe briefed you?" I asked.

"Yes. The girl and her mother are living with Renault pack, in Bougival. Two weeks now."

I glanced at Parker, who tapped her phone. "Confirms with what we got from Gwen's contacts."

"Renaults run the local territory like a fortress," Marcel said. "But it is not impenetrable. We have eyes on three blocks, and a friendly bakery two doors down."

I could almost see Aspen's face light up. "What's the move?" I asked.

Marcel shrugged. "It depends. You want to pull the girl now, or wait for opportunity?"

"Depends on who's watching," I said. "Any sign Steiner's got teams in the city?"

"No. But he has connections. The local police are easy to buy, and if he wants to move muscle, it'll be mercs. Maybe Eastern European. Maybe local. But they do not stand out."

"Great," Parker muttered. "Everybody's invisible except us."

That stung a little, but she was right. We were the only Americans in this equation, and I hated being the loudest color on the board.

We worked through the next hour, mapping likely times for the Renault pack to move as a group—early morning runs, the weekly Friday marché, some nightclubs along the Seine where the young ones preened and fought. Etienne came in, nodded once, and sat at the far end, hands folded. Watchful.

At 7:22, Harper arrived. She wore leggings, an old Army sweatshirt, and her hair pulled back so tight it looked like a golden whip. She smiled at me, then at Marcel. "Bonjour," she said, her accent flawless.

Marcel softened instantly. "Bonjour, mademoiselle."

Wrecker grinned behind his mug.

I introduced her, then caught her up: "They're in Bougival. Renault stronghold."

She blinked, then sat hard, staring at the maps. "Bougival?"

Marcel nodded. "You know it?"

"Familiar. My mother spoke of it. I'd forgotten," Harper said. "It's famous for Impressionist painters. Renoir, Monet, Sisley—they all lived there at some point. There's a little island on the river. Mom talked about it. Said it's some place we'd all need to visit someday." Her voice went soft. "She'd say, 'If I ever got the chance, I'd want to go where the colors blend into magic.'"

Something cold rolled down my back.

"That would be it," Marcel said, catching my glance. "They live on the main road. She paints most days. The daughter—your sister—studies art at the Atelier du Château de Bougival. Uses the name Gemma."

Harper gave a laugh and said, "That was the name of our cat growing up."

She traced her fingertip along the river on the map. "I can just see them there. They'd love shopping in small stores and stopping at small cafes."

Marcel checked his phone, then pointed at the same spot. "You're correct about that. They stop at a small cafe called La Palette on Thursdays. Usually mid-morning."

Parker looked at me. "That's tomorrow."

I nodded. "We'll want eyes on it."

Wrecker cracked his knuckles. "Who's handling the pull?"

Marcel shrugged. "We can do it, or you can. But if you want to keep it quiet, best way is to isolate one at a time."

"Mom first," Harper said, and everyone looked at her.

"She'll trust me. If I come in heavy, she'll think I'm in trouble. She always said, 'Never bring trouble to the doorstep, but if you have to, make sure you close the door behind you.'"

Marcel smiled. "She is very French."

Harper nodded, but her eyes were hard. "Brie won't listen to me if she believes one of the Renault boys is courting her. I need to get to Mom first. If she believes I'm not in danger, she'll help."

I felt pride bloom in my chest, a thing so raw it almost hurt. Harper saw the board as well as any of us.

Marcel passed her a manila folder. Inside were a dozen candid photos, taken from across streets, through cafe windows, at the market. Nanette and Brie, side by side. Brie was taller now, hair cut in a stylish bob, but her eyes were pure Lawson: the kind that could start a fire in a snowstorm.

Harper took a long time with the photos. "Is she happy?" She asked, not looking up.

Marcel said nothing.

I answered for him. "She's safe for now. That's all we know."

She nodded, sliding the photos back. "Then we keep it that way."

The rest of the meeting was about logistics. Wrecker and Etienne would run surveillance from the cafe, using a burner phone with a direct uplink to the penthouse. Parker would monitor local comms and troll the darknet for any sign Steiner's men had landed. Marcel would coordinate with the bakery for an emergency fallback, just in case. I would escort Harper and watch her back. Always.

When the briefing broke, the world was waking up outside: traffic horns, bakery scents, the high song of a street cleaner. Parker drifted off to call Gunner in Dairyville and update him on the plan. Wrecker left to secure the hardware, and Etienne trailed him, silent as a rumor. I poured a fourth coffee and sat at the window with Harper, watching the city come to life.

"You okay?" I asked.

She stared into her mug. "I will be. I just... I miss her, even though I'm angry."

I thought of my own brother, dead and gone for twenty years, and how every night I talked to him in my dreams. "She'll be glad to see you."

Harper snorted. "She'll be furious. But that's better than her being afraid."

I slid my hand over hers, anchor and lifeline. "We do this right, she'll never have to be."

We sat together until the sun made the river outside gleam, and for the first time since we'd landed, I felt the old pack magic: the sense that no matter what hunted us, we'd hunt it right back.

Let the world come for us. We were Iron Valor, and we'd built our home out of war.

We'd set the library up to handle our video conference, linked to secure servers in two countries. We'd patched in Bronc, Gunner, Juliet, and Aspen from Dairyville; Rafe and two of his guys from a secure site in Birmingham.

Bronc looked like he hadn't slept. His hair was spiked more silver than black, and the blue in his eyes shone bright and clear. Gunner was beside him, boots up on the credenza, face slack but eyes sharp. Juliet perched at the edge of the table, hands folded over her belly. Aspen stood a little behind, arms wrapped around herself, a smile softening the lines of her face even though it had to be past midnight in Texas. She wore a bright orange top with white polka dots, her hair piled high in a messy bun. Oscar sat perched on her shoulder. He wore an orange cravat with his navy blazer and plaid vest.

Harper and I sat together, side by side; my hand never left hers. Parker ran the AV from the head of the table, with Wrecker pacing behind her, always moving, always needing to burn off his pent up energy that was more than the massive amounts of caffeine he consumed.

Marcel and Etienne joined us, bringing a whiff of Gauloise cigarettes and expensive deodorant. The air in the room felt like an electrical storm trapped in a box.

Bronc started the call. "Let's get to it. I want to hear it from the boots on the ground."

I outlined the Bougival setup—how the Renaults had shifted their center of gravity. Marcel confirmed: "The Renault Pack is dirty. They have moved girls—some wolf, some not—through their territory for at least six months. It is not common, but enough to be noticed if you look."

Wrecker chimed in, "They're doing it for someone. We don't think it's just for local trade."

Juliet cut in. "Who's paying them?"

"Steiner," Parker said, not even looking up from her tablet. "We've traced three wire transfers from a shell in Luxembourg that maps to his operations in Houston."

Wrecker's voice rang out as he stopped his pacing. "Seems they use the art school to launder cash. And to hide the girls for a night or two before moving them."

Rafe, all polished Southern steel, leaned in to his camera. "So, you have a plan for extraction? I'd caution you that Steiner hasn't made a move yet because he's waiting for you to expose yourselves. He knows you're coming. And it's his plan to stop you."

A muscle ticked in my jaw. "He can try."

Bronc raised a finger. "Arsenal, what's your move?"

"We go after Nanette first. She's the linchpin. If we convince her of the danger, Brie follows. But we have to do it where Renault enforcers won't try to snatch us."

Harper looked up at the screen. "The only place she'll trust me is at the café or nearby museum. If I show up at the house, they'll lock it down."

Gunner finally spoke, slow as ever. "You want to use Harper as bait?"

The idea sent a shiver down my spine. "No. We use her as the messenger. She goes in, draws out Nanette, we cover from outside."

Juliet's eyes never left the camera. "That's bait, sugar."

I growled—an actual, low, throat-rumble. "No. She is not bait. We do not dangle my mate in front of a trafficking pack and hope for the best. That is not the play."

Bronc's voice was a glacier. "Stand down, Arsenal."

I glared, but nodded. I would never challenge my Alpha on open comms, but goddamn if I didn't want to.

He softened. "She's the only shot we have at making this work. If there were another way, we'd take it."

Juliet offered, "We send two shadows with her. Even if the Renaults clock it, they won't risk a public scene. Paris packs still have rules, even if they don't have morals."

Aspen nodded. "She's right. If you can get Nanette to trust you for ten minutes, that's all it will take."

Rafe looked at Marcel. "You trust your team to pull this off?"

Marcel didn't blink. "We are the best."

Wrecker stopped pacing long enough to add, "We have weapons, comms, escape routes mapped. We're not amateurs."

Bronc's eyes bore into mine. "Then it's settled. Tomorrow at 0900, you make contact. If anything feels off, you pull out. No heroics."

I held his gaze. "Understood."

Juliet asked, "Harper, are you good with this?"

Harper's voice was confident. "Better than good. They're the only family I have left, and I'll be damned if I let Brie wind up where I'd been."

Aspen's voice came soft as sunlight, sweet as pie. "You're braver than anyone here, honey. You go and fight for your little family. We'll be prayin' for you." Her Georgia accent seeped through her words.

Parker looked worried for a moment. I saw her bite her lip; then reset her game face.

Bronc wrapped it up. "Full debrief at 1200. We'll be waiting on the call. Make us proud."

The call clicked off. The room went silent except for the white noise of the Paris rain on the balcony windows.

I squeezed Harper's hand so tight I thought I'd snap bone. "You don't have to do this," I said, voice only for her.

She smiled, tired but real. "I'm the only one who can."

Parker closed her laptop with a little snap. "We got this," she said. "If it goes bad, I'll hack every camera in the arrondissement and find you myself."

Wrecker grunted. "Or we just go in and kill everyone."

Marcel actually laughed at that. "I like this one," he said.

I didn't want to laugh. I wanted to rip the city in half, pull the pack out by the roots, and take Harper somewhere nobody could ever find us again. But that was a luxury we didn't have.

For now, we were wolves in the middle of the hunt. And nothing in Paris would stop us from getting what was ours.

The rest of the day vanished in a blur of dry runs and gear checks, but the real test was the next morning. We rolled out of the hotel just after seven, the whole crew running on espresso and spite. Gwen rode shotgun in the lead SUV, her hair in a low twist, lips bare, eyes hidden behind mirrored glasses. She'd spelled the car herself—a glass pebble zip-tied to the rear-view, layered with two kinds of blood and a word I didn't recognize. The charm supposedly scrubbed our scent, our auras, and even our luck from anyone with supernatural leanings.

We dressed the part: jeans, windbreakers, sneakers, nothing that would draw a second look. Wrecker and Etienne went ahead on foot, posing as French joggers in matching neon. Parker, Marcel, and I took the "civilian" route, with Harper on my arm in an old leather jacket and her hair pulled up in a loose bun, sunglasses way too big for her face. She looked exactly like a tourist, except for the way her hand kept trembling on my elbow.

The drive from Paris to Bougival was short—a little over thirty minutes—but it felt like a migration. The city gave way to suburbs, then to the thick tree line and riverside sprawl that had lured painters for two centuries. We passed an old iron bridge, then a block of cafes with terrace seating and battered awnings in faded reds and greens. The rain had stopped, but everything sparkled with the washed-clean light you only got in European spring.

The town was beautiful in a way that made me long for the ability to wrap Harper up and take her sightseeing: stone streets, a slow blue river, the hills dotted with grand old houses clinging to their ledges like stubborn ghosts. The Renault stronghold was a massive manse up on the rise, set back from the main drag by a stone wall and a tangle of hydrangeas that looked half-wild. The windows were shuttered, but two sentries leaned against a Renault-blue delivery van, chatting over a cigarette and watching the street with the bored contempt of men who didn't expect trouble.

Parker whispered through the comms: "Two on the south gate. No movement from the east. Target's not on site—repeat, target's not on site. Proceed to point B."

We followed the plan. Harper and I strolled down to the river, stopping to admire the paint-flaked rowboats and the first flush of pink in the magnolias. A few minutes later, we doubled back, crossed the avenue, and made for the little art gallery wedged between a bakery and a pharmacy. Parker and Marcel peeled off, loitering at a café terrace two doors down, doing a good job pretending not to watch.

The gallery's sign was hand-lettered, a curling script that probably hadn't been updated since before the last world war. Inside, the space was all white walls and bare light, the floors echoing every step. Five or six people milled about, mostly retirees with expensive scarves and bad posture, but one stood out: a slender woman with pale hair, gathered in a loose chignon. She wore a navy cashmere sweater and a cream skirt, her back ramrod straight as she studied a small landscape on the far wall.

Harper froze when she saw her. The old ballet reflexes kicked in—she snapped her chin up, shoulders back, every inch of her body suddenly an exclamation point.

I leaned close, voice low. "Remember, we just make initial contact today. Plant the seed. Nothing more."

She nodded. "Copy."

We drifted through the gallery, pausing at a few pieces. I kept my eyes on the room, counting exits, watching the faces. No Renault muscle inside. One clerk behind the counter, an old man in round glasses, reading the sports pages and not giving a damn about the customers.

When we got within six feet of the target, Harper started humming—just a little, under her breath. A tune I couldn't name, but it was familiar. I guessed it was a song she had danced to once upon a time. The sound, barely a thread, carried to the woman in the sweater. She stilled, then slowly turned.

It was like watching Nanette age in reverse. In the space of a heartbeat, I saw the girl she must have been at fifteen, then the mother she'd become, then the woman who'd lost everything and kept going, anyway.

Nanette's eyes swept the room, not stopping on us. She finished the rotation, then returned to her painting, but her hand had gone white-knuckled on the clutch she carried.

Harper moved closer, this time letting her voice carry just a little: "A demi-plié, then a stretch, then the first note from Mr. Tchakovsky. Always in that order."

Nanette's head jerked. For a second, I saw terror, then calculation, then something that almost looked like hope. She didn't turn, but spoke, voice as delicate as spun glass.

"You shouldn't be here," she said, in perfect English.

Harper swallowed. "Neither should you."

Nanette's posture didn't shift, but her fingers danced a nervous rhythm on the bag. "How did you find us?"

Harper offered a tiny shrug. "Mom, we knew you'd come to the paintings. You always did."

That cracked her a little. Nanette's eyes shone, just for a moment, then the mask slid back into place. "Is it just you?"

Harper lied without a flinch. "Just me right now."

Nanette turned finally, her gaze pinning Harper. The resemblance was uncanny: same jaw, same arched brow, same soft eyes.

"You're safe?" she asked, the words a dare.

"I am now. I got away."

Nanette's smile was awash with relief. "You always were better at running than me."

Harper stepped closer. I drifted left, putting myself between them and the rest of the gallery, just in case. "Mom, we have to talk. It's important."

A flicker of doubt crossed Nanette's face. "Is he here? The monster?"

Harper shook her head. "No. He's not."

Nanette looked like she wanted to believe it, but couldn't. She exhaled through her nose. "We can't talk here. There are eyes everywhere."

I caught the shift in her stance: fight-or-flight, the old prey animal hard-wired to survive at any cost. "Where?" I asked, keeping my voice gentle.

She looked at me, really looked, then at Harper. "You trust him?"

"With my life," Harper said, and I felt that land in my chest like a hammer.

Nanette nodded once. "There's a park. Behind the bakery. It's quiet this time of day."

"Lead the way," I said.

We waited until she left, gave it a five-minute lag, then followed. Outside, the rain had turned to mist, dappling the brick and making the world feel smaller, more intimate. We turned at the bakery, then down a narrow alley to a walled garden. It was empty except for three iron benches and a broken statue of a nymph, worn smooth by a century of hands.

Nanette was waiting at the far end. She didn't sit. She just stood, arms folded, her bag clutched so hard the strap might snap.

Harper hung back, then finally said: "I need your help, Mom. I need to know where Brie is. She's in danger."

Nanette looked away. "She's not herself. She's... she thinks she's in love."

Harper didn't blink. "Is he Renault?"

A tight nod.

I stepped in, voice calm. "We're not here to make trouble for her. We just want to get her safe, and you too."

Nanette's laugh was bitter. "Safe? There's no such thing. Not in this world."

"There are places that are safer than others," I said.

She eyed me. "You found her again? Saved her? After all this time?"

"I did."

She considered that, and then her face softened. "She always loved you, you know. Even after..."

Harper cut her off. "It doesn't matter now. What matters is getting out."

Nanette's breath caught. "There's no way out for me."

"Mom, there is." Harper moved closer, close enough to touch. "If we leave now, they won't be able to stop us. I have people. I have friends. If Brie doesn't come with us, she'll wind up in a crate on a ship to Goddess knows where. Whoever she thinks loves her doesn't. If she won't believe me, make her believe you."

Nanette's eyes were full of tears. "Won't he come after you too?"

"Not this time," I said.

Nanette laughed, a little less bitter this time. "That's what I said, once."

Harper reached for her, and Nanette let herself be held. They stood like that for a long time, mother and daughter, both shaking. I kept watch, eyes scanning the street, the windows, every shadow.

Finally, Nanette broke away. "I'll bring Brie tomorrow, early, past the bridge. We'll have our easels and canvases set up to paint. If you don't meet us, I'll know this was a lie."

Harper nodded. "We'll be there."

Nanette hesitated. "I'm so glad you survived."

Harper smiled. "Me too."

They parted, and Nanette slipped away, a phantom in the morning mist.

We waited a full five before moving. Harper's face was a ruin of emotion—relief, guilt, terror, something like hope. She didn't let go of my arm the whole walk back to the car.

Inside, Gwen and Parker were waiting. Parker handed Harper a bottle of water, then watched as she drank half of it in one go.

"You did good," Parker said.

Harper wiped her eyes. "I'm so afraid she won't be able to convince Brie. Young girls in love can be really stupid."

Gwen's smile was warm. "They can. But you still must try."

I wrapped Harper in my arms, held her until she stopped shaking. "Look around, bluebonnet. You're not alone in this," I whispered, and meant every word.

Out the window, the river flowed on, carrying every secret Bougival ever had. The town was beautiful, but it was also a trap, and we had one more day to get her mom and sister out alive.

Let Steiner come. Let the Renaults try.

We were Iron Valor, and tomorrow, we were bringing the family home.

CHAPTER 23

Harper

The library in the penthouse wasn't really a library, more a shrine to unread books and oversized armchairs. At midnight, it felt like a train station at the end of the world: silent, cold, with every surface made for people who didn't intend to stay. I'd staked out the biggest table by the balcony, the Paris skyline slicing blue neon into the glass, and spent three hours arranging our maps and tablets just so. Jess had said to get some sleep, but I couldn't even remember what that felt like. The plan was all I had.

He materialized in the doorway, arms folded over his chest, watching me with that perfect stillness that always made me nervous. In the low light, he looked more shadow than man. The kind of shadow that could hurt you or save you, depending on the day.

"Come to bed," he said, not moving from the threshold.

I didn't answer. I was tracing the route from the gallery to the bridge to the safe house, over and over, the way a child might rub the edge of a favorite blanket. My finger left little oil stains on the paper. If I did it enough, maybe I'd wear a groove and Brie could just follow it straight out of the city.

He let the silence stretch for a full minute before he came over, boots whispering on the rug. He looked at the map, then at me, and in a single motion dragged a heavy chair beside me and pulled me into his lap.

"I can't focus when you're so far away," he murmured into my hair.

I stiffened, but he just wrapped his arms around me and leaned back, tipping the chair until we hovered on the edge of falling. I wondered if he'd let us crash to the floor just to see if I'd scream.

"Talk me through it again," he said. "One more time."

He didn't mean the plan. He meant the part I was scared to say out loud.

I closed my eyes. "If she runs, we're dead."

He grunted, which was Iron Valor for "you're right."

The maps on the table showed three rings: our approach, the fallback route, and the outer perimeter covered by Wrecker and the Paris wolves. There were backup plans, of course—there always were—but none of them worked if Brie didn't come willingly. Or if she tried to play hero.

"She never believed in monsters," I said. "Not even when we were kids. She'd tell me, 'Monsters are just things people haven't met yet.'"

"Did she believe you when you called from the club?"

I shook my head. "She couldn't believe that Dad would do that to me. He'd never done anything to hurt *her* in her life. Until he ruined the family, and I still don't think she'd take that personally."

Jess's hand slid under my sweater, not for heat, just for the skin-to-skin contact. The touch made my heart slow, like a sedative. "What about your mom?"

"She'll listen to Brie," I said. "She always did."

He nodded, accepting it as gospel.

"Enough of this," He said with a finality I couldn't argue with as he stood and held out his hand for me to take. He led me to our room, which was lit only by the bedside light. It gave a glow that offered comfort and hid secrets. But he didn't stop at the bed; he continued to drag me further.

The hotel bathroom was ridiculous. The floors were heated, the towels the size of blankets, the marble counter littered with tiny French bottles I'd never have touched on my own. He planted me in front of the mirror and peeled off my clothes, folding each piece as if it were mandatory they be neatly stacked.

He caught my eye in the mirror. "Still with me?"

I nodded, but my reflection betrayed the lie: hair wild, dark crescents under my eyes, shoulders pinched in like I was bracing for a punch.

Jess reached for my hand, tugged me under the rainhead shower, and turned the water on full. The instant heat made me gasp. He waited until I acclimated, then stepped in with me, his body a wall between me and the world.

He poured a dollop of something expensive-smelling into his palm—jasmine and green tea and a note of citrus so pure it made my eyes sting. He started with my hair, massaging my scalp with fingers meant for pulling triggers, not making someone feel worshipped. The lather slid down my neck, over my shoulders, and Jess followed it, working the soap down my spine in slow, precise spirals. My knees threatened to buckle.

"Let go," he said, low. "Just for a little while."

So I did. I let my head fall forward and my arms hang limp, and when he turned me to face the spray, I barely noticed the water in my eyes. He tipped my chin up, kissing the salt from my lips, then worked his way down—my throat, my collarbones, the notch at the base of my neck where he sometimes pressed his nose and breathed me in.

The world shrank to water and heat and Jess's hands mapping every inch of me. He washed my breasts with the same care he used on my scalp, fingers slow and unhurried, thumbs tracing circles around my nipples until I forgot my own name. He cupped them in his hands, weighing them, then let them go as if giving them back. His hands slid over my stomach, my hips, and he knelt so he could rub my thighs, calf to ankle, as if he was searching for secret compartments.

I closed my eyes. I could feel his breath against my skin, his lips ghosting over my belly and lower, but I didn't move. I was past moving.

When he stood, I felt the hard line of him pressed to my belly, and I wanted him so bad it hurt, but he wasn't in any hurry. He spun me so my back was to his chest, cradling me there, water sluicing over both of us. His hands explored the front of my body: up to my breasts, down to my stomach, then lower, until his fingers parted me and slid between the folds of my pussy.

I whimpered, the sound embarrassingly desperate, but he shushed me, burying his mouth in my wet hair.

"I need you," I said, barely audible.

"You have me," he answered, and his hand circled my clit, the same slow, deliberate pressure he'd used on the trigger of his favorite rifle. My hips bucked. He anchored me, one arm wrapped tight under my breasts, holding me up as he worked me harder, two fingers slipping inside and curling with ruthless precision.

I came so fast it was almost embarrassing; the kind of toe-curling, stomach-clenching climax that left my legs useless and my lungs on fire. I sagged against him, and he kept his fingers inside me, gentling the rhythm until the aftershocks faded to tremors.

He pulled out, washed his hand, then spun me to face him. I saw the hunger in his eyes, the wolf and the man both clawing at the surface.

He kissed me hard, his tongue filling my mouth with insistence. "You want me to stop?"

"No," I said, desperate for more.

He smiled, just a flash of teeth, and pinned my wrists to the cool marble tile. His other hand found my hip, yanked it forward, and then he was inside me, all the way, in one brutal, perfect thrust. I bit his shoulder to keep from crying out, and he fucked me slow, methodical, like he had all the time in the world.

The water roared overhead. The world dropped away. I wanted to memorize every second: the flex of his arms, the way his jaw clenched, the hitch in his breath when he started to lose control. My whole body lit up, every nerve ending tuned to his, every bit of pain and pleasure the same electric current.

He lifted me, pressed my back to the wall, and drove into me until I forgot why we'd ever been apart. I clung to his shoulders, nails digging in, and let myself go a second time, shattering against him as he came inside me with a growl that made my insides shudder.

We stood there for a long time, breathing each other in, until the water ran cold. He wrapped me in a plush towel and sat me down on the vanity stool. He blow-dried my hair, the motions as careful as everything else he did. When it was half dry, he took my brush and curled the ends, the way I liked them, twisting each lock around his finger. I let him. I let him do all of it.

When he was done, he kissed my forehead and carried me to the bed. He gently laid me on my pillow and pulled the blankets up around me, tucking me in like a child.

He got in beside me, gathering me to his chest, and the last thing I heard before sleep took me was his voice, low and certain.

"I'm so thankful I found you again, bluebonnet. My life had no meaning without you," he whispered. "I thought I'd always be alone, that love and happiness would always be just out of reach. I'm so glad I was wrong." His lips were soft as I kissed him lightly.

I drifted into sleep, muscles warm and heavy, and didn't wake until the sun was already painting stripes across the hotel's velvet curtains.

The morning was cold and absurdly bright, the kind of blue that made the river look less like water and more like a mirror splitting the city in two. I pulled the beanie lower on my head, adjusted the strap of the canvas bag on my shoulder, and kept my chin down as I crossed the Pont de Bougival. The dew hadn't burned off yet; everything was slick, the flagstones shining underfoot. My shoes squelched, and each step sounded way too loud.

According to the plan, I was supposed to blend in with the other artists. That was why we'd stopped at the supply store on Rue Cler, why Jess had insisted on a battered wooden easel, a fistful of graphite pencils, and a block of heavy paper that smelled like it had been milled in the last century. Even the paint-stained smock I wore was supposed to make me invisible. It was laughable. The minute I stepped onto the river walk, some eyes landed on me—either because I looked American or because I was one of only a few people out there before eight a.m.

I scanned the far bank, spotting the tell: a pair of white-haired men, each with a matching baguette under one arm, arguing politics or football over the rail. Behind them, barely noticeable, was the girl with the crimson pixie cut and the rose tattoo on her throat. Parker. She flicked her cigarette onto the cobbles, ground it out with her boot, and melted away before I could blink.

At the other end of the bridge, Jess and Wrecker sat at a terrace café, their chairs turned out to face the water. They wore sunglasses, drank espresso, and tried not to look like the most dangerous men in France. Every so often, Wrecker would make a show of fiddling with a tourist map or pointing at the spires of Saint-Germain, but I could feel their attention, sharp and heavy, as if they could will me through the next hour by force alone.

Gwen was somewhere nearby, blending into the scenery, casting her charms that would hopefully keep us safely obscured from anyone who would mean us harm.

Doc and Big Papa were the only ones truly hidden: parked in a battered white delivery van, engine idling, two blocks away. They monitored the comms, waiting for a code word or the first sound of trouble. I'd checked my phone three times since leaving the hotel, making sure the ringer was off and the battery full. It was the only thing I could control.

I walked slow, trying to get my breathing under control. The bag was heavier than I'd expected, the wooden slats of the easel biting into my collarbone. I clutched it harder, like it was a lifeline, and made my way down the steps to the lower dock.

There were already three painters set up at the edge, their canvases turned to catch the sunrise. The smell of turpentine was thick in the air, along with the sour tang of cheap cigarettes. I continued to make my way towards them.

My stomach tried to claw its way up my throat. Brie looked nothing like I remembered. Of course I'd seen my mother yesterday. I hadn't noticed how much she had changed. Where she used to stand tall and confident, her shoulders now hunched in a way I'd never seen before. She wore a navy trench and a bright yellow scarf; her gloved hands moving with the energy of a bird about to launch itself into the sky. Brie looked older—years older than the last photo I'd seen. She wore her hair in a sassy inverted bob; the ends dyed indigo and the roots black, her eyeliner flicked up into sharp little cat's eyes. The sweater she wore was off-the-shoulder, revealing a silver glitter tank and a mess of necklaces, each more tangled than the last. Her leggings were so tight they looked painted on, and her boots were short, black, and scuffed. She didn't look like a kid anymore. She looked like someone you'd cross the street to avoid.

The plan was to wait. Let them get used to me, let the world settle into routine, and then make the approach. But as soon as I saw Brie, all the air went out of my lungs and I just stood there, frozen.

"Move," I whispered to myself. "You have to move."

A light, deliberate cough sounded a few feet away. Gwen. She stood on the bridge above, dressed in a dove-gray overcoat, her white-blonde hair pulled back in a low bun. Every so often, she'd lift her hand and make a subtle flick of her wrist—a sign for Wrecker and the others that she was keeping the spell up. The veil. If it worked, it meant that anyone watching—Renault wolves, Steiner's men, or the cops—wouldn't see me as a threat. But nothing could keep me invisible to my own mother.

I gathered my courage, shouldered the easel, and started down the path toward them.

My mother looked up when I was ten paces away. Her eyes flicked over me once, registering every detail, then returned to her canvas. Brie didn't move, didn't so much as blink. I couldn't tell if she'd even noticed me.

I set the easel down at the next patch of stone, close enough to see what they were painting, but not so close as to spook them. The cold seeped through the denim on my legs and bit into my knees. I fumbled a pencil from the case and started to draw, hands shaking so bad my first line was more zigzag than curve.

My mom broke the silence. "You're early."

The words came out flat as a tabletop.

I looked up. "Didn't want to miss the light," I said.

She nodded, nothing more.

Brie said, "You're not a morning person. You used to sleep until noon."

Her voice was different, older, with a dry edge I didn't recognize. She didn't look at me when she said it, just kept staring at the river.

"That was before I knew what I was missing," I managed.

Brie shrugged. "If you say so."

My mother's hands never stopped moving. "I'm glad you got out of Houston. And now you're here."

"Yes," I said. "Now I'm here. For you."

Nanette set the brush down, wiped her fingers on a rag, and finally turned to look at me. Her eyes were glassy with unshed tears, but her voice was steel. "Is it safe to talk here?"

I glanced up at the bridge, caught the tiniest nod from Gwen. "It's as safe as we'll get."

Brie snorted. "Is this where you tell us to pack our bags and run? That the bad men are coming?"

Her words hit harder than I wanted to admit. "No," I said. "This is where I tell you the bad men are already here."

I saw a flicker of fear in her face, quickly covered by the old, stubborn set of her jaw.

Nanette shifted on her stool, angled her body to block Brie from anyone watching. "You're not just visiting," she said.

"No," I answered.

I could hear the clink of porcelain from the café terrace, the faint whistle of a cyclist zipping down the dock, and the persistent, low-frequency hum of my own heart in my ears. I tried to look busy, filling the paper with random marks, but my hand wouldn't stop shaking.

Brie finally looked at me. Really looked. Her eyes narrowed. "You're scared."

I nodded. "Yeah. I am."

For a second, I thought she might reach for me. Instead, she just wrapped her arms tighter around her knees, drawing them up to her chest. The bangles on her wrist jangled, too bright for the muted morning.

My mom spoke again, this time in a whisper. "Are they coming for you, or for us?"

"Both," I said, and my voice didn't crack.

Nanette's jaw clenched. "How soon?"

"Soon," I answered. "I have a team. Friends. We can get you out, but only if you want to go."

Brie shot up from the stone, the motion so quick it startled the old painter next to us. "You have a team?" She repeated, all the sarcasm in the world packed into three words. "What are you, a spy now?"

I didn't answer. There was no answer that would make sense.

She glared. "Mom doesn't want to go. She likes it here. So do I. We're not running for your drama."

Nanette reached out, caught Brie's wrist. "Enough," she said, soft but deadly. "You know she wouldn't have come if it weren't real."

Brie jerked away. "You always take her side."

"Not her side," my mom replied. "Our side."

I saw the tears then, threatening to spill over. I wanted to wipe them away, but my hands felt like marble.

Brie sat back down, but her body was coiled tight, ready to bolt.

My mom looked at me, something like hope in her eyes. "We need to finish this painting. When we're done, we'll come with you."

I swallowed hard. I knew what she meant. It wasn't the art she cared about, not really. It was the last normal morning. The last time the three of us could pretend to be a family, before the world came for us again.

I looked up at the bridge and saw Gwen watching, her hands folded at her waist. I imagined Jess and Wrecker and the others, all waiting for the moment we stood up and walked away.

I bent over my paper and started to draw for real. The lines steadied, and soon I lost myself in the familiar motions: the sweep of a jawline, the curve of a cheekbone, the dark slash of a brow. I drew Brie first, then my mom, then the two of them together, side by side against the river. I drew until the paper ran out and my knuckles ached.

When I looked up, the sun had climbed higher, turning the water from blue to molten gold.

Brie stared at the drawing, mouth open. "Is that supposed to be us?"

I nodded.

She rolled her eyes, but there was something softer in her voice. "You never drew me before."

"I know," I said. "I'm sorry."

She looked away, but I saw her wipe her eyes with the back of her hand. I still saw the doubt in her eyes.

CHAPTER 24

Arsenal

I had the perfect angle on the footbridge—a bistro by the Quai de Bougival. We looked like tourists, drinking espresso and checking out maps. There was nothing left to do but wait and watch, every nerve honed to a filament as Harper threaded her way down the riverside toward her mother and Brie. On a weekday morning, the bank belonged to the artists. Easels stood in tight formation along the stones, propped by hunched men in scarves and women in clattering jewelry. I sat pretending not to be the kind of predator I was. At this hour, the river ran gold, with the sun low enough to hide anything ugly in long shadows and reflected glare.

My team was spread in an arc: Wrecker sat with me, city map folded in his pocket like he gave a damn about history; Parker was the second-story, three windows down, pretending to photograph crows with a battered Nikon but really logging every face within a hundred yards; Doc sat in the van with Papa working comms. And then there was Gwen, nowhere and everywhere, holding the spell tight from her own corner of the world.

I tracked Harper, not because I didn't trust her, but because every instinct in me screamed, this was the moment it all went sideways. She wore black leggings and a canvas jacket, hair twisted in a dancer's bun, face scrubbed clean of makeup. She looked impossibly young. I hated that I could see her so clearly, while she couldn't pay attention to me at all.

She slowed as she neared the patch of stone where her family painted. Brie sat on a small folding chair, watercolors and pencils scattered around her, legs crossed at the ankles. Their mother, Nanette, wore a beret and an old camel-hair coat, every inch the expat with a secret. She painted fast, as if outrunning something only she could see. Neither of them glanced up as Harper approached, but Brie's hand stilled on the page, a tremor in the line giving her away.

Harper's voice carried in the stillness. She engaged in small talk; kept her hands visible, palms up, the way she might approach a spooked animal. Smart girl.

Nanette didn't look up. "You came early," she said, painting in quick, nervous strokes.

"I couldn't sleep."

Brie's head jerked, just for an instant. She flicked her eyes at Harper, then away, then at her again, and all the while her hands moved in tiny, pointless circles on the paper. There was something electric between the two of them, a current too bright to hide.

I swept my eyes across the river, hunting for movement, for anyone whose eyes lingered too long on the sisters. There were civilians, sure: two joggers, an old man with a sack of baguettes, a pair of school kids skipping stones near the bank. But there was also the man in the dark puffer vest, hands jammed deep in his pockets, who kept pace with the painters from the far side, pretending to study the river but always glancing back at Harper. And the woman with the pixie cut, leaning on the railing above, her reflection gone wrong in the water's surface. Parker had already flagged them, code names in the earpiece: VEST and PINK.

It all felt off—too easy, too clean. No sign of Steiner, no sign of the Polish mercs, just the familiar lull before a kill box closed.

Harper set her folding stool down and set up her easel.

Brie talked to Harper, accusing her of coming because of so-called "bad men" coming for them.

Harper shook her head. "It's not safe. That's why I'm here."

I waited for the signal. All Harper had to do was touch Brie's wrist, and Gwin would move to shift the veil to invisibility, and they'd move to the van that's only 100 m down the street. Easy.

Harper reached over to tap her wrist. I could hear her words clearly before she made contact. "I have a team here who can get you out safely." But then what I didn't expect to hear.

Brie countered as she rose from her chair. "Luc said we'd go together. You don't understand."

I keyed the comm. "We're blown," I said, and even I was surprised at the calm in my voice. "Brie gave us up."

The world went full color. I caught a shimmer on the bridge—Gwen, dropping the veil—and then the spell collapsed with a ripple that looked like heat rising off tarmac. Every face on the dock turned, all at once, toward Harper and her family.

The first shot came from PINK on the railing, a suppressed .308 that left no muzzle flash but a hot metal streak through the air. The round caught the edge of a trash can, ricocheted, and thudded into the stones an inch from Harper's foot. The second shot went for the real target: Gwen, perched behind a street vendor's umbrella, the bullet ripping through her shoulder in a spray of arterial red.

The glamour died completely. Every person within a hundred yards could see what had been hidden: me, crouched and bristling with hardware; Wrecker, already moving with murder in his eyes; Harper, vulnerable as hell with her hands empty and her heart in the open.

Civilians scattered in all directions. Paint-splattered easels clattered down. The street filled with screams and shouts in French, artists abandoning their gear as they ran for cover. Some tried to drag their canvases; others just ducked behind the nearest bench.

"Go!" I roared into the comm, already leaping from my chair and sprinting towards Harper.

Harper ran to Gwen, and Nanette tried to shield Brie who had jumped up and tried to run to a man in the distance. Luc, no doubt. Another suppressed shot pinged off the iron post inches from my ear. Wrecker vaulted a parked Citroën, closed the distance in five strides, and bowled over VEST with the force of a freight train, both men hitting the pavement in a tangle of fists and teeth.

On the bridge, PINK had reloaded and dropped into a crouch, lining up another shot. I skidded across the stone and tackled Harper and her sister, rolling them out of the line of fire just as a third round snapped the air where Harper's head had been.

Gwen staggered into the open, blood pouring down her arm, her face twisted in pain. She raised her good hand and shouted some kind of spell, but the words fizzled into nothing, her spell broken by the shock. I saw her knees buckle and watched her crumple, white hair soaked with red.

Harper clawed for Brie, desperate to keep hold, but the girl was screaming, fighting her off with surprising strength. "Let go!" she shrieked. "You're ruining everything!"

"Brie, please," Harper begged, but Brie's nails raked Harper's cheek, leaving twin red gashes.

I grabbed Harper's shoulder. "We have to move. Now."

And then I felt it—a hot, stabbing pain in my own neck, a tranquilizer dart glancing off the collar and nicking my neck. For a moment, my limbs went to rubber, world spinning. The next shot was for Harper, the dart thunking into the muscle of her shoulder. She gasped, tried to rise, and collapsed against me, her face twisting with confusion.

I saw the wolves coming before I heard them—two men in dark jackets, their eyes rimmed in gold, breath misting in the cold air. They moved with the lazy confidence of men who'd done this a thousand times.

Wrecker had finished with VEST, leaving him a crumpled heap, but was still thirty yards away, tangled with a second hostile who had come out of nowhere. Parker was gone from her window, probably circling for a shot, but the angle was bad and the crowd too thick.

The wolves descended. One seized Harper under the arms, yanking her upright; the other did the same to Brie. Both girls thrashed weakly, but the drugs were already kicking in. Harper's eyelids fluttered, and I saw the terror in her face as she realized she couldn't fight.

"Let go of her!" I shouted, trying to rise, but my legs were weakened by the small amount of drugs that had crept into my blood. I crawled, hands scraping the stone, every muscle in my body refusing orders.

The wolf holding Harper grinned, like he'd just won the first-place prize. "Stay down, cowboy," he said, voice flat and American. "Not your show anymore."

He slammed a fist into my face for good measure. I tasted blood, saw stars, and hit the ground hard.

They dragged Harper and Brie to the waiting car—a black Peugeot with the plates ripped off and the windows covered in cheap tint. The door slammed, the engine screamed, and the car fishtailed up the dock, scattering fleeing artists as it went.

I tried to rise. My head swam, vision doubling, but I got to one knee, then the other. I stumbled toward the curb, just in time to see the Peugeot take the first turn, Harper's face a pale smear in the back window.

Wrecker reached me, panting, his face split and swelling. "Get up," he snapped, dragging me to my feet. "They have her."

I tasted the words, wanted to spit them out, but I knew he was right.

"We're not done," I said, my voice a slur. "We're not done."

He gripped my collar, shaking me until my eyes focused. "We never are," he said.

We staggered for the van, sirens rising in the distance, the air stinking of smoke and fear. As I collapsed into the seat, I felt my phone buzz—Parker, on the line, her voice tinny and wild: "They're heading south. Fast. I'll track them as long as I can."

Papa put the van in gear and yelled for us to hang on as he took off. I became more alert my the minute since the tranq had barely grazed me. But all I could see was Harper's face, floating in my mind, and all I could taste was the blood in my mouth.

This wasn't the end. Not even close.

But I'd just watched the only person I ever loved get ripped from my arms, and there wasn't a damn thing I could do but hunt them down and start again.

I watched the Peugeot bounce through the street market, dodging a delivery truck and narrowly missing a bakery cart, all with Harper and Brie crammed in the back seat like cargo. My chest twisted in on itself—I could almost taste her fear, sharp and metallic through the frayed cord of our bond. I was already calculating the intercept, every muscle straining for the signal to move.

That's when Wrecker made a great shot out the passenger window. A suppressed single, perfect shot. The rear tire of the Peugeot exploded with a yowl of shredded rubber, sending the car into a wild swerve. For a split second, I saw hope: the rear fender clipped a bollard, the door popped, and Brie's face appeared in the shattered window, mouth open in a silent scream.

Then hope died. A second SUV—a black Dacia with diplomatic plates—lurched from a side alley, cutting off our access to the Peugeot, spraying gravel as it blocked us. Two more wolves, these burly and cropped close like Eastern Bloc prison guards, leaped out with silenced pistols drawn. The Peugeot's driver floored it, fishtailing through the broken glass, and in the chaos, both cars vanished down the service road, trailing black streaks and howls.

Wrecker barked at Papa. "Go! They'll double back through the tunnel under the A14."

I looked to the backseat of the van and saw Nanette huddled in the corner weeping.

"Where's Gwen?" I shouted over the sirens.

Wrecker didn't look back. "Paramedics got her. Doc's with her. He put Nanette in the van and then ran back to ride with her to the hospital."

Papa squealed the van's tires. The van was a civilian Mercedes, nothing fancy, but he drove it like a battering ram. We shot through a red light, horn blaring, and banked hard toward the underpass.

Parker chimed in on comms, breathless but laser-focused. "I have camera pings on both vehicles. Papa, if you cut through the next alley, you'll intercept two blocks ahead."

He grunted and yanked the wheel, sending us lurching over a curb and down a cobbled side street. The G-forces pinned me to the seat, but the tunnel vision was worse: every heartbeat, every breath, was a flicker of Harper's panic, the bond sparking wild in my head. She was awake now, fighting hard, but the wolves had her boxed in.

Nanette moaned in the back seat. "Please," she whispered. "Don't let them take her. Don't let them…"

The Peugeot reappeared at the next intersection, listing hard, metal grinding on pavement. Ahead, the black Dacia spun a fast U-turn, cutting off a city bus and triggering a chorus of horns. For a moment, both cars slowed in the snarl, trapped by traffic and bad luck.

Papa jammed the van into park and popped the side door. "Now!" he barked.

Wrecker and I spilled onto the street, dodging scooters and angry pedestrians. We reached the Dacia first. The two wolves inside had already spotted us, and the passenger lunged out, brandishing a pistol. Wrecker didn't even break stride; he grabbed the man by the wrist, twisted, and slammed him face-first into the hood. I heard the pop of bone and the squeal of pain.

The driver tried to gun it, but I was already there, yanking the door open and dragging him out by his lapels. He went for my throat, but I boxed his ears, then slammed his head against the window until he sagged. All the while, my eyes tracked the Peugeot, where Harper's pale arm flailed in the shattered window, fighting to reach the outside.

Behind me, the Dacia's engine screamed, then stalled. I turned in time to see Wrecker use the wolf's own pistol to shoot out the tires—one, two, three, four, fast as a metronome.

I made for the Peugeot, but the driver had recovered. He floored it again, swerving around the wrecked Dacia and aiming for the open road. I gave chase, lungs burning, but after three blocks the adrenaline ran out and the car was gone, leaving nothing but a haze of exhaust and the echo of Harper's terror.

I dropped to my knees on the curb, gasping for breath. Wrecker caught up, bruised and bleeding. A wince marred his face.

"They got away," I said, the words sour in my mouth.

He put a hand on my shoulder. "Not for long."

Parker buzzed through the comm again. "I'm tracking the Peugeot—last sighting near Nanterre, heading west. They're trying to get out of the city center, probably toward a secondary safe house. I'll keep eyes as long as I can."

I slumped into the passenger seat of the van, wiped the blood from my face, and tried to center myself. The bond to Harper pulsed in my head, an SOS too loud to ignore. She was scared, but she was still fighting.

That was all I needed.

Papa put the van in gear. "What's the plan, Arsenal?" he asked.

I didn't hesitate. "We follow. We hunt. We don't stop until we have them back."

Wrecker grinned a feral grin. "That's the Arsenal I know."

We barreled west; the city blurring past, every nerve tuned to the hunt. I didn't know what waited at the end of the road, but I knew who'd be standing when it was over.

We were wolves, and we'd just tasted blood.

The safe house was a nondescript house at the edge of Versailles: the kind of place that got rented for cash, no questions, no lease, keys waiting in a taped envelope under a chipped terra-cotta pot. Inside, the blackout curtains filtered the noon sun to a nicotine haze, and the furniture was a random inheritance from a hundred other safe houses: a slumped corduroy sofa, a pilled rug, folding chairs around a chipped Formica table. The smell was a chemical war between bleach and ancient cigarettes, but it was safe, and for now that was enough.

We tumbled in, bloodied and wild, and the first thing I did was check the bond. Harper felt farther away than she ever had—a blip on the edge of perception, too faint to track by gut alone. I knew she was alive, but there was a coldness in it, like she'd slammed every door behind her on the way out.

Rafe's men had picked up Doc and assembled a team to help thanks to Papa making the calls. He, Marcel, and Etienne were welcome faces. "Well, amie's you almost got away unscathed. But it seems you just got away, and you seem to have lost precious trésor."

I shook my head. "Not for long. Now, are you fuckers going to help get that treasure back or are you just going to continue to point out the obvious?"

"Let's hear how you're getting her back and how we are going to help."

Parker set up her laptop at the end of the table, eyes gone wild as she hacked into the city's camera grid. Wrecker prowled the perimeter, pausing at the door to sniff the air, then mapping out the nearest exits on a wrinkled city map. Papa parked Nanette at the table, wrapped her in a blanket, and poured two fingers of vodka into a chipped mug. She didn't even flinch as she knocked it back.

I paced the living room, unable to sit, unable to stop moving. My shirt was a mess of dried blood and sweat, my hands still shaking from adrenaline. Wrecker stalked in, gestured with his chin toward the closed window.

"Luc's trail ends at a warehouse near the Nanterre industrial park," he said. "Lots of trucks, lots of noise. They're prepping a transfer."

"To Steiner?" I asked.

He nodded. "Or worse. We need to get there before the crate leaves the yard."

Parker swiveled in her chair, dark circles under her eyes. "I'm running facial on every angle from the last camera hit. The van dumped near a loading dock at 10:17, and three people carried out two bodies. Then the feed glitches." She slammed the keys, teeth bared. "Someone's jamming the next block, or else they're running it off the books."

I stopped behind her, fingers digging into my jaw. "Can you get past it?"

She snorted. "Give me thirty. I'll be running in their veins."

Nanette set her mug down, her voice paper-thin. "I didn't know. I thought—" She broke off, cradling her head in her hands.

Papa hovered at her side, gentle as he could manage. "You did what you had to," he rumbled.

She looked up, face ravaged. "But Brie—she betrayed us. She set us up. My own daughter set us up."

The words hit me like a backhand. I wanted to argue, to tell her Brie was just a pawn, but I didn't have the energy to lie. Instead, I turned and drove my fist into the wall. The plaster split with a satisfying crunch, pain radiating up my arm. For a second, everything in the room froze. Even Parker looked up, startled.

"Sorry," I muttered, shaking the dust from my knuckles.

Wrecker grunted. "We need that temper. Just not yet."

We crowded around the laptop as Parker piped a feed to the flat screen. Rows of cameras, city blocks flicking past in green-tinged night vision. Wrecker pointed to a side street. "There. The van's gone, but a white Sprinter picked up something at 10:30. Tag matches to a shell company tied to the Renaults."

Parker zoomed in. "Warehouse is here. Satellite shows three ways in: loading bay, south gate, and the canal."

Papa straightened, eyes on me. "What's the move, Arsenal?"

I drew a long breath, let it out slow. "We hit it from all sides. Parker on over watch. Wrecker and I take the gate. Papa, you stay with Nanette and keep the van hot. Marcel, Etienne, your team will take every other opening."

Marcel cracked his knuckles. "Sounds like fun."

Doc's phone buzzed, and he snatched it up. "Gwen," he said, listening. His face eased a fraction. "Gwen's out of surgery. She's stable. Says the glamour will hold for another twelve hours, but after that, we're all on the grid. Also—she says good luck."

I nodded, something in my chest loosening. "Let her know we'll bring Harper back."

Doc set his jaw. "Damn right."

We spent the next ten minutes mapping the warehouse on the big screen, marking entry points, sight lines, fallback routes. Every muscle in my body wanted to sprint the whole way, tear the place down brick by brick, but I held the line. Wolves didn't get second chances, and we had to do it right.

At 12:40, a member of the French team checked in: "Six guards at the canal lock. Light armament, local pack. No demons, but Steiner just arrived. Be quick."

Wrecker loaded up, checking his sidearm with practiced ease. "Remember what Bronc said. Let the French team take out Steiner. Or at least incapacitate him so he can be brought back to Rafe."

I wanted his head. But I had to honor my Alpha's wishes. "Understood."

I took one last look at Nanette, slumped at the table, blanket wrapped tight. Her eyes met mine, hollow and pleading.

"Bring them home," she whispered.

I promised, though I didn't know if I could keep it.

We rolled out, black windbreakers and city hats, every inch of us ghosts. The drive was short, silent. Parker tracked the feeds on her phone, murmuring updates as we neared the target.

At the warehouse, the air was sharp with the stench of evil. Big Papa idled the van a block out, ready to run if we called. Wrecker and I circled the perimeter, clocking the guards: three at the front, one smoking at the dock, another two pacing the side gate with a bored slouch.

The French team moved silent as the dead, checking in a larger grid.

CHAPTER 25

Harper

I lost count after the first ten wolves.

Not that I could see them all. The cell was a square shipping crate bolted to the warehouse floor, with chain-link fencing welded over the front and sides, and a caged bulb that cast a sickly yellow cone over everything. I could smell them. When stressed, wolves reeked of canine and testosterone, and here it came in waves, cut with the chemical rot of old blood and diesel. My face burned where Brie's claws had raked me, but the real pain was inside: every time I blinked, I saw the look she'd given me on the bridge, the raw mix of terror and betrayal, as if *I* was the monster.

When I came to, I was in this cage, but not alone. There were other women in here besides Brie and me. One blonde so pale she looked bleached, the other darker, battered around the eyes. They hadn't said a word since we had been tossed in here and sat huddled together on a mat, knees drawn tight, arms locked in a death grip. Brie was at the farthest corner, facing the wall, her boots leaving a trail of black smudges on the filthy floor.

I pressed a sleeve against the blood still seeping from my cheek. "Well, this is a damn mess," I said, but no one replied.

The warehouse was the kind built for trucks, not people: exposed girders, a ceiling high enough to swallow sound, and somewhere up there, was a square of window with the dawn leaking through. They'd turned off the heat, but the place ran warm from wolf body mass and the stink of nerves. I could see through the cell's welded chain-link "bars" to the perimeter: too many wolves to count, all in black jeans and hoodies, shuffling in formation like they'd practiced for a parade. Most ignored us, but one or two made a point of pacing past the crate every few minutes, eyes sliding over the bars. The way they watched, I could tell they were more afraid of their boss than anything we could do.

I took stock of the exits, just as Jess had taught me. Double doors at the front, a single steel panel at the back, maybe a rolling garage door at the far end. The walls were thin, with no insulation, and I could hear the low thrum of traffic on the street outside. I could also hear the wolves muttering to each other, some in what sounded like Polish or Russian; I couldn't tell which.

I ran a hand over my arms to stop the shivering. My jacket was gone; I wore only the thin cotton top from before, spattered now with dried blood. I checked for my phone or anything useful, but the wolves had stripped us clean. I had to count on Jess's relentless skills to find me.

Brie hadn't moved, not even to wipe the blood from under her nails. Her hair was shorter than I remembered; the inverted bob gave her an edgy look. She hugged her knees, head pressed into the crook of her elbow. Every so often, she'd flinch when the wolves barked a command, but mostly she just breathed, slow and shaky.

I slid to her side of the cell. "You want to talk about it?"

She shook her head without turning.

"Because we're probably not going anywhere soon, and I hate the awkward silence."

She said nothing.

The two women on the mat didn't react, but the dark-haired one finally lifted her head. Her nose looked broken, and she had the bruised, faraway gaze of someone who'd seen the inside of a lot of these cages. Her stare was clinical, almost bored. The blonde just stared at her own knees, rocking.

Brie's voice was a splinter. "You shouldn't have come."

I felt my jaw clench. "It was either come or let you wind up in a crate on a cargo ship to Taiwan. I couldn't let that happen."

She let out a hollow laugh. "You don't get it. You never did. You think you're so much better than us—"

"Us? You're all in with these people now?"

She spun on me, her eyes swollen with tears and rage. "Luc loves me. He—he said he'd take me away from all of this. From Mom, from everything."

I glanced at the other girls, then back at Brie. "Yeah, Luc really seems like the prince type. Is that why he sells women out of shipping containers? Real stand-up guy, Brie. Maybe Dad would have liked him."

She lunged at me, hands clawed, but I caught her wrists. She was smaller than me, but she fought like a cornered animal. "You don't know anything! You never did! You just left us, and then you act like you're the only one who ever got hurt—"

"I left because I had no choice!" My own voice echoed too loud, and one of the guards banged the cell with a length of pipe. "Quiet!" he barked, the accent pure Jersey.

I lowered my voice. "You think I wanted to end up in a club, dancing for freaks like Steiner? You think I wouldn't have killed to trade places with you and finish school, be with my *mate*?"

Brie's face crumpled. "Luc said you liked it. He said you made all this up to keep me from being happy."

I looked at the other women, saw the way the pale one shrank into herself at the sound of his name. "Brie, he's a trafficker. They all are. That's the only thing they do. I don't even know if the real Luc exists."

She just shook her head, the tears running unchecked now. "I loved him," she said. "I thought he'd save me."

I pulled her to the ground before she could lash out again, wrapped both arms around her, and forced her to meet my eyes. "We're getting out of here," I said, willing her to believe it. "Arsenal will not leave me here. He'll burn the world down before he lets Steiner take me again."

She sniffed, hiccuped, and let her body go limp in my arms. "You promise?"

I brushed her hair off her face. "On my life."

Behind us, the dark-haired woman made a sound—half laugh, half sob. "They always say that," she said, not unkindly. "But you can't trust men. All they have are words."

I met her gaze. "You've never met *our* men."

Her eyes flicked to my bloodied cheek. "I hope for your sake, you're right."

I sat down with Brie pressed tight to my side. Her hands still trembled, but she held onto my sleeve like it was a rope in floodwater. I kept my own fear under wraps. There'd be time to break later.

The wolves continued to march around the warehouse. I recognized two from the club in Houston, one with a scar down the side of his face, the other with knuckles tattooed in Cyrillic. They never looked me in the eye, just kept pacing or squatting to smoke.

You could pack a room with a hundred wolves, set them barking and jostling and gnashing their teeth, but the second an apex predator stepped inside, it all stopped. Maybe it was pheromones, maybe just learned terror—didn't matter. When the warehouse went quiet, I knew Steiner had come to collect.

Every wolf straightened, eyes fixed dead ahead. Even the guards who'd spent the morning smoking and jawing at us now braced as if about to salute. Brie shuddered against my side; the other two women cowered together on the mat.

Waylon Steiner entered like a king late to his own coronation. He sauntered into the light, hands in his pockets, a smirk pre-installed on his face. The suit was the same as before, navy this time, the shirt blood-red, and I'd bet a month's wages the shoes cost more than my first car. His hair hung loose now, and in the cold light of the warehouse he looked more animal than man.

He stood just outside the bars, his eyes raking over us one by one, pausing on Brie with an extra twist of the knife. "Miss me?" he said, smiling wide.

No one answered. I made a show of dabbing the blood from my mouth, careful not to give him the satisfaction of a flinch.

Steiner jerked his chin at the guards. "Open it."

A wolf with a buzz-cut twisted the padlock, then yanked the gate wide. Steiner stepped in, the guards flanking him with the precision of a firing squad.

He loomed over me, arms folded. "Let's try this again. Where's your boyfriend, Harper? Arsenal, is it? Or maybe he's not as brave as you thought."

I didn't bother answering. He wanted fear, or at least a little awe. I gave him indifference.

His gaze flicked to Brie. "And you, precious? Still think Luc's coming for you?"

Brie cringed. "He promised—"

Steiner cackled. "Luc is Renault's man. He used you as bait, girl, and an easy piece of pussy. He's resting easy back at his pack's compound; likely with a woman prettier than you on his lap. He did what he's paid to do.

And you were as stupid as we counted on you being." He turned to me, shrugged. "Kids these days. So easy to fool."

He bent down, took my chin between two fingers, and smeared the blood from Brie's claw marks across my lips. His touch was obscene, a parody of tenderness. "Did you miss your Master?" he whispered, close enough for me to smell last night's bourbon on his breath.

I met his eyes, steady. "You were never my master."

He didn't like that. The smile slipped, replaced by a chill that frosted the air around us. He backhanded me hard, the signet ring on his middle finger splitting my cheek open, raw and hot. I went down but caught myself on one knee, forcing myself to stay upright. I tasted copper and rage.

"Still got some fight in you," he muttered, shaking his hand. "Good. I want the boyfriend to see what's left of you when he finally shows up."

He straightened, motioned to the guards. "Get her up and bring her out here." He ordered as he strolled out of the cell.

They hauled me to my feet and dragged me out, held me in front of the cell; one on each arm. Steiner circled, slow, inspecting the damage like he was shopping for produce. "You always had a mouth on you, Harper. I had trained it out of you. Looks like we're starting over." He smirked at Brie. "Your sister, though? All she ever wanted was to be wanted. Sad, really."

Brie sobbed, arms wrapped around her waist. I tried to reach for her, but the guards yanked me back.

Steiner's voice dropped, soft and private. "You know what's going to happen? Tomorrow morning, I'm putting your little sister on a jet. She's going to Maltraz, and he gets his pound of flesh. But you? You're staying right here. I'm going to keep you, just like you wanted. My own little wolf on a chain."

He let that hang. The guards laughed, but it was a nervous sound, not a real one.

I worked my wrists, testing the guards' grips. The one on my left was strong, but the other's hands shook—junkie, or maybe just new. I made a mental note.

Steiner loomed close, face inches from mine. "Last chance. Tell me where your boyfriend is, and I'll make this quick. Lie to me, and I start breaking bones."

I spat in his face. "You're gonna die today."

He backhanded me again, harder; the ring rattled my teeth. I tasted air and blood, and this time I fell.

He let me hit the floor, then planted a boot on my spine. The heel ground between my ribs, steady pressure at first, then more and more until something gave with a sickening crack. I screamed; couldn't help it, and the sound echoed off the metal walls.

Brie screamed too, shrill and desperate, her hands gripping the bars of the cell.

Steiner leaned down, whispering in my ear. "That's one. Only twenty-three more to go. He kicked me, lifting me from the ground." This was it; he was actually going to kill me this time.

Through the pain, I scanned for weapons, anything—a pipe, a shard of glass, a loose bar. There was nothing, but I locked onto a hunk of steel pipe sticking out from under the mat. If I could reach it...

The guards threw me against the bars, the pain in my side white-hot. I gritted my teeth, forced my vision to clear.

Steiner stared down at the two other women. "This is what happens to heroes."

The women pleaded, but he just motioned to the guards, who pulled them from the cell. I saw the dark-haired woman mouth "I'm sorry" before they dragged her out.

Steiner was back in my face as his hand clasped my throat. "I was good to you, Harper. Gave you everything." He growled. "And you repaid me by running. I'm going to enjoy punishing you. You think taking Maltraz's demon dick was bad? Just wait. You ain't seen nothin' yet." His fist landed under my ribs over and over. Pain exploded. I struggled for breath from his large hand choking the life from me, and the relentless blows to my gut; had me start to lose consciousness.

One of his men called out. "Boss, we got trouble."

He released my throat, and I fell to the ground, but he kept his foot on my back.

I coughed, blood spattering the floor.

He leaned down to me and laughed. "Don't get your hopes up, slave. Your boyfriend is probably already dead. The French wolves will never let a foreign pack disrupt their territory. My guess is they already took him out."

All at once, the front doors of the warehouse banged open so hard they shuddered on their hinges. For one perfect instant, every wolf in the place froze, then broke for cover as a shape in black tactical gear strode into the light. Arsenal. He looked like a nightmare out of an action movie, every line of his body rigid with intent. Doc had his six, looking just as deadly.

Every cell in my body came awake at once. The bond between Jess and me lit up, urgent and wild, like a wire sparking in water. But I couldn't move—Steiner had his boot on my back, pinning me down with enough force to keep me from even raising my head. Brie cowered in the cell, shaking so bad I thought she might seize.

Steiner didn't even flinch. He watched Arsenal approach, the smirk back on his face. "You came," he said, voice flat with glee. "I knew you couldn't stay away."

Arsenal's gaze was all murder. "Let them go," he said, and his voice was so cold it seemed to freeze the air between them.

Steiner shook his head. "I just took back what already belonged to me, mutt."

He planted his foot harder on my ribs, making me gasp. "You want her, you come and get her."

Arsenal didn't hesitate. He moved forward, gun up, and at the same moment, all hell broke loose.

From the back of the warehouse, the door crashed open and Wrecker with the French wolves—Marcel and Etienne—stormed in, guns blazing. Wolves fell everywhere, some dropping immediately, others shifting mid-run, teeth and claws flashing in the gunpowder haze. Overhead, the skylight exploded, and a member of the French team dropped through in a rain of glass, landing with a shotgun already up and firing.

The guards by the cell scattered, but Steiner kept his weight on me. Through the chaos, I heard him laughing. "This is your cavalry, Harper? I'm disappointed."

I twisted, desperate for leverage. The pipe was still just out of reach, and my left arm hurt but had already started healing thanks to my wolf blood heightened by the proximity to my mate. Steiner had turned toward Jess, and that gave me wiggle room. I used every ounce of pain to drag myself closer.

Brie huddled against the bars, eyes shut tight. "Harper, please—" she whispered.

"Get down," I told her, voice raw.

The shooting intensified. Wolves dropped left and right, the French team moving with the efficiency of men who'd done this a hundred times. Marcel took a bullet in the arm but kept moving; Etienne knifed a wolf through the eye, then used the corpse as a shield while he reloaded.

For Doc to be a healer, his penchant for death was uncanny. He used the Glock in his hand as though it were an extension of his arm. He flew through the warehouse, dropping wolves as fast as he could shoot.

Parker took up position by the office stairs, picking off any wolf who tried to circle behind Arsenal. Wrecker made it to the catwalk above, then threw himself over the rail, landing on two wolves with enough force to shatter bone. I heard a neck snap; the sound crisp as a carrot.

Steiner bent down, breath hot on my ear. "You know what's funny?" he said, voice almost gentle. "You never had a chance. None of you."

He drew a pistol from his waistband, pressing the muzzle to my temple. "You think I won't do it?" he hissed.

I grinned, bloody and unhinged. "I think you'll hesitate, just like you always do."

And then, from the corner of my eye, I saw Arsenal moving. He'd dropped his gun, now empty, and was charging Steiner head-on. Steiner swung the pistol up, but Arsenal was already there—he grabbed Steiner's wrist, twisted, and the gun skittered across the floor. They crashed into the bars; the impact rattled the whole cell.

For a split second, Steiner's foot left my back. I lunged for the pipe, grabbed it with numb fingers, and pulled myself to my knees. Every nerve screamed, but I held on.

Arsenal and Steiner traded blows, neither giving ground. Steiner was stronger, but Arsenal was meaner—he went for the eyes, the throat, anywhere that would slow Steiner down. Blood spattered the concrete. The fight was close and ugly, nothing like the clean choreography of the movies.

Wrecker joined in, slamming Steiner from behind and locking his arms around Steiner's chest. "Now, Harper!" Wrecker shouted. "Do it!"

I staggered to my feet, pipe raised vertically over my head. Steiner saw me coming and laughed, even as he tried to break free of Wrecker's grip.

"C'mon, darling," he taunted. "One last dance?"

I didn't answer. I brought the jagged end of the pipe down as hard as I could, aiming for the place where his shoulder met his neck. The steel entered, crunched bone, and tore through muscle, and this time Steiner screamed. He tried to turn, but Wrecker held him fast.

I drove the pipe deeper, impaling organs, bones, and tendons until Steiner slumped to the ground, gasping.

Arsenal leaned over, voice low. "You're done, Steiner."

Steiner's mouth worked, blood bubbling between his teeth. "You think you've won? There's always another wolf. Or demon."

From behind, Etienne appeared, gun raised. He put a single bullet through Steiner's skull, neat and final. His body jerked, then went slack.

I collapsed. Every part of me hurt. Brie reached for me through the bars, sobbing.

Arsenal hauled me into his arms. "You okay, bluebonnet?" he whispered.

I tried to smile. "Never better."

He kissed my hair, then looked at Brie. "You too, little sister?"

She nodded, mute.

Wrecker and the French team swept the warehouse, making sure every wolf was dead or dying. Parker found the keys, unlocked the cell, and pulled Brie out. Then she pulled me from Jess's arms into a careful hug. "Told you I'd hack every camera in Paris if I had to," she said, voice watery with relief.

I hugged her back, then clung to Jess as he carried me out the door and into the morning light. The warehouse was a war zone—bodies everywhere, smoke still curling from spent gunpowder. But it was over.

On the street outside, Big Papa waited with the van, ready to run.

Arsenal set me gently on the seat, wrapping a blanket around my shoulders. He knelt in front of me, searching my face for something I couldn't name.

Doc was on the phone in the passenger seat. "Gwen's good. Veil is strong. Nobody in the area should be aware of what just went down."

Relief washed over everyone.

Jess climbed in and pulled me close as he held me on his lap. "You did it," he said, voice hoarse.

I shook my head. "*We* did."

He smiled, just a little, then pressed his forehead to mine. "I love you," he said.

I wanted to say it back, but all that came out was a sob. I held him hard until the world stopped spinning.

Beside me, Brie held my hand. She was still shaking, but her eyes were clear.

We were safe. For now.

The van roared to life, tearing down the street and into the waking city. Behind us, the warehouse burned, smoke black against the morning sky.

We didn't look back.

We didn't have to.

CHAPTER 26

Arsenal

The Gulfstream's cabin was set to "hospice quiet," the lights down, windows shuttered against sunrise. The only sound was the background radiation of jet engines and Harper's breathing, soft against my shoulder. Brie and Nanette sat cuddled across from us, sleeping off the stress of the last several hours. Most of the others slept as well. Wrecker sprawled across two seats, mouth open, a thin ribbon of blood dried from a cut above his eye. Parker had curled up like a cat in the footwell of her row, still in her hoodie, one shoe off, arms clutching her laptop. Big Papa and Doc took up a row together, both too big for comfort, both refusing to close their eyes while we were still in the air. Gwen rested opposite the two big men, comfortable and dressed more casually than I'd seen her since we'd met.

I should have been asleep too, but I was wired into the moment, every nerve refusing to lay down. It was a feeling I hadn't had since Afghanistan—after a mission, when the dust settled, and you were still alive, and your hands wouldn't stop shaking.

Harper's head weighed heavy on my right bicep. Her hair, which always smelled like vanilla, was caked now with warehouse grit, and dried blood at the scalp line where she'd split her brow. There was a bruise blossoming down her left cheek, and a crescent of dried blood just under her jaw. She looked peaceful, like knowing the worst of something was behind you and you could finally rest easy. She looked like the girl I remembered: sleeping next to me on a blanket on the shore of an endless lake when we didn't know that evil men and time and distance would separate us.

I couldn't help it—I studied her face like a map, cataloguing every cut, every new scar. I'd almost lost her in that warehouse, and the memory played on a loop behind my eyes, high-def and unforgiving.

She'd been on the floor, bloody and half-conscious, Steiner's boot pinning her ribs. The sound of that bastard's laugh, the way he'd bared his teeth at me as if nothing in this world could touch him. I'd seen Harper's hand groping, her fingers slick with blood, searching for anything—a weapon, a miracle. When she found the steel pipe, she'd barely had the strength to lift it, but the look on her face was pure arithmetic. She knew what had to be done, and she'd done it. Drove the pipe through Steiner's neck like a warrior goddess taking her final revenge.

The moment was burned into me: the blood, the shock on Steiner's face, the sound of his gurgle, and the way Harper had grinned through tears, bloody and victorious. She hadn't killed just for herself. She'd killed for every girl who'd been bought and sold at his hands.

Now, in the hush of the jet, I couldn't reconcile the two images of Harper the soft-hearted girl with the candy-colored ballet shoes, and Harper the woman who would kill a wolf tycoon to save not just her family but strangers. She was an enigma.

I brushed a thumb across her cheek, careful not to wake her. She didn't stir, just nuzzled deeper into my side, muttering something in her sleep. The sound unlocked something old in me, something that had been rusted shut for years.

"You don't get a second chance at this, Jess," Big Papa's voice rang in my head. *"When you do, don't waste it."* The man was not wrong. I had done my best to fuck the whole thing up, but had managed to get my head out

of my ass long enough to realize I had the golden ticket staring me right in the face. Thank the Goddess this woman; this amazing pillar of grace and goodness, didn't give up on me.

The cabin lights flicked brighter as the pilot made a gentle bank. Paris was six hours behind us, Dairyville a mere hour ahead. I should have felt relief, but all I felt was the white-hot terror that I'd lose her again if I stopped watching her for even a second.

I wanted to tell her everything: that I was sorry, that I was proud, that there was nothing in this world I wanted more than to grow old at her side. I wanted to say it and hear her laugh, or punch my arm, or call me an idiot. But right now, she just needed sleep. I could wait. I would wait forever if she asked.

I checked the cabin—no threats, not even the old nightmares waiting in the dark. I let my head rest against the seatback and closed my eyes, still holding Harper close. If this were a dream, let it last a little longer.

I drifted somewhere between sleep and memory, watching the years unspool backwards: the way she'd looked when I first realized she was mine. She was so young and innocent. She hadn't had a care in this world. All she wanted to do was dance and love me. It should have been so easy. And it was until it wasn't. I remembered how excited she was to tell her parents she'd found her fated mate. That very day, it all went to hell.

I remembered her father telling me she'd left for New York, that she'd rejected me. I remembered how I'd told myself I didn't need anyone, how I'd believed it for years, right until the moment I saw her again in Texas, eyes bright and burning with the same impossible light.

The world could end a hundred times and I'd still want her. That was the curse of the mate bond—cruel and perfect, a thing you could never break, even if you tried.

The pilot's voice came through the intercom, barely above a whisper. "Final approach in twenty minutes. Prepare for landing."

I squeezed Harper's hand, felt her fingers twitch. For the first time in a long time, I didn't want to fight the future. I wanted to run straight into it, headlong and reckless, with her at my side.

I looked down at her, the dark smudges under her eyes, the healing gash on her cheek, the little smile tugging at her lips even in sleep. She was alive. I was alive. We were going home.

There are men who go through their whole lives never knowing what it is to be truly loved. I counted myself lucky that I'd lost it once and been given it back, by a miracle or a mercy or just the stubborn grace of a girl who refused to stay lost.

I closed my eyes and let the hum of engines and the warmth of Harper's body lull me. When I woke again, the world would be new. We'd be in Dairyville, and nothing would ever keep us apart again.

They brought the jet in low, cutting north above the old cotton fields and pivoting on a wind that smelled faintly of smoke and spring onions. We landed at Iron Valor's private strip—really just a tarmac and a windsock, with an old fire truck rusting behind a cinderblock shed. Even from the window, I could see Bronc waiting on the edge of the ramp, arms folded, Ray-Bans on, legs spread like he was still guarding the perimeter of some forward operating base. Juliet stood by his side, his ever-present mate, keeping him grounded.

The crew deplaned in silence, except for the hydraulics whining and Wrecker's barely muffled curses as he helped Parker down the steps. Doc, Gwen, and Big Papa spilled out; Brie and Nanette followed. Harper made it down next. I followed, carrying two bags and a head full of trouble, and was the last to hit the tarmac. Bronc didn't move until Harper's feet were on Texas soil; then he strode out and wrapped her in a one-armed bear hug that lifted her six inches off the ground.

"Glad you're home," he said, voice gravel and whiskey.

Harper tried to laugh but mostly just clung to his shirt, her eyes squeezed shut. She'd never admit it, but she needed this—the safe weight of a pack that didn't want to use her, sell her, or turn her into leverage.

Juliet immediately went to Nanette and Brie. She took each of their hands. "You must be Harper's mother and sister. Welcome to Iron Valor. We're so happy you're here and safe."

Nanette spoke for both of them. "Thank you so much for your help and for being so good to Harper. We're eternally grateful." A tear ran down her cheek.

Juliet gave them each a hug. "None of that. We're family. That's what families do. Now, let's get you settled. You look exhausted and would probably love to have a nice hot shower and some clean clothes and a fresh meal. Gunner will take you to the accommodations Parker has arranged for you. It's a home her family owned. It's across the road from Gunner's ranch. He'll be around if you need anything."

Gunner was waiting by his big pickup truck, cowboy hat, scuffed boots, hands in his pockets, looking ready to help. I caught the flicker on his face when he first saw Brie—something raw, almost chemical, like he'd been hit with an emotion he wasn't ready for.

Brie didn't look back. She just hugged Harper, then ran a hand through her hair, eyes darting everywhere.

"Y'all okay?" Gunner finally asked, voice just above a whisper.

Harper squeezed Brie's hand. "We will be. We're home."

Nanette nodded, silent, the lines around her mouth deeper than I remembered. She and Harper shared a glance; it was enough.

Wrecker loitered behind Parker's car. She looked around and got excited when she saw a vehicle approaching.

A beat-up white Silverado rolled up, and for a second I thought it was the pack's handyman, but then Aspen tumbled out in a lime green polka dot dress, her hair wild and her bare feet slapping the concrete. She squealed, literally squealed, and leaped into Big Papa's arms, wrapping herself around him like a happy koala. He caught her, spun her once, and kissed her full on the mouth, not giving a damn who saw. Oscar, the damn prairie dog, scampered up her leg and perched on her shoulder.

"Darlin'," Papa said, voice softer than I'd ever heard it. "You're a vision."

Aspen giggled, burying her face in his beard. "You smell like French cigarettes and blood, you wild animal."

"And you smell like home, Sunshine," he said, setting her down but refusing to let go of her hand.

"Sir, may I say it's lovely to have you back?" Oscar asked him in his most proper British accent.

I hadn't noticed the little black ball of fur that had jumped out of Aspen's truck, but boy Parker did.

"There's my good boy!" She shrieked as Rocket, the world's ugliest dog leaped into her arms.

Wrecker's face surprisingly lit up as well. "Hey kid," he said as his giant hands ran through the wriggling little dog's fur.

Parker handed the dog off to Wrecker, and the monster actually cuddled the thing under his chin. She rolled her eyes, then hugged Harper—quick, awkward, but real. "Call if you need me." She looked at me, her eyes daring me to say something sentimental, but I just nodded. That was enough.

They peeled off, the silver BMW shooting gravel as it vanished up the county road.

Gwen materialized at Bronc's elbow. Her white-blonde hair was down, and for the first time she looked like a person, not a weapon. She eyed me, half-smile on her lips.

"Thought you'd hate me by now," she said.

I considered. "Not today."

She held my gaze. "If you ever need the Paris Accord again, you know where to find me."

I nodded. "I hope I never do."

Bronc put a hand on my shoulder. "Let's get you two to the pack house."

I glanced at Harper. "Let's go home," she said with a sigh.

That was all I needed.

The drive was short, the silence thick but not uncomfortable. Bronc dropped us at our building, then drove off, Gwen in the back seat, her face turned away. The street was empty; the grass starting to turn green; the air fresh with the hint of spring flowers. I unlocked the door, held it for Harper, and let her step inside first.

The apartment smelled the way it always did—coffee grounds and gun oil, with a trace of her perfume in the sheets. Harper slumped into the armchair, toeing off her boots, and just sat there, eyes closed, breathing in the ordinary.

I knelt in front of her, took her hands in mine. They were shaking, but I didn't mention it.

"Want to sleep?" I asked.

She shook her head. "Don't want to wake up and have it all be a dream."

"It's not," I said. "You're here. You're home."

She smiled, small and tired. "So are you."

I kissed her knuckles, then her lips, then pulled her onto my lap, just holding her. We stayed that way a long time, the world outside fading to nothing, the only sound the slow, steady drum of two hearts trying to remember how to beat together.

Eventually, she fell asleep, arms around my neck, breath warm against my cheek. I stayed awake watching her, memorizing every detail. I'd lost her once. I would never let it happen again.

The sun rose higher, cutting long shadows through the blinds. I blinked against the light, but I didn't move.

For the first time since I could remember, I wanted the day to last forever.

"Church" didn't always mean God; sometimes it meant a table full of eggs, sausage, and the people who'd pull you out of hell. Bronc called the meeting for 6:45 sharp, which meant everyone was there by 6:30, hair damp and eyes red, but shirts tucked and boots shined.

Pearl herself manned the kitchen, refusing all help, and if anyone complained about the noise she made with the pans, she'd threaten to serve them grits with no butter. The air was thick with the smell of coffee, frying bacon, and the soft undercurrent of wolves and a mix of vanilla and jasmine. I'd never loved a place more.

The long table was packed—Bronc and Juliet at the head, Wrecker to his left then Parker, and Doc was next rounding out that side. Big Papa sat to Bronc's right with Aspen next to him (Oscar was perched upright on the sugar caddy, looking dapper). Harper was happily filling her plate next to Aspen, and I was doing to same on the other side of her. And then Gunner sat at the end, cowboy hat and all.

Bronc started with the food. "Eat," he commanded, and nobody argued. Plates clattered, biscuits passed from hand to hand, gravy ladled until it ran off the edge of the plate and pooled on the tablecloth. For ten minutes, it was just eating, no talk except the occasional "pass the salt" or a low chuckle when groaned at how good everything tasted. That was tradition. You never did business on an empty stomach.

I watched Harper through it all, making sure she got enough to eat, enough coffee, enough warmth. She'd woken up stiff and bruised, but by the time she finished her second biscuit, her eyes had a little spark again.

She even nudged me under the table when Gunner told one of his famous dumb jokes.

Aspen and Big Papa sat hip to hip, every so often exchanging little grins like they shared a secret sweeter than the cinnamon rolls. I'd never seen Papa so relaxed. Even Oscar looked happier, his tiny paws folded primly in his lap.

Wrecker demolished four eggs and a mountain of bacon, glancing at Parker every so often to see if she'd say anything about it. She didn't. Instead, she typed on her phone with one hand and shoveled grits with the other, multitasking in a way that only made sense if your mind held so much information that you constantly needed it moving.

Once everyone was fed, Bronc wiped his hands on a napkin and got down to business.

"All right," he said, voice dropping a full octave. "Who did we kill, and how are we going to explain it to the Council so they don't come for us?"

Nobody laughed. Not even Gunner.

Wrecker leaned back, crossing his arms. "The official list is twenty-two Renault wolves, plus Steiner, plus two civilians who tried to interfere. Unofficially, there's three or four we didn't confirm. Could have run, could have bled out."

Parker spoke up without looking away from her phone. "Cameras were on a loop. The only live witness was a French cop who's in Rafe's pocket. As long as we play it right, nobody in the States ever has to know. Well, except for the dead Alpha of the Morgantown Pack. I mean. We kinda did it again. What's our tally now? Three dead Alphas, two dead kings? Hot damn! We're on a roll!"

Bronc gave Parker a look that said he was not amused.

She kept the grin on her face but at least tried to look contrite by lowering her head. "Sorry, Alpha."

Juliet poured another cup of tea, no coffee for the pregnant Luna, and asked, "What about the Council?"

This was my cue. "We did what we had to do. Steiner was the real target, and the Renaults were acting as his proxies. The French wolves will confirm that, if we need them to. Plus, it was the French who actually made the kill officially. Steiner was trafficking on French soil."

Big Papa cleared his throat. "We still have two women in protection, Nanette and Brie's gonna need a more permanent place to stay." He trailed off, leaving the rest unsaid.

Bronc raised a brow. "As long as Brie wants to be here, she's part of this pack. Nanette too. We take care of our own."

Aspen squeezed Papa's hand. Oscar said, "Hear, hear," and the whole table cracked up.

Wrecker looked at Bronc, then at me. "You want to patch Rafe in for the rest of the debrief?"

Bronc shrugged. "We need to. Let's do it."

Wrecker connected his laptop to the big TV on the wall, and in seconds King Rafe appeared, suit pressed, hair perfect, eyes twinkling like he'd just won a bar fight.

"Y'all alive?" he asked, drinking coffee from a mug that said "Roll Tide" on it.

Bronc grinned. "All accounted for, Rafe. Appreciate the assist."

Rafe nodded. "The Parisian wolves will take full responsibility for the mess. You're squeaky clean with the Council. Tell your people to lie low for a week, let the news cycle die, then go about your business."

Juliet asked, "And Steiner?"

Rafe's smile turned cold. "I understand that thanks to Harper, with an assist from the French connection, he won't bother anyone again. I'm sorry you took some hits, Harper. But great work on improvising the weapon to end that son-of-a bitch."

I looked at my mate, pride shining in my eyes.

She nodded at the camera. "Yes, sir."

Rafe continued. "I know Maltraz has to be pissed. Steiner's docks were how he could get his cargo loaded without detection. Now he's got to figure out another way. Yet again, Iron Valor has gotten in his way. He might get over it, or he'll come for you, and then you can send him to hell yourself."

Nobody disagreed.

Rafe continued. "If you could let Gwen know the plane will be ready to bring her back to Birmingham at noon today I'd appreciate it."

Bronc agreed. "Thank you for loaning her to us for this mission. Her help, as I understand it was invaluable."

Rafe nodded and ended the call, leaving only the sound of silverware on china and the clink of coffee cups in the room.

Bronc looked around the table. "Anything else?"

Gunner said, "Need more bacon," and everyone laughed, just a little too loud.

For the first time in years, the air felt safe.

Bronc squeezed Juliet's hand, then stood. "Go home. Rest. There's nothing on the horizon but spring and sunshine. Let's enjoy it for once."

The meeting broke up in the usual Iron Valor way—slow, with a lot of half-hugs, shoulder claps, and promises to meet again soon. Aspen dragged Papa out by the hand. Oscar waved from her shoulder. Gunner lingered, talking low with Bronc. Wrecker and Parker left together, arguing about who had to fill the tank on the way to the city.

I lingered with Harper, finishing the last of my coffee. She stared into the mug, then at me.

"I can't remember a time when my heart has felt so full," she said.

I pulled her to me. "I can't remember a time when I felt so much love."

She smiled and said, "Me neither."

This was our home. This was our family. And for once, I had everything I ever wanted.

EPILOGUE

Gunner

I'll be honest, County Line on a Thursday night was never my first choice. I preferred Sam's, even if the beer cost a dollar more, but County Line was neutral territory, and Bronc said I had to make myself "seen" here once in a while, let the locals remember whose name ran this county. So I nursed a Shiner and tried not to look like a wounded animal, even as the local pack girls prowled the shadows, waiting for my scent to slip.

You could tell a lot about a bar from its woodwork. Sam's was slick, lacquered, with round corners polished by decades of elbows and bellies. County Line's was hard, unfinished, gouged with pocketknives and stained with spilled High Life. All the barstools had at least one broken rung, and the only thing keeping the beer fridge from toppling over was a cut-up phone book jammed under its front leg. The whole place stank of desperation and Fritos. If you wanted to disappear, this was the place to do it.

I watched the dance floor, all but empty this early except for a couple of college kids with dollar bills pinned to their shirts, and a pair of local farmhands doing a lazy two-step with one girl between them. Usually, I'd be scanning for prospects, but tonight, I had no interest in local talent. Not when my mind was stuck in a loop over the one girl who'd been driving me crazy since she'd stepped off that plane almost two months ago.

From the jump, she acted like Dairyville was beneath her, like every store was one step away from closing, and the locals were lucky if they could read a stop sign. She didn't try to fit in, not once. She tried to exude sophistication. Except she forgot her daddy was shot dead in a parking garage because of his illegal financial dealings and she and her mama were living on the kindness of strangers now.

The thing that pissed me off most was that it worked. She had every man in the county, wolf and otherwise, noticing her, and lots of the women hated her on sight. It seemed to me she really was just out of control.

I shouldn't have cared, except for one tiny detail.

My wolf knew her the second she stepped off the plane.

It was like getting hit with a cattle prod—one look at that face, the way her hair whipped in the wind, and every cell in my body screamed, *Mate.* I tried to fight it, but the truth was, I'd been hard for her since the night I met her, and nothing was going to change that.

It made me mean, and it made her meaner. Bronc kept sending me over to Parker's family home to "help out," as if I was some kind of butler for the pack. Brie would always answer the door with a look like she'd just stepped in dog shit, and then act like she'd never even heard of a hammer. Her favorite game was calling me by a famous cowboy name. Marshall Dillon, Doc Holliday, Jesse James. The last one she said with a wink, like she knew I'd stolen a candy bar from the Shell when I was nine and felt guilty about it for years.

If I'd been a better man, I'd have stayed away. But I wasn't, and I didn't. The only reason I came here tonight was to get her out of my head. It was working about as well as you'd expect.

Two girls from the Sun Valley pack outside of Canyon sidled up next to me at the bar. I recognized them—Kimmie, who ran barrels in high school and had a reputation for biting, and the one called "Kat" even though her real name was Denise. Kimmie flicked her hair and smiled.

"Haven't seen you in here for a while," she said, voice honeyed and just a little mean.

"I'm a busy man," I said.

"You too good for us now, Gunner?" Kat/Denise chimed in.

"I'm good, period," I said, not giving her the satisfaction of a look.

They made a show of laughing, then retreated to a corner, whispering about me like I was a prize steer at the fair. I didn't mind. Let them talk.

I took a pull from my Shiner and stared at the old Texas flag nailed to the wall above the pool table. It had never been new; even the white stripes were a sickly yellow, and the blue was almost gray from decades of smoke. There was a comfort in things that never changed. I thought of Bronc's face, all hard edges and black and silver hair, the way he could clear a bar with just one look. I wanted that kind of authority. I wanted to be the man people shut up for.

But tonight, all I could think about was Brie and the way she'd tried to get a rise out of me the last time I was sent to their house to fix their air conditioner. She just couldn't leave me alone and let me get the job done.

She squatted down next to me, not caring if her shorts rode up. "So, is it true what they say about cowboys?"

I felt my face go red, which pissed me off. "What do you mean, what do they say?"

She smiled, slow and sly. "That y'all think you can ride anything."

It was the first time I'd wanted to kiss her and throw her off the porch in the same heartbeat. Instead, I fixed the A/C, told her, "You're welcome," and drove straight to County Line, where I drank six Shiners and ended up throwing hands with a Hollow Ridge enforcer who thought I was looking at his girl.

Now, two weeks later, here I was again. Same bar, same beer, same obsession with a girl who'd never once looked at me the way I wanted.

My phone buzzed. It was a text from Bronc:

Heard you're at County Line. Don't do anything stupid.

I thumbed out a reply: *Never do.*

He answered: *That's the problem. My idea and your idea of stupid seem to differ.*

I drained my beer, debated another, then caught a flash of movement in the mirror.

She walked in with Maddie. Bronc's sister was always up for fun. She had a nose ring and the kind of laugh that made every man within a five-mile radius look up. They were arm-in-arm, ready to have fun or get into trouble. I'd bet on trouble.

She was wearing leather pants so tight they looked like they'd been painted on, and she was clearly dressed to turn heads. It looked like she expected to end up on someone's Instagram before midnight.

Maddie made her way to the bar and ordered them both whiskey sours and took them back to the hi-top they had commandeered.

I couldn't stop watching. I hated myself for it, but I was a dog and she was the steak on the table.

Maddie's eyes went around the room, evaluating the crowd, but Brie just sipped her drink, cool as a movie star. When the music changed—Luke Combs, of course—she leaned into Maddie, and they started swaying at their table, singing along to the chorus. She was having a better time than I'd seen since she came to town.

County Line's dance floor was nothing to write home about—a rectangle of fake wood that warped every time it rained, a handful of tables pushed up against the wall, and a speaker system that made every song sound like it was underwater. But when a girl like Brie hit the floor, the whole place might as well have been a damn bar on Broadway in Nashville.

The air shifted, and I felt it in the static, the way every male eye zeroed in on her silhouette. She moved like she owned it, hips rolling with every step, her arm slung around Maddie's waist, both of them laughing as they wove through the bodies already moving to the music.

Brie was a walking violation. The leather pants hugged her so tight it made my teeth hurt. Her top hung off one shoulder, bare except for a narrow black tank-strap. The boots had thick heels, but they were tall, which said she liked making an entrance but didn't plan on running. Her bob had grown out, and she'd dyed the ends blue, which framed her face every time she whipped her head to the side. The makeup was dialed up to maximum—black wings at the eyes, gloss on the lips so shiny it caught the light from the neon signs.

On the second song, the beat changed to something slower. Brie didn't miss a step—she just rolled her hips a little more, hands over her head, letting her hair fall forward and hide her face. It should have looked ridiculous, but instead it was hypnotic. I watched her, one drink deep and already half out of my mind.

That's when I saw the problem.

Guy was maybe six-three, built like an oil derrick, bald except for a ring of fuzz above his ears. He wore a Black Rifle Coffee tee stretched tight across his gut and had a tribal tattoo snaking up one arm. The kind of guy who thought "no means try harder." He hovered near the edge for a few songs, then made his move—sidled up behind Brie, reached for her waist, and tried to pull her back against his crotch.

She stiffened for a second, then turned and gave him a look that should have put him six feet under. But he didn't back off. Instead, he grinned, said something I couldn't hear, and doubled down, his hand low on her hip, his mouth close to her ear.

My wolf went red. Not white-hot, not explosive, but surgical—a scalpel to the brainstem.

I sent a text to Arsenal on instinct: *Your sister-in-law is at the County Line with Maddie. Better come get her.*

He replied in less than a second: *FUCK. We're on our way.*

I didn't wait for backup. I set down my beer and moved across the room, every step deliberate, every muscle coiled for violence. I never used to be the jealous type, but Brie made me want to fight for her, even if it meant getting my ass kicked.

The crowd thickened near the dance floor, so I had to push my way through. Kimmie and Kat were already watching, eyes wide, waiting to see if the new drama would end in blood or a hookup. A few of the college kids noticed me coming and gave me space, but the big man with his hands on Brie didn't clock me until I was three feet away.

I didn't make a scene. I just stepped up, put a hand on the guy's wrist, and squeezed.

He jerked like he'd been grabbed by a pair of vice grips. "What the fuck, man?"

"She's mine," I said, keeping my voice low. "Find someone else."

He sized me up, then noticed the cut—the Iron Valor MC patch, clear as day. His attitude did a 180. He let go of Brie, held up both hands, and backed away with a muttered, "No problem, brother. Didn't know."

I slid in behind her, taking the place of "Grabby McHandsy" and started moving with her to the slow groove of the song. Her body fit against mine like a loaded gun in a custom holster. I slid my hand lower, catching the strip of bare skin between her tank and her pants, and that's when it hit us—both at once. The jolt, the thing no wolf in the world could mistake. My fingers burned on her stomach, and for a split second, her whole body tensed.

She sucked in a sharp breath, her eyes flicking up to mine, the pupils gone black and wide. We just stared, not moving, letting the song fade into background noise. For the first time since I'd met her, Brie didn't have a comeback.

Then she found it as she started moving again. "Billy the Kid, fancy meeting you here."

I groaned. "I'm no outlaw, sugar, but that doesn't mean I'm the good guy."

She bit her lip, then twisted in my arms so she was facing me, her hands draped around my neck, pulling me closer. I felt every inch of her, the way her chest brushed mine, the heat off her skin. Her perfume was expensive but not too sweet—something floral, but with enough bite that it reminded me of sunburnt grass.

"You always this touchy-feely?" She asked, but her voice was breathy, not accusing.

I ran my thumbs in slow circles over her sides, just above the curve of her hips. "Not usually. You bring out the worst in me."

She slid her fingers up through the back of my hair, twisting the longer parts, tugging a little just to see if I'd stop her. I didn't. My wolf liked it; he wanted more.

The rest of the world dropped away. I felt nothing, but her, saw nothing but the blue flicker of her eyes in the dark. I leaned in, close enough to feel her lips brush my cheek, but I didn't go for the kiss, not yet. I wanted to watch her squirm.

She did.

I glimpsed Arsenal coming through the door then I let my mouth graze the line of her jaw, my stubble scraping her just enough to make her shiver. Then in a voice barely above a growl I told her, "I don't know if I want to kiss you...or take your pants down and spank your bare ass until it's red and throbbing."

She froze, her brow giving an adorable look of confusion.

Then, I leaned toward her ear. "Your ride's here, sugar." And I kissed the top of her head and headed for the door.

As I made my way out of the bar, I heard her call after me. "This isn't finished, cowboy! Finn Walsh! We're not done here!"

I stopped, turned, and let her see the smile on my face. I tipped my hat as she'd almost made it to me. "You're goddamn right, little girl. We're not done here. Not by a long shot."

Thanks for Reading

If you've reached this page, you've survived the emotional whirlwind of Arsenal. I need a moment to catch my breath right here with you. Writing this story was like holding my heart in my hands as my own memories of the loneliness of rejection flooded my soul. If you've ever felt that sting, my desire is that Arsenal and Harper's story sparked the hope that a second chance at love and acceptance is waiting for you as well. This book was born from moments of self-doubt and the beauty of resilience.

And how 'bout that epilogue? Brie only *thinks* she's running things! And our boy Gunner...wow! Who knew he had those bad-boy vibes? I can't wait to see those sparks fly. I'm excited to write his story. He's the guy that everyone underestimates. The nice guy that everyone goes to for a helping hand. But that hand is itching to do unspeakable things to the little brat who thinks the world owes her everything. Just because his wolf is screaming *'mate'* in his ear doesn't mean he is going down without a fight. Brie has some lessons to learn, and while he's teaching her what it means to be his, there's a demon king plotting their demise. If you thought Arsenal was a wild time, just wait for the ride Gunner will take you on.

Thank you, from the depths of my ink-stained soul, for reading. For loving my characters. For always coming back for more.

With endless gratitude,

Dex

P.S. If you ever need to debrief after this emotional rollercoaster (or demand more details about the guys), find me on my socials: Facebook (www.facebook.com/dexhavenauthor) Instagram (@authordexhaven) or Tiktok (@authordexhaven), or for autographed copies of my books, visit my website (dexhavenauthor.com).

ALSO BY DEX

If you loved Arsenal, and you somehow missed books 1, 2, 3, or 4 in the Wolves of Iron Valor MC series, you need to read them NOW! BRONC Book 1and MENACE Book 2 and Wrecker Book 3 and Big Papa Book 4

And if you're a fan of romantasy, my first series is a fun tale of an orphan from Texas who realizes she's actually not so much from Texas as she is from an entirely different realm. She's tasked with saving the realm from destruction by a power-hungry goddess. Along the way she meets her mate, a dreamy shadow-wielding vampire king, as well as a host of other fabulous creatures, including dragons, of course. Read the completed hot and steamy Kingdoms of Eldoria series **Claiming Starlight, Starlight & Luna Rising, and Starlight & Fire**, where you'll meet Olivia and Cade as well as the Dragonia and group of wonderful friends and family she comes to know and love. You'll find yourself on the edge of your seat with the heart-stopping action and needing a fan to cool yourself off as the steam heats up between several couples.

www.ingramcontent.com/pod-product-compliance
Lightning Source LLC
Chambersburg PA
CBHW071202100726
47908CB00002B/482